ROSE DOYLE

# Gambling With Darkness

Hodder & Stoughton

Copyright © 2003 by Rose Doyle

First published in Great Britain in 2003 by Hodder & Stoughton
A division of Hodder Headline

The right of Rose Doyle to be identified as the Author
of the Work has been asserted by her in accordance with the
Copyright, Designs and Patents Act 1988.

1 3 5 7 9 10 8 6 4 2

All characters in this publication are fictitious and any resemblance
to real persons, living or dead, is purely coincidental.

A CIP catalogue record for this title is
available from the British Library

Cased edition ISBN 0 340 82740 8
Trade paperback edition ISBN 0 340 82741 6

Typeset by Palimpsest Book Production Limited,
Polmont, Stirlingshire

Printed and bound in Great Britain by
Mackays of Chatham Ltd, Chatham, Kent

Hodder & Stoughton
A division of Hodder Headline
338 Euston Road
London NW1 3BH

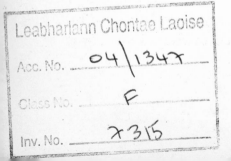

# ACKNOWLEDGEMENTS

I found memories of the so-called Emergency years alive and lively in all sorts of places and people: I am enormously indebted for knowledge generously given and books generously lent. In particular I would like to give thanks to:

The *Irish Times* library staff for patiently giving me access and time to browse the files and make my way into the years 1944–45. To the paper's editor, Geraldine Kennedy, for permission kindly given to quote from the *Irish Times* of the day. To Howard Williamson, for allowing me to quote from his father's beautiful poem, *Afternoon in Anglo-Ireland*. It made all the difference.

To the staff of the National Library, helpful and forbearing to a woman and man, and the building itself for the peace it bestows.

To Brendan Culleton, Gerry Mullins and Elgy Gillespie for kick-starting and pointing me in the right directions. To Gerry Mulvey (once and always a News Editor), Arthur Reynolds (infallible about the sea and boats) and Bernie Doolie and Phyllis Behan for their memories of Shelbourne Road, Turners' Cottages and Ballsbridge.

The following books did an invaluable job of shoring up my ignorance of the politics, propaganda, food, fashions, passions and prejudices of the war years in Ireland. *In Time of War* by Robert Fisk; *On the One Road – Political Unrest in Kildare 1913–1994* by James Durney; *Spies in Ireland* by Stephan Enno; *The World War 11 Years* by Helen Litton; *Irish*

*Voices – an Informal History 1916–1966* by Peter Somerville-Large; *The Shelbourne Hotel* by Elizabeth Bowen; *An Irish Childhood*, anthology edited by Norman Jeffares and Antony Kamm; Cunningham's *Manual of Practical Anatomy (vols. 1 and 11)*; *From Newman to New Woman, UCD Women Remember*, edited by Anne Macdona; *Irish Traditional Food* by Theodora FitzGibbon, and Phyllis Gaffney's remarkable *Healing Amid the Ruins*, the story of the Irish Hospital at Saint-Lô, 1945–46.

Thanks to the Army Archives, for help past and present. For the inspiration for the title, my thanks to Brendan Kennelly for the image, in one of his *Glimpses*, of a young woman dancing with the darkness.

And to Hodder and my editor Sue Fletcher, of course, because if they hadn't given me the extra time, there would be no book at all.

# I

'We can only be a friendly neutral . . . Any other policy would have divided our people, and for a divided nation to fling itself into this war would be to commit suicide.'

Taoiseach Eamon de Valera, December 1941, on Ireland's decision to remain neutral.


The body was fat, female, forty-eight years old and seven days dead. Its yellowy grey flesh fell in folds on to the table and its face was full of an angry resentment. The mouth was pursed, ready to speak: death had come unawares.

'Make the cut, Miss Cusack.'

The dead woman was so very alone, so mercilessly exposed. What had she been thinking of, donating a body like hers?

'We're waiting, Miss Cusack.'

Let them wait, let him wait. The woman on the table was in no hurry, palms turned upwards and lumpy fingers curled and pleading. She'd never been pretty and death had done her no favours.

'Maybe you would prefer to observe, just for today?' The demonstrator was at her shoulder.

'No, it's all right. I'll do it.'

Honor nodded without looking at him, afraid to take her eyes off the body now she was about to begin. She'd seen his demonstrating style with other students. He was helpful enough, in a detached sort of way. Patient too, after the same fashion. God alone knew how many bodies he'd cut up in his time as a surgeon and teacher. Better to learn to do it on her own, from the beginning. She ran a finger from one end of the clavicle to the other, wishing she'd been given a lower limb or foot to work on, to be where she could have avoided the woman's disappointed mouth.

She took a breath and was immediately sorry. The smell of formalin, reeking and choking, caught at the back of her throat.

'Want a drag?' The student next to her held a cigarette under her nose.

She'd noticed him too. He was skinny, younger than she was and slightly green about the gills. The entire class was younger than she was; no one else had come from nursing to study medicine.

'Thanks.' She took a long drag on the cigarette and let the smoke out slowly. It helped, blessedly masking the smell.

'I've seen happier-looking bulldogs.' The student spoke loudly enough to raise a few laughs.

'Perhaps you'd prefer to study veterinary science, Mr Lynch?' The demonstrator sounded conversational. He might have been joking, of course. He was German and, though the word was that he'd been in Dublin since before the war, still had a bit of an accent. He'd a reputation for precision and thoroughness and his class was popular, which was why Honor had signed up for it. His name was Raeder. Dr Oscar Raeder.

The skinny student shrugged, retrieved his cigarette and put it back in his mouth. He kept it there while he worked. Most of the others were doing the same thing. There might have been a tobacco glut instead of shortages and rationing.

'Do you need help?' Dr Raeder was still beside her.

'No. Thank you.'

Rain, hard and fast, had begun to beat against the windows. Honor didn't look up for that either, just swore under her breath. Bloody bike. She'd left it in the open. The wireless had warned it might rain. So had her aunt Grace, with whom she lived. She should have paid heed to both and caught the tram. Thing was, she liked to cycle and she liked her bike. She'd brought it from home when she came to Dublin and painted it yellow.

She lifted the scalpel and held her breath. Any of the deceased she'd seen before now had been freshly dead and greatly mourned. The woman she was being asked to cut open was nakedly spiritless.

'Please be careful how you hold the knife,' Dr Raeder warned, 'the consequences of infection are deeply unpleasant.'

'I'm aware of that.' Honor bent over the corpse.

The rain sounded heavier. The pack of Craven-A Gold Flake she'd forgotten in the bike's basket would be sodden. If they weren't stolen already.

She inclined the blade to a forty-five-degree angle and pressed on its back with a forefinger. It went easily through the skin, right to the other end of the line of incision where, suddenly, the tension went and it was loose in the slimy morass of the woman's fat. It was like cutting into butter.

'The fat of the superficial fascia is usually more plentiful in the female,' Dr Raeder said. Precise he definitely was.

Honor lifted a corner of skin with the forceps, detached it from the fascia with the edge of the scalpel and held it between her thumb and forefinger while she carefully drew the edge of the knife across and removed the skin. The slender delicacy of the exposed nerves and arteries surprised her.

'Nicely done, Miss Cusack.'

Dr Raeder touched her shoulder and she turned, this time, to look at him. He was smiling, glasses pushed back into his longish brown hair to keep it out of his eyes. She wondered if that was their only purpose; they'd been there since the beginning of class.

'Thank you.' She gave him a quick half-smile, unsure whether or not he was patronising her.

'You must educate your fingers to recognise the feel of the various structures.' His own long, blunt-tipped fingers hovered over her piece of the body. 'With practice you'll recognise the differing sensations when you touch fascia, nerves, vessels and muscles . . .'

'Yes,' Honor cut him short, 'I've been listening.' She'd done the reading too. Cunningham's manual was very clear.

'This is your first dissection class, Miss Cusack, you've missed a full two weeks.' He pulled down the glasses. Their lenses were tinted and made it hard to see his eyes. 'The first principles of medicine are found in anatomy. You've got some catching up to do.'

'I'd intended speaking to you about that after the class . . .'

'Very well. We'll talk when the others have gone.' He took a watch from the pocket of his white coat. 'That will be in another ten minutes.'

He was thorough, too. And definitely hiding behind those glasses.

She concentrated, for five of the ten minutes, on the delicate beauty of the nerves streaming downwards across the clavicle, carefully traced their branches through the fat with a seeker, felt the soft bulging of a large muscle.

For the other five she wondered, with bleak uncertainty, what on earth she was doing in the dissecting room. She was twenty-four years old and a trained nurse. She'd grown to like nursing, over time, even if it had been her aunt Grace's choice for her in the first place. She owed Grace a lot. Maybe putting her heart into the study of medicine was just a matter of time too.

She worried about the bike. The rain was heavier, a torrent

now against the long windows. The beret covering the saddle would be ruined. So would the saddle. The class ended, as Dr Raeder had promised, in ten minutes. She put her scalpels, scissors and forceps into their box. Dr Raeder covered the cadaver with its brown rubber sheet and answered questions from departing students.

'You didn't faint anyway.' The skinny student lit another cigarette. 'The other women and a fellow all fainted on the first day. Half of the rest of them went green in the face.'

'Which lot did you belong to?' Honor relieved him of the cigarette, took a pull and handed it back.

'Very funny,' he said, scowling.

Dr Raeder was at a desk, writing. All of the bodies were covered, a dozen of them on as many long tables. Honor stood at the desk. He went on writing.

The last of the students and other demonstrators left and the room became still, if not exactly peaceful. Too many reminders of death for that, too many skeletons hanging from gibbets, too many bones, skulls, livers, lungs and gall bladders on display. And at either end, like barricades, there were the rectangular, formalin-filled tanks in which embalmed, greying, helplessly floating bodies waited for dissection.

Honor cleared her throat.

'Be with you in just a minute.' He kept his head down, his hair falling forward so that it almost touched the page. Honor rehearsed what she wanted to say.

'Sorry to keep you.' He looked up, smiling. She hadn't noticed before how lopsided a smile it was. Some might have thought it shy; she wasn't so sure.

'I'd like a chance to go over some of what I've missed,' she said. 'I was hoping you might have time to give me extra tuition.'

'It's not usual.' He stood. 'But it's not usual to miss the first two weeks of term either.'

5

'My grandfather died,' Honor said, 'I was needed at home.'

Peadar Cusack's timing had been immaculate in life and he'd died suiting himself too. He'd been eighty-seven and living proof that age neither softened nor mellowed a raging temperament.

'My sympathies,' Dr Raeder said. 'Was he an old man?'

'Yes. But his death was unexpected nevertheless.'

'It happens that way with the elderly sometimes. The will to live goes and the heart gives out . . .' He hesitated. 'I'm sure you don't want my medical musings on the cause of your grandfather's death.' He looked embarrassed.

'It's all right,' Honor said, 'he won't be missed.'

'By anyone?'

'By his wife, I suppose,' Honor said, 'my grandmother.'

'Elderly people can sometimes be difficult,' he said, and smiled what was definitely an awkward smile. But Honor had had enough chat about her grandfather, who would have thought Dr Oscar Raeder soft and a fool.

'Perhaps I could have an hour in the dissecting room tomorrow?' she said. 'If you're free.'

'I have time in the morning, early. Since it's Saturday there shouldn't be a difficulty getting the room. But I'll need to make the arrangements. I'll do it straight away.'

'Thank you. I've done nursing you know . . .'

'That should be helpful.' He sounded brisk. 'Why do you want to become a doctor?'

Honor, unprepared for the question, hesitated. 'Isn't it a natural progression?' she asked.

'It can also be a retrograde step,' he shoved the glasses off his face again, 'depends on the person.' His eyes were grey with blue in them and he needed a shave as well as a haircut. 'I presume you've discussed it with some-one?'

'Of course,' Honor said. She'd discussed it with Grace,

who'd been a nurse herself for a while and had also, for a while, wanted to be a doctor.

The next classes began to arrive.

'If you could come with me, I'll arrange a time when we can use the dissection room.' Dr Raeder was all energy, gathering up his papers to make way for the next demonstrator. 'You'll also need to purchase a half-skeleton. I may be able to help you with that too.'

'My bike,' Honor said, 'it's outside, in the back laneway . . . I'll need to put it in the shed.'

'Meet me in the Shelbourne in half an hour then,' he said, 'we can discuss arrangements over coffee.'

She hoped he was paying. Her budget was limited. 'Grand' she said, 'I'll rescue the bike and meet you there.'

'Use the lift,' he suggested, indicating the closed gates at the end of the room, 'it goes to the embalming room, which leads into the laneway. It'll save you going all the way around the building.'

'I don't mind going round . . .'

'I'll show you how to use it,' he insisted. 'It'll save you time. I've another class in an hour.'

Meaning he couldn't wait all morning in the Shelbourne. 'Thank you,' Honor said, reluctantly.

She didn't want to go to the embalming room, but neither did she want to explain to him why not.

He went ahead of her, weaving carelessly through tables of small body parts laid out for study. His white coat was ink-stained. Honor wondered if he did his own laundry.

At the lift he pressed the bell. When nothing happened he gave a sharp kick to the end of the cage and pressed it again. Something clanked into action.

'Always works,' he said.

While they stood by the body tank and waited Honor watched, mesmerised, as one of the bodies disentangled

7

itself from the others and floated free. A woman, it looked like. Then they massed together again, united and waiting. God, how she hated death. Always had. The idea of it, the finality. The bit she liked about medicine was the healing.

'There's no escaping death these days,' she said loudly, the silence making her nervous, 'so many being killed, every day and every hour, in the war . . .' She stopped, a flush beginning at the base of her neck. 'I'm sorry,' she said. 'That was insensitive. It must be the bodies, the dissection . . .'

'And the fact of my being German?' he finished for her. 'Please don't worry. The war's a hard reality for us all. But at least it's ending.'

So everyone said. The papers that morning were full of the American capture of Aachen and other German towns, full of pictures of the Western Front aflame. God alone knew how this man was feeling about it all.

When the lift arrived he yanked open the gate for her, nodded and left quickly. She watched him for a minute as he made his way through the dissecting room. He didn't look back. She presumed their coffee date for the Shelbourne was still on.

Going down in the lift the clanking was merciless, the shuddering descent slow enough to give her time to brace herself for what her gut feeling, and sod's law, told her was about to happen.

Bernard Corkery was sure to be waiting in the embalming room, larger than life and twice as tormenting as he'd been during the years they'd grown up together. Grace was responsible for *his* presence in the medical faculty too: with blundering magnaminity, and an arrogant urge to end the history of bad blood between Corkerys and Cusacks, she'd used her influence to get the youngest, and last, of the Corkery sons a technician's job.

Honor could no longer remember when childhood's taunting had turned to a fondness for her on Bernard's part.

Nor did she want to remember. It was enough that she couldn't return it. Not in the way Bernard wanted her to anyway. He was sure to misunderstand her arrival in the embalming room after her first class on her first day in college. She damned her own stubborn streak again. If she'd caught the tram she'd be in the Shelbourne by now, her childhood and everything that went with it in the past where it should be.

She saw him through the gate when the lift stopped. He pulled it open from the other side, hiding his surprise well. In his white coat he looked nothing like the Bernard she was used to and had last seen, briefly, at her grandfather's funeral. He looked grown-up. A stranger, almost.

'Nice of you to drop down,' he stepped back to let her out, 'if a little unexpected. Have you got the kettle on, Dandy, my man?' He turned his handsome, red-haired head and wide smile on the second technician in the room. 'We're being honoured by a visit from the love of my youth. And of my life, too, if she'd only encourage me.' He took Honor's resisting arm and led her out of the lift. 'I'd like you to meet Miss Honor Cusack.'

What she could see of Dandy Lyons' head above a news-paper was covered in a soft felt trilby. When he lowered the paper she saw a black, pencil moustache in a sallow face. When he put it down and stood up he was about five inches shorter than Bernard Corkery, who was more than six foot tall. He looked to be twice Bernard's age, which was twenty-six. The trilby was the same dark green as his silk tie.

'Am I right in thinking I've the pleasure of meeting the niece of the esteemed Mrs Grace Sayers?' Dandy Lyons smiled and pushed the hat to the back of his head.

'You know my aunt?' Honor said.

'Only by repute. And that's she's responsible for the pres-ence here of my colleague, Mr Corkery.' His gave her a slow look and nodded his approval. 'You're a fine-looking woman, all right.' He bent over two saucers of dried tea-leaves on the window sill. 'Do you prefer your tea to come from China or the Indian sub-continent?' He pointed to a saucer. 'Guaranteed used only once, fifty percent of the flavour intact. Rationing has not defeated us, nor shortages laid us low.'

'I won't have any, thanks,' Honor said. 'I'm here to collect my bike and I'm in a hurry.'

'Your bike?' Bernard, frowning, peered about the room. 'No bike here. Did you hide the beautiful Miss Cusack's bike anywhere, Mr Lyons?'

'No bike. I'd notice a bike. I've worked with bodies for thirty odd years and in all that time our clients have tended to arrive by hearse. I've known some to be carried in, of course, but cycling's never suited.' He folded the newspaper. He'd been reading the sports page. 'If you were to ask me about a horse, Miss Cusack, or even a dog, that'd be a different matter.' He gave a small shiver. 'Close the lift gates, Bernard, my lad. It's cold enough in here without the draught coming down that shaft.'

Honor looked but couldn't see the bike from the window. She couldn't rightly remember where she'd left it either. Rain, overflowing from the gutters outside, poured in a deluge past the iron bars securing the room.

Behind her, Dandy Lyons gave a loud sigh.

'Unfortunate thing, leaving your bike outside in that rain.' He put a match to the primus. 'Sure we can't persuade you to have a cup of something while it eases off?' He put a kettle on the flame when it hissed into life.

'Thanks. But I'm on my way to have coffee.'

'We're only a whistle stop in Miss Cusack's morning.' Bernard shrugged. 'Best to let her be on her way.' He threw open the door to the laneway. 'Don't let us keep you.' The door banged on its hinges, gusting rain across the floor.

'Shut the door and behave yourself, Bernard,' Dandy said,

'and you'd best be sensible too and sit for a minute, Miss Cusack.' He hooked a stool with one patent-leather-clad foot and pushed it her way. 'It's only a passing rain storm. Ignore our soured friend here and tell me how you're getting on upstairs with the dissecting? We don't get that many student visitors.'

'That's because the lift's forbidden to the student body,' Bernard said irritably, 'it's there for the transportation of the embalmed dead and attending staff.'

He sounded like his grandfather. And like her own grand-father too, for that matter. She resisted telling him so: there were enough dead people about without dragging them into it too.

'I won't be using it again,' she snapped.

Bernard studied the sky before closing the door. 'My colleague's right about the rain passing. There's a break in the clouds. I must warn you, Honor, not to be otherwise taken in by Mr Lyons. You might think him a kindly soul but the truth is that all he's interested in is gossip.'

Honor sat on the stool, next to a couple of trolleys with embalmed bodies under oil cloths. Dandy Lyons put tea into a china pot.

'Nothing wrong with a bit of gossip,' he said, 'it's what keeps this town alive. Gossip feeds the great self-regard we have for ourselves.'

While he arranged china cups in saucers to match the pot Honor looked around the room, which was square and lit by low-hanging electric light bulbs. A map of Ireland covered one wall, shelves with specimens in jars lined another. The iron bars on the window and the high stone walls of Iveagh Gardens opposite kept daylight at bay. The empty embalming table awaited a body.

Dandy Lyons, tut-tutting fussily, cleaned ash from a saucer and looked at Honor. 'Might I suggest you avoid the Annexe for your coffee. What they brew there has the consistency and taste of watered down, warmed up clay.'

'I'm going to the Shelbourne,' Honor said. 'I'm meeting Dr Raeder.'

'You never were one to let the grass grow under your feet,' Bernard said.

'He's going to give me extra tuition,' Honor was curt, 'I need to catch up.'

'Of course you do,' Bernard was soothing, 'and of course he is.'

'You were in Raeder's class then?' Dandy poured tea into the cups. 'They say he's very good at teaching the dissecting. I find him easy to deal with myself, for a German. Always manages to get a fresh cadaver for his class too, even when supplies are low. No desiccated old bones for him. No half-skeletons or ancient plastic models either. Which reminds me.' He lifted a corner of the nearest oil cloth; the corpse beneath wore a serene expression. 'He wants this lad tipped into the tank during the lunchtime.'

'It'll be done.' Bernard gave a mock salute and looked at the clock on the wall. 'There's a hearse due any minute. Laneway's no place for the bike, Honor. It's kept clear for incoming bodies. You'll have to pay more attention to the little ways of the college, m'dear, if you're to be the social success here you were at home in Cloclia.'

'Time to put the green-eyed monster back in his bottle, Bernard.' Dandy Lyons, pouring the tea, was mild. 'It's not Raeder's fault the women in this college are pathetic in their adoration of the German male. It's the whiff of cordite attracts them. There was a fellow last week, a prisoner on parole from the Curragh, who marched right down the steps of the first arts theatre and gave the lecturer the Nazi salute. You wouldn't get Raeder doing the likes of that now.'

'Not in public anyway.' Bernard Corkery shrugged. 'Not

now that the war's all but over and they've lost. They're putting manners on them in Aachen. We'll soon have the truth too about the German outrages that're being reported.'

'They were all at it,' Dandy said, 'all as bad as each other with the brutality. Did I hear you say you'd have a cup of tea after all?' With exaggerated politeness he filled a third cup for Honor. 'Rain's easing, as I said it would. Give it another minute and you could save destroying that lovely white coat.'

The coat was old and too long and a man like Dandy could see as much. Honor went to the window with the cup of tea. The laneway did indeed look to be lightening up. Dandy came and stood beside her, peering out.

'The unclaimed bodies are buried out there.' He held his cup delicately, small finger in the air. 'Once they're dissected, of course. When the flesh decomposes and falls from the bones they're dug up for study purposes.'

'Rain's stopped at last,' Honor said.

The bicycle, when she found it, was on the ground, the beret and saddle in a pool of muddied water. The basket was empty; so much for her Craven-A. The spokes were sound, though, and the brakes seemed to be all right too.

The hearse was almost upon her before she heard it, the soft splash when it stopped making her spin round. The driver blew the horn and stared while he waited for her to move out of his way. She gave him a wave which he ignored.

The door of the embalming room opened.

'Give me the damn' thing,' Bernard took the bike from her, 'and go on back upstairs in the lift. I'll put the bicycle into the shed when the hearse is gone. Go on.'

Waiting for the lift to arrive she stood again by the window of the embalming room, watching the hearse back silently up to the door. It came to a halt just a couple of feet from where Bernard had parked her bike under the window.

'Fags are on the shelf,' Dandy was washing his hands, businesslike, 'take one.'

Honor helped herself to a cigarette from a packet of damp Craven-A. She blew and studied a perfect ring of blue smoke while behind her the body was taken from its coffin and laid on the table.

'It's one of the Fitzgibbons from the North Strand.' The voice had to be that of the driver. 'Cantankerous auld divil he was. Gave his body to science so as to deny the family a funeral. Doesn't look to have brought him a lot of joy.'

Honor didn't turn. One disgruntled dead face was enough to be going on with for the day. She smoked resolutely while they stripped the body, while the driver left with its clothes and backed the hearse out of the laneway. Rain dripped down the stone walls of Iveagh Gardens from what was left of the leaves on the overhanging trees.

She checked her watch. Dr Raeder, if he was still there, would have been waiting twenty minutes by now. The lift arrived with a clatter.

'I'd rather take you to the pictures than quarrel with you.' Bernard pulled open the gates. 'Any chance you'd come to the Savoy tomorrow night? I've tickets for *The Call of the Wild*.'

'Thanks for looking after the bike,' Honor said.

'That's your answer then, is it?'

'Let it be, Bernard, please.' She got into the lift.

'I'll take the tickets off of you,' Dandy Lyons called, 'wouldn't mind a night with Clark Gable myself. Fine-looking man.' He giggled. 'I'll take the old mother along with me. She'd like the night out.'

Bernard, closing the gates, said softly, 'The day will come when you'll need me, Honor Cusack.'

'I hope not,' Honor said.

# 2

'As long as Ireland conducts herself in a neutral fashion it can be counted on with absolute certainty that Germany will respect her neutrality unconditionally . . .'

Joachim von Ribbentrop, German Foreign Minister, to Irish Government, July, 1940.

D r Oscar Raeder was standing, rooting through his pockets for money to give the hovering waitress, when Honor arrived in the Shelbourne. He sat down immediately he saw her come in and said something which made the waitress disappear, quickly.

'I was delayed,' Honor said, feeling as wet as this sounded. A tree along St Stephen's Green had shaken the rain from its leaves down her neck as she passed.

'That's all right,' he said, standing again, 'I didn't mind waiting.' He indicated the armchair opposite and they sat.

'My bike was in the way of a hearse,' Honor said, 'I'd to wait while a coffin was unloaded.'

Only half the truth but that made two of them; he'd definitely looked like someone tired of waiting when she came in. He was wearing brown corduroy instead of the white coat and the specs were now in his top pocket.

'You'll have coffee?' He signalled the waitress.

'And a scone,' Honor said, looking at the creamy-white crumbs on his plate, 'and jam.'

Bread these days was mostly grey and had the laxative powers of syrup of figs. None of that for the Shelbourne, obviously, which probably had its flour supplied by one of the nasally county women customers sitting too close for comfort to Dr Raeder's table.

Further along the room there was a group of American GIs, down from the North, awkward-looking in the stuffed armchairs. They were a lot more subdued than the county matrons, very likely because they were hungover. American and British soldiers only ever came to Dublin to drink, smoke and meet prostitutes.

The waitress, when she came back, managed to take the order from Dr Raeder without once looking at him.

'I've only been here once before,' Honor said, looking around.

'Not your kind of place, or not your kind of people?' Oscar Raeder followed her gaze around the room.

'People, now you mention it.' Honor smiled. 'You do know this place has a reputation for sheltering both variety of spies, German and British?'

'At the same time?' He was interested.

'So rumour has it. The same rumour has them drinking together as well as sharing lovers and girlfriends. Last week's variation on the story had the women of Dun Laoghaire baking cakes and delivering them daily to German spies all over the city.'

'I've heard that spies are like fleas.' He shrugged. 'Find one and you start itching everywhere.'

'I'm sorry,' Honor said at once, 'you probably hear so-called amusing German spy gossip all the time.'

'Not so much these days,' he said, 'not with the war coming to an end. Why don't you take off your coat?'

Honor slipped off the bulky, belted tweed, and immediately felt naked without it. The skirt she'd worn for the bike was too long and too grey for the room's pale walls and floral cretonne. Her shoes were too brown and too plodding and her hair was sodden on her shoulders. While the waitress fussed at the table she unwound and shook out her plait.

'I'll hang this outside.' The waitress removed Honor's coat from the arm of the chair, carrying it from the room like something contaminated.

'Coffee's not bad,' Honor said, sipping. While she buttered her scone she waited for Dr Raeder to speak. When he didn't, and she looked up, he was staring at her.

'Is something wrong?' she said. Now she felt hot too, and flushed.

'My turn to apologise,' he said. 'Your hair is very beautiful and I am very rude.' He was half smiling. 'Sorry.'

'Beautiful . . .' She put more jam than she needed on the scone. 'I'm wet, that's what I am.'

'Wet and beautiful.' He was brisk. 'Now tell me why are you studying medicine?'

Why couldn't the man ask her something she was able to answer? To give herself time to think, Honor crossed her legs and made the table, which had thin, spindly legs, wobble. She concentrated on balancing it again and spoke slowly.

'I want to make decisions for the sick . . .' She did too. Or part of her did. 'Nursing didn't give me that chance. I want to know all that's possible to do.'

Also true. But did that mean she had to be a doctor? Grace had persuaded her medicine would be an escape, which to her aunt meant a catapulting up the social ladder. Escape to Honor meant something else altogether.

'Why did *you* study medicine?' she asked, and looked up at him. He shrugged.

'My father was a doctor.'

Honor waited for him to go on. When he didn't, and

because she hated silences, she said, 'Mine was a farmer. I never wanted to work the land, though.'

'Would it have been possible?'

'No,' she said. Her brother was still waiting to take charge of the Cusack forty acres, one-third of them a mountain and not a field with her name on it. 'Your coffee is going cold,' she said.

'I've had enough. What part of the country did you grow up in?'

'A small place called Cloclia. It's a peninsula with a couple of farms, a few hills we like to think are mountains, a river, a great many stone walls and some hard-working people.'

'Sounds familiar,' he said, 'where is it?'

'I suppose it could be anywhere along the coast,' Honor agreed and pulled a wry face, 'but it's in County Waterford.'

She didn't want this conversation. There was too much to tell and too little she wanted to talk about.

'Will it be all right for me to use the dissecting room tomorrow?' she said.

'Yes. I've made . . .'

He stopped when one of the county women at the next table raised her voice above the wailing of a police car in the street outside. The conflict was too much and he grimaced, lifting his coffee and drinking while he waited for her piercing tones, and the police siren, to die down.

'The sooner this war ends the better.' The woman tucked a curve of hair under a tweed hat with a feather. 'We've had low-flying planes over our lands all through the autumn months.' Her eyes passed briefly through Oscar Raeder. 'They've been circling, causing panic, terrorising our labourers and the animals. Even the pigs ran wild. I saw them charging at walls with my own eyes. One of the planes came down a couple of fields from the house. It was German, of course. Neutral territory or war zone, it's all the same to the Hun these days.'

'The pilot?' One of her companions was mildly curious.

18

'Killed instantly.' The woman shrugged. 'The people were like bees to a honey pot after the salvage. I heard of a man installing the pilot's seat in his donkey cart and of another coming away with a German helmet . . .' She managed a laugh and simultaneous wrinkle of fine nose. 'Quite unpleasant, really, since the owner's jaw bone was still inside. Shows you how merciless war can be.'

'Not merciless enough,' Honor muttered. The siren had died away.

'She's no different from most people.' Oscar Raeder turned so that his back was to the woman. 'The war's a drama to the majority of the Irish people. Their neutrality allows that.'

'You disapprove?'

'I neither approve nor disapprove.' He shrugged. 'After all, I'm neutral too.' He took out a packet of American cigarettes.

'Posh,' Honor said when he offered her one.

'The black market is something else which thrives in this hotel.' He lit hers and then his own. 'Now, tell me about your family?' He paused. 'Please.'

The 'please' did it.

'My father's dead. My grandfather, his father, died three weeks ago. His was the funeral I went home for. My mother, brother and grandmother live on the farm. I live in Dublin with an aunt, my mother's sister. She was a nurse once, for a while, and was helpful in getting me the place in UCD.'

She stopped and took a drag on the cigarette, which was strong and made her catch her breath. Her family sounded quite normal when put into words, spoken quickly.

'Your father died a young man then?' he said.

'He died for Ireland.' The family phrase came automatically.

'When was that?'

'In 1922. I don't really remember him. I was two years old. He was away a lot, on the run, and then he died . . .' she paused '. . . for Ireland.'

Hard to know if his dying had done his country any good. It hadn't done a lot for his family.

'To have a hero for a father is the sign of a young country,' Oscar Raeder said. 'This is a young country, newly independent. It's very much younger than my own.'

'It's a decrepit country,' Honor said, 'full of the past. I'll be gone from here as soon as I get my degree.'

'Ireland's the future,' he said.

What did he know, with his head bent over specimens and his hands dissecting dead bodies all day long?

'What about Germany?' she said. 'What about the future there?'

'Who knows?' He shrugged.

They'd both seen the day's headlines. She didn't press him.

'How is it that you're here?' she said instead.

'My mother was Irish. I studied here. I came in 1938, before the war.'

'Your mother is dead?' she said.

'A long time. She met my father in Baden Baden in 1910, before the Great War. She was there with *her* father, who went to take the waters. My father was a doctor working in the spa. He and my mother married and she never returned to Ireland.'

'Not even to be married?'

'They married in Baden Baden. She died when I was very young. I don't remember her any more than you remember your father. I was reared by mine, and when the time came to study medicine I decided I would combine university with getting to know the other side of my heritage, so to speak. I live in my grandfather's old home in Lansdowne Road.'

His family story sounded normal enough too, told quickly.

'So you didn't go home when Mr Hitler called on all able-bodied men over sixteen to take up arms for Germany?'

'No. I didn't go home to fight.'

20

'Why *didn't* you join the war?'

'Medicine is more important than war.'

'You could also argue that there's little point practising medicine in a world without peace,' Honor said.

'I'm not arguing. Merely stating a belief. And wars end.'

'Do they?'

The war her father fought for Ireland was still being fought. The field in which he'd died had never been, and probably never would be, tilled.

'I didn't think this one would go on so long,' he said, 'and I still don't know why you did nursing, and now medicine. It's not the only alternative to farming.'

'You tell me first.' She smiled. 'Did you do medicine because your father was a doctor?'

'I wanted to do medicine and I wanted to get away from him,' he said. 'He didn't want me to come to Ireland but he did want me to do medicine. We compromised.' His gaze drifted towards the window and stayed there. The sun had come out to sparkle on the wet glass. Honor watched him. He looked serious, in profile. When he turned she dropped her eyes and felt him staring at her. An eye for an eye, she thought, and cleared her throat to smother a nervous giggle.

'What had your father got against this country?' she said.

'He was besotted with my mother, never resigned himself to her death. He believed her country would take his son from him too.' He turned from the window and looked at her. There was no expression that she could read on his face. 'By denying it a place in our lives he merely made Ireland more alluring.'

'Us? You have brothers and sisters?'

'I was referring to my father and myself. By denying Ireland he made it a place apart, to himself as well as to me.'

Not such a normal family, then. 'Was he right to fear Ireland would take you from him?'

Oscar Raeder shook his head. 'He was wrong. I'll go home after the war. Germany will be rebuilt and there will be a great deal for me to do.'

'Has it been hard? Living in a neutral country while your own is at war?'

'Yes, of course it's hard.' He signalled the waitress. 'My question to you remains unanswered, Miss Cusack. Why did you choose to become a nurse in the first place?'

'I didn't choose.' She stubbed out the end of the cigarette. 'My aunt, who's a widow and childless, put me through school and got me a place in St Vincent's Hospital to train.' She shrugged. 'Opportunities are limited in this country. I found I was good at it. That I liked it.' She stopped. 'My aunt is what they call a healer. She has healing hands. It's a gift.' She looked at him, expecting disbelief.

'You have this gift?' He looked curious.

'No. I'm dependent on medical science for any healing I might do.'

'A pity.'

'You believe then, in the healing gift?'

'Why shouldn't I? Do you think us Germans such a dull, unimaginative lot? You think we rely on rationalism at the expense of intuition? You may be right, of course,' he smiled, 'but I'm also Irish, you know.'

'I believe it myself only because I've seen my aunt bring great relief to people,' Honor said. 'I believe what I see, what's proven.'

'What about things yet to be proven?'

'I leave them to science and the mystics.'

'Tell me about your aunt?'

'She lives in what was her dead husband's family home in Clyde Road. Not far from where you live yourself.'

She stopped when the waitress arrived, her white lace cap high on a nest of curly hair.

'Two scones, wasn't it?' She looked from Honor to her pad. 'And three coffees. Am I right?'

Tapping her foot and without waiting for an answer, she totted the bill and put it in front of Oscar Raeder. Carefully ignoring him, she folded the carbon copy and put it to the back of her pad. Her foot didn't stop tapping either until he handed her a £1 note.

'I'll be back with your change,' she said. Her black skirt bristled against Honor's leg as she left. Passing the GIs she stopped and joked, laughing with them.

'The war is already over for some people,' Oscar Raeder said.

The sun streaked through the thinning leaves as they walked by the railings around St Stephen's Green, drying the pavement ahead of them as they went. Fallen leaves blew in small drifts.

'My aunt Grace came to Dublin in 1914.' Honor broke the silence when they were halfway to the college. 'She was training to be a nurse when the rebellion broke out.'

'That ended her training?'

'No. A man did that. He was one of the wounded fighting in the College of Surgeons. They already knew one another when she helped get him out of there. To save him from jail she took him home with her. The landlady of the boarding house betrayed him anyway. But my aunt stuck by him and they married when he returned from Wakefield Prison.'

'A romantic story.'

'Not so romantic as all that. He developed TB in Wakefield and she spent the rest of his life nursing him. The healing gift doesn't always work; she brought him comfort but no cure. He took six years to die. She didn't marry again.'

'Sad, but still romantic.' They stopped at the end of the footpath to let a tram pass. 'Come to the dissecting room at nine tomorrow morning. I can give you an hour's tuition then.'

'Thank you.'

The tram passed. Honor was the first to see the police cars and gathering crowds on Earlsfort Terrace.

'Something's happened!' She began to run.

There were two black Ford garda cars blocking the front steps and a large number of guards had corralled what looked like most of the student body inside the gates. Honor pushed a way through the rest, who were spilling out on to the pavement.

'What is it?' she asked as she went. 'What's happened?'

'They found a body,' someone told her, 'a woman . . .'

Wire-thin fingers grabbed her arm. 'She was there all the time.' The skinny student called Lynch spoke into her face, his grip pincer-like. 'She was in the tank all the while we were cutting . . .' He stopped, swallowing. He was more green about the gills than ever.

'Who was in what tank?' Oscar Raeder, by her side, was sharp.

'Some woman. She was in a tank in the dissecting room.'

'But the tanks are where the bodies are kept,' Honor said slowly.

'They're usually donated first.' Another student, older and less shaken, spoke directly to Oscar Raeder. 'This one was what you might call an involuntary donation, dumped in the tank without her own or anyone else's permission. Reluctantly dead too, is what they're saying . . .' he turned a short laugh into a cough '. . . and embalmed.'

'They're questioning a technician,' the skinny student still held Honor's arm, 'the big fella with red hair. He found her. He was tipping another body in . . .'

'The guards want to talk to everyone connected with the dissecting room,' said the other student. 'Wouldn't fancy the chances of the likes of demonstrators, or anyone else with keys.'

# 3

# The Basement

'For us, life was a long hunger. The rarest food turned to ash on our tongues, the most delicate wine went sour in our cellars.'

Bruce Williamson, 'Afternoon in Anglo-Ireland'

I knew before she knew herself what was happening to Honor Cusack. It wasn't difficult to see, for anyone who chose to pay attention.

I pay attention to everything.

Her aunt didn't see it, of course, or not in the beginning anyway. My daughter-in-law only ever saw what she wanted to, which was her fatal flaw. Her niece's flaw was altogether different, but just as fatal.

I pay close attention to them both, and to everyone else who comes and goes from the house. It gives me something to do, now that decrepit age has been tied to me like a dog's tail.

I met the poet who wrote that, once, when he and I were young. He's dead now, lucky man. But I am not and I will be here, watching and waiting in the basement of the house that was once my home, for some time yet to come.

Living here, and like this, is my solution to my late husband Lionel's will, an odious document which left this house jointly to me, his wife of nearly forty years, and to Mrs Grace Sayers, née Danaher, the widow of our only child, Douglas. It was

Lionel's to give, of course, but she charmed him as she charmed our son into her bed and marriage.

I will be revenged but death is too good for her. All I need do is wait.

After Lionel's funeral I moved myself and my long memory here, to the part of the house once occupied by servants, and dedicated myself to being a thorn in the underbelly of her life. She will have everything when I am gone but for now she is poor. I control the money and she will not get a penny more than her allowance until I die.

I had everything and she took it from me. I had my looks and my beautiful son. I had this house and money. I had my husband, whom I loved. Her destruction of it all began when she seduced my son for herself and her cause, exposing my family to betrayal and sickness and death. Nothing was ever the same again. But there is a price to pay for everything.

I'm of little consequence to anyone, any longer, but I have some living to do yet. Anger and bile keep me alive, as well as a desire for revenge.

Time was when I mattered, when people like me were listened to. But that was in another Ireland, before land wars and rebellions and the twentieth century changed the way of things forever. Before my son died, and then my husband, leaving me to live on, watchfully waiting for death and my own release. But as long as I live Grace Danaher is thwarted and that, alone, gives me purpose.

Those who live in the rest of the house, and those who come and go there, make the mistake of thinking that, because I am waiting to die, I don't see what is going on. This is as foolish as many of the other assumptions they hold dear. Their posturings and the ugly little pageant of their lives are diverting. I see everything and I hear everything and, as a consequence know, almost, everything.

I could be wrong about the calamity I see waiting to

happen. But I've never been wrong before so why would my perception fail me now? Certainly not because I am old. My years are what give me knowledge and make me more likely to be right.

The only thing which gives me cause for pause, and doubt, is the unpredictability of men, and women to a lesser degree.

And, always, of war. I listen to the wireless. I hear what is said as well as unsaid. I pray that I am right and a German defeat is inevitable because when it happens Grace Danaher will be exposed for the dangerous fool and harbinger of evil she is. That exposure will destroy her. She will become an outcast, socially unacceptable overnight.

For my daughter-in-law this will be worse than any death.

The first inkling that events are going my way at last came yesterday when Honor Cusack called. She visits me daily out of duty and, I sometimes think, a sort of affection too. She trusts me, sometimes, with her secrets. A safe confidant is a rarity in this gossiping city and I am ideally isolated.

Also, her judgement is poor.

It was early-afternoon when she came through the front garden gate, home too early for her to have attended all of her lectures in the university. She was frowning as she put her bike into the ugly, lean-to contraption her aunt had erected in full view of my window.

I knocked on the glass with my cane and she came in to see me.

'How're you today, Mrs Sayers?' she said. She is invariably polite. She knows to call her elders by their correct title. 'It's dark enough outside to have the light on in here. There's no fun in sitting in the dark.'

She flicked the switch and the electricity came on, filling the place with a sickly yellow light. I'd have preferred the gloom.

'I like the dark,' I said, but half-heartedly because I knew she didn't care for it and I wanted her to stay. She has been changing since the summer and I am less certain of her than I used to be.

Buried in the gloom I could observe those who came and went without being seen myself. It suited me also not to look too long or too often at the four walls, at the pictures and reminders there and elsewhere of those I'd loved and outlived. Hard as I found it to look at them, I would have found it harder to inhabit my cellar rooms without them.

And my cats. Walter and Algernon move, sulky and spoilt, through the remnants of my life and suit me fine. Grace Danaher, as she must be called since she in no way merits the Protestant name Sayers and did not even produce an heir for my son, hates my feline companions. The feeling is mutual.

'We need a bit of cheer in here,' Honor Cusack said.

She took the long-strapped satchel she always carried from her shoulder and busied herself at the fire, raking the ash before putting fresh sods of turf on top.

I could have done for myself but let her at it. She seemed agitated to me, and to need the activity. She shooed the cats out of her way too, which wasn't usual. They moved bad-temperedly. They like her, Walter more than Algernon, and were not used to her treating them brusquely. I waited for her to tell me what was wrong.

'That'll light up any minute.' She straightened herself. 'Will I make you some tea?'

'No.' Tea was rationed and I don't care for it anyway. Never did. 'Pour me a glass of brandy. Please.'

When she brought me the drink I didn't encourage her to have one herself. There is a level of familiarity beyond which I will not go.

'You're home early,' I said.

She didn't answer and I had to suffer her silence and

ministrations while she settled the rug about my knees. Her hair was wet and smelled of the autumn wind. It awoke in me memories of long walks at that time of year with Lionel when we were first engaged and I still living at Skelfort. My family still had land then too, and a place among the gentry of County Meath. But all that was ending.

Honor Cusack had long, efficient fingers, useful in a doctor no doubt, should she ever become one. But after a minute I'd had enough of her fussing. I poked a chair forward with my cane and indicated that she should sit there. It was a bentwood, light but not very comfortable. I didn't want her overstaying her welcome.

'You're right, I'm back early.' She spoke eventually as, much to my alarm, she began to remove her scarf and the unpleasantly bulky tweed coat she wears in the winter. But she knows me, if not well then better than anyone.

'Relax,' she said, 'I won't stay long. Just making sure I don't catch a cold sitting in these wet things. I've been out in the rain a lot today.'

She has the sense too to humour me. Her aunt could learn from her.

'Has Grace been down to see you today?'

This was a trick question. What she really wanted to know was if my son's widow was at home; if she herself could slip into the house without having to account for her early return from the college.

Honor Cusack had something on her mind and was not very good at hiding it.

I could see it in the way she stared sightlessly through the window and set about a fidgety unplaiting of her heavy, wet hair. She'd all but forgotten I was in the room. It was part of the straining at the leash I'd been been noticing in her since the summer. She was a cauldron of frustration, held in place by guilt and a misplaced sense of gratitude to her aunt.

'Your aunt called earlier, as I was taking my luncheon.'

I spoke loudly so as to get her attention. 'She tells me she intends serving mutton tonight.' I made a disgusted sound. 'She's very likely boiling some ancient animal as we speak.'

'Yes,' Honor Cusack said. She hadn't heard a word.

I dined once a week, on Friday evenings, in the dining room over which I'd presided for nearly forty years. My daughter-in-law's way of entertaining was not mine and her guests not the type of person I'd have had at my table. The houses on this and the roads around had once been the homes of judges, colonels, leading lawyers and gentry. We saw no need to welcome in people we did not know, who might not know how to behave. All that is changing.

Grace Danaher entertains the same guests every Friday, a group she chooses to call her 'troupe' and which gossips about the events of the week, their own little lives and the war. Two of her guests are long-time admirers whom she keeps, mostly, at arms' length. They are encouraged by her still considerable beauty and by the fact that she will one day own this house.

The longest standing of these is Lennox Mangan, a vain man of epicurean tastes who spends his time in the study of folklore. The other is Flor, otherwise known as Florrie, Mitchell, a greedy, noisy person who made his name as a bad portrait painter and now buys and sells *objets d'art* for a living.

The other regular guests are the bespoke tailor and his wife who rent rooms at the top of the house. Grace Danaher says she cannot afford to run the place without such an arrangement and so the Gibbons, Ernest and his shop-assistant wife Delia, not only live here but must be fed on Friday evenings too.

A young man called Bernard Corkery also dines from time to time. Large and red-haired, he has the blunt hands of the Irish peasantry but is intelligent enough and clearly besotted with Honor. Not that he will get anywhere. Grace Danaher's ambitions for her niece don't include a coupling with a yokel from their own, inbred back yard.

Nor, for that matter, do Honor's ambitions for herself. Grace Danaher is making a doctor of her niece for reasons of vanity: she wants in Honor a reflection of the things she didn't do herself.

My daughter-in-law cultivates the young Corkery man in a patronising attempt to subvert history. But the Irish countryside breeds tribal wars with long memories and it will take more than a few badly cooked dinners to put the war between the Corkery and Cusack families to rest.

None of her guests is what he or she seems. I know them well: the hostess and her two Lotharios very well indeed. Each and every one comes to Grace Danaher's table wanting something. I wouldn't have had a single person among them at my table. But Grace Danaher has no such discrimination about her.

It amuses me to observe the 'troupe', and to use what is left of my wits reading them and what they are up to. Lionel would not have approved. But Lionel is dead and I am alone and must pass my time without him and our son somehow.

'We will no doubt be served mutton broth as an *entrée*.' I spoke more loudly. Honor Cusack heard me this time and stood up.

'You never eat dinner anyway, no matter what's on offer. I must go. I'll be back to help you up the stairs later.' She picked up the coat.

'Sit,' I said. She would leave when I wanted her to, which wasn't just yet. 'You're not yourself,' I said. 'Something happened to you today.'

'Nothing happened to *me*.' She was irritable, looking out of the window again. Then she sighed. 'Something terrible's happened to another woman though . . .'

She sat back on to the chair, facing the fire and looking into the awakened flames. The way in which they lit the wet sheen on her loosened hair and the high bones of her cheeks lent her a dramatic beauty which wasn't quite true. Her looks were of the handsome sort and would endure longer than beauty's simplicity. I gave her time and at last she took a deep breath and began to speak, quickly.

'A woman was murdered and put into one of the tanks of formaldehyde in the dissecting room at the university . . .' She looked up. 'Maybe I shouldn't be telling you about such an upsetting thing?'

'How was she killed?' I was impatient with her feeble conscience and studied concern about my age.

'How was she killed . . .' She repeated my question absently and looked at me for a minute before going on, with a shrug, 'That hasn't been made public yet. All everyone knows is that after she was killed she was embalmed and put into the tank.' She stopped and I'd the sense, again, not to push her. When she went on she was clearly thinking aloud. 'Maybe her murderer meant to keep her hidden there for a few days only, until he could get rid of her by another means. Or maybe . . .'

'Or maybe,' I became impatient, tired of waiting for her to state the obvious, 'he meant to have her dissected and got rid of that way?'

'Yes.'

'Could it have happened?'

'I suppose so. She could have been laid out on a table and . . . once in the tank it would have been presumed . . .'

It was difficult to curb my impatience when she fell silent again and walked to the sideboard where I keep what she calls my altar of framed photographs. Lionel and Douglas are there, alongside pictures of Skelfort and of myself as a young woman. 'God knows what kind of life she had.' She picked up a picture of Lionel and me on board the *Queen Mary* before Douglas was born. 'Rumour has it that she was a prostitute, that she was known to the American and British soldiers who come here on leave.'

I resisted an impulse to order her to put the photograph down. 'To sup with the devil one needs a long spoon,' I said, instead.

'So they say.' She touched a faded bunch of rosemary, which I keep for remembrance, and turned with the picture still in her hand. I was less inclined to take her impudence on this occasion.

'Replace the picture, if you please, Honor,' I said, 'it is very dear to me.'

'I would have liked to know you when people were dear to you, Mrs Sayers.' She gave me a wry look but put the photograph obediently back in its place. 'You were a handsome woman,' she looked from it to me, 'still are. Not beautiful, exactly, but certainly handsome.'

Strange the way she echoed my thoughts about her own looks.

Even so, I didn't need an unformed girl to tell me I hadn't been beautiful. As a young woman I'd been tall and big-boned with heavy hair and a high nose. I'd been lucky to catch Lionel's eye. Or so I'd thought.

'Beauty was what your aunt had.' I was curt, disliking this descent into the personal. 'As a quality it cannot be said to have contributed noticeably to the world we live in. On the contrary, it can be much abused when possessed by women like her.'

'You're like a broken gramophone record.' Honor cut me short, rudely, and turned her back to poke again at the fire. 'We agreed not to talk about Grace. I'll stop visiting if you're not going to stick with what we said.' She put the poker down and picked up her coat, 'I'll go on up through the house. The rain's back.'

It was. Falling heavily from the darkened sky and running in a small river down the steps leading to my front door.

'You brought her into the conversation,' I sounded querulous, even in my own ears, 'and it's hard for an old woman to avoid mentioning the person who ruined her life, killed her son . . .'

'Stop it,' Honor snapped. 'Your son made his own decision when he decided to fight for his country's independence.'

'He wasn't himself. He was young and impressionable. She was older than he was and seduced him with her experience and her body into believing he could be important, a hero . . .'

I stopped, as she had warned me to. Honor had tightened her lips in an unpleasant way she sometimes had. She was quite capable of leaving me now, an old woman, without so much as a by your leave. There were still one or two more things I wanted to ask her.

I was, in any event, becoming emotional, caught up again in the horror of the Civil War which had killed my son and stopped my heart's natural beat forever.

The son I reared would never have espoused the rebel cause, unrealistic and bloody as it was. The son I reared believed in the Union between Ireland and Great Britain, and had been to Loyal and Patriotic concerts and meetings with his father and I. He would not have gone out to fight alongside the thieves and adventurers and misguided of the nationalist cause but for Grace Danaher.

He would not have gone to gaol. He would not have died at twenty-eight years of age.

He would have lived to fight for the Allied cause against Germany because he would never have countenanced the hypocritical, neutral state we now inhabit.

'Have the Civic Guards arrested anyone for putting the woman in the tank?' I asked.

'Not yet. They're questioning a lot of people . . .' She examined her coat, testing how wet it was. A delaying tactic. There was something she wasn't telling me.

'Were *you* questioned?'

Her head shot up. 'Why would I be questioned?' She sounded quite sharp.

'You're a student of the faculty. You have access.'

'She was murdered three or four days ago. I wasn't even in Dublin then.'

'Do they know that? Is that why they didn't question you?'

'Students have access during class times only. They're apparently questioning those who have keys. Staff members.'

'How interesting,' I said. 'We may find that a learned academic doctor lost his head over a lady of the night. A man dedicated to the preservation of life may have taken one.'

'It can't be that difficult to get a key.' She became suddenly brisk, throwing the coat over her shoulders and winding the long satchel strap round and round her hand. 'Especially for the kind of people the dead woman is said to have known.'

So. The city's scandal-mongering machine was at work already.

'She was consorting with our politicians and businessmen then?'

'American and British soldiers on leave, as I told you.' She frowned. 'And maybe Germans too. What they're saying is that her murder had something to do with security.'

'Of course it had,' I cut her short, 'the woman was clearly consorting with spies, passing on her pillow-talk with American and British clients to her German customers. It looks as if her death was the wages of many kinds of sin.'

Her eyebrows shot up at my mention of pillow-talk. She knows so little of me really, nothing of the real person I am. Or was.

'That's what they're saying.' She shrugged. 'Though there can be precious few German spies left in the country by this stage.' She picked up Walter and rubbed her face in his fur. He closed his eyes, hedonist that he is, and enjoyed the feel of her. She was still keeping something from me.

'There could be hundreds, for all the army and Civic Guards know or care,' I said, 'for all any of us know.'

'It's hardly worth Germany's while having spies here at this stage, surely.' She put the cat down and watched as he stretched himself by the fire.

'Why not?' I said. 'A dying beast is the most vicious, and the most desperate. It will do anything to survive. Nazi Germany has not, as yet, accepted the loss of the war.'

'They must surely be using all the manpower and intelligence they have defending their cities and towns . . .' She spoke firmly, as if convincing herself of the truth of what she was saying. 'What good would information from this country be to them now?'

She can be frighteningly naive. Or deliberately blind. I'm never quite sure which it is.

'It could help them get the Irish government they want into power.' I was patient. 'A German-backed government in this country could be a great advantage to their post-war recovery. Or they may still decide to invade. They would have an easy victory here since, with our having denied the Royal Navy the use of our ports, Britain certainly will not help defend us.'

'It's over,' she was flatly categorical, 'Germany is being destroyed, her cities bombed into ruins . . .' She paused. 'The city of Aachen has been taken.'

'You've sympathy for them?' I lost all patience. 'How very quickly you forget the horrors they have inflicted on the world beyond these shores. Horrors we have escaped.'

I stood and shook my cane at her before walking slowly to the sideboard.

She stepped out of my way as I stood looking at the photographs. At Douglas on his wedding day to her aunt, wearing his IRA, or Oglaigh na hEireann as he preferred to call it, uniform. At myself, alone, in the doorway of this house on the very spot where, just a few years before, Lionel had been beaten and accused of being a British recruiting agent. He'd given advice and references to young men wishing to join the Royal Navy. He would later espouse another cause altogether. Lionel was mercurial, very different from myself. That was part of his charm for me.

'Have you forgotten how the city of Warsaw and three hundred thousand Polish people were destroyed?' I confronted her. 'Or how German bombs on the North Strand killed twenty-eight people here, and how in County Wexford innocent country people were bombed at a creamery?'

She looked at me in silence, and with the expression of surprise which is always so insulting from people of her kind. It's a look which excludes me and *my* kind, says I am not Irish because I am of a religion and a class not that of the majority on this island and so cannot be party to Irish pain and suffering.

But I am Irish too, as is my seed, breed and generation. They forget that, or don't care to acknowledge it, those who are building this twentieth-century mockery of a nation. A Protestant woman from a landowning family has as much place here as anyone else. My son died for Ireland too, in the same pain and discomfort as many of their sons. And for the same beliefs, God help him.

'I haven't forgotten,' she said at last, 'it's just that I'm trying to understand. Terrible things are done on both sides in war.'

The moral uncertainties were beginning. War will do that. So will love for a man.

'Of course they are,' I said, 'but one must take sides. There is justice and injustice, even in war.'

'Yes.'

'I imagine your dead prostitute understood that rather better than you do,' I said.

'Why do you say that?'

'Her murder has nothing of the *crime passionel* about it.' I made my way back to my armchair and watched, as she had done earlier, the rain against the window. It had a soothing effect. I dislike becoming agitated.

'It seems to me too clinical for that,' I went on, 'and the embalming the action of a pragmatist. She was murdered by someone clever. It's unlikely they would have gone to such trouble for whatever paltry sum of money a creature like her might have had. The gossips have it right this time. Espionage is most likely to have been her downfall. Are there any German medical students or employees in the college?'

I had turned and was looking at her when I said this and, even in the murky light, could see how she blanched. She had indeed not told me everything.

'A murderer in college would hardly be likely to betray himself so obviously,' she said. 'Anyone so clever as you credit him with being would hide the body as far away from his place of work as he could.'

'So there *are* Germans employed? Who is it you suspect? A professor, perhaps? A clever German doctor?'

'I don't suspect anyone.' Honor reddened. I had struck home. 'The guards took some people to be questioned. They took Bernard Corkery. He's a laboratory technician. He's called here a few times . . .'

'I remember him,' I said. Corkery's wasn't the name she was keeping from me. 'Who else?' I said. She was taking a very long time time to tell me what I wanted to know.

'They took another technician too, a man called Dandy Lyons who works with Bernard, and they took the porter. They'll be questioning everyone in the faculty, in time.'

'Doubtless,' I said. 'So you might do me the courtesy of telling me who exactly it is you're worried about.'

'I'm not worried. Concerned perhaps . . .'

'Tell me?'

'The German doctor who demonstrated my first dissecting class this morning promised to give me extra tuition. It was to be tomorrow morning.'

'Was this before or after the murder was discovered?'

'Before. We had coffee . . .' She stopped. But I knew enough anyway.

'And now you're concerned about him?'

'A little. He's been here since before the war. This is where he studied to become a doctor. He doesn't agree with the war. With any war.'

'And why do these few facts make him innocent?' I said. She had obviously spent more than a little time over her coffee with him.

'They don't,' she was curt, 'but they don't make him guilty either. My concern is that he might be picked on, scapegoated by the gossipmongers because of the turn in opinion against Germany, with the war ending.'

'And you don't think he can take care of himself? Don't you think the German Minister, Dr Hempel, will protect him, if he's innocent?'

'Of course he's innocent!'

'You like this man,' I pointed out, 'so naturally you don't think he could be a murderer.'

'Today was my first day in college,' she snapped. 'I know only that his mother was Irish and he lives in Lansdowne Road. I met him very briefly.'

It had been long enough, apparently. I knew the signs. Even if she hadn't faced it herself she was attracted to the man. I gestured to my drinking glass and carried Walter back to my armchair with me.

'I'd be obliged if you would pour me another brandy,' I said, 'a small one.'

She poured carefully, her expression intent, and I knew she

was angry with me. I would have abandoned my rules about such things and invited her to have a drink with me had I not been aware of the abundant supply of alcohol her aunt kept upstairs in one of my best cabinets. War-time rationing does not exist for women like Grace Danaher.

Also, though she protested, I knew Honor Cusack coveted the German medical man. She might lack her aunt's vulgarity but was still of the seed of the Danaher women. Their righteous Catholic morality didn't get in the way of fornication and they took what they wanted by way of male flesh. Grace Danaher had ensnared my son within a week of meeting him, seen him into his grave within six years and given free rein to her appetites ever since. Her sister Faith had married Tim Pat Cusack in haste, produced a son within five months and Honor four years later and been repenting her rashness ever since.

'I must go.' Honor put the glass of brandy on a coaster on the occasional table

She meant it. I wasn't going to get much more out of her just then. But there was always tonight at the dinner table. The conversation there would be of little else but the murder.

'What is your German doctor's name?' I tried anyway.

'It wouldn't mean anything to you,' she said and was gone, clattering in her heavy shoes along the hallway to the rear of the house.

I could still hear her as she climbed the stone steps to the first floor of her aunt's part of the house, the banging of the door as she went through to the kitchen. She could be bad-tempered at times.

She was wrong about her doctor's name not meaning anything to me. Everything about him, and her, had interest and meaning for me.

# 4

'. . . Ireland is despised more than any other neutral but we must remember her struggle to maintain her newly found freedom and independence . . .'

German Radio, April 1944

'You're wet,' Grace Sayers was busy making soup, 'and bedraggled. Why, in the name of God, didn't you shelter from the rain?'

'What's the soup?' Honor sniffed. 'Leek?' Her aunt hadn't heard about the murder then. She'd have pounced on the subject first thing if she had.

'With potato,' Grace said, 'and parsley. Tell me what you think?' She offered some on a wooden spoon.

'Needs pepper,' Honor said.

Grace definitely hadn't heard. Honor relaxed, unbelted her coat and acknowledged to herself a huge relief at not having to face an impassioned interrogation. Dinner, where ghoulish interpretations and speculation would be the order of the night, would be soon enough. Unless she could avoid that too.

'I've been having trouble with the range,' her aunt said, 'I haven't been out of this kitchen for three hours.'

That explained it. That and Lord Haw Haw on the wireless, his tinny, scolding voice warning that England would take revenge on Ireland: 'Because she was neutral in this war instead of sacrificing her life for the Empire.' It looked as if Grace had been tuned in to German National Radio and had missed the local news.

'Have you been listening to him all afternoon?' Honor turned the knob to off.

'I *was*,' Grace said, frowning.

'I don't know why you bother with that warmonger.'

'It's as well to be informed,' her aunt said.

'He doles out propaganda, not information.'

'It's information, and given by a Galwayman,' Grace said. 'It informs us how Germany's thinking, in the way that listening to the BBC informs us how the Allies are thinking.'

'Both sides tell us what they *want* us to think,' Honor said. 'And well you know it.'

'Your generation has forgotten the past so quickly.' Her aunt shrugged, the rings on her long fingers flashing as she sprinkled pepper on to the soup. 'You never seem to give a thought to what this country has come through, how hard-won our independence has been.'

She stopped and turned and waited for her niece to defend herself.

But Honor, with the wisdom of experience, kept her mouth shut. There was nothing she could say that would please a woman who'd fought in her country's armed struggle, tended the wounded, watched her young husband die – and couldn't understand why others' lives couldn't be as heroic.

Grace sighed.

'I worry about Ireland's future,' she said, 'I worry about the hands we've put it in, about the lack of passion in your generation. You don't give a thought to how bitterly the English regret ever having given this country the liberty to remain a neutral state. We must bear that in mind, now the war is ending. We must be on our guard against them.'

'No one wants more fighting,' Honor, watching her aunt's hand movements become more frantic, was placatory, 'and no one wants any more wars. Not Germany. Not England. Not America. Are you going to change or is that what you're wearing tonight?'

Grace was dressed in purple; long, velvet, and with *crepe de Chine* insets. On her feet she wore slim-heeled, green leather shoes, a legacy of a long ago holiday with a long-ago lover. Grace Sayers was a woman who treasured memories, friends and belongings.

'I'll stay as I am,' she said.

'I need to wash my hair.' Honor helped herself to a glass of milk from the enamel pail inside the door.

The kitchen had once been a sun room and carried its origins in its wide windows, flagged floor, rattan chairs and long, low table. Rationing didn't much affect Grace Sayers' household. Turf burned recklessly in the range and tea-leaves, once brewed, were used to feed the potted plants in the window.

'You've been with Lavinia.' Grace resumed her stirring.

'She's fine, since you ask,' Honor said, 'tells me we're having mutton for dinner.'

'Needs must.' Grace stopped to secure her dark, white-streaked hair in its loosely coiled chignon. 'You're not usually so interested in the menu. You mustn't allow Lavinia to agitate you so.'

Honor ignored this too. Going into battle with Grace about Lavinia Sayers would have been an act of madness. Grace frowned and checked the pendulum clock on the wall.

'You were home early then?' she said.

'A little,' Honor said, and added, vaguely hopeful, 'I'm feeling tired. Would you mind if I skipped dinner?'

'I would mind very much indeed, my darling.' Her aunt turned, wooden spoon held aloft. 'I can't be expected to deal with the lot of them on my own.'

'You'd be superb,' Honor said, 'you always are. A one-woman show . . .'

'Your confidence is reassuring,' Grace cut her short, 'but it's your show tonight, my darling. Everyone will want to hear about your first day in the medical faculty. I can't wait to hear myself.' She shook head. 'You're being extraordinarily taciturn. I'd hoped you'd be full of news and views and things to tell me.'

'I will be. At dinner.' Honor, muttering, picked at the apple tart cooling on the scrubbed table.

'I don't understand why you're so difficult about my little Friday dinners.' Grace gave a weary shake of her head. 'We've had so many fine and entertaining evenings. The company's a bit older than you, it's true, but they all adore you. Each and every one of them, whatever you may think. We're like family, dining together once a week and catching up on news. You can be very contrary by times, Honor, really you can.'

'Must be something in the blood.' Honor, muttering still, draped her coat on the clothes horse by the range to dry.

'I heard that,' Grace said, 'and all I can say is that I wish you were *more* like me and less like your mother. For your own good.'

Honor sat at the uncomfortably low table with her milk. She would become as crazy as the rest of her aunt's guests if she had to endure another winter of Friday dinners. Though there was always Lavinia, of course, whose frozen detachment contributed a sort of sanity.

Grace, who'd a fondness for drama and belonged to an amateur dramatic society, was the star of the Friday dinner show and the focus of it all. The others were support players: scholarly Lennox Mangan and disillusioned Florrie Mitchell ardently pursuing their leading men roles; Delia and Ernie Gibbons bit players wanting a place in a world they imagined more prestigious than it was.

'I'll wash my hair and change.' Honor stood; the table was cramping her legs. 'I'll sort out the dining room when I come down.'

'You're more than withdrawn, my darling, you're distracted.'
Grace's smile was meant to disarm. 'Is there something wrong?'

'Nothing that won't keep until dinner,' Honor said. Grace
would be furious not to have details before the others but
would have to live with it. 'Apple tart looks good.' She backed
towards the door with a smile that matched her aunt's for
dazzle. 'Won't be long.'

'Gretta Harte called,' Grace said as Honor reached the
door, 'I sent her packing. She was wearing a fawn raincoat
and looked like a streak of lard growing limbs.'

'The coat's a new one,' Honor said, coming to a halt in the
doorway, 'she bought it in Galligan's men's shop.'

As a defence of her friend it was feeble stuff, prompted by
guilt that she hadn't been to see Gretta in weeks.

Gretta Harte, the postmistress in nearby Shelbourne Road,
had become a friend during Honor's first weeks in Dublin, a
time when she used to haunt the post office for letters from
her mother. Now, with the man Gretta had loved for years
missing in action in Northern France, her friend could do
with the company. The fact that she'd loved Arland Magee
unrequitedly only made it worse. All hope, as Gretta saw it,
was now extinguished. Gretta coming to the house, risking a
meeting with Grace, could only mean she'd heard about the
murder. If Grace had taken time with Gretta, hadn't so readily
given in to their healthy, and entirely reciprocal, dislike of one
another, she'd have heard the day's news for herself by now.

'See you later.' Honor turned to go.

'What happened at the university today?' Grace, suddenly
angry, raised her voice. 'What're you keeping from me?'

'I was planning to tell you over dinner,' Honor leaned
against the door jamb, 'it'll be the night's topic, believe me.'
Remembering her encounter with Gretta had clearly got her
aunt worked up.

'So I don't warrant an individual word about this event?

I'm to be given the generalised version?' Grace glared. 'Have you any idea how offensive you can be, Honor? How hurtful?'

'I'll go and change . . .'

'You're just like your mother,' Grace's voice was dangerously quiet, 'avoiding things, evading and ignoring. I do all I can for you. I always have. You'd be stuck on that Godforsaken hell-hole of a farm still if it weren't for me. The least I can expect is your confidence, to be told how things are with you. I would like you to talk to me, Honor, just talk to me.'

'You're right. I should talk to you.' Honor stopped. 'About a lot of things.'

The murder was the least of what they had to say to one another, she and Grace. The day of reckoning with her aunt had been a long time coming but was well and truly nigh. Nigh but not upon them. Maybe in a few weeks. Definitely before Christmas.

'Could we do it some other time?' Honor said. 'I've done a lot of talking today . . .'

'You're doing it again,' Grace snapped, 'just the way Faith does. Think about it, Honor: Where did prevaricating get her?'

'Why wouldn't I be like my mother?' Honor shouted, aware she was using anger to side-step the issue. 'Isn't it more natural for a daughter to be like her mother than her aunt?'

The leek soup simmered in the quick, pungent silence. Grace, with icy calm, moved it off the heat.

'Natural doesn't always equal right,' she spoke with her back to her niece, 'nor do we have to be prisoners of the natural or of our birthright. We have choices. We can change ourselves. Change the world, for that matter.'

'My mother, your sister, is a good woman,' Honor said. 'She gives without expectation and cares unconditionally. She doesn't make a drama out of the smallest event. I wish . . .' she walked to the sink and turned on the cold tap '. . . I wish to God that I was more like her.'

She held her hands under the water until her anger cooled. She'd meant what she said but what she'd left out mattered too. Her mother was downtrodden and fettered.

'If you want to repeat my sister's life then go ahead,' Grace's quiet bitterness was performance free, 'but you will not, by Christ, do it in my house. As long as you live here, as long as I am putting time and money into your future, you will do things my way.'

'I can't be you, Grace. I can't even be my mother.'

Only the God of her adolescence knew how hard and long she'd tried to be her free, beautiful, daring aunt.

'You can at least learn from me.' Grace sank into a rattan armchair. Her eyes were bright but no tears fell, yet. They would be her last resort.

'It may be that I've learned all I can from you.' Honor shook the last drops of water from her hands into the sink.

'You'd better get changed.' Grace let a tear fall. 'I'll hear your news over dinner.'

Honor knelt and took her aunt's hands in hers.

'Why do we fight?' she said, hating the way Grace made her feel guilty, herself even more for making her aunt feel the need to. 'Friends?' She brushed the single, silver tear from her aunt's face.

'Of course we're friends.' Grace smiled her dazzling smile. 'Why wouldn't we be?'

Why indeed? Honor smiled back and stood.

There would be other rows, other amend-makings. They were too alike, and too different, herself and Grace, too full of confused affection for one another for things to be otherwise.

But they would not be together for life, as Grace seemed to imagine. This house and its past, Grace herself, had no part in Honor's future.

Whatever it might be.

47

# 5

'. . . there will come a day when we shall see who were the bloody fools to go to war and risk everything for the sake of the Lion of Judah.'

German Radio, 1944

T alk of the murder of the young woman didn't altogether dominate the evening. Delia Gibbons, arriving downstairs breathless and pink, clutching the arm of her husband Ernie, saw to that.

'I've got something to tell you all.' She stood inside the door, smiling and blonde in the yellow jumper she'd knitted for herself the winter before. 'I've been saving it since yesterday. Haven't told another soul.'

Ernie Gibbons, shorter than his wife and pinned to her side, looked like a man torn between jumping a hurdle and running for his life.

'A whole day!' Lennox Mangan, by the cabinet dispensing drinks, adjusted his monocle. 'We're honoured, Mrs Gibbons.'

He replenished his brandy glass, as well he might since he was the one supplied the house with alcohol. Grace, wise in such things, never questioned his source.

'You are indeed honoured, Mr Mangan,' Delia, sensitive to the jibe about her talkativeness, led with her chin as she advanced on the fire with Ernie, 'and I'm very glad you realise it.'

She stood with her back to the room, warming her hands at the flames. Her taffeta skirt came neatly to her knees but she'd drawn a stocking seam on one of her rounded calves and not the other. Delia unkempt was unknown.

Ernie Gibbons eased himself off his wife's arm.

'We, had a little celebration of our own before coming down.' He smiled self-consciously and smoothed the tight, greying curls circling his pate. 'I felt it incumbent upon me to open the bottle of champagne given me by a grateful customer last Christmas.' His pale eyes shone and he was smiling hard. 'We're in fine form for the evening, the pair of us. Fine form.'

He lifted his customary, pre-prandial whiskey and Delia's vodka and lime from an occasional table.

'We're still waiting to hear.' Grace was carefully kindly.

Her top-floor tenants could be tiresome but, on the whole, suited her purposes. They paid their rent on time, were clean and quiet enough, and confined themselves to their own part of the house.

'We're also in need of livening up.' Florrie Mitchell, already seated at the table, beamed between a pair of candles. 'So I hope your news is cheerful, Delia. The news from the city today is anything but life-enhancing.'

His laughter brought a nervous, disapproving throat-clearing from Ernie Gibbons.

Florrie, in black tail coat and white scarf, leaned forward encouragingly. 'Come on, you temptress, tell us your news.' He smiled at Delia, his curling black-grey hair and beard giving him the look of a devil-priest in the candlelight. Delia simpered and moistened her pink-painted lips.

'The floor's yours,' Honor said to her.

'I'm to be a mother,' Delia blurted her news, 'and Ernie's to be a father.'

'Hah!'

49

Lavinia Sayers' exclamation was followed by the sighing collapse of a burning sod of turf and then silence. Ernie Gibbons, a fit sixty year old, had been married to Delia, née Maguire and with an acknowledged age of thirty-five, for seven years. Parenthood was something they'd long, and in Delia's case loudly, denied any interest in.

Ernie Gibbons dabbed tapering, white fingers against his mouth and gave a small cough. 'We're surprised,' he said, 'and of course delighted.' He hesitated. 'It will mean changes.'

'Aren't you the right auld devil, Ernie!' Florrie Mitchell left the table and grabbed the tailor by the hand. 'More power to your elbow, man, more power. Best news of the day. Confirms what the righteous among us believe about the Lord giving and taking away. Calls for a drink too.'

Delia, fiddling with her string of pearls, gave a giddy laugh as Florrie raised his glass and cried, to murmured agreement, 'To Delia's motherhood and a fine job on Ernie's part.'

'When will your child be born?' Grace said.

'Not until next summer.' Delia, gap teeth uneven between her shining lips, took her customary place at the table. 'Early in May. With the help of God the war will be well and truly over by then. If it's a boy we've decided to call him Clyde, after the road he's to be born and reared upon. If it's a girl,' her smile widened, 'we'll call her Grace.'

'Please don't do so on my account.' Her landlady turned a shudder into a swift straightening of her shoulders. 'The soup will go cold,' she said.

Grace liked the appearance of order. The top seat was hers, Lennox Mangan and Florrie Mitchell sat to either side of her, and Ernie and Delia Gibbons side-by-side next to Lennox. Honor sat beside Florrie with Lavinia on her other side, as far from Grace as was possible. When they'd taken their places Grace ladled out the soup and passed the bowls down the table.

She deserved an award, Honor thought, for that minute's performance alone. Her aunt must have been devastated by the Gibbonses' news. Long and reluctantly reconciled to her own childless state, Grace couldn't have bargained on an infant tenant in the top of the house. Her style of living didn't include a pram in the hallway and squalling echoes everywhere else either.

Grace's style involved a great deal of candlelight, for its 'kindness', and the opulence of curtains in jewel-coloured ruby and green. She'd had Florrie Mitchell cover a wall with *trompe l'oeil* inspired by Celtic mythology, and paint another, of stage curtains, across the double doors dividing the dining and drawing rooms. Hard to imagine a child fitting in.

'Let us begin,' Grace said, and lifted her soup spoon.

It was no great surprise that Lennox Mangan was the one to raise the subject of the murdered woman. Urbane, learned and posturing he might be but he also took an unbridled interest in the life of the town. Or death, in this case.

'Since you were at the eye of the storm, Honor,' he looked at her as he broke his bread, 'do you feel able to share the news of the day with us? Or should we hold fire on unpleasant things until we've finished eating?'

'It's not exactly a dinner-table topic,' Honor said.

Grace went on eating, everyone else looked up. Delia put her spoon down and clutched the side of the table.

'They're saying only a madman, the sort that might kill again, could have done what was done.' She made the sign of the cross on the heaving chest of her yellow jumper. 'The talk in the shop today was of nothing else. I'd to listen to customers going on about how we're in danger for our lives, all of us. They could be right too,' her voice rose, 'and to think I'm to bring a child into . . .'

'Doesn't anyone have control over that woman?' Lavinia Sayers interrupted in a weary, flat voice. 'Such histrionics!

*She's* far more likely to harm her unborn child than any marauding executioner.'

Ernie Gibbons loosened Delia's grip on the table.

'It's been a hard day for my wife.' He cast a cold eye on Lavinia. 'She has an amount of adjusting to do at the moment.' He looked fondly at Delia's round, clear-skinned face. 'We both have,' he added, holding her hand.

'Only a savage would do what was done,' Delia blinked as a tear fell, 'only a savage. Nobody's safe any longer . . . nobody. There's danger everywhere. Until now we only had to worry about being over-run by either the English or the Germans, neutral or not. Now there's this new danger . . . I don't think we should even be talking about it.'

Grace stopped eating. 'Then you might be better off finishing your meal in the kitchen, Delia, because I'd certainly like to discuss whatever happened today.' She looked along the table, expression enquiring. 'I appear to be alone in this room, maybe even the entire city, in my ignorance of today's events.'

'I'll stay,' said Delia quickly, and finished her soup.

'The body of a woman was discovered in a tank in the dissecting room at UCD,' Honor explained quickly. 'College was closed for the afternoon.'

'Isn't that what the tanks are for?' Grace dabbed her mouth with her napkin. 'To hold bodies?'

'Donated ones. Not murder victims.'

'Ah, I see.' Grace studied the lipstick marks she'd left on the napkin.

'I heard she'd been pumped full of poison,' Delia put a hand to her heaving chest again, 'and thrown into a tank of another poison to finish her off!'

'She was dead before she went into the tank,' Honor said, 'she was there while classes were going on in the room this morning.'

'Did you see the body?' Delia leaned across the table. 'Did you see the wounds?'

'Now, Delia, don't be upsetting yourself.' Ernie, still attached to his wife's hand, made a small, alarmed sound. 'You should stay calm, dearest, do what the doctor says.'

'I didn't see her,' Honor said.

'There all the time? Jesus, Mary and holy Saint Joseph!' Delia crossed herself again. 'Dead in a tank of poison! And you were in the same room with her and didn't see her?'

'I swear, Delia, that I will murder you myself if you don't shut up.' Honor didn't look up from crumbling a piece of bread on her plate while she spoke. Delia gave a gulping sniff and glared and fell silent.

'You're upset, Honor, and understandably so.' Ernie Gibbons pulled his silvery-grey wool waistcoat more firmly over his flat stomach. He liked to display his best work on his own dapper frame. 'We're all upset. The preparations in the shops for All Hallows' Eve might be a more cheerful topic for the dinner table. I was noticing today that there were great mounds of hazelnuts in the windows but that apples are in short supply. The barm bracks are more miserable than they've been for many a year too, on account of a shortage of sultanas . . .'

'That was delicious, Grace, as always.' Lenox Mangan laid his soup spoon across an empty bowl. 'Another culinary success.' He shook his head, sighing. 'I'd heard, naturally enough, about events in the medical faculty. A most unpleasant business. The Civic Guards will no doubt get to the bottom of it but they'll need all the help they can get.' He looked in concern down the table at Honor. 'I hope, young lady, that it won't interfere too much with your studies?'

'Of course it will,' said Honor, belatedly deciding on a policy of discouragement.

'How was she found?' Lennox sounded only mildly curious

but was never quite so laconic, nor disinterested, as he seemed. Honor had often enough seen his urbanity slip when things didn't go his way.

'Bernard Corkery found the body,' she said, 'he was putting another into the tank. They took him away for questioning, along with Dandy Lyons and . . . some others.'

'Bernard can be a fool, by times, but he's not a killer.' Grace stood, 'He has neither the wit nor the daring to carry out anything as planned as a murder. Delia, do you feel able to help me carry the rest of the food from the kitchen?'

'I'm not incapacitated.' Delia laughed nervously. 'Not yet at any rate.'

The men left the table to stand by the fire, smoking, a custom Grace encouraged so as to prolong the meal. Honor lifted the soup bowls and rearranged the table. Lavinia had for once eaten her soup.

'My, but you're well-behaved tonight,' Honor said.

'That's as much as I'll have.' Lavinia pushed herself out of her chair. 'I'll sit by the fire for the rest of the meal.'

'Be a shame to treat us to too much of a good thing,' Honor said.


The men made way for Lavinia, who went to sit in a wing-backed armchair before the fireplace. Honor built up the fire: Government offices and the rest of the city might be short of fuel but Grace had done her bit for Ireland and knew how to extract her dues. Turf came from the bogs in barges to the nearby Turfbank in Percy Place and, while others queued with prams and handcarts and children scrounged for single sods, Grace strode majestically in and ordered her needs delivered.

'There's never been a shortage of murdering bastards in this town,' Florrie Mitchell laid shreds of tobacco along a paper wrapper, 'but they've not shown much imagination before now. They've more flair for it over the water.' Using one hand

54

he deftly began to roll the cigarette. 'Anyone remember the acid bath case?'

Lennox Mangan shook his magnificent silvery head as he snipped the end off a cigar and slowly lit it. 'Afraid not,' he said. 'Not my area of interest.'

'Nor mine.' Ernie Gibbons sucked on the weekly, ritual cigar given him by Lennox.

'Torrid stuff . . . torrid.' Florrie licked the paper and lit up slowly. 'Most of the body had dissolved into charred, fatty residue.' He took a deep drag. 'And what about the Luton sack murder a couple of years ago? Strangled woman found naked, trussed up in potato sacks in a river.'

'Most interesting,' said Lennox dryly, 'we're indebted to you, Florrie. I'm sure Honor and Mrs Sayers are particularly grateful for your contribution.'

Honor sighed. 'Give the murder talk a rest for tonight, Florrie.' She put a hand on his arm. 'Please?'

'For you, m'dear, anything.' Speaking with the cigarette clenched between his lips, the painter touched her cheek with one finger: 'Just trying to put things in perspective. Death's a funny old business,' he shook his head, spilling ash on to his white silk scarf, 'but murder's downright peculiar.' He rubbed at the ash, leaving a grey stain.

Grace and Delia arrived with the meat which Grace served, in thick slices, from a warmed serving dish while Delia repaired her lipstick. There was a caper sauce to go with the mutton, as well as boiled potatoes and carrots and a red Burgundy courtesy of Lennox Mangan. Grace left her own plate empty.

'My appetite's gone.' She pushed her plate aside. 'I'll neither eat nor sleep until I know everything there is to know about this murder business. Delia tells me the woman was a prostitute and that she serviced the soldiery of all and any army she came across.'

'She who sups . . .' Ernie began. Grace silenced him with a glare.

'She must have been supping with a devil we know, to end up in a formalin tank. Not too many soldiers have keys to the dissecting room, or know how to embalm a body for that matter.'

'Any fool can do an embalming,' Florrie said.

'Is that a fact?' Lennox dissected a piece of mutton.

'Well, any half-competent idiot anyway.' Florrie tossed a lock of hair out of his eyes. 'It's not what you'd call one of life's mysteries. All it needs is a basic knowledge of anatomy and a gadget to pump fluid into the body. The Egyptians did it five thousand years ago.'

'The Egyptians, Florrie my pet, were a little more than half-competent idiots.' Grace patted the artist's hand where it rested on the table. 'But you may be right.' She raised an eyebrow. 'You're a man knows a *lot* about the human form. Are you saying you could embalm a body?'

'If I'd a mind to.' Florrie shrugged. 'It's not a pastime I've ever considered. Time spent on anatomical drawing in the dissecting room cured me of that. A most unattractive sight, the embalmed body.' He raised a sympathetic eyebrow in Honor's direction. 'You'll have discovered that for yourself today?'

'Yes,' she said, the fat woman's disappointed face floating into her mind's eye, 'yes, I did.'

'We've a deal of anatomical knowledge between us here tonight, in fact.' Smiling Grace held up the elegant fingers of her left hand. 'There's Honor whom you might call our novitiate', she began ticking them off. 'Then there's you, Florrie, with your drawing experience, while Lennox, as we all know, dallied with medicine before finding his true calling in history and folklore.' She looked impishly over her splayed fingers at Ernie Gibbons. 'And you, Ernie, owe your mastery of the tailoring trade to a fine knowledge of the bodies you clothe.' She made a fist of the hand and extended her thumb. 'Last but not least there's the familiarity I myself picked up during my years as a nurse.'

'What about me?' Delia widened her eyes and smiled. 'I spend eight hours a day, six days a week, behind counters in Woolworth's helping customers select everything from sweets to gloves. You'd be amazed what I've learned about people from their hands and stomachs.'

'I don't doubt it for a minute.' Grace held up and inspected her glass. 'Cursed turf dust,' she said, brushing it off with her napkin.

'I hope, Mrs Sayers,' Ernie gave a small, stiff smile, 'that you're not suggesting either myself or anyone else around this table had anything to do with the day's terrible event?'

'Grace is playing games,' Lennox said impatiently, 'merely making the point that most of us, for one reason or another, are familiar with the map of the human body.'

'How well you think you know me, Lennox,' Grace gave a low laugh and refilled her wine glass, 'but don't be so sure that I'm not, in fact, pointing a finger.'

'At whom?' Florrie Mitchell looked around the table.

'Dear, dear Florrie,' Grace wagged a teasing index finger, 'so fearless and, as ever, so very much to the point. Sorry to disappoint you but my speculations must remain a secret.'

'I'm compelled to say, Mrs Sayers, that what happened today is no laughing matter.' Ernie Gibbons held his knife and fork poised over his plate, leaving his food untouched. 'Impending fatherhood has made me increasingly concerned about the current state of affairs in this nation of ours and drawn me to the regrettable conclusion that the woman's murder, horrible though it be, is the least of our difficulties.'

Delia, lips damply parted, watched by his side as her husband went on, brandishing his cutlery. Florrie whispered loudly in Honor's ear: 'The long-suffering are only waiting for the right moment to avenge themselves on life. Keep your eye on that man.'

'We must ask ourselves serious questions about what lay behind this,' Ernie went on, 'why she was killed in the first place and, more importantly, if a situation exists which may lead to further killings.'

'Why should we ask ourselves any of these things?' Honor said. 'That's what the guards are there for.'

'We have a duty as citizens to look out for the safety and security of the state,' Ernie intoned, 'and I for one am not satisfied that the job is being properly done by the Civic Guards.'

'You're dead right, Ernie, absolutely spot on.' Florrie was cheerful. 'The nation would be found slaughtered in its bed if we were to rely on our police force. I could tell you stories . . .' he caught the tailor's angry glare '. . . but I won't. The rest of us are lucky to have men like yourself keeping a weather eye on things for us.'

'Tonight's facetious tone is distressing, in the circum-stances.' Ernie slowly laid down his knife and fork. 'It's clear to me, at least, that the dead prostitute was keeping company that made her a danger to the state. A woman of her loose morals would have had no scruples about spying, if money were offered.'

'The woman was probably no more a spy than I am.' Florrie was dismissive.

'In that case you must be one, Florrie Mitchell,' Delia said, 'because they were saying in the shop today that the pickled woman was a spy – that pickling her was a way of showing us there are people living among us we don't even think to question. They're everywhere, blending in like mummies.'

'Like *mummies*?' Honor queried. 'Are these the same people think the world is flat?'

'You may sneer,' Delia tapped a pink fingernail against her glass, 'and you may disparage, but the critics will be confounded. The country's full to overflowing with spies. Everyone knows it. You can't deny there was that fellow they threw in jail, that Herman Goertz, arrived here with twenty thousand dollars in his pockets. Dollars! And what about the forty-eight German sailors they interned in the Curragh camp only last week? What were they doing in Irish waters?' She stopped, briefly, to examine some damage to the nail. 'Not that I think the Germans are the worst of them. They're all right really. Not so different from ourselves, when all's said and done. Just fighting to keep what's theirs for themselves.'

'Eat your spuds, Delia, there's a good girl,' Florrie sighed, 'you're eating for two after all.'

'It's not German spies we need to worry about,' Ernie was clearly a man exercising patience, 'Germany has been an ally in the past – we'd have no Shannon hydro-electric scheme if it wasn't for the Siemens-Schuckert group coming in and building it for us.' When he leaned forward his pate shone in the candlelight. 'No, it's the old enemy we need to fear. It wasn't the Germans murdered and robbed our people for seven hundred years.'

'The war's over, man, all bar the shouting.' Florrie brandished a bottle of wine. 'No more need for spies. Government might as well open the Curragh gates and send the couple of hundred Germans they're holding down there home. They're nothing but a drain on the economy. Let the crowd imprisoned in Athlone go too. No one'll miss them but the local girls. We should be drinking to a plague on all their houses.'

He helped himself to more wine, and Grace too when she held out her glass. Lavinia appeared to be sleeping.

'We would seem to have moved a distance from the subject of today's tragedy.' Lennox Mangan looked thoughtfully at Honor.

59

'We haven't moved away from it at all,' Ernie spoke loudly enough for all at the table to turn his way, 'our discussion is of the greatest relevance. What happened today is an indicator of the way things are going for the country. The dead woman benefited from the patronage of the American and British soldiers who spend their time in the Republic. Does anyone even question any longer what they're doing here in the first place?'

'Ernie . . .' Delia began, but settled back into her chair, looking helplessly pretty and smiling her bad-teeth smile when he went on more insistently, 'Did the misfortunate woman herself ask questions? Is that why she died? She may have been no better than she might have been but she was Irish for all that . . .'

'I hope, my dear Honor, that you weren't too upset by today's unpleasantness?' Lennox, cutting across the tailor's rant, was loudly polite.

'I didn't see her,' Honor reminded him, 'though I suppose I must have without realising it. I stood beside the tank while I waited for the lift to the embalming room and saw the bodies then. I didn't know one of them was . . .' She hesitated, then said defensively, 'Dr Raeder was with me. He didn't notice her either.'

'Oscar Raeder? German, isn't he?' Lennox looked thoughtful. 'I heard he was giving lectures.'

'He gives dissecting demonstrations. I'm in one of his classes.'

'And is he a suspect?'

'Why would he be?' Honor was coldly off-putting.

'Opportunity, medical knowledge,' Lennox shrugged, 'motive too for all we know.'

'Everyone in the department has the same opportunity and knowledge,' Honor replied, 'but of course the rest of them are Irish and Celtic and Catholic and know right from wrong so would have no motive to murder or commit violence.'

'My, my, but you're protective of Dr Raeder.' Lennox peered at her through his monocle, smiling. 'But you're quite right and I offer my apologies. Dr Raeder, like everyone else, is innocent until proven guilty. You, knowing him well, are best qualified to defend him.'

'You know him well?' Grace sat quite still.

'I do *not* know him well,' Honor snapped, 'and neither do I know where Lennox gets the idea that I do. I'd a cup of coffee with him, nothing more.'

'Where?' Grace said. The table had fallen silent.

'Where what?' Honor said. The expectant air around her was like an imprisoning clamp.

'Where did you have coffee?' Grace began eating and Florrie winked at Honor over his glass.

'In the Shelbourne. We were there when the body was discovered.' She couldn't believe she'd told them. She'd meant to keep Oscar Raeder to herself. But they did the same thing, every Friday, one or other or all of them preying on her life until she offered them her small secrets.

'I hope you at least discussed the classes you've missed,' her aunt commented stiffly.

'*Carpe diem*, Honor, turn events to your advantage,' Lennox advised. 'The faculty will be closed for a few days so you'll have time to study, catch up with your colleagues.'

'That hotel is full of soldiers and other questionable sorts.' Ernie was on his feet. 'It's no place for you to take coffee, Honor.'

'Sit down, Ernie, please.' Delia pulled at the hem of his jacket. 'Your food will go cold.'

'I have the floor, Delia, and I'll say my piece.' He tapped his glass with a spoon. 'This shocking murder's the tip of the iceberg. We're blinded in this country to the terrible dangers on the way if the war is lost by Germany. It's no coincidence that the Jews are everywhere in America. The US was once glad of the Irish, glad to have them in the police and fire departments and running the unions. But the Jews are ousting our people even in the US – you don't hear the names Kennedy and McCarthy any more, all you hear is Bernstein and Goldwyn and the like.' He punched the air with a fist. 'If we don't watch out for ourselves the Jews will over-run us too . . .'

'You're exciting yourself,' Delia warned, and tugged at his jacket again.

'I will have my say!' Ernie moved out of her reach, back from the table and closer to Lavinia. 'And what I have to say is this: Ireland must remain neutral to the end so as to keep us from Jewry. We must safeguard our holy Catholic faith.'

He stopped and stood breathing heavily, his hands behind his back, feet apart. Everyone looked at him. Lavinia's half-open eyes glittered.

'Bravo, Ernie.' Grace clapped slowly in the silence. 'But I really don't think we need worry about our faith, nor about being run over by . . .'

'You are wrong, wrong, wrong, Mrs Sayers!' Ernie, wagging a finger, ignored Delia as she moved to stand beside him, frowning prettily. 'The father of An Taoiseach, the revered Mr De Valera, was a Portuguese Jew. Erskine Childers' grandmother was a Jewess. Jew is written all over the face of our great Minister Lemass at the Department of Supplies. Practically all of the Fianna Fail TDs are in the clutches of the Jews.'

Delia took hold of his arm, firmly. 'Come upstairs, Ernie,' she said, 'you're getting far too excited about things.' She looked around the table. 'It was the champagne did it. He's not used to anything more than the wine and whiskey.'

'We must be vigilant.' Ernie took her hand and held it in

both of his. 'Today's tragedy could very well be a warning shot across the bow, the poor creature in the tank put there as a warning to us all.'

'The tank was used as a way to dispose of her body, nothing more.' Lennox was amused but brisk. 'We should be glad it was discovered. It could easily, if you'll pardon the pun, have gone the way of all flesh in the dissecting room.'

Honor felt her stomach lurch. 'That's not funny, Lennox.'

'It wasn't meant to be. It is, however, true.' He smiled apologetically.

Ernie Gibbons belched and Grace's face glazed over.

'Excuse me – please excuse me.' Ernie was elaborately apologetic, his curls bobbing. 'Disgraceful thing to happen . . .'

'I think, Ernie, that you've had enough to drink and that we've heard enough of your views for one night,' Grace told him.

'Then I'll go.' Ernie retained his dignity. 'But I stand over what I said, and I'll say it any night, to anyone who cares to listen, whether I've drink on me or not.'

On Delia's arm, taking careful steps and with his head held high, Ernie Gibbons exited the room. Just outside the open door he stopped.

'I should go back,' he began, 'they don't understand . . . I should make them see . . .'

'No one disagreed with you, Ernie,' Delia said, 'it's just that they've a different way of putting things.' She pulled the door closed.

'Apple tart, anyone?' Grace said.

# 6

'. . . civilians now leaving besieged Dunkirk under sixty hours truce . . . Germans will be allowed to restore mines and demolitions which block road. Then battle will start up again.'

*Reuters*, October, 1944

The storm ended and frost came in the night. Honor, on her bike going down Shelbourne Road at nine the next morning, caught a wheel in the tram tracks and came off in front of a coal cart outside the post office.

'You'll be killed next time, riding that scrap heap!' yelled the boy driving the cart.

'There's nothing wrong with this bike.' Honor pulled it clear of the threatening wheel and sat on the pavement to catch her breath.

'Throw the fecking thing up here and I'll get rid of it,' the boy said.

'If you so much as look crooked at it I'll call the guards.' Honor grabbed the handlebars and pulled the bike closer.

'Just offering to do you a good turn.' The boy cracked a whip over the horse's back and moved on.

A crowd of gaping children gathered. An adult coming off her bike was more diverting than playing about the stationary trams.

'Your stocking's in flitters and your knee's cut,' said a small girl.

The child was right. One of Honor's goodish, dark blue stockings had blood and skin showing through a hole in the knee. There was gravelly stone in the wound and it hurt when she stood to walk.

'What in the name of God's happened to you? Why're you limping like that?'

Gretta Harte came from behind the counter as Honor hobbled with the bike into the post office. She was paler even than usual, her bony frame bonier.

'I came off the bike.' Honor swore as a warm trickle of blood travelled down her leg. Gretta bent and had a look.

'Needs washing and disinfecting.' She pulled a green baize curtain across the grille. 'Come into the back.' She hung out a Closed sign. 'They can wait for their coupons. The feet are frozen off me standing here anyway.'

She lifted the wooden counter flap and Honor followed her past the mail bags and map-covered walls of the sorting room to Gretta's haven at the back. She'd been reading the newspaper earlier and had the fire blazing. The newspaper had a picture of Earlsfort Terrace on the front.

'Sit,' Gretta said, 'you'll need a glass of port.' She put the kettle on the primus and a bottle of Sandeman on the draining board. Honor sat in the only armchair and rolled the stocking down her leg.

'Damned bike's more trouble than it's worth these days,' she said. The gash was deepish and embedded with grit. But it had stopped bleeding, the blood drying on her leg already. 'Left it in the wrong place yesterday and almost lost it under a hearse.'

'You got it back, that's the main thing.' Gretta handed her a glass of port. 'Put the leg up on a stool.' She poured water from the kettle into a basin and TCP into the water. Honor sipped her port while Gretta bathed the knee clean.

Gretta Harte was one of the most practical and well-prepared women Honor had ever met. She was also, usually, one of the most talkative. Her restrained mood indicated serious hurt that Honor hadn't called before now.

'I've a half-pound of tea for you,' Honor said. 'I'll bring it next time.'

'That'll be nice,' Gretta patted the wound dry, 'whenever you've the time.' She applied a liberal amount of Germolene and bandaged it in place with a piece of lint. The tiny room reeked of TCP.

'You called yesterday.' Honor rolled up her stocking and secured it with a garter.

'I did.' Gretta poured herself a tincture of port and added hot water. 'I was worried about you, but Grace put the run on me.' She sat on the stool. 'I'd heard all about the carry-on at the university. The customers were full of it. I'd to listen to them all yesterday afternoon.'

'I'm sorry I haven't called before now,' Honor said, 'I didn't get back from the funeral until two days ago. I'd have called yesterday but . . .'

'Were you caught up in it?' Gretta demanded.

'Yes,' Honor said, 'and no.'

'Give me the yes bit first.'

'I may have seen her in the tank,' Honor said, and explained about waiting for the lift to the embalming room. 'It might have been her, floating loose. I don't know.' She told of meeting Bernard Corkery, whom Gretta knew, and about having coffee in the Shelbourne, a venue Gretta said she 'wouldn't be caught dead in'.

'The no bit is that I don't really know anything,' Honor said, 'except that the dead woman was a prostitute, embalmed after she was killed and then put into the tank.' She reached for the newspaper. 'Does this have any more details?'

'Indeed it doesn't!' Gretta gave a snort. 'I'd have done a

better job of writing it up myself. There's not a thing printed there that I haven't heard from customers and the people around.'

'What've you heard?'

'A lot of it's likely to be untrue,' Gretta acknowledged, 'but I always maintain that you have to put everything through a sieve to get to the nitty-gritty of things. That's where the truth is, in the nitty gritty.' She clipped back a vagrant strand of dull-blonde hair with a slide. 'It's my view that respect for the truth is what separates us from the savages. That and knowing right from wrong.'

Honor stood up, testing her knee. 'Truth's in short supply, if the stories you heard are anything like the tripe Delia Gibbons dished up to the dinner table last night.'

She walked to the window, three feet away in the tiny room. The yard to the back was still covered in silvery frost. It had been filled with sun and red geraniums the day Gretta had told her she loved Arland Magee. It had been her twenty-eighth birthday and she'd never, she said, loved any man before him.

Gretta stood beside Honor now and emptied the disinfected water down the sink.

'I'm privy to a much better class of gossip than anything Delia Gibbons hears in Woolworth's.' Gretta's grin, always sudden and mostly fleeting, was impish. 'My informants are my neighbours – she's to listen to riff-raff from across the city.' She dried the basin. 'You can take it from me, Honor Cusack, that there's no shortage of riff-raff around. This city's a sewer, running with decadence.'

And Gretta knew her city well. She shared a small, nineteenth-century dwelling in nearby Turner's Cottages with her mother, a sister who danced every Friday night with soldiers in the RDS and the sister's three children. Word on the city's life was as core to life in the cul-de-sac cottages as its damp stone walls.

'Tell me everything you've heard,' Honor said.

'I got the unfortunate creature's name right, which is more than they did in the paper for all their reporters and their questions.' Gretta leaned, arms folded, against the sink. 'Marigold Keogh they're calling her in the paper, but that's only the name she used for working. Her proper name was Bridie, the name her mother gave her. She was Bridie Keogh and she was twenty-two years of age and grew up on the north side, in Eccles Street. In no great splendour either. Will you have a glass of milk now?'

'I will,' Honor agreed. Gretta needed to be kept busy.

'Bridie Keogh was on the game at sixteen years of age.' Gretta filled two mugs from the morning's delivery of fresh milk. 'I'm not judging her but there's a lot of them saying she got her just desserts.'

'The wages of sin?' Honor watched a magpie in the yard try to peck open a canvas bag. One for sorrow.

'They're without sin, of course, those of them throwing the stones,' Gretta commented sarcastically. 'They're the kind attend Masses on the top of Croagh Patrick and ignore the tortured world below.'

'No word from Arland then?' Honor watched a second magpie join the first. Two for joy.

'None.' Gretta was watching the magpies too. They stood quietly together, sipping their milk. A third magpie swooped.

'Three for a death,' said Gretta.

'Three for a wedding,' Honor corrected her.

'The way I learned it,' Gretta said dourly, 'it was one for sorrow, two for mirth, three for a death and four for a birth.'

'Shows you can't even believe the old proverbs.' Honor tapped on the window, hard. The magpies relocated to the top of a nearby wall. 'My mother used to tell us it was one for sorrow, two for mirth, three for a wedding and four for a birth. Makes more sense, if you think about it.' She paused. 'Wedding, birth.'

'Only in a perfect world,' Gretta turned from the window, 'and there's not much perfection about these days. At home or abroad.'

'Lord, but you're in cheerful mood this morning!' Honor put her hand lightly on her friend's shoulder and studied her face when she turned. Gretta's eyes, indigo blue and her finest feature, were slightly red-rimmed. She'd been allowing herself a few tears then. 'He could turn up in a hospital,' Honor said, gently, 'or maybe it's just that he's deserted. You know Arland.'

She knew Gretta too. She might not get over Arland but she would get on with life. Gretta was a warm-hearted stoic.

'I know Arland,' Gretta agreed. 'I know too that he should never have gone. It's not his war to fight.'

'No, it's not his war. God knows whose it is any more.'

Honor had tried to get to know Arland herself, once, for Gretta's sake. Silent, unremarkable Arland who'd worked as a butcher and whose long, thin fingers had been forever carving animals out of wood. When she asked him why he was going to fight in the war he'd said,

'If Hitler conquers England then Ireland will be next. He'd only have to send a platoon of donkeys to capture this country because we've no army worth talking about. I've been thinking I should do my bit to stop it happening.'

He didn't speak about it again and was gone to war within a month.

'I know Arland,' Gretta said again, 'and I know he's not coming back.'

She pulled her cardigan across her chest and tucked her hands under her armpits. Pessimism wasn't her usual approach and Honor, wanting to believe it and wishing Gretta would, said, 'You don't know that.'

'I know he never cared for me in the way I did for him and that I was living in a fool's paradise thinking he'd come round.' Gretta pulled a wry face and shrugged. 'I used to have a fantasy that he'd come into the post office with a single red rose and tell me, in front of everyone in the place, that he'd woken up to the fact he couldn't live without me.' She took the empty glass from Honor. 'I'll wash that.'

'It's not like you to give up,' Honor put her arm briefly about the other woman's shoulders. Gretta, who'd rarely encountered displays of affection, would have considered anything more an imposition.

'It's not like me to avoid reality either.' Gretta dried the glasses. 'I'm growing old and eccentric before my time. I'll find no one to please me now, ever, and that's maybe because I don't want to be pleased.' She looked out the window. 'The magpies are back. All three of them.' She made no attempt to frighten them away.

'Let's see what they've to say here,' Honor said, picking up the newspaper.

There wasn't a lot to read. Marigold Keogh, the paper reported, hadn't been seen for four days before being found in the tank of formalin. The pathologist's report indicated she'd been poisoned before being embalmed. Academic and administrative staff of the medical faculty had been questioned and the body removed. The college president was appalled and horrified, the entire medical faculty in shocked upheaval, the student body unnerved and frightened. And the writer, Honor thought as she put down the paper, was the possessor of a great store of adjectives.

'What did you hear,' she tapped the paper, 'outside of what it says here?'

'They're saying she was living in a flat with a German by the

70

name of Clemens Hauptmann. Had told half a dozen people, in secret, that she was going to be married to him. Poor, silly creature.'

'Is he the one killed her then?'

'He's disappeared anyway. So it looks likely.' Gretta sighed, watching as a thin ray of sun found the window and slanted across the draining board. 'No one could say why he was here. One of the spies, most likely. But there seems no doubt she was fierce fond of him and he of her. Something terrible must have come between them.'

'Do they know why he embalmed her and put her in the tank?'

Gretta rested a hand in the warmth of the sun's ray before answering. 'Why he killed her's the real question. Why he put her in the tank is common sense – he did it to get rid of her body. Should make it easier for the guards to find him, though, if he's still in the country.'

'Why's that?' Honor said, knowing the answer.

'Because he'd have had to get equipment to do what he did and help from someone with medical experience.'

'Lennox Mangan says it would take very little knowledge to do what was done . . .'

'That fella should take his head out of his books and use his common sense more often,' Gretta snorted, 'if he has any, that is. Any man who'd put an eye glass on a perfectly good eye has a lack in him somewhere.' She shook her head. 'Can you imagine a person without medical experience even *thinking* of it as a plan?'

'No,' Honor agreed, 'I suppose not.'

'They'd be left with a terrible mess if it went wrong and what would they do then?' Gretta frowned, 'what's up with you?'

'Nothing.'

'Why're you unplaiting your hair then?' She stared at

Honor. 'I suppose the guards have been talking to Bernard and the fella that works with him?'

'They have . . .'

'And to the doctor you had coffee with?'

'Yes.'

'What do you know about this Dr Raeder?'

'Very little . . .' Honor turned from Gretta's probing stare.

It would have been asking for trouble to tell her friend she'd been searching the morning crowds for Oscar Raeder when she'd fallen off the bike. If he'd been about she'd planned to hop off the bike and walk along with him. If he'd been alone, that was. If he'd been accompanied, and by a woman, she would have felt quite sick.

The realisation had shocked her. She'd no rights in his life. She hardly knew him, for God's sake. They'd had coffee, exchanged a few details of their life stories and shared the experience of hearing about Bridie Keogh's murder. That was all. But it had distracted her enough to send her tumbling from the bike.

'Tell me the very little you know,' Gretta, raising her voice, was insistent.

'He's been here since before the war,' Honor said, slowly, 'he came to study medicine. His mother was Irish.'

'Was she, indeed?' Gretta raised her eyebrows. 'Have you asked yourself, Honor, why he's not fighting for his country?

'Yes. I asked him, too,' Honor snapped, 'and he's a pacifist.'

'They're all pacifists,' Gretta said, darkly, 'according to themselves. De Valera's a pacifist too, and Frank Aiken, and so are half the English and American soldiers walking around the town with army uniforms on them. Has this Raeder a wife or girlfriend?'

'No wife.' Unless he was lying.

'And?'

'Don't know about a girlfriend. He lives around the corner in Lansdowne Road.'

'Does he, indeed?' Gretta raised her eyebrows again. 'Don't know that I've ever seen him in here. Doesn't he have anyone in Germany to send letters to?'

'He's got a father there. Friends too, I suppose,' Honor shrugged, 'if they're not all fighting in the war. Or maybe he uses the post office in Leeson Street, or the GPO even.'

'Maybe that's what he does,' Gretta was brisk. 'And maybe you'll introduce me some day. I've work to do now though, in this particular post office.' She squinted at Honor's knee. 'Stopped bleeding anyway, from the looks of it. If you're feeling up to it you could put your mind at rest about your Dr Oscar by popping round the corner and paying him a visit.'

'I might just do that.'

'Never seek to tell thy love,
Love that never told can be;
For the gentle wind does move
Silently, invisibly.'

William Blake, 'Never Seek to Tell Thy Love'

D r Oscar Raeder had said nothing to Honor about Mr Terence Delaney. The first she knew about him was when he appeared at the bottom of the granite steps leading to the front door of the house in Lansdowne Road. She was about to drop the brass knocker when he shouted at her,

'What do you want?'

The hobnails on his boots cracked against the granite as he came up the steps. He was wearing a cap and long, brown coat tied with a belt. A black haired dog, old and doleful, followed him.

'I came to see Dr Raeder,' Honor moved away from the door. 'This *is* the right house?'

'Might be.' He stood beside her, short and bristling, 'and then again it might not. Who wants to see him?'

The cap made it hard to distinguish his face or tell his age. He could have been anywhere between sixty and ninety. The dog looked older in canine years. He staggered the last few steps before lying with his head on his paws and his eyes closed.

Honor gave the man her name. 'Is Dr Raeder at home?'

'He might be,' he looked at her closely, 'and then again he might not. Didn't know he'd any friends on Clyde Road.'

'And I don't know you,' Honor said.

'You don't need to know me,' the man said, 'it's enough that I've the measure of you. Get up,' he poked a boot gently under the dog's belly, 'you're supposed to be on guard.' The dog stayed where he was.

'Why did you ask me my name if you know who I am?' Honor said.

'I said I had the measure of you, know where you live, not that I knew what you were called.' The old man stood between her and the door. 'He won't want to see you.'

The morning was slow to warm up and Honor was cold. It didn't look like it was going to improve either; the house faced the Botanic Gardens and the leaves on the palms there were still white with frost. She didn't feel at all like humouring Oscar Raeder's cantankerous caretaker. Or whatever the old man was.

'He can tell me himself if he doesn't want to see me.' Quickly, without warning, she stepped sideways round him and dropped the knocker, twice and echoingly, on the door.

The dog gave a half-hearted bark and wagged his tail.

'You'd no right to do that!' The man shook his fist in the air. 'I'll have the guards on you. You're disturbing the peace and you're trespassing. Get on out of here.' His fist, when he lowered it, was distorted by arthritis. 'And you're upsetting the dog,' he finished.

'I wanted to talk to Dr Raeder, I'm a student of his . . .'

'Student? Student be damned!' The man had stepped back and was staring at the ground by her feet. 'Students don't come here to drip blood on to the granite I scrub twice a week.'

Gretta's dressing had come away and the cut knee was bleeding again. The climb up the steps must have done it.

'It's a ploy, a woman's trick,' the old man grumbled. 'You're here to persecute and pursue a man who's never done a scrap of harm to anyone. He's had enough bother these last few days. He needs a bit of peace and quiet. Go on now, get yourself out of here, you hussy, back to Clyde Road with you.'

The wretched man clearly thought she had the curse.

'Dr Raeder invited me here.' It was almost true. 'In fact, he's waiting for me.' A lie. When she dropped the knocker on the door again the old man didn't try to stop her.

'We'll see whether he is or not,' he looked her straight in the eye, 'he's coming now. You've disturbed him at his studies.' The door opened.

Oscar Raeder looked her straight in the eye too, a shocked expression on his face. The dog wagged its tail and barked at him.

'Honor,' he said, 'I wasn't expecting you.' He looked tired and was unshaven.

'I knew you were lying to me!' The old man was triumphant. He called the dog to heel and repeated to Oscar Raeder, 'I knew she was lying. I told her to go. I told her you wouldn't want to see her.'

'It's all right, Terence. Miss Cusack is a student . . .'

'She's bleeding,' the old man shouted.

'You're bleeding.' Oscar Raeder followed the old man's gaze to the ground at Honor's feet.

'Yes, I know.' Honor looked down too, at the small, almost circular pool of blood between her feet on the granite. 'I fell off my bike.'

'I'll talk to you later, Terence,' Oscar Raeder said and took her arm.

Then the door was closed and she was in the hallway, being walked to the back of the house while, distantly, she could hear the old man's hobnails receding down the steps. The house was cold and dark and needed, at the very least, a fresh coat of paint on the walls.

'It's only superficial, a nasty graze . . .' She pulled her arm free when they came to damp, inner lobby and Oscar Raeder stopped to shoulder open a door. 'It's been cleaned already. There's nothing to worry about.'

'No harm in taking a look anyway.' He turned on a light and went ahead of her into a kitchen. A modern electric cooker stood white and isolated against a blue-painted wall. It was as cold as the lobby had been.

'Take a seat.' He switched on an electric plate under a kettle on the cooker.

Honor sat into a wooden chair with arms. The alternative was a bench seat by a wall. Oscar Raeder put an enamel bowl of water on the floor beside her.

'This is embarrassing,' she said, 'it's just a scratch, nothing more. I was passing. I thought I'd see how you were . . .' she hesitated '. . . after yesterday.'

'That was kind of you.' He smiled and she relaxed a little.

'I'd kill for a cigarette,' she said hopefully.

'Sorry.' He looked it. 'Would a pipe be any good to you?'

'Thanks, but no.' She shook her head, smiling. 'Not quite what I had in mind.'

He stood with his back to her, taking a First Aid box from a shelf, and she looked around. It was a kitchen without a table, just worktops. The window had iron bars over it and the garden beyond needed to be cut back. The flagged floor shone like black ice. Honor shivered.

'I wanted to arrange about the dissecting class too.' She spoke to his back, more loudly than she needed to. 'We left things a bit unsettled. I suppose the dissecting room will be out of bounds for a while.' She paused when he turned round. 'Will it?'

'First things first. Where exactly did you fall off your bike?' He came back with the box. 'Open this.'

'You're a bit short on chairs,' Honor said, and opened the First Aid box.

'One is usually enough. I don't use the kitchen much.' He poured warm water on to the cold already in the basin. 'Terence had the cooker put in but I eat in the university mostly. Is there cotton wool in there?'

'Yes. Sorry, I've probably left a trail of blood through your house . . .'

'Take off your coat, and your shoe and stocking.' He took the cotton wool from her.

'I'll clean it myself,' she offered quickly.

'Here you are then.' He handed her the cotton wool and watched while she unlaced her shoe, rolled down the torn stocking and pushed the skirt above her knee. 'A longish laceration but you're right, it's not serious.' He hunkered down and touched the broken skin. 'There's wool from your skirt in there. We don't want infection to start.'

'No. *We* don't,' Honor said, and dabbed at it. To distract herself while she worked she told him about Gretta and the cut's earlier cleaning. 'This is a terrible fuss about nothing.'

'It's not terminal,' he agreed, 'but there's always the danger it could go septic. There's some potassium permanganate in the box. Put some on now and take the rest with you. Ideally,' he emptied the bowl of water into the sink and ran a tap, 'you should put the sound stocking on the wounded leg to keep the dressing in place.'

Ideally . . . Did he mean here, now? He was waiting. He obviously did.

'I don't have far to go,' she said, 'it'll be all right. I've taken enough of your time.'

Someone knocked on the front door, hard.

'Cover it up,' he was smiling, 'only sensible thing to do.'

She pulled up the torn stocking, covering the bandage as best she could. The knocking went on, louder now, a drumbeat from another world.

'Aren't you going to answer the door?'

'No. I would like to offer you a drink, however.'

'A drink?'

'There's brandy, whiskey, port, red wine.' He hesitated then said abruptly, 'I don't do much entertaining. The drawing room's where I live, mostly. It's warmer up there.'

'It's early in the day and I've already had a glass of port.' She heard and hated the stilted nature of their conversation. 'From Gretta,' she added. They'd got along fine the day before.

But the day before they'd been surrounded by people, with the diversions of other conversations. This vast, lonely, lifeless kitchen gave her the creeps.

'Have another,' he offered.

'Lead on,' she said, smiling, and followed him back along the hallway to the front of the house.

Maybe he was a drinker. Maybe that was his story. Maybe she'd have a quick drink with him and make her way home when the frost had melted.

The drawing room was definitely, as he'd promised, more lived in than the kitchen. On her way to an armchair Honor waded through drifts of paper and newspapers, skirted armchairs sinking under books and sat, in the end, on what she thought was a cushion but quickly realised was a wet bathroom towel.

'Sorry.' Oscar Raeder took it from her and dropped it into another chair. 'I've been a bit distracted.'

'Understandably,' Honor said and smiled and stood in front of the lazily smouldering fire.

The fire didn't do much to heat the room, which wasn't a lot warmer than the kitchen and was darker. Heavy, tightly drawn curtains kept the heat in but the light out. What there was came from a reading lamp and heavy chandelier. The fire was burning coal slack mixed with turf and pitch, notoriously unresponsive when it came to fostering a warm glow.

'Do you mind if I open the curtains?' Honor said, and went to the window without waiting for his response. 'Habit,' she said, half-turning, 'my mother hated to keep the daylight out.' He was staring at her, again.

'What is it?' she said.

'Stay that way,' he said.

'You're embarrassing me,' she laughed, glad of the cold sun on her cheek, the way it cooled the flush coming up from her neck.

'You're lovely in the sunlight,' he said. 'What would you like to drink?'

'What about a brandy?' she suggested, and moved away from the light. 'That's a sort of daytime drink, isn't it?'

'Let's pretend it's night,' he moved quickly and closed the curtains, 'then we can both have a brandy.' He cleared a space for a bottle and two glasses on the table. 'Terence hates the curtains opened before midday. Says the morning sun fades the furniture.' He poured. 'I can only take his word for it.'

'Thank you.' Honor took a glass and wondered how the sun could be expected to penetrate the paper blanketing the room. She stood awkwardly with her drink.

'It's a hell-hole, I know,' Oscar Raeder suddenly grinned, 'but it's my hell-hole. I don't think about it until somebody like you sees it for the first time. Here.' He cleared an armchair for her to sit in.

He sat on the table himself, one leg swinging and the glass resting on his knee. He was trying hard, Honor thought, but he was not relaxed. At least the knocking on the front door had stopped.

'Tell me about Terence' she said. 'He appeared behind me, out of nowhere.'

'He appeared from the basement, where he lives. Please

don't worry about him. His bark's definitely worse than his bite.'

'Who is he?' Honor persisted.

'His name's Terence Delaney. He's eighty-four years old. My grandfather called him his butler but he was caretaker, nurse, everything . . .'

'Why does he think he owns you?'

'Yes, I should explain this,' he gestured vaguely around the room, 'the way I live . . .' He stopped talking again.

'You don't have to,' Honor said.

'I think I must,' he said, and looked into his glass of brandy. He hadn't yet taken a drink from it; Honor hadn't touched hers either.

'I left Germany because I knew what was coming and like many others could do nothing to stop it.' He looked up at her, briefly, gave a slight nod before going on. 'I found, of course, that I couldn't totally leave it behind. I'd seen certain things . . . because I'd heard rumours about them and sought proof for myself. I knew that gypsies and retarded people were being forced to labour in camps. That those who questioned the Nazi Party and Adolf Hitler were being flogged or imprisoned, even killed. The secret police were everywhere. The Jews were being persecuted.' He drank some of his brandy. 'I knew that German industry had been brought back from the dead and that unemployment had ended.' He didn't look at her when he stopped speaking.

'We read . . . things in the paper,' Honor said, 'but I don't know that many people really understood.'

She hadn't, anyway. Nor had she tried to. There was nothing she could say to comfort him, nothing. She held on to the glass for dear life.

'It seemed to me that if I studied and worked and achieved medical expertise then I could be of some use to Germany when it's all over.' He finished his brandy. 'I have been

81

doing that, and precious little else. And that is my story, Miss Cusack.'

Honor sat very straight in the armchair. 'I think I understand,' she said. In fact, she understood him very well and wished she knew of a way to tell him so. But she didn't so she added, after a minute or two of not uncomfortable silence, 'I'm not a lot wiser about Terence Delaney.'

'Ah, Terence.' He shook his head and smiled his lopsided smile. Honor smiled back.

'Well?' she prompted.

The knocking came on the front door again, four sharp raps in a row. Oscar Raeder gave no indication he'd heard.

'The door . . .' Honor began.

'Terence will deal with it and I'll tell you his story. It's the story of the family who lived in this house, really.' He spoke quickly.

There were another four raps on the door but no sound of Terence Delaney thumping up from the basement in his hobnails.

'He came to work for my mother's family sometime around 1880. My grandmother died a young woman and my grandfather left Terence looking after this place when he took my mother, whose name was Eleanor, to Baden Baden. She stayed in Germany, as I told you, which left my grandfather to live out a reclusive life alone in this house. Terence looked after both him and the house and they grew old here together. It's Terence's house now, my great-grandfather left it to him. He just prefers to live in the basement, where he's always been.' Oscar smiled. 'He has his own story too, our Terence. He fought in the Civil War with Michael Collins. Went missing and turned up four years later. He doesn't talk about it.'

'So you've taken your grandfather's place in his life, in a way?'

'I suppose I have, in a way.'

The knocking had stopped. Honor sipped her brandy

and stood up. Her knee was still covered and she moved around, testing it for stiffness. On a low table she came across a gramophone player, an uneven pile of wax records beside it.

'There's someone living in the basement in Clyde Road too. She's about Terence's age. Maybe they're both in retreat from the new Ireland we keep hearing about. It's very likely she and Terence know each other.' She looked at him. 'You could come to dinner on Friday, if you like, and meet her?'

She regretted the invitation immediately. He couldn't meet Lavinia without meeting the others, Grace too. Not a good idea. Not yet anyway. Maybe in the future, if their friendship *had* a future.

'That would be interesting,' he said, polite but nothing more. He didn't really want to come then. She could forget she'd said anything.

'The police took my fingerprints,' he said, and the day before came alive again, there between them in the bewildered hurt of his words. 'They didn't fingerprint anyone else, no one in the college anyway. They just took statements from the others.'

'Why you then?' Honor said.

'They clearly suspect I had something to do with the woman's murder.'

'Why would they think that?'

'Why *wouldn't* they?' he countered. 'She had a German lover. I have keys to the dissecting room. I was the last person to request a body from the tank. There's a war on. It might seem more natural to help a fellow country-man get home than to hinder him. All truly patriotic Germans are going home to fight after all.' He looked at her, eyes studying hers as if he could read in them what she was thinking. 'They seem to imagine that at the very least

83

I helped Hauptmann embalm the body. Though maybe they imagine I strangled her too. Who knows what they've dreamed up?'

'She was strangled? I'd heard poisoned . . .' Honor's mouth had gone dry. She sat down on the arm of the chair and held on to the back of it, tightly. Strangled. Killed by external compression of the throat. Horrible.

'That's what the post-mortem revealed.' Oscar Raeder rubbed his eyes with one hand. 'Poor woman,' he said, 'it was a terrible way to die.'

'Not much of a burial place either.'

'The police say I can't leave Ireland, though God knows where they expect me to go. I'm to tell them too if I travel anywhere within the country.' He got off the table and walked over to where the brandy bottle stood. 'You can hardly blame them, I suppose.' He stared at the bottle without touching it. 'They have to start somewhere.'

'If there's anything I can do . . .' Honor began

'The dissecting room's sealed off,' he interrupted, 'but I'll do that hour's work with you as soon as it's open again. That'll be in about a week, according to the guards.'

'Thank you.'

A dog barked in the silence. It sounded far away but was probably Terence Delaney's dog in the basement. 'Terence calls his dog Setanta,' Oscar said.

'That was the warrior Cuchulain's name when he was a boy,' Honor said.

'Yes,' Oscar Raeder said. When the dog stopped barking the silence had an echoing quality. Honor sat quite still, staring at the dead-looking fire, wishing she could find something reassuring to say to him. She couldn't think of a thing.

'I must go,' she stood up.

'How's the leg?' He was on his feet too, face worried as he looked at her.

'Dressing in place. Bleeding stopped. Thank you, Doctor,' she smiled at his serious expression, a rush of affection warming her. He smiled too.

'I'll drive you home,' he offered.

'It's less than ten minutes walk. There's no need. It would be a total waste of your emergency petrol.'

'How I use my petrol is my business,' he sounded irritable.

When he took her elbow she didn't resist. He held it firmly, even when he opened the door and ushered her into the hallway.

There was an envelope on the mat inside the front door. Oscar Raeder left it where it was when he opened it to a blast of icy air and the cawing of seagulls. The weather must be bad at sea if the gulls were coming inland in such numbers.

The pale sun had melted the frost from the windows of the car, a two-tone Ford 8 in cream and brown. When the engine started on the second turn of the key Oscar Raeder gave a low, triumphant whistle.

'Got her,' he said.

Honor, looking back when they got to the end of the road, saw the black dog standing on the footpath outside the house. Terence Delaney was probably there too, skulking behind him in the garden.

When they stopped in Clyde Road she couldn't open the door on her side.

'I'll do it for you.' He leaned across and she held her breath and stared straight ahead. If she moved their faces might collide. She had no idea what she would do if that happened.

The door fell open and he moved back.

'I'll see you on Friday then, for dinner,' he said.

'Yes. Yes, of course.' She didn't look at him while getting out of the car. 'My aunt is a good cook. She'll be glad to meet you. And Lavinia, of course.' She was babbling. Grace would be no such thing. Neither would Lavinia. God, what had she done, inviting him?

'What time is dinner?' He was smiling.

'Half-seven for eight.' It was what Grace would have said.

'I'll be there.' He hesitated, then got out his side of the car and leaned against it.

'Would you like to come for a drive to the mountains tomorrow?' He rapped on the car roof with his hand. 'I rarely use this thing and I've a tankful of petrol.' He made it sound as if she would be doing him a favour. Maybe that was how he felt.

'Sounds like a good idea,' Honor smiled.

It was a great idea. Freedom and the mountains for a day. A chance too to rearrange Friday . . .

'What time will you pick me up?' she said.

# 8

# The Basement

'. . . We rest on a trestle of shadow
And joke that we're dead but uncoffined. Our one expectation
Is never to be forgiven.'

Bruce Williamson, 'Afternoon in Anglo-Ireland'

It's dangerous, they say, to get what you wish for. Honor
Cusack is in danger of getting what she's long, and uncon-
sciously, wished for and of proving the old adage right.

I could see all of this yesterday, Sunday, when she came to
see me in the late-afternoon. She was restless and didn't want
to be with me at all but I provided a refuge of sorts. She'd been
disappointed by her German and was still forlornly hoping he
might appear.

I watched her as she paced my rooms. She was wearing
a two-piece costume in Glen Check with a velvet collar and
buttons. The skirt had three pleats in the front and three in
the back and was short enough for me to see where she had
a bandage on one knee. She'd bought the costume for thirty
coupons, most of which were donated by me when she didn't
have the £6.10.6d. it cost in Switzers. The coupons were of
no use to me anyway.

'You're restless,' I said at last.

'Sorry.' She sat down in the Charles II chair brought with
me from Skelfort when I married Lionel. I didn't like her
sitting there but at least it kept her back straight while she

87

was speaking to me. She had coiled and pinned her hair up in a way that was new.

A woman changes when she falls in love with a man. It happened to me and it happened to Grace Danaher when, God help him, she fell in love with my son. Now it's happening to Honor Cusack. She has never been in love before and is confused and resisting. But love's madness has its way with all of us and she is no different from anyone else.

Love is many things. It can be wishing for another's happiness before one's own or it can be wanting possession of that other. It can also be a mistake. Someone filling a need in one's life makes them an object of love but not always a loved one. Love and need do, however, often coincide.

The German fills a need in Honor Cusack's life.

'I like it here.' She crossed her legs at the ankle, quite elegantly, and stretched her wounded leg in front of her. She has long legs. 'I like the lavender smell. I like having the sideboards and mahogany bookshelves all around me. I even like seeing those ancestors of yours looking down on me from the walls.' She smiled. 'God knows why . . .'

She liked them for the same reason her aunt did; such things stood for security and wealth and, since they both came from the nothingness of the Irish peasantry, they knew well the value of such things.

'I like them too,' I said. 'Now that my family is dead, murdered by this state and history and the woman upstairs, they're all that I have . . .'

'Don't start on all that, Mrs Sayers.' Her eyes glazed over and she looked annoyed. 'It won't bring your son and husband back and it gives me a headache.' She left the chair. 'Also, I'm not in the mood today.'

I sulked for a while after this. Part of the reason I tolerated her was a need in me to vent my spleen and she had often,

88

in the past, been good enough to lend me her ear. Love was already making her selfishly intolerant.

'What has affected your mood?' I said when it was clear she was prepared to pace by the window indefinitely.

'I had an arrangement with the doctor I told you about.' She stood with her back to me, looking out of the window. 'The German one who teaches anatomy?' She turned to ensure that I remembered. I nodded and she turned away again. 'We were to go driving in the mountains today. He should have been here hours ago. It's almost dark. He won't come now.'

'Perhaps he forgot,' I said cruelly. Did she really think herself suitably dressed for a mountain drive in her velvet-collared costume?

'Perhaps.' She didn't look back at me.

'Or maybe he has been arrested for murder,' I offered.

'That is less likely.' She turned to frown at me. 'You hate him without even knowing him. Not all Germans are the same, Mrs Sayers, any more than all Irish people are.'

'How wise you are,' I said, 'about Irish people. Tell me about him. Your friendship would seem to have deepened since last we spoke.'

And since her defence of him at the dinner table too. I'd noticed then how she'd defended from a well of ignorance, how nakedly she'd exposed herself, and how her aunt had been forced to control her own possessive fear for the young woman.

'Obviously not as much as I thought.' She was sour-faced, leaning against the window sill while she unpinned her hair and shook it free.

'He lives on Lansdowne Road,' she said, 'I called to see him about the classes I missed. I'd cut my knee and he drove me home. That's all.'

It wasn't quite all but I let it go. 'I'd be obliged if you'd build up the fire for me,' I said, 'I'm feeling the cold today.'

'Are you all right?' she said immediately.

I gestured impatiently to the fire. I needed her to be quiet for a minute while I considered what to do with the information she'd just given me.

She had confirmed what I'd suspected by telling me he lived in Lansdowne Road and had had an Irishwoman for a mother.

Her Dr Raeder was a scion of the Leahy family, once reasonably respectable for Catholics but destroyed by a young woman's ill-advised marriage to a German. I'd known them, though not well. They weren't really my kind of people.

The marriage which led to the Leahy family's downfall took place in Germany in the year 1910. I had arrived in Clyde Road as a not so young bride of twenty-nine in 1894 and had come across the Leahy patriarch a couple of times socially with Lionel. His name was Desmond Leahy and he was a nodding acquaintance of my late husband. Lionel was a *bon vivant* and met everyone locally. I was always more discriminating about the company I kept.

The third time I met Desmond Leahy I was out walking alone. He was walking too, along Lansdowne Road with a retainer fellow for company. We spoke briefly and he told me he was in mourning for his daughter who'd both married and died in Germany.

Much later I'd come across his own death notice in the paper. Not before his time either; he'd been ninety-four. That was in 1939, just before the outbreak of war, when I'd still been inclined to go out occasionally. I called to the house on the funeral morning with a condolence card and the retainer, changed hardly at all from the first time I'd seen him, took it from me at the door. A thin young man had appeared behind him in the hallway and offered me a sherry.

There were no other callers or mourners that I could see, so I stepped inside and accepted the drink. The young man, as I sipped, introduced himself as Oscar Raeder, grandson of the dead man. He was, he explained when I asked, the son of Desmond Leahy's daughter Eleanor, here in Dublin to study medicine.

I had decided, once I was sure of the facts, that I would tell Honor I'd had a sudden recollection of meeting her friend. It would make her more inclined to keep me informed of future developments, and so keep me a step, if not several, ahead of Grace Danaher.

'I am fairly certain that I've met your Dr Raeder,' I said, and told her the circumstances. She listened attentively, hands in the pockets of her costume, leaning against a sideboard.

'Dublin's such a close-knit place,' she said when I'd finished, 'everyone knows about or is connected to everyone else. Whether it's Clyde Road or Turner's Cottages, it's all the same.'

She stood with her head down, thinking. She was cross, as I'd known she would be, because I'd incorporated her new friend into the life of Clyde Road. Honor Cusack very much wanted something of her life to be separate and her own. But that was her problem and something she would have sort out for herself. It didn't suit my purposes to help her.

'I don't know why they call this a city.' She was harsh-voiced when she spoke again. 'I believed, before I came to live here, that a city was a place where people minded their own business, not everyone else's. I was sure I would be able to live my life without being watched,' she traced a circle on the carpet with the toe of her shoe, 'but it's as bad here as Kilmacreen, or even Cloclia. Worse, in fact,' she corrected herself bitterly. 'In the village and countryside around they're still fighting the Civil War and you've to watch your neighbour in order to protect yourself and your family. There's no excuse here other than nosiness and interfering and mischief-making.'

She was only partly right. The Civil War was no more ended in Dublin than in any other part of this wretchedly incestuous island.

'And of which of those three vices are you accusing me?' I spoke harshly. Better to stop her meanderings before they led us somewhere I didn't want her to go. She didn't answer immediately.

'I don't know,' she said at last, no apology in her tone, 'there are times when I don't know what to make of you, Mrs Sayers, and this is one of them.'

'I'm coming to the end of my life,' I spoke with quiet dignity, on safe ground with this at least, 'and would like to be given the respect my years warrant.'

She laughed, quite cheerfully and certainly dismissively. 'The feeble old lady role doesn't suit you, Mrs Sayers, it never will,' she said. 'The fact that you're *not* a feeble old lady is what I like about you. But, as a favour to me, would you please, please not tell my aunt you know Oscar's family?'

Oscar. So he'd stopped being Dr Raeder, or even Oscar Raeder.

'If you insist,' I said.

Nothing binds more firmly than a secret shared. Things were exactly as I wanted them to be.

I said nothing to her about comparing Clyde Road with Turner's Cottages, but it was an affront I would not forget.

'He was questioned by the guards and his fingerprints taken,' she went on, 'but there's no word of them arresting anyone for the woman's murder.'

'That would call for intelligence and efficiency,' I said. I was feeling more tired than was usual for me and wanted to lie down. I closed my eyes and leaned back in my chair. 'You're right in imagining your aunt will not approve of your affair with the German . . .'

'I'm not having an affair.'

'. . . and nor will her cohorts Mangan and Mitchell. What the Gibbons pair think is of no importance, but you are wise to be careful.'

'It's no concern of theirs what I do, or who my friends are.'

Brave words, but untrue and she knew it – otherwise she would not have asked for my silence. She was a core part of the closed world her aunt had constructed with her cronies and would not be allowed to escape easily.

Grace Danaher loves her niece. Honor is the child she didn't have but she is also her own, younger self, the young woman who threw away the opportunity of being one of the first women in medical school and opted instead for a life of manipulation and gross sensual indulgence. She seeks now to relive her life through her niece and, up until this summer, it seemed as if she might succeed in doing so.

But persuading the young woman Honor has become into the medical school was, I suspect, a bridge too far. Honor is not unintelligent. Nor is she without dreams of her own, even if she is afraid to contemplate them.

She is not, either, the stuff of which doctors are made. For that she needs a certain detachment, a cooler intelligence than the often dreamy, if sometimes sharp, mind I've observed. I suspect she has in her the stuff of a teacher or poet *manqué*. The change I've observed in her has to do with a growing fear and dread at the prospect of years of study followed by life in a profession for which she has no passion.

She is on the point of rebellion. And the German doctor is to hand. Honor Cusack wants to flee her life and he offers her a way out. How long it will be before she fully knows this herself, sees freedom and flight in her German doctor and not love at all, is the question.

'You saw how they were at dinner,' I pointed out, 'all the signs are that Mangan would annul your affair, Mitchell scoff it out of existence, and your aunt diminish it. The

93

Gibbonses' histrionics count for nothing but will be an annoyance.'

I heard Algernon arrive, scratching at the window. Walter would not be far behind.

'Let him in,' I said, 'and then you should go. I need to rest.'

I kept my eyes closed, discouraging further talk, and she went to the window and opened it, letting in a blast of air that was full of winter. The dark months and long nights were upon us.

'You could call to Lansdowne Road,' I suggested as she put Algernon in my lap, 'ask him why he broke his promise.'

'No,' she said, quickly, 'I won't do that. It's for *him* to explain to *me*. He could have sent the old man who lives there with him to explain. Or he could have come himself.'

She has pride. But it won't save her. It never does.

'You'd better apply yourself to your books then,' I said, 'make some use of your time.'

'I suppose so,' she said. Her lack of enthusiasm had never been more clear to me.

'Bring me a footstool and rug,' I said, 'I will rest by the fire until Walter comes home.'

She did as I asked, fussing too much for my taste but leaving me alone at last.

Walter took his time about coming back. Tom cats, like the male of all species, will spread their seed and breed whenever and wherever the mood and fancy takes them. But like all males too they return in due course to home and comfort and the hand that feeds.

They never expect it to bite as well.

Algernon, older and like myself a little tired, sat with me while I remembered another year, another turning season, and the joys of having a son.

Douglas gave no sign, as a boy, that he would become a Republican and a so-called patriot. I remember him, at ten

94

years old, reading a copy of *The Spirit of the Nation* and writing on it, very clearly, 'Patriotism is the last refuge of the scoundrel.' I praised him for his perception and he smiled up at me and said, 'You believe that, Mama, I know you do.'

And so I did.

My own upbringing had been a chequered one. My father's family could trace its line back to one of Cromwell's officers, a fact of which my father was proud. He believed that half the people in Ireland, especially the stronger and healthier ones, were descended from Cromwell's soldiers.

I was an only child, like Douglas, and to compensate for the lack of company my parents took me most places with them. As a consequence I didn't know much about being a child and worried about my character and being good from an early age. A governess started me on this path, strongly supported by my mother. I was a child who worried.

Skelfort was set in a wilderness of heather which stretched for mile upon mile and covered the low hills all around. A river ran through the heather, and two roads which I was forever watching for signs of activity from the long window in my bedroom. When I saw the crusaders from the Evangelical Movement coming I ran with my governess to welcome them. They preached that there was a dreadful hell, with everlasting pains, where sinners must with devils dwell in darkness, fire and chains. I feared this for years.

I was twelve years old when I noticed my mother's joy going from her, fourteen when she died, and a year older than that when my father brought home his second wife.

She was a sad misjudgment and was, in the end, the cause of our losing everything. Because of her my father began wintering in Egypt, and because of her my father, until then a cautious man, entered into any number of risky ventures.

I don't blame him. Men are feeble in matters of emotion and their loins, and he was no different. No different from

95

my son, his grandson, who was a sensitive child and who inherited his weaknesses.

It was my father's second wife who, by her example, helped me stop believing, and fearing, the Evangelical word. Watching her taught me a lot of things, not least to value and use my power over men.

He died at this time of the year, my golden-haired son with the beatific smile. Disease had thinned his hair and strained that smile, but death gave him back the look of boyish innocence the woman he married had taken from him.

Grace Danaher nursed him, in this house, to the end. But nursing was what she was trained to do and he said he would rather die in a short time at home with her than take longer in a sanatorium. Her so-called healing gift did him no good, no good at all. He already had tuberculosis when he returned to us after his imprisonment in Wakefield Prison, where they took him after his capture for his part in the abortive rebellion of Easter, 1916. Notwithstanding, he went back to fighting in the Civil War, until he became too ill to continue. She nursed him then, for two years, until he died in 1923.

She looked after him well, I will give her that.

But she looked after herself even better, never denying herself the company of other men nor the pleasure of their bodies. She was not fond of men from her own peasant class. She met both of the men who are her lap dogs still through her interest in medicine.

Lennox Mangan was wealthy and she met him when he was toying with the study of medicine. Florrie Mitchell was something of a society artist at the time and she came upon him when he was doing anatomical drawings in the medical faculty. She enslaved both by giving her body and keeping her heart.

All this while my son was dying.

Lionel was enslaved, too, but I put a stop to that, a long time ago.

My musings on all of this stopped when Walter came at last and I had to go to the window to let him in. He circled my legs, rubbing himself ingratiatingly against me, as I stood for a while remembering again, this time the late-autumn day on which Douglas died.

I'd insisted he be buried in the small graveyard not far from Skelfort. I will lie there in time myself, next to where Lionel lies waiting in *his* grave. The autumn was a glorious affair that year, dry and cold with leaves of all colours bright against the sky. We took my son's coffin off the train and carried it along the narrow country roads on a day bright with impossible hope.

By the time it was over, and we were waiting for the train back to Dublin, the sky had become thick and stormy.

It is my belief that while the malignant deeds of the past merely appear to lie dormant they are in fact growing, taking on new life. They touch everything and everyone who comes in contact with them, the innocent and the guilty both.

I have done wrong in my time but, unlike the Catholics, I do not expect to be forgiven.

What I do expect is that there will be a day of reckoning. There always is.

# 9

'To the traveller arriving from England's black-out Dublin's sea of lights is like a magic lantern . . . the enjoyment of leisurely gossip reminds the visitor of long-forgotten times.'

*Neue Zurcher Zeitung*, Switzerland, 1942

The Black Hob cafe, early on Monday morning, was thick with smoke and black with clerically garbed students. Bernard Corkery, sitting with Dandy Lyons at a table by the window, discouraged would-be occupiers of a third, empty seat at their table.

'Push off,' he told a hovering clerical student. With the young man's companion he was more impatient. 'Go rest your arse on some of the hot air filling the rest of the place,' he advised.

'Steady on, lad,' Dandy Lyons said, 'Maisie's not half so fond of medicals as she is of her clericals. You'll get us thrown out.' He flicked the lace curtain along its brass rod and cleared an eye-hole in the window. 'Your fancy woman's coming. No good you losing the head and both of us our seats before she gets here.' He angled his hat more firmly on his head.

'It's losing my effing job I'm worried about,' Bernard said. 'I'd membership of the ranks of the unemployed for too long to want to rejoin.' He helped himself to a cigarette from Dandy's packet of Kerry Blues. 'You're sure she's headed this way?'

'Almost upon us,' Dandy Lyons confirmed. 'For a Catholic country lad you're very down on the clerical students.'

'It's profound conversation over coffee I'm not keen on.' Bernard shrugged.

'You'll need to avoid this place on Monday mornings so,' said Dandy. 'It's their sanctuary at the beginning of the week. Maisie's ministrations ease them back into the real world.'

'Won't be hard to keep away from here,' Bernard said, 'medical faculty's likely to be closed for reasons of murder for a while to come.'

Dandy Lyons examined the burning end of his cigarette. 'Perhaps. But one can never be too sure of anything in this life.'

The Black Hob had an ochre-painted door and permanently steamed-up windows. Inside it was long and narrow, its customers packed around square wooden tables covered in plastic lace cloths, drinking weak, overpriced coffee. A chicory substitute was stronger and cheaper and, for those who could do without the caffeine, better value. It came in bigger cups too. The third alternative, made from cocoa husks and much sweetened, was a speciality of the house called chock.

Honor came through the door too quickly and Maisie Moran, who ran the place, had to sidestep smartly to save the mugs of chock she was carrying.

'We're full.' She jerked her head at the open door. 'You can take yourself back out every bit as fast as you came in.' Maisie preferred her customers male and grateful.

'She's an invited guest.' Dandy, on his feet and smiling, put one arm around Honor and the other around the cafe's owner. 'Don't be hard on her, Maisie, she's a famished innocent and an old friend of our esteemed Mr Corkery. We found her wandering and cold earlier and asked her to join us. She's . . .'

99

Whispering in Maisie's ear, he eased Honor into the third chair.

'I'm not sure I believe you, Dandy Lyons.' Maisie put the mugs on the table and eyed Honor. 'But she can stay anyway. I'll get her the chock. She could do with it, from the looks of her.'

'*What* did you tell her?' Honor shrugged herself out of her coat. She wouldn't have had room to move at the table with it on. 'And I don't want a cup of boiled cocoa husks so you can . . .'

'A polite "thank you, Dandy" is all that's needed.' He brought his knees primly together and sniffed. 'You'd be back outside in the street if it wasn't for me so be glad and be grateful for what you're about to receive. I am also constrained to say,' he drummed his manicured nails on the table top and hissed, 'that if yourself and Bernard here can't display better manners and a bit of humour then I'll leave ye alone with the clericals.' He raised his voice. 'See how ye like *that*.'

'Sorry, Dandy, and thanks, Dandy,' Honor smiled, 'and please don't go, Dandy. Don't leave us alone.'

'That's more like it,' he said, 'only remember, there's things other than listening to the pair of you I could be doing with a free morning. Maisie, you're a jewel and a flower.' He beamed as Honor's chock appeared. 'That'll make all the difference in the world to her health and well-being.'

'Who's paying?' said Maisie, who hadn't survived in business alone, into her sixties, without commercial acumen. 'You or her?'

'What was it you told her?' Honor sipped and grimaced, after Dandy had paid.

'That you were alone in the dissecting room with the murdered whore for a full hour, studying,' Dandy said. 'That you're in shock and having nightmares.'

'Is that true?' A freckle-faced clerical student turned to face them from the next table. 'You were there all the time she was in the tank?'

His companions sat hunched and waiting for her answer.

'Leave the woman alone.' Bernard Corkery cracked his large knuckles. 'Be more in your line to pray for the departed's soul. There's enough practising calumny and detraction in this town without would-be princes of the church cashing in on a sinner's misfortune.'

'How did you know she was different from the other cadavers?' The freckled cleric turned his back on Bernard and his chair to face Honor. 'Was she . . . newer-looking, or what?'

'Didn't I tell you to leave her alone?' Bernard Corkery leaned over and tapped the cleric on the shoulder. 'Whether they're living or dead you fellas can't lay off the women, can ye?'

'I was only . . .' the man began.

'Well, don't. Stick to your own table and your own company and we'll all be a lot happier.'

'Watch it, Bernard.' Dandy aimed a kick at his leg as Maisie approached. 'Terrible the amount of upset poor Marigold Keogh's death's caused,' he said when she stood over them.

'Is that what the problem is?' Maisie was looking hard at Honor. 'Monday mornings are usually peaceful times in here. If you medical lot are bringing your troubles in with you then you'd better clear off.' She frowned and wiped ash from the table with a damp, yellow dishcloth. 'I don't need your business and I won't have my regulars disturbed.'

'Let them be, Maisie,' the clerical student said, 'they're no doubt disturbed by what happened, especially with a member of the medical faculty staff's being arrested. It's all very sad, very sad indeed. Reflects on all of us.'

'Who've they arrested?' Bernard said.

'Didn't you know? Monsignor Lamb was able to tell us first thing this morning. Isn't that so, lads?'

'That's right, Sean,' one of his companions said, 'seems they arrested the German doctor, Raeder, sometime yesterday. Caught up with him on the Curragh, trying to escape.'

'Funny place to go to escape.' Honor's voice sounded, to her own ears, almost normal. 'No airport, no port, not even a place to hide . . .' She was beginning to sound hysterical. Better stop.

'The Monsignor has it on good authority that the work of the Civic Guards revealed the man's roguery and spying activities.' Older than his companions and with the high brow of an ascetic, a priest sitting with the students was impatient. 'He was attempting to make contact with some other of his kind, a prisoner in the Curragh camp, when he was apprehended. We must thank God for a speedy end to an unpleasant incident.'

'Is your Monsignor always so very well-informed?' Honor sipped at her drink. Unable to stomach the mixture, she pushed the cup away.

'Always.' The man counted out coins and gave them to Maisie. 'We should be going now, lads.' He stood and so did the clericals in The Black Hob, getting to their feet as one body and leaving in ones and twos. 'I'm sorry to have been the bearer of bad news,' the priest looked from Honor to Dandy to Bernard, 'but it will all be for the best. A decent Irish doctor will be brought in by the college to take his place and the medical department will be the better for it.'

'You're right, Father Breen, you're right.' Maisie gathered up and counted the coins. 'An Irish Ireland for the Irish people is what I always say.'

'The women will be safe at least.' The student Dandy had whispered to nodded to Honor as he backed out of the door. 'They won't need to be watching their backs as they go about their studies.'

'The women students of this college are God-fearing and Catholic.' Father Breen stood in the open doorway. 'Their virtue and their God will protect them.'

The door banged shut, sending a blast of icy air through the cigarette pall. Maisie began cleaning the empty tables with great swipes of the yellow cloth.

'I'll have a coffee, please,' Honor called.

Her stomach was turning. The chock had been a mistake. The news of Oscar was a mistake too. It had to be. She would catch a tram to Lansdowne Road and find out. After the coffee. She caught Maisie's eye.

'I keep what coffee I have for my regulars.' The woman frowned. 'It's only fair. You can have a cup of chicory.'

'I won't have anything then.'

'That's probably best,' agreed Maisie.

There was a small silence in the empty cafe while Bernard smoked the end of his cigarette and Dandy opened out his newspaper. Faced with the front page Honor saw that General Patton's Third Army had taken the city of Metz and that beef in the west of Ireland was sixpence a pound as compared to two and ten in Dublin.

There was nothing, on the front page anyway, about Oscar Raeder's arrest. Maybe she should leave now.

'I think I'll go . . .'

She was halfway out of her chair when Bernard, turning a wide smile Maisie's way and restraining Honor with a hand on her arm, said, 'I'd be indebted if you'd stretch a point and make a coffee for Miss Cusack. She needs it more than most this morning.'

'Since you put it so nicely,' Maisie said, 'I'll get one for her!'

'Well, there you have it.' Bernard stubbed out his cigarette. 'Case solved. Done and dusted, according to the druids.' He helped himself to another of Dandy's Kerry Blues.

'Steady on there.' Dandy retrieved the package. 'I don't manufacture the buggerin' things, you know.' He put the paper down. 'Not a nag running that's worth putting a bob on either.' He shook his head.

103

'I've an order in with my tobacco supplier for this evening.' Bernard lit up and took a drag before stubbing out the cigarette, carefully, and putting it behind his ear. 'The sight of all of those clericals is more than I can take!'

'Christ Almighty, Bernard, but you're hard on the men of God.' Dandy wet a finger and smoothed his pencil moustache. 'Was it one of them put your nose out of joint?'

'This was nobly come by.' Bernard stroked the small lump on his nose. 'I took on every comer in the schoolyard to get it.'

He'd taken them on defending his dead father, who had been violently killed and then denounced from the pulpit by the parish priest. Honor waited but he didn't enlighten Dandy Lyons. She inched the newspaper closer.

'I've a problem with the scenario we've been offered here.' Bernard was watching her. 'I never liked Raeder and I've no doubt he knows something. He might even be involved. But I don't see him doing the deed, strangling that woman with his bare hands.'

'The reports said nothing about a strangling,' said Honor, carefully. Oscar had but Bernard didn't need to know that.

'You're right, they didn't,' Bernard was casual, 'but the dogs in the street know what the papers won't until they're told. Still, as I was saying, I don't see Raeder taking a life.'

'Nor do I.' Honor opened and began scanning the inside pages of the paper as Maisie arrived with the cup of coffee.

'I made it good and strong,' she said.

'Thank you.' Honor sipped and looked grateful. Maisie hadn't exaggerated its strength. She had a couple of long gulps and went back to the paper. There was nothing that she could find about an arrest for the murder.

'I don't see Raeder doing the deed because I've an idea who did.' Bernard, to get her attention, raised his voice. 'Or at least an idea who might have been responsible. They're saying there's a group broken away from the IRA that's disposing of German spies who've infiltrated their ranks. There's stories going the rounds about a split in the IRA.

'Seems some want to go with Germany in the cause of the Republic and the rest want to go the Sinn Fein route, as in ourselves alone and to hell with the rest of the world, including Germany. The dead woman got caught between the two camps, is my view, and was killed for her trouble.'

'You might be right,' Dandy said, 'and you might not. But the guards'll be back. They've plenty questions for us yet. They still don't know exactly when she was put in the tank, poor creature.'

He leaned back in the chair, removed his hat, took a comb from his pocket, ran it through his Brylcreemed hair and put the hat back on. Honor and Bernard watched and waited.

Dandy turned to look at Honor. 'Appearances are every-thing, m'dear. Even a corpse would tell you that, if it could. Take the dead woman, for instance. If she'd been buried or thrown in the river we wouldn't be talking about her now. She'd be long gone. As it is, we're all immersed in talk about her appearance in the tank. Now what does that tell us?'

'What does it?' Bernard sounded puzzled.

'That the murderer was either arrogant or stupid,' Dandy pronounced.

'He was both,' Bernard said. 'He thought he'd found the perfect means of disposal. Only he forgot to put a copper disc on a toe. That's how I noticed her.'

'How long do you think she'd been there?' asked Honor.

'Can't have been long.' Bernard said. 'She was a few days dead is all. The hair hadn't been properly shaved, that was another giveaway. There was stubble all over her head. Could have contaminated the tank.'

'How do you think she got in there?' Honor said.

'How the fuck would I know?' Bernard exploded, then hunched into himself when Maisie glared. 'The police are mad to get someone and all but accused me of putting her there.'

He cracked his knuckles again and held Honor's eye. She'd forgotten the depths of his anger.

'Are you accusing me too? I was the one found her. I was the one reported her. They owed me gratitude for that, not abuse. If it hadn't been for me she'd have been cut up, made pieces of by people like you and gone into the back lane for bones like all the rest of the bodies. A clerical error's all she'd have been when they couldn't account for her.' He straightened up. 'And what thanks do I get? Questions and more questions, as if I was a black murderer!'

'They were civil enough,' Dandy soothed him, 'doing their job, is all. You didn't help yourself by being truculent about the company you keep and your work for the Supplementary Intelligence Service. Do you no harm to be a bit more civil.'

'The SIS is no business of theirs,' Bernard said, 'it's security work, and some of those gob shites of guards are the biggest security risks in the state. In any event,' he gave a sudden, wide grin, 'they'll have a fine time of it when they start investigating *your* little pastimes, Dandy old girl. That'll stretch their civility.'

'I didn't know you were part of the SIS,' Honor said.

'Nor should you,' Bernard grunted. 'Dandy here has ears as well as eyes in the back of his head. It's security work, part-time.'

'They're the lads'll keep us safe from invasion.' Dandy moistened a finger and smoothed his pencil moustache. 'My own life and hobbies are a threat to no one.' He sighed. 'Impetuous youth is so very attractive . . . but so very dangerous. Try to remember, Bernard, that the guards too have ears everywhere.'

'What're the guards actually questioning you about?' Honor met Bernard's angry eye.

'They want a time for when she went into the tank,' he said. 'I say she was put in there on Thursday night and no one'll persuade me otherwise. The first time I saw her was on Friday when I was tipping in a new body. She wasn't there before that.'

'They're looking at us because of what we do,' Dandy said, 'but the truth is that anyone with a modicum of knowledge could do an embalming job.'

He took a corner of the newspaper, and a pen, and began to draw.

'All you need is a table. Your body on the table. A vessel – a bucket would do – to hold the formalin solution, say about ten litres of it, a way of suspending the bucket over the body and a way of pumping in the fluid. All clear so far?'

'Yes.' Honor looked at the drawing. It was cartoonish, and clever.

'You put your body on the table,' Dandy pointed, 'your fluid overhead and going into the body via a tube into the femoral artery. The entry point would be a cut in the groin. Gravity thus created,' he pointed to the bucket suspended over the drawn body, 'allows a good flow. You keep filling the bucket with formalin until clear fluid comes out and you know all the blood has gone. All you're doing, basically, is replacing dead blood with formalin. I suppose,' he looked thoughtful, 'that you could do it without even opening the vein, just allow the whole thing to wash through. The formalin goes through the vascular system, fills all the arteries and heart, goes through the capillaries, perfuses the veins . . .'

'I must go.' Honor stood up hurriedly, pulling on her coat.

'What's your hurry?' Bernard caught her hand. She pulled it free.

'I've got study and . . . things to do,' she said.

She left quickly, passing the window without a glance inside, her jaw squared and long legs striding.

'She's fairly keen to get to the books,' Dandy Lyons said, thoughtfully.

'Yeah,' agreed Bernard, 'keener than I've ever seen her.'

# 10

'I hid in the Wicklow mountains . . . exhausted through the effects of hunger and rain . . . knocked at the door of an isolated farmhouse and asked for food. This I was given but told I could not stay.'

Statement of Herman Goertz, German spy in Ireland

It didn't occur to Honor to climb the steps and knock on the front door of the house in Lansdowne Road. That, as Gretta Harte might have pointed out, would have been a far too obvious and sensible a thing to do. And Honor, Gretta liked to maintain, had a way of making life more difficult for herself than it already was.

She was right, but also wrong when she accused Honor of being simply contrary. Honor Cusack had grown up expecting the world to cave in around her, in a household forever tormented by the horror of her father's death and the threat of poverty. She did things the hard way because she didn't know any other. Afterwards, when it was too late, Honor would reflect on the speed with which her feelings had grown for Oscar Raeder and wonder if stepping back would have made any difference. She hadn't meant it to happen. She was confused enough about herself and her life without falling in love with a man whose country was losing an ugly, battering war, whose own life was about to fall into chaos. It was asking for trouble.

But it had happened. Or something had. Insidiously, without a choice on her part, she found Oscar Raeder was in her head all the time. He was on her mind when she woke in the mornings and was the last thing she thought about before falling asleep. There was nothing pure about her thoughts either. They were wanton, full of imaginings about how it would be to have him beside her, the warmth of his body pressed close, his mouth covering hers.

She did nothing to stop them. If impure thoughts were to be the cause of her roasting in hell's fire then let them be impure thoughts about Oscar Raeder.

She didn't expect him to be at home. On the off-chance that he might be she didn't want the humiliation of calling on a man who'd stood her up. So she called to the door of Terence Delaney's basement flat looking for news, or otherwise, of Oscar Raeder's arrest.

This decision inadvertently gained her an ally.

It took the old man a while to answer but she could hear him moving about inside and waited.

'You're back,' he said tersely when he answered the door. He was wearing a tweed jacket and wool shirt. His hair, now he wasn't wearing the cap, was black with surprisingly little grey.

'What is it you want this time?' He was impatient, but a lot less belligerent than he'd been two days before. The dog wagged its tail.

'I came to enquire about Dr Raeder,' Honor said. 'Do you know if he's been charged?'

'Charged?' His eyebrows came together. 'What would he be charged with?'

'I don't know . . . Is he here?'

'The college has suspended him so where else would he be?' Terence Delaney began to close the door. 'I'll tell him you called.'

'Can I talk to him? Please?'

'You could, if he's got the time. What message will I give him?'

It came to her then why Terence Delaney's attitude had changed. His civility was the giveaway. He'd spent a lifetime as quasi butler. As long as he was deferred to, seen as the first port of call, he would be obligingly polite. She'd done the right thing. She took a deep breath and smiled.

'You could tell him I'm round in the post office in Shelbourne Road,' she said, 'that I'll be there for the next hour or so and would like to see him.'

'What name will I give?'

Honor told him, confident he knew already. The dog followed her back down the path. He sat watching as she crossed the road and walked along by the Botanic Garden trees to the corner with Shelbourne Road. There was no sign of Terence Delaney, or anyone else at any of the windows of the house, when she looked back before rounding the corner.

She took her time getting to the post office, walking slowly past the Swastika Laundry and the tramway yard, talking for a while to children playing in and around the telephone box. It took will-power but she didn't turn again until she was at the door of the post office.

Oscar Raeder was nowhere to be seen in the street behind her.

Gretta, adding long columns of figures when Honor came in, affected a leisurely surprise.

'My, oh, my!' She pushed her chair back and put her hands behind her head. 'But isn't university a fine thing! Allows people all the time in the world to wander the streets. Chance would be a fine thing . . .'

'Yes, it would,' Honor snapped, ''and so would a rest from the sarcasm.'

'My, oh, my,' Gretta said again, 'but we're in bad form today. Your knee doesn't seem to be giving you any trouble so might it be to do with your friend, Dr Raeder?' When Honor frowned she held up a pacifying hand. 'Relax,' she said, 'but be warned. If the mood's to do with that aunt of yours, I don't want to hear about it.'

'I just dropped by to see how you were.'

'Liar.' Gretta sounded cheerful, leaning forward and taking a coupons book from a customer just arrived. 'You've worry written all over you and you only ever call when something's the matter.'

Honor stared at her, aghast. She went on staring as Gretta joked with an elderly customer and filled in a form for a man who couldn't write. Her friend was right. Their friendship relied on Gretta listening and understanding and always being available. It was one-way traffic, pretty well.

She shifted from one foot to the other, waiting for Gretta to be finished. On the wall behind her friend's head there were the words of a Local Security Force marching song. Arland had been an LSF member. He'd persuaded Gretta that displaying the song would help recruiting. Then he'd left. Honor hadn't listened to her about Arland either. Not really listened.

She felt Gretta watching her. There were no more customers.

'It's all right.' Her friend was half-smiling. 'Arland did what he had to do, I'm learning to accept it now.' She looked behind Honor, towards the door. 'There's someone here looks as if he wants to talk to you.'

Oscar Raeder looked good, uneasy but smiling and wearing a maroon wool scarf. He was all right then. Not under house or any other kind of arrest. Relief almost floored Honor and she leaned against the counter for support.

Relief also made her angry. 'I was worried about you,' she said sharply. 'I didn't know what had happened when you didn't turn up for our drive.'

'I wrote you a letter, explaining . . .'

'It's a pity you didn't deliver it to me then.' Honor, aware of Gretta listening, didn't let him finish.

'Sorry,' he said. He was holding out an envelope. 'You can have it now.'

Honor took the letter from him. A woman with a crying infant in her arms stepped around them.

'You're in the way of my customers,' Gretta said lightly. 'If ye want to talk, go on into the back and discuss whatever business you have there. Fire's lighting.'

When Oscar merely stood awkwardly, not making a move, and two more customers arrived, Honor said hurriedly, 'We'll do that.'

Gretta gave Oscar an assessing look as they passed.

The door of the back room refused to close properly and the voices of postmen in the sorting room outside were clearly audible. The postmen would hear whatever they said too.

'Maybe you should read what I wrote,' Oscar said, 'it explains things.'

He left her to it and stood at the window, looking into the small yard as she'd done only two days before. There were no magpies today. No portents of any kind. Honor stood beside him. He didn't turn when she slit the envelope open, nor when she began to read.

His handwriting was precise and he used black ink. He began with a formal 'Dear Miss Cusack' and went on to give full details of how he'd lied to her previously.

*I am not the only member of my family in Ireland. My brother, who is younger than me, is here also. His name is Stefan and he has been an internee in the Curragh internment camp for nearly eight months now. He believes in the war. He joined the German Navy when the war began. I heard nothing of him until last New Year's Day when he was picked up off the Irish coast after his ship went down.*

*He was brought to the Curragh and has been held there as a prisoner-of-war ever since.*

*Stefan and I have always disagreed about politics. It began with our opposing views on National Socialism and Adolf Hitler's Nazi Party. Fearing I would be used to make him reveal naval secrets, he asked me not to visit him at the Curragh camp. I considered this madness on his part and have been visiting him in the camp every Saturday.*

*This weekend, because of the murder of the young woman and the police following me, I decided not to do so in case it would involve Stefan. But a note was delivered saying he had to see me, would I please come on Sunday instead. And so I did. It was for this reason I did not meet you, as promised, for our trip to the mountains. I apologise, most sincerely.*

*The police were waiting for me when I came out of the camp. They accompanied me back to Dublin where I was questioned for many hours. But of course there is nothing to be proven against me and so they released me, though I am under suspicion because I did not tell them of my brother's presence in the Curragh. They wonder what other secrets I may have, and I suppose cannot be blamed for that.*

*I hope you can understand my situation.*

*With sincere apologies and my very best wishes, I am*

He had forgotten to sign the letter. Honor believed every word of it. She also wondered what else he hadn't told her.

'Do you understand?' he said as she folded the square of paper, then folded it again, and again. He was looking at her intently. She could feel a pulse beat in her neck.

'Your brother . . .' she paused, remembering the postmen in the next room, and lowered her voice '. . . I suppose he brought the war with him when he came to Ireland? Made you a part of it whether you wanted to be or not?'

He shrugged. 'It's true that we have a right to stand aside, but it's not an inviolate right. Sooner or later we all become a part of the madness.'

'That knocking on the door on Saturday was the message from him?' She turned her face up to the sky above the back yard, hoping he wouldn't see how close to tears she was. 'You knew and didn't want to answer while I was there?'

'Yes. Terence disapproves of Stefan and keeps away if he suspects a caller is a messenger from my brother.'

'Which was how you knew . . . ?'

'Yes. Only we were both wrong.'

He put a hand on her shoulder and for a moment she thought he would hold her against him. Then he dropped his hand.

'Stefan says he didn't send any message. He'd read about the murder and thought it would cause work problems for me and that I might not be able to visit on Saturday anyway.'

He had shoved his hands into his pockets. Honor thought about leaning her head against his shoulder, then reconsidered. Instead, unable to stop herself, she kissed him. She didn't draw back when she felt him freeze, just for seconds, and touched his face when he returned the kiss, warm and long and with his hands gently holding her shoulders. My feet, she thought, they've left the ground. She was light headed when they I broke apart.

'I'm sorry,' she said, without being sorry at all.

'Why?' he said. He was smiling.

'Taking advantage.' She smiled too.

'Is that what you were doing?' he said and ran a finger down her cheek before turning to the window.

They went on standing side by side, both of them staring at the empty geranium pots. He was no more than two inches taller than she was.

'Who sent the letter then?' she said. 'Did you say to anyone you weren't going to the Curragh?'

'Perhaps the same person who brought it to the attention of the police that I had a brother in the Curragh. Internment is the business of the army and I've been very quiet about Stefan. Secretive in fact, for everyone's sake.' He stopped. He seemed to be thinking. Honor didn't help him. 'I mentioned it at the legation,' he said eventually. 'I called there on Friday afternoon. Usually I would collect cigarettes and chocolate to bring to him but didn't on Friday. There were quite a few people about.' He shrugged. 'Someone obviously thought it their duty to expose my dark secret and my brother's existence.'

'I'll make tea,' Honor put the envelope into her pocket, 'Gretta will be taking her lunch break soon. Strong tea is what the three of us need.'

It was what she needed anyway, as well as the reassurance of actually making it. He watched, in silence, while she filled the kettle, found the matches, lit the primus and put the kettle on the flame. She didn't once look at him.

'Do you want to know what they're saying in college?' she said when she was putting three cups and three saucers on the draining board.

'I'd prefer to hear it from you than anyone else,' he said.

So she told him the clerical students' version of things, and Bernard's defence of Oscar's innocence. She spoke quickly. Too quickly. Her voice was babbling. She stopped when the kettle began to boil.

'I'm suspended from the college,' he said quietly, 'indefinitely suspended. I won't be able to give you any help with the dissecting class.'

'Suspended?' Honor turned her head, staring up at him. 'Why?'

'Because they say it's damaging to the university to have a staff member under suspicion of murder. I could be the cause of bringing it into disrepute. College lecturers must be morally above reproach, an example in all things to the young in their care. A shadow over one is a shadow over all, so they tell me.' He paused and pulled a wry face. 'They're right. I'm sure I would do the same in their place.' He hesitated. 'But for different reasons.'

'What reasons?' Honor began making the tea.

'I would suspend me because students will pay no heed to anything I say, or try to teach, until all of this is cleared up. I will be a bogey-man, a *cause célèbre*, and a waste of everyone's time in the dissecting room.'

'What about the notion of a person being innocent until proven guilty? Isn't upholding that principle something they should be doing also?'

'They have a university to run,' he said, 'that comes first. They had no alternative. Especially since they already knew what had happened, or a version of it, when I arrived to tell them.'

'Monsignor Lamb,' Honor said, and put a cosy on the teapot.

'Monsignor Lamb?'

'That's who told them,' she said. 'Busy spreading calumny and detraction and being an example to his student flock.'

'You may be right,' said Oscar, 'but in the end it doesn't matter who told them. Someone was bound to. If not Monsignor Lamb then someone else.'

'Someone was bound to,' Honor echoed. 'If there's anything I can do, Oscar, to help . . .'

She looked up. The intimacy of saying his name had narrowed the space between them. Somehow, without moving, they were almost touching. 'Please tell me, anything at all?'

'Is the tea made or did I imagine I heard the kettle whistle?'

Gretta, coming briskly through the door, didn't fool Honor. She'd heard, and probably seen, enough from the half-open doorway to put her on her guard against Oscar. She gave him a cool-eyed stare as she took the cosy off the tea pot.

'Don't bother to introduce yourself,' she said, 'I've wit enough to know who you are. There's a stool under the sink, Dr Raeder, if you want to sit down.' To Honor, as she poured the tea, she said, 'If you don't want the listeners in the other room to hear every word we're saying you'd better turn on the wireless.'

The wireless was playing fiddle music.

'Just the job.' Gretta handed round the tea. 'Now tell me what's going on?'

Honor, cradling her cup and without once looking at Oscar for corroboration, or even to see if he approved of her telling Gretta, gave her friend all the details.

'It's a terrible business,' Gretta said when she'd finished, 'truly terrible.' She shook her head and sighed. 'Had you ever come across poor Bridie Keogh, Dr Raeder?'

'No.' Oscar looked surprised. 'I didn't know her.'

'They'll hang you in this town, whether you did or not.' Gretta looked at him, hard. He'd declined her offer of the stool and was leaning against the wall while he sipped his tea. 'The compassionate and Christian Sean Citizen wants a scapegoat for that poor woman's murder. Laying the blame on you means he won't have to accept it could have been one of his own did it.' She shook her head and tightened her lips. 'You'll have to gird your loins against the slings and arrows.'

'What about the real murderer?' Honor said sharply. 'Surely the guards will be doing all they can to find him?'

'They'll be doing only as much as they have to do,' Gretta said. She pulled out the stool and sat on it herself, poking the fire. 'Strange, Dr Raeder, that I've never seen you in the post office before.' She spoke with her back to him.

'I drop off what letters I need posted at the Legation. They go from there.'

'I see. We've one of the best postal services in Europe, Dr Raeder, but you must do as you see fit. Pity you didn't make it your business to be more a part of the neighbourhood before this. The people around are decent enough. If they knew you at all they'd be more inclined to be sympathetic, to look out for you now you're in a spot of bother. Six years you've been here?'

'Since 1938,' he said, 'and please, my name is Oscar . . .'

'You've kept very much to yourself up 'til now,' she put a shovelful of slack at the back of the fire, 'before meeting Honor. You live with the blocky, heavy-set set old man with the dog?'

'I do,' Oscar, behind Gretta's back, shot Honor a questioning look. She smiled, but didn't try to rescue him. Gretta's questioning had to be going somewhere. It always was.

'The guards will be watching you, everywhere you go,' Gretta said, 'it's their job. They'll be watching the company you keep too. Could create difficulties for people around you. I don't know if you want that.'

Too late, Honor realised what Gretta meant. Stupid of her to have been so complacent. And so trusting.

'Any difficulties I might have are my own business, Gretta,' she said sharply.

'I was speaking to Dr Raeder,' her friend replied, 'and I'd like to hear what *he* has to say.'

'It wasn't my intention to involve Honor.' Oscar straightened up, standing awkwardly before them. 'Now I think I will go.'

Gretta stood too. 'I said what I did because there's been a man outside watching since you came in here,' she said. 'I wanted the both of you to be aware of how things are before Honor becomes any further involved . . .' she spread her hands '. . . with your troubles.'

'You're sure about the man?' Honor said.

'Sure enough to go out to him and tell him Dr Raeder was making a social call and to take himself off,' Gretta said. 'He told me to get back to licking my stamps. Not a nice class of person at all.

She stood, putting her hands into the small of her back and stretching.

'Your best plan of action for whatever length of time it takes them to find the murderer, is to go about your life in as open a manner as possible. More open than before, at any rate. Get out and about the neighbourhood now you're not going into the university. I'll take your letters for you here and Mr Treacy'll be glad to see you in the chemist's shop. You'll find the newsagent's friendly too. No need to be going into town for your bits and pieces, or sending the old man out to do your messages. Cut the snoopers and troublemakers and the guards off at the knees, that's my best advice.'

'I appreciate your concern,' Oscar said, 'but I have work to do, papers to write. Why should I change my habits when I've done no wrong?'

'Innocence is no guarantee of safe conduct through life,' Gretta warned, 'so you take my advice and things'll go easier for you.' She paused. 'You're going to need friends.'

She was right, but Honor wasn't fooled this time. Her advice was double-edged; a more visible Oscar Raeder would allow Gretta to keep an eye on Honor's meetings with him.

Oscar smiled. 'My habits are being changed for me. Honor has asked me to dine at her home on Friday evening.'

'Has she indeed?' Gretta widened her eyes. 'That will certainly broaden your circle of acquaintances.'

## 11

'Deportations ... to ... centres of mass executions
continue unabated ... May our heavenly father ...
make you providential agent for salvation millions innocent
men women children facing imminent threat of
annihilation.'

Telegram to De Valera from Isaac Herzog, 1942

Friday's dinner was late. Grace had prepared baked stuffed
herrings which she refused to bring from the kitchen until
everyone was in place. Florrie Mitchell was late. So was Oscar
Raeder.

'Florrie holding us up is one thing,' Grace fumed, '*your*
guest not coming on time is entirely another. Shows ingrati-
tude. Given his situation, he can't exactly be inundated with
dinner invitations.'

She was wearing green tonight, an olive-coloured shawl
over a long, pale lime skirt. Honor's hair was loose and she
was wearing lipstick as well as a blue crêpe dress she knew
flattered her. Grace, ominously, had already said she hoped
Oscar Raeder was 'worth the effort'.

'He may not come at all.' Lennox Mangan, languid by the
fire, checked his watch on its chain. 'Man may be in jail, for
all we know. When did you last speak with him, Honor?'

'Monday.'

'Is he a reliable person?' Grace shook her head. 'Ridiculous
question because how could you know? The accounts I've
heard of him myself are variable.'

'Of course he's reliable,' Honor said hotly. 'He's also my guest.'

'It wasn't your place, Honor, to extend our little group,' her aunt said, 'but since you've done so he will naturally be made welcome.' She placed a hand to her ear in an exaggerated listening gesture. 'There's someone at the door now. Might be him. At last.'

Florrie Mitchell stood on the doorstep in a wide-brimmed hat and long, belted coat. He was carrying a single yellow rose.

'The last rose of summer.' He came inside and kissed Honor's cheek. 'Though not for you, my lovely, for that aunt of yours. Your day will come.'

'I'm sure yours will too, Florrie,' Honor said as he hung his coat and straightened his bow tie.

'I was wrong not to bring you a bloom as well,' he stroked his beard into shape, 'you're out of sorts, I can tell.' He lowered his voice. 'I'm late. Has anyone noticed?'

'She's noticed. We've been waiting for you, Florrie, as well as for a friend I've invited too.'

'Anyone I know?'

'I've invited Oscar Raeder, he'll be here any minute.'

'You may well be right,' Florrie said as the knocker sounded on the door behind them. 'Hope the fella sings for his supper. We could do with hearing his version of events.'

Oscar was holding a bunch of white roses.

'I'm very sorry,' he said, stepping inside. 'I was delayed at the Legation. I hope . . .'

'I'm glad you're here,' Honor said.

She held the roses in her arms while she introduced him. Grace was extravagantly charming.

'I'm so very glad to meet you at last,' she held his hand in both of hers, 'and I do hope the week hasn't been too trying for you. We were just about to sit down. Delia,' she took the roses from Honor, 'perhaps you could look after these while Honor and I serve dinner.' Smiling, she swept her niece from the room with her. Delia, dressed in a cerise-coloured dress already too tight, followed at a trot.

'White's very tasty, Honor,' Delia found a vase for the roses in the kitchen, 'but don't you think they look a bit like a wreath for the dead?'

'No, Delia, I do not.'

'Put them on the table,' Grace said firmly, 'and stick Florrie's rose with the crysanthemums on the sideboard.'

'Crysanths really *are* the flowers of the dead,' Delia said. 'His rose will die if I . . .'

'It will definitely die, and you along with it, if you don't do as I say!'

Delia fled with the flowers.

'Your guest is pleasant enough-looking,' Grace lifted a salver of herrings overstuffed with oatmeal, parsley and peel, 'but hardly handsome. I'd expected better of you, Honor.' She went ahead out of the kitchen.

Honor took a couple of steadying breaths. I'll leave, she promised herself, if she follows that crack with one more like it. And I'll take Oscar with me.

She picked up the vegetables and followed her aunt up the steps and along the hall. The white roses were in the centre of the table.

'Herring?' Lavinia Sayers looked disbelieving as Grace put a fish on her plate. 'I don't eat herring.' Her pearl tear-drop earrings gave a shimmering tremor.

'There's no fish more Celtic than the herring.' Grace continued serving. 'Please, all of you, begin. I didn't spend hours over a stove to have good food go uneaten. I've made it just as Tomas Ó Crohan tells us it was cooked on the Great Blasket.'

'I thought it was their young they ate out there.' Delia, one hand covering her teeth, giggled childishly.

'I often wonder,' Grace, taking her place, was conversational, 'if there's any end to your ignorance, Delia.'

'We were told that in school,' she protested, 'by a nun from Donegal.'

'There actually *are* some primitive Blasket Island practices on record . . .' Lennox began.

'Have you lost your mind, Lennox?' Grace, interrupting him, sliced open her herring. 'You're pursuing far too lonely a Celtic Studies furrow if you're starting to believe such things of our people.'

'It's necessary to keep an open mind,' Lennox said, 'in order to move forward with what is best in our national identity. Wouldn't you agree with me, Dr Raeder?'

'Of course,' Oscar said, 'and an open heart too.' He smiled. 'Mr de Valera would agree with you also, I'm sure.'

'In what way?' Lennox looked surprised.

'Isn't it true that with his policy of neutrality he hopes to maintain an Irish national integrity?' Oscar said.

'Yes, yes, of course he does.' Lennox was impatient. 'You sound like your German Minister, Dr Hempel, and just as full of diplomatic protocol, if I may say so. The fact is that with the war ending we must move on. My own belief is that this country of ours, having come through the last six years with its national identity intact, *must* now play its part in the building of a new Europe.'

'That depends on what you mean by a new Europe.' Oscar spoke carefully. 'What are you proposing exactly?'

'I'm simply talking political reality. Ireland *belongs* to Europe while England does not. Ergo Ireland's future lies with the new, post-war Europe and no other.'

'I've always seen Ireland's neutrality as pro-Irish,' Oscar said mildly, 'rather than anti-British or pro any other country.'

'Of course it is those things too,' Lennox said, 'but the future beckons and we must prepare our thoughts if nothing else.' He smiled. 'What sort of future do you see for your country, Dr Raeder, and for yourself?'

'For everyone's sake, not just Germany's,' Oscar watched his interrogator as he spoke, 'I would like to see an international community of *all* peoples built up in Europe.'

'Wouldn't we all, my lad, wouldn't we all?' Florrie dabbed at his mouth with his napkin. 'And how will you be playing your part in this frenzy of building?'

'I'll be in Germany,' Oscar said, 'there will be a greater need for me there than anywhere else.' He studied his plate briefly. 'I've always liked herring.' He smiled at Grace.

'Then you may eat mine as well,' Lavinia pushed her own plate aside, 'and tell us, if you please, why the police have been questioning you to do with this unfortunate murder? The papers give us very little information and Honor has been practising discretion for your sake all week.'

'When did the papers ever know, and when were they allowed to tell us, what's going on?' Florrie Mitchell energetically piled food on to his fork as he spoke. 'This war is a conflict between major powers fighting for world domination. The evils we hear of are part of a struggle which has nothing to do with Ireland.' His hands became still momentarily. 'The papers did say, Dr Raeder, or maybe I just heard it said, that you were given your freedom because of lack of evidence?'

Oscar slowly filled a glass of water. Now, Honor thought, it's starting now and I'm leaving. She pushed back her chair but was forestalled by a delighted, tinkling laugh from Grace.

'You must excuse Florrie's bluntness, Dr Raeder,' he aunt said, 'but the fact is that we're all eaten alive with curiosity about the recent excitement in your life. We'll none of us be able to enjoy our food if you force us to wait.'

'Understandable,' Oscar smiled politely, 'though there's not a lot to tell. I was brought in for questioning following a visit to my brother, who is interned in the Curragh camp.'

He glanced around the table. 'There's really no more to it than that.'

'Is your brother a spy?' Delia was breathless.

'My brother is a prisoner-of-war,' Oscar said, 'and will remain so until the end of hostilities.' He paused. 'We do not agree on politics. He was in the German Navy.'

Lavinia snorted. 'I suppose we are expected to believe his ship merely foundered in our neutral waters? That he was not captured coming ashore with no good purpose in mind?'

'Dr Raeder is not his brother's keeper,' Lennox put in, 'and you of all people, Lavinia, are in a position to understand how political loyalties can differ within families.'

'Understand? I never understood my son's position, Mr Mangan, merely tried to accept what I couldn't change. He was influenced when young, as you well know.'

'What age is your brother, Dr Raeder?' he asked. Lennox looked at Lavinia for a moment, sighing, then turned away.

'Twenty-three.'

'And in the navy since he was seventeen, no doubt? And you were what age when you found you could not support National Socialism?'

'I was a teenager.'

'My point is made, Lavinia, I need say no more.' Lennox resumed eating.

'How right you are about that last, Mr Mangan,' she sighed, 'and how cleverly you extract what you want to know.'

Honor, blessed with a good appetite, ate her herring. Oscar ate his too, with what looked like pleasure. She caught his eye, briefly, and smiled. He smiled back. The white roses reflected beautifully in the polished wood of the table. Grace had been right to put them there.

'The directors of the Abbey Theatre have been asked to resign.' Honor chose her change of subject carefully and spoke loudly. 'The most the actors are paid is seven pounds three shillings – and they only get half that when rehearsing. There's an almighty row brewing.'

Grace took the bait, and cast it aside quickly. 'If the government takes over it'll be worse,' she said, 'infinitely worse.' She looked down the table. 'I'm told by my niece that you've been a neighbour of ours for a number of years now, Dr Raeder. You appear to live as reclusive a life as your grandfather did.'

Honor swore under her breath. Her aunt had clearly been making enquiries.

'Not at all reclusive,' Oscar said, 'I've been both studying and working in the Mater Hospital.'

'And does your brother visit you on parole?'

'No, though he does visit the town of Newbridge.'

'Ernie has made suits for some of those fellows.' Delia put a playful, gagging hand over her mouth. 'Oops!' she squealed. 'Shouldn't have said that. That's one of the little jobs he likes to keep quiet about.' She put a hand on her husband's rigid arm. 'Sorry, Ernie, but we're among friends so it's all right.'

'We can't always be sure, even of friends.' Ernie Gibbons agitatedly pushed his fork around his plate. 'And Dr Raeder, if you'll forgive me, sir, is a stranger to us. Just by way of setting the record straight,' he focussed on a point to the right of Oscar's ear, 'I have made very few suits of clothing for the Curragh prisoners, and none at all for your brother.' He gave a small cough. 'Those I tailor for want their suits cut in the styles of Leipzig, Hanover and Munich. They're very pleased with my work.'

'By God, but you get around for a trouser-maker,' Florrie laughed.

'Ernie's a tailor,' Delia was suddenly shrill, 'there's a big difference between a trouser-maker and a tailor. Not that you could be expected to know, Florrie Mitchell, since you've no idea of dress.'

'The baby . . .' Her husband's hand covered hers warningly. 'Don't upset yourself, Delia. It's only Mr Mitchell's way.'

'Ernie's more private than he should be about such things but he tailors for the best,' she said, 'don't you, Ernie?'

'All of my customers are of equal importance to me.' He shifted in his seat. 'And their secrets as safe as if I was bound by the confessional seal.'

'Ernie's making for a minister of the government,' Delia said breathlessly. 'Criminals on the Curragh are the least of his business.'

'Can't say I've noticed any sartorial improvement in the way our leaders dress,' Florrie commented.

'Delia shouldn't have said what she did.' Agitation had drained the colour from Ernie's face. 'I'd be obliged if you'd all forget what you heard.'

'As if they could!' Delia, smiling, re-clipped her hair into its cerise slide.

'My livelihood is of the greatest concern to me,' her husband said, 'I am daily having to defend myself against the threat of cheap imported labour.'

'*What* are you talking about now, man?' Florrie, frowning, looked down the table at the tailor.

'Jewish labour,' Ernie said triumphantly, '*that's* what I'm talking about – and they're here already. We must be on our guard against the growing menace of alien immigration. There are an undue number of Jews in the country and . . .'

'You'll be safe enough, Ernie,' Florrie said dismissively.

'My brother tells me that many of the German prisoners had never had a suit tailor-made until they arrived in the Curragh,' Oscar said, and smiled at Ernie Gibbons.

'They're nice lads,' Ernie muttered, 'the most of them. Doing their duty by their country's no sin.'

'You're talking about a country which saw fit to destroy the city of Warsaw and three hundred thousand Polish people.'

Lavinia looked directly across the table at Oscar. 'The same country we're now told has extermination centres for such as Jews and gypsies all over Germany.'

'You can't believe everything you hear,' Ernie said. 'We're fed propaganda night and day, on the wireless and in the papers. We don't know any of these things to be true.'

'Dr Raeder knows they're true,' Lavinia said.

'Yes,' he said, 'they're true.'

Florrie shrugged.

'The leaders of this country know them to be true also but it's not their war, nor ours. And this man,' he held up his glass to Oscar, 'has enough troubles on his shoulders without our putting the war there as well.'

'You were fortunate to be able to spend the war years here, away from it all.' Delia beamed at Oscar. 'You'd very likely have been fighting, like your brother, if you'd stayed in Germany. I mean, how could you not? You'd have had to take the side of your own, wouldn't you?'

'It's usual,' Oscar agreed.

'People here have a lot of time for Germany, but I suppose you know that and it's why you're here.' Delia refilled her own and Ernie's wine glasses. 'I'm not for any of them, myself. I say a plague on all their houses – but a bigger plague on the English than anyone else. Hitler at least gave them a bit of a run for their money.' She lifted her glass in salute to Oscar. 'I don't believe half the things we're told about him being the devil incarnate and all of that.'

'Maybe you should . . .'

But Oscar was interrupted by a sombre Ernie Gibbons.

'Solomon tells us,' he said, 'that the wise traveller never despises his own country. It might be hard for a man like yourself but you'd do well to heed his advice.' He shook his head. 'Not a good thing to abandon the fatherland in its hour of need. Not a good thing at all.'

'You misunderstand, Mr Gibbons.' Oscar spoke carefully. 'I do not despise Germany, I fear for my country. And for my countrymen and women.'

Honor looked at him. If he resented Ernie and Delia's lumbering intrusions he was hiding it well.

'Do you have any views, Dr Raeder, on who might have murdered the young woman found dead?' Lennox had finished eating.

'None at all.'

'We were surmising at this table last week,' Florrie began, 'that it might have been someone interested in medical science, keen on keeping up the supply of bodies.'

'God, but you're tasteless, Florrie!' Honor couldn't bring herself to look at Oscar's reaction. 'I really think we should drop the subject entirely.'

'You're right,' Florrie agreed. 'With millions dying in Europe and the Pacific, what's the death of one little whore in Dublin? Wouldn't you agree, Dr Raeder?'

'Of course not.'

Honor stood up.

'We're leaving,' she said.

# 12

'The battle for Germany has started in deadly earnest . . .
it is evident that the Germans are determined to defend
their soil with the utmost tenacity.'

*Irish Times* editorial, 31st October, 1944

The night was cold, the sky clear with a few bright stars. Conversation was difficult. The confines of respectability and the late hour lent a hushed stillness to Clyde Road which made their footsteps sound like small thunder claps in the silence. A late tram, clanging past as they turned into Ballsbridge Road, sounded like an explosion. Honor shivered when a dog howled.

'Does Setanta come out at night?' she said.

'Yes. But he doesn't howl.' Oscar took her arm and they walked on like that, their steps matching.

'I bet you didn't even like the herring,' she said as they came up to the Lansdowne Road house. She was certain they were being watched from the shadows of the trees opposite.

'I did,' Oscar protested. He pushed open the gate. 'Your aunt is a fine cook.'

'She is,' Honor agreed. 'It's a sort of performance with her.'

She walked past him and went ahead up the steps. Terence Delaney and Setanta were nowhere to be seen or heard, the basement in darkness.

'I'm sorry I inflicted the evening on you,' she said, standing waiting while Oscar searched for his key.

No point telling him how lack-lustre the invitation had been, that she'd known in her heart there wouldn't be enough generosity of spirit at her aunt's table to take him in.

'I'm sorry I inflicted it on myself,' she added.

He was frowning as he searched and she resisted an urge to smooth his brow. Things were moving fast enough, she didn't want them to spin completely out of control. Not here on the doorstep anyway.

'I'm glad you invited me,' he'd found the keys, 'and I'm very glad you're here.' The door swung open. 'You're coming in, of course?'

'Are you offering me a nightcap?'

'Whatever you'd like.' He stood aside, closed and locked the door once she was in the hallway.

In the kitchen he took milk from the cold box and filled two glasses. She kept her coat on, tightly belted. Oscar dropped his over a chair.

'It's cold in here,' Honor said, making fists of her hands in her pockets.

She wanted to kiss him again but felt too breathless, her heart beating somewhere outside her body, as if she wasn't responsible for its reactions.

'It's always cold in here,' Oscar said.

Never in her life had she felt less like a glass of milk. 'So – what happens now?' she said. Inelegantly put, for a seduction line. So inelegant he misunderstood.

'Nothing much. The police will continue their investigation and keep a watch on me at the same time. I'll continue to visit Stefan on Saturdays. Hopefully, and sooner rather than later, they'll find the murderer and I'll be forgotten.'

She looked away from him, at the chill walls and white cooker.

'My aunt will wait up for me to come home,' she said. 'Lennox and Florrie will try to outstay one another until she tells the both of them to go. The Gibbonses will leave their door open so as to hear me coming in. Lavinia will watch from her window.'

'What do you want to do?' He took her hand in one of his and traced the knuckles with a finger. She knew what he wanted her to say.

'I want to stay here,' she said, 'please?' And smiled. 'And I don't want that milk.'

His bedroom was filled with dark wooden furniture, nineteenth-century landscapes and tartan coverings. An old man's room with a dark blue rug on the floor. At least it was warmer than the kitchen.

Honor stood in the window. Oscar joined her and they looked together at the brooding trees opposite and the bare beginnings of a frost on the ground.

'Do you think these were hanging here when your grandparents married?' Honor touched the curtains. They were blue as well, made of heavy velvet that had no doubt been opulent before wearing and fading.

'I don't think so,' he said. 'My grandfather had this room redecorated for himself when my grandmother died.'

'Maybe we should close them,' Honor said.

'Maybe we should.' The curtains came together with a loud sigh. He took her hand. 'Maybe you should take off your coat,' he said. When she gave it to him he dropped it on a chair. 'Your eyes were the first thing I noticed about you.' He took her by the hand to the bed and sat her there. 'Your face had turned white, looking at the cadaver, and your eyes the darkest of dark blues.'

'Is this a medical observation?' she said as he laid her on the bed and looked down at her.

'It's a personal one,' he said and kissed her, holding her face in his hands. She kissed him back and it was all right. More than all right.

Oscar drew away and leaned on an elbow, looking at her. 'You're very beautiful,' he said, for the third time since they'd met. She'd been counting. He must mean it.

'There's no accounting for taste,' she said and smiled. She *felt* beautiful.

'You're beautiful by any standard, any taste,' he said.

'Thank you,' she said and he went on looking at her, as if he would say something more. When he didn't she said,

'I'm glad we met . . .' but stopped because she'd no idea how to tell him just *how* glad. Nor even if he wanted to know. To explain she would have had to tell him that the world around her had changed because of him, that obstacles had become possibilities, the unbearable bearable. She'd never felt so alive. Because of him she knew what it was to really want a man.

'I feel I have always known you,' he said.

'I'm a bit afraid.' She pulled away, just far enough to see his face clearly, to be certain he wanted her there. 'But I don't want to be.'

'Don't be,' he smoothed the hair from her face, looked at her mouth, then her eyes before kissing them shut.

'I'm relying on you,' she kept her eyes closed, 'to teach me.'

'This is not on the course,' he said, his mouth close to hers, 'but an exception can be made.'

She opened her eyes and smiled into his and said, 'I'd like that.'


She hadn't meant to stay the night. That had never been part of the plan. All she'd had in her head when she'd left the house was a walk to Lansdowne Road, then maybe a talk before going home – to her own bed.

But it was the early hours when she woke to the strange, and wonderful, long, warm length of Oscar's body beside hers and knew she'd been fooling herself. *This* was what she'd wanted, and planned, all along. She stretched, finding his toes with hers, and pressed herself closer. He didn't waken.

She lay there and took deep, luxurious breaths, letting them in and out softly and slowly. Dear God, she prayed, and dear anyone else who cares to listen, please, please don't take this from me. Let me have it, and him, a while longer. Please.

'Are you saying something?' Oscar's eyes were open and he was smiling.

'My prayers,' she said, and laughed at his disbelief.

They lay for a while and listened to the rattle of the milk cart and bottles in the street. 'My life's changed forever,' Honor said.

'Mine too,' he said.

'I meant in practical ways.' She pulled an exposed shoulder under the heavy bedclothes. The bedroom was icy. 'My spending the night here will change everything. This,' she turned and kissed where her head had lain at the base of his neck, 'and what we've shared separates my aunt and me. She can never be part of it, and she can never know it, and I don't know how she's going to be about it.'

'Are you sorry?'

'God, no.' She turned to lie on her back, holding his hand, still close. 'I'm glad,' she said.

'I'm glad too.' He laughed, his breath warm on her neck before he kissed her there.

Honor, as they started to make love again, knew that whatever happened Oscar would be a part of her from now on. Together or apart it made no difference.

When she woke the second time the sounds were the day-time ones of trams on tracks, the call of a paper boy, a distant car backfiring. When she sat up there was enough light to see her discarded clothes on a chair: blue frock, white slip, stockings, suspender belt. They could stay there for another while.

'What time is it?' she said as Oscar reached for her and she sank back beside him.

'Early,' he said, 'Terence comes into the house about ten on Saturdays. We'd have heard him. It's not ten yet.'

'Does he come up here?' Horrified. 'To the bedroom?'

'Just to the kitchen. He makes breakfast and spends the time it takes to eat it trying to persuade me not to go to the Curragh.'

'He's so very against your brother then?'

'He disapproves of what he calls "the German virus" in the Leahy family.' Oscar held her hand against his mouth as he spoke. 'He sees the war as vindication of his view of the Germans in general, my father in particular. Stefan, in his opinion, is nothing but trouble. He may be right. My brother is impulsive and immature.' He kissed her hand. 'Stefan maintains that the problem is mine, that I'm a renegade and traitor. Our mother dying when he was less than a year old didn't make us close in the way you might imagine.'

'Did you mind growing up without a mother?'

'I was bookish,' he said. 'And you, how was it for you without a father?'

'His memory was kept alive,' Honor said grimly. 'So Terence wants to save you from your brother?'

'He wants to save me *for* this house, which he doesn't actually want for himself and would prefer to be owned by me. His attachment was to my grandfather.' Oscar paused. 'He's a good man.'

'What do *you* want?' She propped herself on an elbow and watched him as he answered.

'I'm not free to have what I want,' he said, 'not until the war is over. Maybe not even then. And you?'

'I'm not sure. All my life I've felt like a prisoner of circumstance,' she put her feet under his legs, hogging the warm spot there, 'that I had no personal choice, should be grateful for whatever opportunities were given me.' She looked at him,

135

unsmiling. 'It's the Irish way. Being grateful for things you don't even want.'

'It's the way of those who've known poverty,' he said, 'wherever they are.'

'I suppose it is.'

After a minute, afraid she might drift into sleep again, she slipped from the bed, wrapped herself in a blanket and went to the window, opening a narrow slit of curtain.

'Just checking the world's still there. The sun's shining.'

'Come back to bed,' he said, 'please.'

In bed again she kissed him on the mouth. 'I'll burn in hell, I've committed a mortal sin and taken far too much pleasure in it. I'll burn for eternity.'

'We both will,' he said, lazily.

Downstairs, the sound loud in the empty house, the front door opened, then shut again, and Terence Delaney's hobnails punished the tiles all the way to the kitchen.

'I'd better go.' Honor wrapped herself in the blanket again and shuffled to her clothes.

'You don't have go.' Oscar stood beside her in a dark wool dressing gown. 'Stay for breakfast.' The layers of wool negated their earlier intimacy.

'I'm not hungry,' Honor said. She was ravenous. She was also full of dread about going home. 'I'll dress in the bathroom.' She clutched her clothes to her chest.

'Come to the Curragh with me today,' Oscar said, speaking quickly. 'I'd like Stefan to meet you. I'd like you to meet him. You'll understand things better once you have.'

'I might,' Honor said.

'. . . my sphere of action was only small, set against the pattern of the war as a whole. However, it was up to me to make something of it.'

Herman Goertz, German spy in Ireland

The plains of the Curragh were bleaker and less green than Honor had imagined they would be. And she'd imagined them often; the limestone-rich, rolling centre of Ireland they'd been told about in school but which she'd never, until now through the dusty window of Oscar Raeder's two-tone Ford 8, actually seen. Famously hospitable to horses and sheep, the Curragh's wide, open acres now just as famously prevented the escape of the IRA prisoners kept in the army camp there since the early years of the war.

The German sailors, spies and airmen held in a separate, barbed-wire-surrounded internment compound, had every chance to escape, but didn't. A parole system allowed them daily hours of freedom; a code of honour meant attempts at escape were rare. Oscar told her all about it as they drove across the plains.

'Stefan's allowed to leave the camp between two and five o'clock to go into one or other of the nearby towns,' he explained, 'all he has to do is give an undertaking to return. The Germans prefer to use the Grand Hotel in Newbridge; probably because the RAF internees preferred the other one, the Central Hotel, when they were here. He gets four free hours in the evening too.'

'All that and tailor-made suits as well?' Honor commented. 'Doesn't sound such a bad life.'

'Having a suit made isn't Stefan's style,' Oscar said wryly. 'He's one of a group who took sewing classes and learned to make their own. Matter of pride, he says.' He changed gear and turned towards the internees' compound. 'Pride's a funny thing. Too often it drives young men to their deaths.'

Stefan Raeder was stiff with dignity and very handsome. Taller than his brother, he wore side whiskers and seethed with frustrated energy. They met in the grassy centre of the compound where he shook hands formally with Honor, nodded briskly and immediately stepped back.

Oscar had told her his brother was twenty-three but he might have been seventeen, a boy playing at being a man. The lapels on his brown sports coat were uneven and his whipcord trousers had turn-ups large enough to cultivate seeds. He wore a collar and tie.

'You have the car outside?' he said to his brother.

'Of course.' Oscar put a hand on his shoulder. 'We'll leave for Newbridge straight away, if you like?'

'I like,' Stefan said.

His English was less fluent than Oscar's so Honor gave his apparent rudeness the benefit of the doubt. It was less easy to dismiss the way he sat in the front of the car and left her wrestling with the back door. And the way, in spite of Oscar's repeatedly breaking into English, he spoke German all the way to Newbridge. They spoke about the murder, and Oscar's suspension from the college, and even, she gathered, about the dinner party of the evening before.

'It will be all right,' Oscar said as they drove up to the hotel, 'please don't worry about it.' Stefan's reply, in German, was monosyllabic.

In the wood-panelled bar of the Grand Hotel Stefan Raeder said he would have a neat whiskey, Honor said she would have hers with water and Oscar ordered a pint of Guinness. Most of the bar's customers were German internees. Most of them too were accompanied by women.

'You will want, of course, to ask me if I am a member of the Nazi Party?' Stefan Raeder looked languidly around him. 'All of the Irishwomen I meet ask this question.'

'I suppose it's a natural enough thing to ask,' Honor said.

'How could I *not* be a member of the Nazi Party?' He leaned forward suddenly, dangling his hands between his knees. His knuckles were red and raw. 'You join when you are eighteen.' He scratched at his knuckles, making them worse. 'I went to sea to serve my country when the war began. It was my duty. My brother does not agree with duty to one's country but I suppose you must know this, and agree, or you would not be his lover.' He smiled, looking from one to the other of them as he said the last word. The smile revealed a platinum tooth.

'Friends and lovers are no more obliged to agree with one another than brothers,' Honor said, lightly. 'I rarely agree with my own brother, if it comes to that.'

'I was twelve when Hitler came to power.' Stefan Raeder might have been alone and talking to himself. 'In my heart I will always be a National Socialist. I've never known anything else.'

'Things will be different after the war,' Honor said. She didn't look at Oscar, sitting next to her, his drink untouched on the table.

'You are right. They will be different.' His brother made fists of his hands and thumped his thighs. 'You will see, in a year the English and Americans will be fighting the Russians.' His voice rose and his clear boy's skin reddened. To Honor it seemed he might cry. 'This is what I think: Germany didn't start the war. Austria was always a part of Germany and the Germans and the English are of the same stock. I can never understand why they would want to fight one another.' He downed his whiskey in a gulp. 'Never.'

A small silence was broken by Honor.

'Do you come here every day?' There was a homeliness about the scene, sun shining through the windows onto the worn carpet, even about the hunting prints and stuffed, mounted foxes. 'It seems . . . nice.'

'Most days. Always when my brother comes,' Stefan said. 'He and I have nothing to say to one another, that is why he brought you with him. But, of course, you and I have nothing to say to one other either.'

'I thought, Stefan, that it would be interesting for you to meet Honor,' Oscar said. 'I thought it would be interesting for her to meet you too.'

'Why would you think it would interest me to meet her?' Stefan Raeder straightened his shoulders and stared at his brother. 'That she would be interested to meet me I can understand. I am a sort of circus animal in this country, a beast to be observed as a curiosity, a member of a race many Irish would like to learn from and whom they hoped would win the war.' He held up his glass, indicating to the barman that he would have another. 'Victory may still be ours. We may still prove invincible.'

'We should go,' Oscar stood, abruptly. 'You are in no mood for civilised company, Stefan. It was a mistake bringing Honor to meet you. I will not have her exposed to your infantile rudeness.' He stepped back from the table, reaching a hand to Honor. 'It's probably best if you walk back to the camp, Stefan. You seem to me in need of the exercise.'

Stefan Raeder didn't budge. 'You never change,' he said.

'I will always be a child to you, always wrong. What did you expect from me today? That I would be boyish and charming to your trollop? That I . . .'

'Enough, Stefan!' Oscar took Honor's hand and pulled her to her feet beside him. 'You're a child, a ridiculous and dangerous child. We're leaving. But first you will apologise to Honor.'

'I'm sorry.' Stefan rose suddenly to his feet. He looked oddly deflated as he stood stiffly to attention and extended his hand. 'My brother is right and I was wrong. I should not have called you a trollop. I am certain, even on our short acquaintance, that you are a woman of virtue.' He brought his heels together and bent forward. 'Will you please accept my apology?' His face was flushed.

Honor took his hand. It was firm and long-fingered.

'You're forgiven.' She smiled. 'Now maybe we could all sit down and start again?' She sat down herself, holding her breath and hoping for the best. Stefan sat too. Oscar remained standing.

'I'm not so sure I should inflict any more of my brother's company on you,' he said. 'This trip was not a good idea. It is I who should apologise.'

'I'm seriously hungry,' Honor told him quickly. 'Do you think you could ask them if they serve afternoon tea here?'

'If you're sure . . .' Oscar studied her face. 'Okay. I'll see about it.'

Honor sat watching him leave. When the bar door closed behind him Stefan said, 'He is lucky to have you. It's a lucky man who has a loyal woman by his side.'

'Do you have a sweetheart at home?'

'Yes. I have known her two years and it is a year now since we met . . .' He produced a photograph. 'This is what she looks like.'

The picture showed a smiling, round-faced girl of about

eighteen. Across the top she'd written her name, Micha, and the word *Vergissmeinnicht*.

'What does it mean?' Honor traced the bold, hopeful letters with a finger. Stefan pulled the photo away and put it back in his wallet.

'She has written "Forget me not".' He looked away. 'But I think by now she is the one who will have forgotten me.' He paused. 'Micha's brother was my friend. He is dead.'

'Do you write to her?'

'How can I? It would be different if I was an ordinary sailor but since I was sent here on a mission of secrecy my situation is different. I may not send letters until the war is over.' He shrugged. 'Which may happen soon, if all we hear is true.'

'You were sent as a spy?'

'As an agent, yes.' He shrugged. 'Did my brother not tell you? I was captured coming ashore off County Wexford. Bad luck or betrayal, I may never know.'

'Oscar didn't say . . .' He had told her his brother was a sailor, rescued when his ship went down.

'He was always discreet,' Stefan gave a sudden laugh, self-conscious and jerky-sounding, 'much better than me at keeping secrets.' As suddenly as he'd laughed he became brooding again. 'It's an open secret that my country had hoped the IRA would attack the English in the north of Ireland. You must realise,' he looked straight into her eyes, 'that the Celtic race will come into its own if England collapses.'

'Is that why you were sent here?' she said. 'To help the IRA attack the north?'

He gave his short, jerky laugh. 'I cannot, obviously, answer that question.' He looked past her and stood. 'Oscar is beckoning from the door. We must follow him to the dining room.'

The dining room was bright and sunny and smelled of the cabbage and potato which had been on the lunch menu.

Honor sat with her back to the window at a round table covered in a white linen cloth with a Raeder brother to either side of her. They were the only people there.

The menu offered currant scones and caraway seed cake with tea or coffee. As an alternative there was hot chocolate or milk, but they would take longer. There were two varieties of jam on the table, as well as butter and a single paper rose in a bud vase in the centre.

Stefan, taking control, ordered scones, cake and a pot of coffee.

'Your brother tells me he came here as a spy,' Honor said. She was pleasant, even smiling a little as she held Oscar's gaze. 'I must have misunderstood when you said he was rescued when his ship went down.'

'You said that?' Stefan, buttering a scone, looked amused.

'If you remember, Stefan,' Oscar was icy, 'that is what you yourself first told me. It was also the version the Legation gave me.'

'It's true.' He turned to Honor. 'We agreed on this story for Oscar's protection, so that his life here should not be disturbed by the facts of war. But he has known the truth for a long time now.'

'I see,' Honor said.

The waitress came back. She served Honor first, in silence, then chatted brightly to the Raeder brothers about the freshness of the seed cake and the quality of the jam. Honor, picking the currants from her scone, lined them round the rim of her plate. It was a habit from childhood. Like the child she'd been she felt confused and, another familiar feeling, fearful.

She understood Stefan Raeder's truculent, young man's frustration and ill-temper at his incarceration. What she didn't understand was why Oscar had lied to her, again. She waited until the waitress left before pushing her plate aside and turning to him.

143

'Why did you lie to me about how Stefan came to be here?'

'Because I didn't want you involved,' he said.

'But I was already involved when you made that decision.'

'There is no longer anything for you to be involved in.' Stefan spread a thick, fast layer of blackcurrant jam on a slice of seed cake. 'The talk in the camp is of nothing but Germany's defeat. The war is over and Germany's cause is lost. For now. They say Mr De Valera will hand us internees over to the British. My brother chose well when he decided to be neutral.' He put down his knife and stared at his plate. 'For the rest of us it is the end.'

'Only the end of the war,' Oscar said.

'For you, perhaps,' said Stefan, 'but you have always been able to put your head into a book and hide from life's realities and duties in lofty thoughts. And I have always thought Germany and the German people worth fighting for.' He didn't look up.

'You will be able to go home when the war ends.' Honor touched Stefan's hand and he recoiled, then rubbed it. 'You can go home to Micha.'

'You know nothing,' he looked across her to his brother. 'Things are so bad for Germany now they allow us listen to the news in the camp.' The words came in a bitter torrent, accompanied by much scratching of his knuckles. 'Morale is very low. One man tried to commit suicide. But he is old already, nearly fifty. Some are saying they are no longer Nazis, some denying they ever supported the Nazi Party. Others say they will not go home to Germany when it is all over, that there is nothing to go home to, except perhaps to see their mothers and fathers who may well be dead anyway.'

'Our father is alive,' Oscar spoke quietly, 'and Germany will need to be rebuilt. There will be work for both of us. For all Germans.'

'Not for me,' Stefan said. 'The rebuilt Germany you talk about will not be the one I fought for.'

They drove back to the camp slowly, Stefan in the back this time, silent except when he asked Honor for a cigarette. Oscar had barely come to a halt in the compound before his brother left the car and began to walk away. When Oscar followed him Honor stayed where she was. They needed to be alone. She should never have come.

She lit another cigarette and watched them through the smoke as they walked to a hut fifty yards away. When they disappeared inside there was still light in the sky. When Oscar reappeared, alone, it was an inky blue.

'Sorry to have left you so long.' He started the engine. 'You must be cold, waiting all that time.' He reached into the back seat. 'Wrap yourself in this.' He put a blanket on her lap.

For long stretches of the thirty-five-mile journey back to Dublin theirs was the only car on the road. For even longer stretches they drove in silence. The first of the city lights had appeared in the distance before Honor asked, quietly, 'Why did you lie to me? Why didn't you tell me your brother was a spy?'

They drove for another while in silence.

'What I said to you was the truth. It was because I didn't want you involved and didn't think it concerned you,' he said at last. 'I was asked to keep quiet about it, for diplomatic reasons.'

'Diplomacy be damned!' Honor said. They had turned and were driving along by the Grand Canal.

'My brother's stupidity is not your affair,' Oscar said, 'and nor is the war. You are no part of it, any more than this country is. In the ridiculous situations created by war ignorance is the only way to keep yourself safe. I'm sorry Stefan told you. He shouldn't have.'

'Then why did you bring me to the Curragh?' Honor said. 'You know your brother. Surely you must have . . .'

'I didn't think even he would be quite so stupid,' Oscar said curtly, 'and I wanted you with me today. Nothing more.'

Honor, staring through the windscreen, wanted to believe him. She'd made the journey to be with him, nothing more. She'd trusted him.

'You should have trusted me,' she said.

The headlights caught the white glide of a swan on the canal waters, then a second and a third, before the water became dark again, and reed ridden.

'It's not a question of trust,' he said. 'You don't need to know such things. You shouldn't be touched by war, Honor, ever. You should know only peace, and what joy there is.' He gave her another quick, sideways glance. 'I am truly sorry to have hurt you.'

'I'd like to go straight to Clyde Road,' she said, 'before Aunt Grace mobilises the army to look for me.'

She would have more than a little explaining to do. Grace breaking the sexual rules of church and society was one thing, her niece doing so another. Honor wished she felt more buoyant facing her aunt; more certain about Oscar and that spending the night with him had been the right thing to do.

# 14

# The Basement

'. . . we can only summon a shiver
Of remembrance, that our love has betrayed such a lover.'
Bruce Williamson, 'Afternoon in Anglo-Ireland'

I know evil and I can smell it. Not the evil of the faraway war either. The stench is close by, coming and going in this house.

I recognise evil in others because it is in me. The longer I live the better I know it, the more I belong to it. You could say we've become one, evil and I.

Evil stalks the world and is not always apprehended. We all live with it, are a part of it and have a role to play in its unfolding. Mr Hitler is evil manifest most strongly. In the rest of us it sometimes goes unnoticed. It may be disguised by charm, urbanity, stupidity, a twinkling eye.

I have exercised evil myself, and thought it well worth my while to do so. I have also, easily, disguised it.

I killed my husband because of Grace Danaher. There were other women but Grace Danaher was the *coup de grâce*, for me. I could not let him get away with bedding our son's widow.

I have kept my secret for eleven years now. I was no doubt evil long before I murdered Lionel or I wouldn't have done what I did. I have yet to decide whether I was born evil, chose to be or had it thrust upon me.

Others would have tolerated an unfaithful husband, or left him. Perhaps the fact that I chose to kill Lionel because of the pain thrust upon me means that I was born with evil in me. It's a conundrum which gives me pause for endless and amusing speculation. I speculate too on how things might have happened differently, but didn't.

I brought all that I owned to this house when I married, and most of what my family had owned too. I was almost thirty years old, the year 1894 and it was a shameful thing then to be unwed at that age, much more so than it is today. Just as shameful was the fact of my family's penury and the forced sale of Skelfort. Before retiring abroad with my step-mother my father gave me half of the money and all of the furniture and pictures he'd salvaged.

The gift was conditional on my marrying Lionel, and it worked. He agreed to marry me. He would have lost this house without my money.

I first met him at a house party given by friends in County Tipperary in the summer of 1892. It was bright in the sun, and hot, the air filled with the sound of men scything in the long meadow as we gay young things lounged in deck chairs under the trees. Lionel came walking across the lawn, hands in the pockets of his white flannels, and I knew, in the brief moment he looked at me, that he would be mine. There had been other men, at other parties and in other countries, but none that I had so instantly wanted, and forever.

We knew each other, in the Biblical and other ways, before the weekend ended. I seduced him by the river, with the moon casting shadows about us and the sounds of the dancing and music from the farewell ball drifting from the house.

'They're playing that damn' primitive fiddle and flute music,' Lionel said after a long time, after we'd kissed and explored and built a hunger for more of one another. 'Means things are coming to an end. We should go back inside.'

'We must, I suppose,' I said.

We held each other as we walked in and out of the moon shadows on the lawn, and went through the front door arm in arm. Lionel's fiancée screamed when she saw us, and began weeping.

And so, in our beginning, there was our end.

Honor Cusack has displeased me. She did not keep me informed of the progress of her affair with the German. I had to wait to find out at the dinner table, along with everyone else, that he has as a brother a 'guest of the nation', as being a prisoner of any kind is so quaintly put in Ireland.

She brought him here, for them all to see. Worse even, she had told Grace Danaher beforehand about his family and that he lived in Lansdowne Road. Grace, of course, would not have known the Leahys so the only import of this was in Honor's making a mockery of the promise she'd extracted from me not to speak of the family.

She called on me only once, and then briefly, during the week. She was businesslike and quiet, lost in her own thoughts and telling me little. When I questioned her about this she appeared surprised, as if the promise were of no importance because, as she put it, 'Events have moved on, everything's changed.'

For her, perhaps, but not for me. A promise broken dismantles loyalty. Whatever allegiance I felt towards her is gone.

She did what I would have done myself at her age when she left the table with her German and didn't return until next evening. From a woman's point of view, and leaving his nationality aside, I thought his rakishly dishevelled appearance attractive enough.

But what comedy! What theatre! What outrage and frenzy she left behind!

Lennox Mangan was only restrained from following them by Grace Danaher who, quite rightly, said this would merely inflame her niece's passion for the man further. Florrie

Mitchell was jealous, pure and simple, revealing feelings for Honor he'd kept well hidden until then. The Gibbonses, of course, were righteously indignant, the wife Delia announcing she would 'do the nine Fridays in Clarendon Street Church for Honor's immortal soul'.

The pity of it was that a German had the benefit of her body, and for what (unless she is a liar and I am a fool, and neither is the case) was the first time too. She came to me tonight, chastened after her adventure. I was sympathy itself. I still need her.

'His brother is childish and rabidly for the war.' She walked about the place, a habit of hers when she's agitated. She was, as usual, smoking a cigarette. I still like the smell, but have no inclination to smoke any longer. She, in any event, smokes inferior tobacco.

'In a strange way the war and Hitler's dream for Germany are all that he is,' she went on. 'There is nothing else to him. Except for a girl in a photograph, and if you ask me she's a dream too.' She paused and sighed. 'He's handsome, of course. And tall.' She said this last as if feeling she had to say something good about him.

'He just sounds German to me,' I said. 'What did you expect?'

'I don't know.' She sat down opposite me in an armchair where firelight played on her face. Her eyes had the beginnings of circles under them. Sleep is the first casualty of an uncertain love affair. 'Someone more like Oscar, I suppose.'

How she could have thought a soldier of the Third Reich would have anything of the bookish Oscar Raeder about him I failed to fathom.

'It was misguided of you to go to the Curragh,' I said.

'I know. I wish I hadn't.'

'Oh?'

'He's a spy,' she said. 'Stefan Raeder was arrested as a spy.

That's why he's interned. He wasn't rescued when his ship foundered at all.' She hesitated. 'Oscar lied about that.'

'Why are you surprised?' I said, knowing full well it was because she'd slept with him, believed in him, and very likely believed herself in love with him too. She didn't answer, not directly. She asked a question instead.

'Does love die of its own accord or does it have to be destroyed?'

'In my experience,' I said, 'affection of any kind between two people needs a little help before dying. Lies, deceit, cruelty all help.'

Walter went to her and she picked him up. 'I've never been in love, Mrs Sayers,' she concentrated on stroking the cat's silky fur, 'but you have. You loved your husband. How can I be sure? How do I *know*?' She paused. 'Is instinct betrayed by love? Is judgement affected?'

So she had doubts about him. She was afraid of love blinding her, and worried that he'd lied about his brother. She was so unformed: as a lie it was nothing, in the scheme of things.

'Judgement is affected,' I said, 'and instinct is unreliable anyway.'

'And love? Is there a way of telling if it's real and will last?'

'Of course not,' I said. 'You may imagine there is love without limit, and on both sides. Not so. There is one who loves and one who is beloved. There is no other way it can be.'

'Were you the one who loved?' She looked at me curiously.

'Have you shared his bed?' I was equally direct.

She cannot be allowed to probe my past and personal life. Also, I had my own measure of curiosity. She reddened in the firelight and I had my answer. Her burning excitement made me feel even older than I am.

'He might give you what you want,' I said.

He might give her escape, a new life as a German Frau, in which case she would discover too late what being German was really about.

He might also, as she already feared, betray her.

'You could have chosen more wisely,' I said. If she insisted on taking a German for a lover then she would have to live with the consequences.

'His nationality is the least important thing about him,' she said slowly, and I wondered, not for the first time, if she knew me better than I gave her credit for. 'He is the person he is first, a German second. If you just knew him . . .'

I waved a dismissive hand and silenced her. 'The days left me are too few to spend getting to know a representative of a race which would enslave the free world. And this country too if it got the chance.'

'He is as repelled as you are by this war.' She sounded impatient. She was truly an innocent; far more so than I had been at her age.

'You set great faith by this pacifism he attributes to himself,' I snorted, 'but I have never known a pacifist who was not at heart a coward.'

'Is there anything you need?' She put Walter gently on to the rug by the fire and stood up to go. 'Someone gave Aunt Grace a casket of Robt. Roberts coffee. Would you like some?'

'Someone' was always giving Grace Danaher commodities the rest of the country had to do without.

'I prefer tea,' I said, thanking Providence I still had my own supply of *that* at least. 'Why don't you talk to your aunt about your feelings?' I said. 'She has loved men. Is loved by men still.'

'Aunt Grace can't help Lennox caring for her.' She was leaving now, the ugly satchel under her arm, the lumpy tweed coat bundled about her. 'He's an old friend and she can't just banish him. Florrie she encourages as a sort of protection against him. She's not being disloyal to your son. You know I'm right.'

She was, too, up to a point. Her theory that Florrie Mitchell was there purely for protection was interesting and could be right. I hadn't thought of it myself, since I knew there was another, more odious, reason for his being a regular visitor to the house. His own wants and greed are being served and come before any loyalty to Grace Danaher.

And Grace herself is wrong to imagine Lennox Mangan will remain her obedient lap dog. He will do nothing of the sort. He wants to marry her and he is a man who gets what he wants. Grace Danaher and this house are part of what he craves and will have.

I shrugged.

'My son is long dead, her disloyalty to him no longer matters.' Not to Douglas. Only to me. 'There is something I should perhaps say to you,' I added, 'a small piece of advice, though I doubt you'll listen.'

She leaned against the door with her legs crossed at the ankles. The movement was womanly, with a woman's assurance about it. She was changing already. I greatly feared it was too late to say what I had to say.

'Give up your German,' I said. 'I lived through the Great War and its ending. I know what I'm talking about when I tell you there will be whispering and conniving against Oscar Raeder by the very people who most espoused the German cause when the Hun looked like winning.' I waited but she said nothing so I continued.

'You will be a weapon for them to use against him and you will be ruined in the process. You will be presented by the gossips as an innocent student, a country girl seduced by her teacher, himself a man suspected of murder whose brother came here as a spy to endanger this country's neutrality.'

I stopped again. She'd opened the door and was tapping one foot on the floor. Such impatience irritated me intensely.

'I've said what I have to say,' I waved her away with my cane, 'you may take my advice or not, the decision is yours.'

'Please don't worry about me, Mrs Sayers.' She smiled easily, pleasantly. 'I know what I'm doing.'

She didn't know at all what she was doing. As always with the young, she'd wanted my wisdom but was not prepared to take my advice. It's said that advice is seldom welcome, and that those who want it the most invariably like it least. I've always found this to be true and knew at once that I was not too late and that I'd just driven Honor Cusack back to the arms, and unreliable charms, of her German. Which was exactly where I wanted her to be.

And where Grace Danaher, and others besides her, least wanted her.

'I'll be off now then,' Honor said from the door in the common way she sometimes had, 'I'll come back to see you soon.'

She was smiling and light-hearted again and I knew without doubt that she'd made up her mind to return to her German. She was so stupidly predictable. As I'd been myself, at her age.

I was right, of course. Within minutes I saw her from my window, wheeling the bike from the lean-to and along the front garden path. She was swallowed for moments into the great, leafy maw of the laurel by the gate, a bush the Danaher woman should have long ago had clipped back, and then she was cycling away, standing on the pedals for speed, in the direction of Pembroke and Lansdowne Roads.

'She is so completely without guile,' I said to Algernon, the one who understands me, 'that she deserves what's coming to her.' Walter turned to stare. Maybe he, too, understands more than I give him credit for.

I'd found the dynamics at Friday's dinner table *most* interesting, even if they were more or less what I'd expected.

They all saw, as I did, that Honor is changing. Florrie Mitchell, carefully safeguarding his own position, maintained a distance from the problem. Lennox Mangan listened and heard what he wanted to, while Ernie Gibbons was revealed as the man with secrets that he is. His wife merely proved herself more of an idiot than usual.

Grace Danaher, worried to a frenzy, had them all dispatched by midnight. A watchful light in the drawing room was still flooding the front garden by three a.m., the hour at which I gave up the wait for Honor myself and fell asleep.

When I awoke at six a.m. the light had not been turned off.

I pray that Grace Danaher now feels something of the betrayal and loss I felt when Douglas first brought her to meet me. And I pray too that she feels something of my desolation, and fury, when she took Lennox Mangan to her bed as my son lay dying.

The general antipathy to Dr Oscar Raeder on her guests' part was understandable. The situation suits them and they do not want it to change. They rightly see an inevitable end to the *status quo* if Honor continues her friendship with the German.

Perhaps I should have left it to someone else to put to him the questions which needed answers. But it gave me pleasure to cause him discomfort. His country has destroyed Europe and he himself may well be involved with the death of the streetwalker through the carry-on of his brother the spy. His presence brings the war and German evil closer and makes it easier for me to bring down Grace Danaher.

But things will need to move swiftly if I am to enjoy my revenge in full health and awareness. My aches and pains are, I fear, more than those of old age these days. A pain like nothing I've known afflicts me with increasing frequency. I will not win the battle with this one but before I go I. *will* see my daughter-in-law destroyed. If her niece is a casualty of my revenge then so be it. God is not merciful and neither will I be.

# 15

'Flushing almost in our hands . . . Canadian troops within . . . mile of the last remaining big German gun . . . final chapter is being written here.'

NBC Report, 2 November 1944

Honor's mother would have written the letter which arrived on Monday morning sitting in the window of her bedroom. There was nowhere else in the house she'd have been allowed the privacy, or where she would even have had enough light. The letter, as a consequence, was filled with a sense of watchful claustrophobia. It was long, as all her letters were.

Faith Cusack's precise but sparsely punctuated handwriting covered the first page with details of how pressed she was for time, how her son and mother-in-law would be needing her, and how she herself was desperate to get out of the house for an hour before the daylight failed.

Then she got down to the real purpose of her letter.

*You haven't been home in nearly a month Honor not since your grandfather's funeral. It will be his month's Mass on Sunday and I will be expecting you. I needn't tell you how hard things have been here since he went your grandmother misses him something terrible and I have to listen to her without cease from the time she gets up in the morning 'til I lay myself in my own bed at night.*

*They were together sixty years as you know and though
they fought like cats and dogs every day of that long time I
suppose it's true that old habits die hard. She'd got used to
him and his ways and misses him now he's gone. She fights
with me more than ever she did when he was alive so I
suppose she misses the arguing too it's wearing me out as if I
wasn't worn out enough already.*

*It would be a great ease to me if you would come home
for the coming weekend and the Mass. November's short
days are dark enough without the perpetual rain we've been
having and the shortage of candles in the village. Maybe
you'd bring a few with you I know my sister will have plenty
to spare. Red candles would be nice if she has that colour
though I'll be grateful for whatever you bring with you.*

*Your brother works as hard as ever but is still talking
about going for the army or one of those jobs building up the
country that the papers and wireless are always telling us
about. He doesn't mean a word of it of course he'll not give
up the farm now with only his grandmother holding on and
unlikely to live forever. Even so you might talk to him when
you get here tell him how he upsets me when he gets into one
of his furies and moods.*

*I worry about you more than ever since I read about the
misfortunate creature that was found dead in the university
and I had a nightmare in which yours was the body in
the tank of poison. I prayed for the dead woman at Mass
on Sunday I hope you're attending Mass every week
yourself.*

*It's hard to get your brother to the church or anywhere
other than the pub and fields for that matter. The priest has
been good to us regardless and comes to the house to see your
grandmother Cusack once a week.*

*I'm going walking to the village with this letter so that
your grandfather Danaher can take it to the post office for*

*me tomorrow. He keeps well but is less and less able to tend the shop and would sell up if he could find a buyer. If you were at home you would be of great help to my poor father but you have made your choices in life and may God provide they are the right ones.*

*It's nearly a month to Christmas and of course you'll be home then but the wait is too long so I'll expect you on Friday evening from the train or Saturday on the bus. Say hello to my sister and tell her I'll be writing to her soon and that our father sends his best wishes too and would be glad of a letter from her. Or better still a visit though I suppose she hasn't the time to spare for such frivolities.*

She signed it, as she always did, 'Your loving mother Faith Cusack (née Danaher)'. Honor's theory was that her mother signed in this way because reminding herself of the woman she once was gave her a feeling of security she hadn't had since the day she married.

There was also, of course, her mother's own explanation.

'That's the way we were taught to end a letter when I was at school,' she'd said when Honor asked her, 'it made sense to me then and it still does.'

Sitting at her own bedroom window with the letter, Honor watched her mother's sister go down the garden path in her musquash coat and fox fur hat, and shivered at the thought of the difference a marriage could make. Her mother was a slighter, more delicately pretty version of Grace, to whom marriage had bequeathed raw hands, stout shoes and a double-breasted coat she'd been wearing for twelve years.

Marriage to Tim Pat Cusack had also, as her mother-in-law liked to point out, put a stop to Faith Danaher's gallop. This it had done by tying her to forty rock-strewn acres of farmland, a possessive husband, his parents and two children. Poverty and circumstance had done the rest.

Poverty and circumstance had taken the joy out of her too, but not her good looks. Faith Cusack, née Danaher, was a head-turning widow in her old coat, but one who lacked the energy or will to do anything about it.

Faith could have more accurately described her father-in-law's funeral, with its three days of hypocritical lamenting and watchful keening, as a release. She put a gloss on her son Liam too; Honor's older brother's hard-working days were sporadic. Honor didn't blame him. She marvelled that he could put any heart at all into the stony soil whose acres were owned by grandparents who vetoed any change, big or small. He was twenty-eight years old and demented with impatience to assume ownership of the land.

Honor had been glad to read that Father Duffy made calls. He was a comfort to her mother, even if he'd an eye on a bequest to the church from Honor's grandmother, Mary Cusack, when she died.

'I'll be going down home on Friday,' Honor said to Grace when her aunt got back. It was Monday. 'It's Grandfather Cusack's month's Mass on Sunday. Mother's written.' She waved the letter.

'I saw it arrive.' Grace opened the day's newspaper. 'How is she?'

She put her feet on the footstool and held the paper in front of her. She was wearing a skirt that barely reached her knees and silk stockings. Her shoes had two-inch high heels and white laces.

'Her general health seems fine,' Honor said, 'or at least she says nothing to the contrary.'

'Good. That's good,' Grace said. 'Why are you going down there then?' The newspaper headlines were about German resistance and Allied victories in Holland.

'Because she wants to see me and she's my mother.' Honor thought about tearing down her aunt's paper defence.

'And because she's got no relief from Grandmother Cusack's nagging since . . .'

'All she has to do is pack her bags and walk,' Grace cut her short. 'Our father would be more than glad to see her. He could do with the help in the shop.' Her ankles on the stool gave an impatient twitch. 'Then your lump of a brother might learn to wash his own socks and the old woman would shut up or die. Preferably the latter, making everyone happy.'

'Mother asked about you,' Honor said, and walked to the window. It was just after three o'clock but there was a fog and the streets and garden were dark and murkily blanketed. 'She'd like you to write to her.' She paused. 'Or visit.'

'Will you tell her when you go down that you're sharing his bed with a German doctor?' Grace said. Honor didn't turn. She could hear her aunt put down the paper. 'Will you tell her you're putting your medical degree at risk? Not to mind your future.'

'There's a shortage of candles in the village.' Honor still didn't turn. 'She wants me to bring some down with me. She'd like some of your red ones.'

'Take the lot.' Grace raised her voice. 'Take her the yellow and green and gold too, anything that might illuminate that stagnant life of hers. But the answer to my question first, if you please?'

'I'm going to bring Oscar home to meet her.' Honor turned. The firelight on her aunt's face made her appear to twitch but she was unquestionably immobile, her black eyes staring. 'Do you want me to close the curtains?' Honor said. 'The damp will come creeping in otherwise.'

'This is your home,' Grace spoke slowly, 'this is where you are cared for and given what you need. Why would you bring that man to meet Faith?' She stood, the paper falling from her lap. 'Unless you intend marrying him. Do you?'

'I intend going home for the weekend to see my mother.'

Honor turned away again to close the curtains. 'And I intend bringing a friend to meet her. That's all.' The curtains were heavy and closing them took a while. Her aunt, behind her, was silent.

When Honor at last turned back Grace was standing in the way of the door. There would be no leaving the room without further debate.

'He's using you.' Grace stood very straight. 'If he had any regard for you he would leave you alone, not involve you in the unholy mess he finds himself a part of. The guards will have to be told he's leaving the city and you'll be followed. Do you want that? Do you want to expose my sister to the ugliness of what happened to that dead woman? To a man who's under suspicion, and to being watched herself – and maybe not *just* by the gardai?'

'You don't give a damn about your sister.' Honor stood in the middle of the room and hugged herself in the blue jumper her mother had knitted for her when she was eighteen and leaving home. 'You didn't keep any of the ugliness of your own life from her when you needed her. *Don't* tell me how to be with my own mother, nor when I may see her and what friends I may bring to meet her.'

She stopped, studying her aunt's expression and ordering her thoughts so that the rest of what she had to say would be less harsh. Grace Sayers' face was stiff with shock, the lines at the side of her slightly open mouth deeper than Honor had ever seen them

'Don't,' her aunt said, 'please don't say any more.' Her voice was older than it had ever sounded.

'I must.' Honor tried hard to keep her voice from lurching into a shout. 'I must say what hasn't been said between us before. I know that you love me as a daughter and you know that I love and regard you deeply.'

The words came out awkwardly. She'd never had this kind

of conversation before, with anyone. She wouldn't again either, if she didn't begin to feel better about it soon.

'But you are not my mother, Grace, and you must leave me my mother even though I would not have survived if it weren't for you. You were all that I wanted to be, had all I wanted, a life beyond the one I grew up in.' That was it. Enough said.

'Well, that's fine then.' Grace, smiling brilliantly, opened her arms. 'Everything's all right and there's no need for any of this.'

She took an inviting step closer and Honor panicked. Nothing had changed.

'You inspired and gave me courage, Grace, but I can't be you. I've tried and I can't.' Honor stayed where she was, arms by her sides now, nails dug into the palms of her clenched fists. 'And now I don't want to be.'

'I understand,' her aunt said, 'don't think that I don't.' She dropped her arms and looked immediately smaller, defenceless. Honor had seen her do the same thing on the stage, once. 'I've never wanted that either. I want the best life there is for you, that's all. You have the brains and ability to become a doctor – you cannot imagine the doors this will open, the stature it will give you. You will beholden to no man and answerable only to yourself. That's what you want, isn't it?'

'I wanted to heal. But I don't know if I can or even if I still want to,' Honor said. 'I've decided to finish this year and see then what I will do. Please, Grace,' she shook her head, 'I can't explain my confusion, to you or to myself. Just let me sort it myself. I'll move out, if it's easier for you that way.'

'Where will you go?' The fear in Grace's voice was real. 'Will you go to him?'

'Of course not.'

'It's a ridiculous idea anyway,' Grace said.

'I suppose it is,' Honor agreed, 'I couldn't afford to live

anywhere else and I'd miss you terribly.' She smiled. 'I'd worry about you and Lavinia alone together too. One of you would be sure to take an axe to the other.'

'I may still do it, even with you here.' Grace moved quickly and put an arm about her niece's shoulder. 'Don't frighten me like that again,' she said, 'you're all I've got.'

Honor closed her eyes, shutting out a feeling, old and familiar and frightening and now recognised by her as suffocation. She hadn't wanted this conversation and she'd been right. It had changed nothing.

But she did want to take Oscar to Cloclia, and she did want her mother to meet him. She wanted him to see the headland and farm she'd grown up on, and the village of Kilmacreen where her aunt and mother had grown up and where their father, her grandfather Danaher, still kept his shop.

'I'll go on Friday,' she said.

'Your grandmother Cusack will misbehave and make him feel unwelcome,' Grace warned. 'Your brother will sulk or get drunk. Faith will fuss and fluster and make a fool of herself.'

'Oscar will drive,' Honor said, 'Terence is working on the car to make sure it's in good order.' She paused then added, 'It'll be nice to arrive by car.' Her usual bus journey meant she had to cycle the last four miles from the village to Cloclia.

'No,' Grace said, shakily, stubbornly, 'I won't let you go. There's dinner on Friday. We cannot do without you and he cannot have you. You are too precious to me. I have . . .' she shook her head and ran a finger down Honor's cheek '. . . I have put too much of myself into you.'

'You can come with us, if you like,' said Honor, knowing her aunt would never agree.

Honor took a long time getting ready on Friday morning, brushing her teeth twice and tying the scarf at her neck three different ways. She tied up her plait with it in the end.

Oscar arrived at last, ringing twice on the front door and a third time as she galloped down the stairs. She got to the door just ahead of her aunt.

'We'll be back on Sunday night, late.' Honor kissed Grace quickly, hugged her briefly. 'Enjoy tonight's dinner.' She stepped through the door and handed Oscar her suitcase. 'Say goodbye to Lavinia for me,' she called without turning. Grace closed the door before Oscar, hand raised and a smile on his face, had finished his goodbyes.

'What a wonderful day to be travelling!' Honor looked skyward. 'Nothing but blue skies and the prospect of more.'

# 16

'. . . poverty is still a general thing . . . houses . . . extremely primitive of rough stones with straw roofs . . . in which large families huddle . . . possibilities of billeting troops . . . described as bad . . .'

German Intelligence Report on Ireland, 1940

'Glory be to God, I didn't expect you to bring anyone home with you!' Faith Cusack rubbed her hands on her pinafore before sliding them out of sight behind her back. 'You're very early too, the bus doesn't get in until eight as a rule. The house isn't ready for you.' She hesitated. 'Or for a visitor.'

She spoke quickly, her eyes on Oscar, a slight woman in heavy boots standing full square in the narrow doorway, blocking his way into the kitchen directly behind her.

'This is Oscar Raeder, Mother.' Honor spoke just as quickly. 'We drove here in his car. We made good time. We wanted to get here before dark.'

It had been wrong not to prepare her. Honor should have sent word somehow. But things had been difficult, not least because Terence had fiddled with the car for the entire week, only reluctantly handing it over to be driven at the last minute. For a while it had seemed they might have to catch the bus.

Wind rattled the door on its hinges and blew a strand of hair across Faith Cusack's face. She made no attempt to brush it away. Honor did it for her and took her by the arm.

'We're famished.' She turned her mother round and steered them both into the open kitchen. 'We didn't stop to eat on the way.'

She was taller than Faith by several inches but in profile they'd the same longish nose and sculpted mouth. She had none of Faith's diffident way of moving and would never have her wide and cautious dun-coloured eyes.

'You should have said.' Faith fretted by the fire, using black iron tongs to build the turf sods higher. 'You could have telegraphed. I haven't even the bread baked.' She hung a kettle of water from the crane and lowered it over the flames. Her navy sprigged-cotton pinafore was heavily dusted with flour.

'I'm sorry if I've disturbed you, Mrs Cusack.' Oscar spoke for the first time, from the middle of the stone-floored kitchen, his head two inches below the low beams. Faith spun round from the fire to stare at him.

'Perhaps it would be best if I went into the village now and returned in the morning,' he went on, awkwardly. 'Honor has explained already that there is no room for me to sleep here.'

'I thought your name sounded foreign,' she said, 'and that's not an Irish accent you have.' She stood with the tongs in her hands, waiting.

'I'm German,' he said.

'I thought as much, but then we all have our cross to bear. Mine was to be married at eighteen and widowed at twenty-six. Where are you off to?' Her voice rose in alarm when Oscar took a step backwards.

'Honor has arranged for me to stay with your father,' he said, 'in a room over the shop. We stopped on our way here.'

'Don't be foolish, man,' Faith was gently irked, 'there's no need for you to go running off the minute you arrive. I'm vexed at myself now for upsetting you.' She gave her daughter a wry look. 'It would seem the entire county has been informed about Mr Raeder's visitation.' She paused. 'Entire but for me.'

'We stopped at the shop for a minute coming through the village, that's all,' Honor said. It was warm in the kitchen and she took off her coat. It was also dark, though the wintry, midday light was still palely blue outside. 'I brought you the candles. A dozen of them.' She put her suitcase on the settle seat. 'We could do with lighting a couple right away.'

'You'll have to forgive our country ways.' Faith, securing her hair into its bun, smiled at Oscar. 'We like to be at our best before guests.' She smoothed her hair at the sides and sighed. 'One candle will be enough, Honor. You can forego your extravagant city ways while you're here. I'll give you eggs to bring back to her, and butter.'

'You don't have to . . .'

'Yes, I do. I'm not a charity case. Now,' she beat at the pinafore, puffing flour into the air, 'sit up to the fire, both of you. You'll have a glass of whiskey each while we wait for the kettle to boil.' She took a deep breath. 'Before your grandmother comes down from her nap.'

She poured the whiskey into glasses painted with shamrocks. 'They were a wedding present,' she said, and poured one for herself, 'to get over the shock'.

'You're welcome, and I'm delighted to make your acquaintance.' She stood between them, sitting on hobs to either side of the fire, and raised her glass to Oscar. 'We don't get too many Germans calling since the war. There used be plenty of them, studying folklorish matters. Stories and the music mostly. My father has a great store of songs and poems in his head. Are you interested in such things?'

'Reasonably,' Oscar said, 'though I'm ashamed to say I don't know a lot about the folklore of either Ireland or Germany.'

'Oscar is a doctor, Mother,' Honor explained.

'Is he, indeed?' Faith studied the outline of a shamrock on her glass. 'You met in the university then?'

'We did.'

'Honor doesn't bring a whole lot of her Dublin friends to see me.' Faith used the toe of her boot to anchor a sod of turf. 'But then, we're a bit cut off and there's not much excitement here for people used to the glamour of the city. I worry . . .' she shook her head and smiled, widely and bleakly, at both of them '. . . I worry about foolish things, like any mother would. But I pray and I suppose I must believe in God's goodness.'

Honor resisted her usual compulsion to hug her mother and tell her to please, please stop worrying. Her daughter wasn't going to forfeit her immortal soul, not in pursuit of mammon anyway, and wasn't going to turn into her sister Grace either. She resisted because her mother would have thought such a display 'woefully emotional' and been more embarrassed by it than reassured.

'It's the lot of a mother to worry,' Oscar said, smiling a little.

'It's true.' Faith was rueful. 'I suppose it's a relief to your own mother that you're in Ireland, away from the war?'

'My mother is dead. She died when I was a boy,' Oscar said.

Faith Cusack was silent for a minute, looking at him with what could have been either compassion or puzzlement. Honor, catching her eye as she looked away, willed her not to ask him about the other members of his family. Her mother obliged. 'May the Lord have mercy on her soul,' Faith sighed, and finished her drink, and fussed at the bread baking in a skillet in front of the fire. 'I'm sorry for you that you're an orphan.'

Honor knew exactly how her mother's mind was working. Oscar was the first man friend her daughter had ever brought home. He was a doctor, even if he was a German one, and if by any chance he was also a Catholic then he'd the makings of a good husband and Honor's salvation.

'Will you be staying to the month's Mass for Honor's grandfather on Sunday?' She asked.

'If you think it appropriate,' Oscar said, leaving her real question unanswered. He could be well-mannered and Catholic, or well-mannered and belonging to any faith under the sun. Faith sighed.

'Bernard Corkery hasn't been home since the murder of that woman,' she said, 'your brother tells me he was the one found her dead body.' She looked apologetically at Oscar. 'I didn't read the paper myself. The less a person knows about these things the better, is my way of thinking.'

'Where's Liam?' Honor said. 'Where's Whiskey?'

The absence of the eight-year old collie dog was a sign her brother was out, not lying in bed as he often was.

'Your brother's gone fishing. He went down to the rocks in the early-morning.' Faith stopped talking and raised her eyes at a thumping on the floor upstairs. 'He thought you might fancy a nice bit of fresh fish after your journey.' She hunched inwards and hugged herself. 'Your grandmother's awake. I suppose the fact of us getting twenty minutes' peace was a miracle in itself. I must go on up to her, she likes a cup of milk when she wakens.'

The stairs were at the end of the kitchen, deep steps that had defeated Honor as a child and meant her grandmother now descended on her behind, step by careful step, using her stick for support. She would die before sleeping downstairs, Mary Cusack said, her bed in the loft being closer to God should she pass on in the night.

'I'll take the milk up to her,' Honor said.

Mary Cusack sat waiting, an eighty-four-year-old wraith

with pale, tenacious eyes. She was brushing her long, yellowy-white hair in the low-ceilinged gloom of the loft.

'You took your time about coming to see me.' She put away the brush and cupped the glass of milk in elegant, blue-veined hands. 'You can sit into the chair but be careful with your grandfather's hat and coat.'

Honor put the hat on the floor and sat forward so as not to touch the coat. 'You look well,' she said, which was true and could be affirmed now her eyes had accustomed themselves to the murky light. Frail Mary Cusack might be but there was an inherent vitality and wiry strength about her.

'I heard a man's voice,' her grandmother said.

'You did,' said Honor, who could play the game too.

If her grandmother wanted to know who'd come with her, let her ask. Age had not softened Mary Cusack's heart, nor gentled her disposition, and her granddaughter had too many harsh memories to be herself softened by Mary's great age and the inevitable approach of death.

Mary Cusack waited, staring straight ahead at the small rectangle of window, balancing the glass of milk on the double peak of her knees. She'd sewn the patchwork quilt covering the bed herself, when a girl. It had been made to last; Mary Cusack had never been given to extravagance.

Her son Tim Pat, Honor's father, had shared this and other characteristics with his mother.

'Mother says Father Duffy's been good about calling,' Honor said.

Her grandmother didn't reply immediately and Honor, following her gaze, saw the tide was high and crashing against the rocks in the inlet below the house. The weather was changing. Liam wouldn't stay fishing much longer.

'He does his priestly duty,' her grandmother said at last, 'nothing more.'

171

'I'll go on downstairs then,' Honor said, 'let you drink your milk and finish doing your hair.'

Time was when she would have offered to do her grandmother's hair for her. But that had been a long, long time ago, and not very often even then.

'Take yourself off so,' Mary said. 'A fine doctor you'll make, without an ounce of kindness in you.'

'You know, Grandmother, that you only have to ask for what you want.' Honor spoke quietly.

'You can wash the milk out of this quilt then,' Mary upended the glass on to the bed cover, 'and you can tell whatever friend you've with you that this house is still mine and that I'm the one will decide who stays here.'

'I'll bring you soap and water,' Honor walked to the opening where the stairs climbed downwards from the loft, 'and my friend will be staying in Mother's old room over the shop.'

'You're your mother's daughter,' Mary's voice followed her down the steps, 'bad cess to you but you're every inch the trollop she is! You'll have no more luck than she's had either. You turned your back on duty and a neighbour's child and the right thing to do by your family. The man that's dead always said you'd have no luck.'

Oscar and her mother, drinking tea at either end of the table, continued talking when Honor arrived in the kitchen. They didn't for a minute fool her. Her mother hoped to obliterate the sour rasp from upstairs, Oscar hoped to convince Faith she was succeeding, that he hadn't heard a thing. Their conversation involved Faith explaining the tradition of month's Mass to him.

Honor left them at it and went back upstairs with the soapy water. Her grandmother, sitting on the side of the bed, had put on her boots and grown silent again. Honor placed the water within easy reach. She'd got as far as the top of the stairs going down again when Mary Cusack spoke softly.

'It would be a mistake for you to imagine I'm losing my faculties,' she said, 'or to imagine grief has softened my brain.'

'I vaguely entertained some hopes,' Honor didn't turn round, 'but to no avail, obviously.'

'You will be punished for that,' her grandmother promised, 'by God if not by man.'

'I don't doubt it,' Honor replied.

The house was long and low, one gable end facing the sea, the other a low mountain that in summertime blazed with flaming montbretia. It was one of only two farmhouses on the peninsula, itself an outcrop of uncertain land which seemed about to slide into the sea at any moment. From the front door of the Cusack home there were wide views of the winding road which gave access to the promontory, and of the precariously inclined fields and stone walls of both farms. High cliffs with snapping rocks gave it a fortress feel.

As a small child Honor had thought Cloclia the true end of the known world. As a woman she knew she'd been right.

The Cusack house itself had six rooms; the kitchen with a bedroom at either end on the ground floor, the loft with storage for grain, flour, horse tackle, and two bedrooms upstairs.

It had a slate roof, put there early in the century and the reason it had withstood the battle with the elements when the thatched roofs of the less farsighted had fallen into decay and their occupants opted for the emigrant boat. The Cusacks' slate roof set them aside, confirmed their status as a family who for generations had considered themselves more forward-looking and generally superior to their neighbours.

None of which had safeguarded them from the tragedies of civil war, greed, poverty, politics, and the inexorable march of changing times.

'You shouldn't have agitated your grandmother.' Faith

wrung her hands. She was the only person Honor knew to do such a thing and she always expected frantic perspiration to squeeze from between her mother's fingers. 'She'll be upset now for the night. We'll have no peace, even at the dinner table.'

'Speaking of which,' Honor squinted from the doorway at the coastal rocks, shiny and black in the sunlight, 'I think I'll take Oscar to meet Liam, see if he's caught anything for us to eat. The sea's getting rough.'

'He said he'd try the north side.' Her mother sounded relieved; she'd been worried about him then. 'There would be less of a swell there, he said.' She glanced at the votive lamp, burning red under a picture of a thorny-crowned and bleeding Sacred Heart. 'He's been gone since daybreak. Six hours.'

She'd have counted the minutes too, Honor knew. Worry about her son had been the real root of her agitation when they'd arrived.

'We'll bring him back with us,' Honor assured her.

A blue sky and light wind was no guarantee of good weather on the peninsula. It could turn with hideous speed, the wind become a gale and the skies black and thundery. November was the worst month of all twelve for such mercurial behaviour. Honor knew this as well as her mother and grandmother and all who'd lived before them on the forty Cusack acres, which was why she was worried herself about Liam as she set of with Oscar to cross the low mountain to the north-side fishing spot.

'I'm sorry about my grandmother,' she said. 'I'd hoped good manners and hospitality might make her behave.'

'It evens the odds.' He took her hand. 'Stefan's manners and hospitality weren't much on show when you met him.'

Honor smiled, wryly. 'Grandmother *can* behave, when it suits her. She may even be charm itself when we get back to the house.'

'She doesn't have to be.' Oscar took her hand. 'I'm glad to be here with you. It helps me understand.'

'Understand?'

'You.'

He was uncertain on the strange terrain, cautious about pushing his way through furze as they went uphill, slow to plunge through bracken, suspicious when they came to a plateau of long brown wet grass. Cool-eyed, languid sheep watched unimpressed as Honor, several times, had to wait for him to catch up.

'You didn't tell me your home place was anything like this,' he said when they at last stood on the prow of the hill. The sea, where it curled and met the gentler rocks of the other side of the headland, was a smiling blue. 'It's beautiful.'

'It's savage,' Honor said. 'What it gives it takes away.'

She went downhill ahead of him, sure-footed and quick, leaving him to follow on his own. She'd seen her brother on the rocks below. Better to get there first and explain who Oscar was to him.

Liam would be a different proposition altogether from her mother. Disaffected he might be but he was intelligent and alert to the world and its affairs. He would have read the fine detail of Bridie Keogh's murder.

The dog ran to meet her as she came near and she laughed as he careered round her in excited circles, jumping goat-like from rock to rock. Liam was on his haunches smoking a cigarette when she got to him. Beside him a conger eel, long, thick and dead, soaked in the blood-red water of a rock pool. Its head had been bashed in with a nearby bloodied stone.

'Devil from hell tried to drag me into the water with him,' her brother said as Honor hunkered down next to him. 'But I had the better of him. I'd be damned if I'd let him best me, or let the sea have him back either. I fought the bastard for three solid hours. Must be ten feet long, if he's a black inch.'

He shook his head, smiling and dragging on a cigarette, dark hair heavy and damp on his forehead. 'But, by Christ, I took him. I took the devil.'

'You should know better.' Honor, tight-lipped, stared at the eel. Liam could have drowned so very easily. 'Do you want to kill yourself?' She kept her voice low, the fury otherwise unrestrained. 'You could have gone in after him! *You* could be the dead one. You can't even swim. One wave would have been enough. One sudden wave. Have you lost your mind completely? What in the name of God is wrong with you, Liam? It could be you at the bottom of the sea . . .'

'The conger eel is bad luck.' He shrugged, interrupting her, taking a cap from his pocket and putting it to the back of his head. 'But this is one bastard won't foul any more nets. He won't destroy any more lobster pots either.'

'That's not why you did it,' she said, 'so don't play the fisherman's saviour with me, Liam. Or with yourself either.'

'Good to have you home, sister mine.' He gave her a brief, hard hug and handed her a cigarette. Clouds had begun appearing from nowhere and a snapping wind flustered the waters.

Hunkering together, dark-haired, blue-eyed and angular, they were of a type, but different. A permanent, simmering fury in Liam Cusack gave him a blunt edge and reckless indifference akin to the rocks around them. Honor had more of the rocks' hard, enduring core about her.

Liam jerked his head towards Oscar who had stopped at the edge of the rocks to peer seaward through binoculars.

'You brought a man with you then,' he said, 'he's taking his time getting here.' He took a long drag on the cigarette.

'He's a city man,' Honor said. 'From Berlin.'

'What does he want coming here for?' Liam studied Oscar, on the rocks now and clambering cautiously towards them.

'Shouldn't he be flying a Luftwaffe aeroplane or some such?'

'No more reason for him to be doing that than there is for you to be drilling in the mountains with the IRA.'

'You like him then or you wouldn't be defending him.' Liam shrugged. 'How long've you been keeping him a secret from us?'

'I'm not defending him,' Honor said, 'merely putting you in touch with reality. Not all Germans agree with the war, any more than everyone in Ireland agrees with bombing England for a united Ireland.' She took the cigarette from between his lips and lit her own from its burning end.

'Be careful, Honor.' Her brother, retrieving his cigarette, spoke softly. 'Be very careful how you speak for me. Putting the ballot box before the gun is not at all the same as disagreeing with the cause.' He flicked the end of his cigarette moodily at the dead eel.

'Did I say it was?' she flared. 'You were the one brought the subject up. But what you call your pacifism is no more than carrying the past on your back like a cross.'

'I told you to be careful . . .'

'You've no authority to tell anyone anything, Liam.' Honor's voice was bitter. 'You've crippled yourself with self-pity. You'd rather wallow in the past than work, make something of the place. You were a child . . . what happened wasn't your fault. None of it. Worrying about what people think, brooding and drinking and working one day out of seven, is making you an old man before your time.'

'Did you come from Dublin to tell me this?' Her brother got to his feet and the dog gave her a reproving look. 'Because I can hear that kind of talk from our mother any day of the week. Or any night for that matter.' He looked out at the sea, heaving and unfriendly now as the wind turned round. 'I'm considering my options,' he said. 'McAlpine and Wimpey are recruiting the able-bodied for builders every day of the week and the countryside's practically empty with the numbers going to work in English factories.'

'I've heard all this before,' Honor said, 'and I certainly didn't come from Dublin to hear it again. This is the only place you'll rid yourself of the past, here, where it happened.'

Liam stood with his hands in his pockets, jabbing the eel with the toe of his boot. It twitched and coiled reflexively, as if there were still some life there. The water darkened.

'Bastard,' he said. 'Bastard won't stay dead.' He grabbed the fishing pole.

'It's dead,' Honor spoke quietly, 'let it go, Liam. You can't make it any more dead than it is.' She paused. 'The dead don't come back.'

'So they say,' her brother replied.

'Did you catch anything we'll actually be able to eat tonight?' Honor lightened her tone.

'A few bass, some herring. There's enough.' A hessian sack wriggled when he lifted it. 'Fresher and better than anything you'll get in Dublin anyway. Your friend's just upon us.' He was smiling, face shadowy and teasing under the peak of his cap. 'What was it you said made you bring him with you? Was it to encourage tourism? Or did he come for the bird watching?'

'I brought him to meet you, Liam,' Honor said, smiling while cursing under her breath and praying he would behave. He could, when he chose to. Just as her grandmother could be charm itself, when she chose to. They were more alike than either of them would acknowledge.

Liam swung the sack across his shoulder and held out his hand as Oscar reached them. The dog sniffed at his ankles and waited, assessing.

'You're welcome,' Liam said, and the dog, reassured, sat

with a slow-wagging tail. 'Though you've made it just in time for us to turn back.'

He was right. The sea and sky were looking less hospitable by the minute. Honor, standing in the way of the eel's corpse in the rock pool, steadied herself against a spiteful gust of wind.

'We should go,' she said.

'What's that?' Oscar stepped round her to study the pale, brown corpse of the conger. He squinted, taking in the measurement from its bloodied head to black-tipped fins. 'Must be two-and-a-half metres long. You landed him on your own?'

'Do you see anyone else around?' Liam, moving ahead of them off the rocks, was short with him. 'It's a conger eel. Fishermen hate the bastards.'

'You're leaving it here? Surely it's edible?' Oscar said.

'Not eaten by the people round here anyway, though I can't speak for Germany.'

'I would think there are many in Germany would be glad of an eel for dinner these days,' Oscar said. 'So you're leaving him here, on the rocks?'

'The sea'll reclaim him soon enough, there's a storm coming.'

They moved quickly and silently, the early flurries of the storm whipping up the long grass and sending scurries of rain across the bay as they came down the other side of the mountain. Oscar took Honor's hand when they were in sight of the house. Liam looked away.

'You were mentioned in the papers, Dr Raeder,' he spoke with his back to them, 'in connection with the misfortunate murdered woman found in the university. Must have been a bothersome thing to have happen.' He paused. 'For the dead woman especially.'

'It was . . . is . . . a terrible thing,' Oscar agreed.

'My mother doesn't read the papers,' Liam said, 'she's afraid of what she might read there since Honor went to Dublin. She gets as much news as she wants from me.' He slowed down and looked sideways at Oscar as they came alongside. 'She's unlikely to have put two-and-two together as to who you are but you might want to keep quiet about your involvement. She'd be inclined to worry more about Honor.'

'Of course,' Oscar said. 'I'll do that.'

'There's a car on the road above the house.' Liam stopped in his tracks. 'A garda car.' He turned again to look at Oscar. 'They've no business with me. Would they have any call to be looking for you, Dr Raeder?'

# 17

'You in Ireland have had many great men . . . Therefore . . .
you will regard the struggle of the German nation and the
work of the Führer with understanding.'

German Radio's Wartime Foreign Service

Mary Cusack was sitting where she always sat, in a
chair by the table with her back to the kitchen's only
window. Her spine was straight and her hands gripped the
chair's wooden arms. It had been made by her husband forty
years earlier. The light behind her made it hard to see her face.
Since hers was the only raised voice it was equally hard not to
hear her.

'I did not invite him,' she said. 'He's no guest of mine. You can
take him away with you, and good riddance. You can take my
granddaughter too, since she was the one brought him here.'

'We're not here to take anyone away, Mrs Cusack.' Sergeant Healey, long-bodied and pebble-eyed, stood with his
legs apart and backside to the fire. The young garda with
him stood looking seriously uncomfortable at the other end
of the kitchen.

'Who asked you here, Healey?' Liam dropped the sack of
fish on the stone floor. It landed with a slow slither. 'What
little you and I have to say to one another can be said in the
barracks.' A writhing in the sack moved it several inches closer
to the sergeant's muddy boot.

'It wasn't you I came to see, Liam.' Sergeant Healey's face expressed apology. 'It was your guest, Dr Raeder. I'll only take a minute of his time now he's here.'

'Are you sure you've the right to take any of his time?' Liam upended and emptied the sack. Fish and a couple of crabs slipped in a pile to the sergeant's feet. The crabs began an immediate sideways crawl. 'As you rightly said, he's a guest in this house. Cannot your business wait until morning? We're about to eat.'

'As God is my judge, Sergeant Healy, I'd no idea . . .' Faith began.

'You've been upsetting my mother.' Liam stepped close to the sergeant. His face was inches from the older man's beaky nose when he said, 'If it can't wait 'til morning you'd be better conducting your business outside in the yard.'

'That's a good idea.' Oscar, just inside the door, looked at the policeman. 'We can talk outside, Sergeant.' He turned to Faith Cusack, standing by the table, turning an enamel jug of milk round and round between her hands. 'I'm sorry, Mrs Cusack, to have brought my difficulties to your home.'

'God in heaven, I'd no idea . . .' Faith began again. Her mother-in-law cut her short this time.

'This is my house,' she said, 'get him out of here.' She drummed her fingers on the arms of the chair. 'I'm afraid for my life with him under my roof.'

'You're the only person anyone need be afraid of in this house,' Honor stepped between her grandmother's pointing finger and Oscar Raeder, 'and if you're not careful you'll end your days here alone and rotting.' She lowered her voice to a murmur, leaned forward and put a hand on each arm of the chair, pinning her grandmother where she sat.

'There's something you should know, Grandmother, and you might as well be told now since you've so much to say for yourself.' She was smiling and very calm. 'My mother might be persuaded to leave here and come and live with me in Dublin. Things have changed now Grandfather's dead. Nothing's the same; the war's ending and Liam might not wait much longer to be given his head. I'd watch myself from now on, Grandmother, if I were you. Liam and I care more for our mother than we ever did for you. Remember that.'

'You don't frighten me.' Mary Cusack gave her a black-eyed glare. 'This family has done its bit for Ireland and I'll not have it soiled and brought down by the likes of your fancy man.'

Honor straightened up and stood away from the chair.

'I warned you,' she said, 'what happens now is on your own head.' She faced the sergeant. 'I've never known you bring good news to this house, Sergeant Healey. What is it you want today?'

'I'd like a quiet word with Dr Raeder,' the sergeant said, 'that's all. We'd a request from Dublin. Just a minute of his time's all it's take.' He paused. 'Outside in the yard might indeed be the best place.'

'Dr Raeder's done nothing wrong,' Honor cut him short.

'Of course he hasn't.' The sergeant rubbed his hands together. 'But my orders are my orders and must be obeyed.'

'I'll start the dinner,' Faith said. 'You might gut the fish for me, Liam, there's a good lad.'

The young garda stood a nervous six feet away while Sergeant Healey spoke to Oscar in the walled yard to the front of the house. Honor stood by Oscar's side. The wind was climbing to gale force and filled with splattering rain.

'It's an embarrassment to me to have to do this,' the sergeant began, 'but as I said inside, orders are orders.'

'Of course,' Oscar said.

The sergeant cleared his throat. 'I was told to tell you to stay close and around the place,' he said, 'and to go straight back to Dublin after your visit.'

'I've already been told that by your colleagues there,' Oscar said, politely. 'It is not my intention to do otherwise.'

'Why're you really here, Sergeant?' Honor said. 'It's to cause mischief and embarrassment, isn't it? There was no need for you to come out here at all.'

'There was no need either for you to bring this man among us.' Sergeant Healey frowned before signalling his younger colleague back to the car. 'You brought the consequences upon yourself. And upon your friend.' He looked towards the open door of the house, and at Liam standing there. 'The same law applies to us all, the high and the low. It even includes the Cusacks of this world.'

The dinner preparations in the household were time-worn and unchanging. Even Faith's nervous efficiency, as she cooked the potatoes and fish on the open fire, was usual. Honor lit the tilly lamp, as she always did, and hung it on the wall above the table. When its white gas light flared over the oil-cloth cover Faith put down a platter of boiled potatoes and a dish of her own butter. Honor brought the fish to each plate as it was ready.

Faith broke the silence as they began to eat. 'We're poor but we've no shortage of good food, thank God.'

'You've no need to apologise,' Liam was short with her, 'there's far greater poverty in Dublin. I'm sure the doctor is aware of it too.'

'Aware but not affected,' Oscar said. He sounded apologetic.

'I read that more than five hundred poor go every day for thrupenny dinners to the Meath Street Dining Rooms,' Liam said, 'and that in the same rooms, for just a penny, they can get a bowl of meat soup.' He gave the patiently waiting dog a potato. 'For an extra halfpenny there's a slice of bread with it.' He looked at Oscar. 'I do a great deal of newspaper reading.'

'You do.' His mother cleared her throat. 'It's as well to be informed.'

'Since you read so widely,' Honor said, 'you'll know that Oscar is in no way suspected of being implicated in what happened to Marigold Keogh.'

'I don't think we should be talking about such things at the dinner table.' Faith put her cutlery down with a clatter. 'We should be enjoying our food.'

'The fish is excellent,' Oscar said.

'Tell us how Bernard is then?' Liam prompted. 'He's always good for a conversation piece. Saw his name in the paper too.'

'Bernard's fine,' Honor said shortly.

'You see a fair bit of him then?' Liam was smiling. The dog, with a sigh, went and stretched himself out in front of the fire.

'He works in the medical faculty. As you well know.'

'So he does.' Liam professed astonishment. 'I'd overlooked for a minute how well Aunty Grace had stitched things up around herself. She's got that old goat Lennox Mangan still in attendance too, I suppose? And that other, though less old, goat Mitchell?'

'Yes. But Bernard's his own person,' Honor said.

'He is. In a way. He did well to get away from this place, at least. I presume, Dr Raeder, that you know our neighbour, Mr Bernard Corkery?'

'Of course,' Oscar said, 'though not well. He's a good man at his job.'

'The milk, Liam, if you please.' Faith didn't look up. 'I forgot to put the milk on the table. This morning's fresh is by the back door.'

The meal continued and ended in a silence which made the sounds of the gathering storm more ominous. Wind came in gusts down the chimney, sending billowing shrouds of grey smoke into the room and making the dog whimper in his sleep. Mary Cusack, finished with her food before anyone else, sighed deeply and left the table. She pushed her chair in front of the fire and sat packing a clay pipe with tobacco.

'I should go,' Oscar said, 'I don't want Mr Danaher to delay going to his bed on my account.'

'Only the tinkers eat and run,' Liam said. 'I'll be going to the village myself in a while so you can give me a lift in your motor car. It's early yet. We'll have a smoke first.'

'It's a bad night, Liam, to be going to the pub,' his mother said.

'There are too many bad nights to pay heed to them.' Liam offered round one of the packets of Woodbine Honor had brought with her. 'Might do a bit of lamping on my way home, if the wind dies down.'

'Lamping?' Oscar was interested.

'Rabbit hunting,' Liam said shortly. 'Their numbers are increasing by the hour around here. The dog flushes them out, I dazzle them with the lamp, down comes the club and bob's your uncle.' He grinned. 'There's a fella I know exports them along with chickens to England. I get four and sixpence each for a rabbit. Used to be one and sixpence at the beginning of the war but hunger and shortages have improved things. England's difficulty, as they say, is Ireland's opportunity.'

'The storm will get worse, not better,' his grandmother said. 'You know that yourself. The wind's from the east or it wouldn't be coming down the chimney.' She turned to Oscar. 'It's a bitter wind that comes from the continent. Good for neither man nor beast.' She shook her head. 'A sad fact, but true.' She sounded pleasant enough, sadly smiling.

'If ye'd brought Bernard he'd play a tune on the whistle for us at least.' Liam fiddled restlessly with the knobs on the wireless. A squawking sound emerged and he turned it off in disgust. 'Batteries are low on the bloody thing.

Bernard owes us a tune, since he didn't come to the auld lad's funeral.'

'He couldn't get the time off,' Honor said, 'you know that.'

'Honor could have married Bernard Corkery.' Liam, straddling a chair, looked Oscar in the face.

'I'd be surprised if half the young men in the county hadn't wanted to marry her.'

He was smiling, refusing to be baited or to play Liam's game. Honor, for an abandoned moment, wanted to throw herself into his arms and kiss him. Hard.

'She'd have resolved a lot of old family problems if she'd taken him on,' Liam said. 'Created a lot of new ones too. I suppose she's given you the family history?'

'We've spoken of your family,' Oscar said, 'and of mine.'

'Civilised chats, by the sound of it.' Liam leaned his arms on the back of the chair. 'But did my sister tell you why our mother is a widow? Why the two of us grew up without a father?'

'No. But if she'd wanted me to know then I presume she would have.'

Oscar's voice held a warning note which Liam, in truculent mood, ignored. Her brother might be intelligent but wasn't half so clever as he thought he was. Honor knew exactly what he was up to. Nothing that had been discussed so far had yielded him the information he wanted about how close exactly his sister was to Oscar Raeder.

Nor had he been given a chance to test Oscar's mettle against the story of their father's life, and death.

Honor had a choice. She could suggest they leave for the village now, walk out and kill the conversation stone dead.

Or she could take part, let what had to be said be said. That way it would be over and done with, Oscar would know what there was to know and *she* would know how, as a pacifist, he

187

dealt with the intimate and very real tragedies of civil war. Or if, as Stefan had accused, he buried his head in books and lofty thoughts when life's uglier side shuffled his way.

Faith also saw the way things were going. Her son ignored her small, protesting sound.

'You'll know, of course, that we've had our own war in this country,' Liam began. 'It wasn't so easy to escape either, or for people to stand aside. It was the worst of wars, brother against brother and father against father.'

'I've read about the Irish Civil War.'

'You do a lot of reading?' Liam asked.

'Probably too much,' Oscar acknowledged.

'You'll know then that there were terrible atrocities committed in the name of justice and freedom. Inhuman things. Neighbour against neighbour.'

'All wars are terrible,' Oscar said.

Mary Cusack, pulling on her pipe, sighed deeply and drew herself into a narrow, collapsed shape.

'Of course they are.' Liam was curt. 'But you've avoided the latest one by being here while your own country fights.'

'Deliberately,' Oscar confirmed. 'I don't agree with this war. With any war.'

'You're a lucky man to have had a choice.' Liam's voice was harsh.

His mother stood and put a hand on his shoulder. She shook him, gently, and would have spoken if he hadn't moved himself, and the chair, abruptly away. He was close enough now to Oscar for their faces almost to touch as he leaned forward.

'If you were born in the month of the year your country rose in rebellion,' Liam spoke slowly, 'and reared with a dead hero for a father and his death on your hands,' his mother, behind him, left the room, 'then you might not find it so easy to distance yourself.'

The kettle, hanging from the crane over the fire, began to sing. The dog, fast asleep, thumped his tail once against the floor. Oscar's head and shoulders made a hulking shadow on the wall behind him and Honor, getting up to lift the kettle, thought how her grandfather's shadow, when he used sit in the same spot, had so often terrified her as a child. It had, she knew, become confused with her hatred of the old man.

The silence when the kettle stopped singing had a brooding quality to it.

'I'll have a hot whiskey, if you please,' Mary said, smiling.

'Do you understand what I'm saying to you?' Liam said to Oscar.

'What you describe sounds difficult.' He offered Liam a cigarette. His eyes followed Honor, at the dresser getting whiskey and sugar. 'Confusing.' He held out a match to Liam who, ignoring him, lifted a sod from the fire with the tongs and used it to light his cigarette. 'Your father is dead many years, Honor has told me. How could a child, which you must have been when he died, have been the cause of his death?'

'My father was murdered in 1922.' Liam checked the burning tip of his cigarette before replacing the sod in the fire. His movements were slow and provocative. He looked into the fire as he went on.

'He took the Republican side in the Civil War. This family has always stood for a republic, for a united Ireland. My father's father, the man we buried a month ago, fought for the Republican cause too, long before my father went out to do his bit against the army of murderous irregulars the Free State government had doing their filthy work for them.'

'It's history, Liam.' His mother had reappeared from the bedroom at the end of the kitchen. 'What you're telling the man is nothing but history now.'

189

She was wearing her coat; brown tweed with a half belt, and a beaver collar Grace had sent her from Dublin.

'I'll take a lift from you as far my father's shop.' She moved up the kitchen, tying a scarf about her head, speaking directly and purposefully to Oscar. 'There'll be time enough for you to drop me home too before you settle in there for the night. It's a long cycle there and back this time of year and I might as well make use of the car now it's here.'

The scarf was a pale square of silk with horses' heads on it. She'd had it as long as Honor could remember and usually wore it on Sundays only.

'I'm ready to go.' She stood between Oscar and her son, hands clasped in front of her, waiting.

'I'll finish what I've started, Mother.' Liam raised his voice, but not a lot. 'Better he hears it from me, now, than in the pub later tonight or tomorrow.' The cigarette between his long fingers sent up a coil of smoke. 'Better he hears the truth of it than some local shyster's version of things.' He blew at and dispelled the curling smoke.

'You don't have the truth of it to tell,' his mother spoke quietly, 'only your burden to share. Let it go, Liam, there's a good lad.' She moved towards the front door. 'Let the man enjoy his couple of days with us without having to take on the family's woes.'

'He should know,' Liam said stubbornly, 'if he's to be any sort of a . . . decent friend to Honor, he should know what happened to her father.'

'You're right.' Oscar touched his shoulder. 'Tell me.'

'Tell if you must, Liam,' Honor said quietly, 'but don't pretend you're doing it for my sake. I'll speak for myself in my own time. If I need to.'

'Let him.' Mary spoke with distanced impatience. 'Since he must be forever talking about my son's death, let him get on with it.'

Liam flicked the cigarette end into the fire.

'The truth is that I was the cause of my own father's death. The Black 'n' Tans came here, looking for him, following a bit of a skirmish further up the county. There was also the matter of the bombing of a barracks. My father had nothing to do with either event but he knew they'd be out for him anyway and had gone on the run. They came unexpected though, on a day when he was home visiting us. His friend, our neighbour Frank Corkery, was also on the run and with him here, in this kitchen, talking. We knew nothing 'til my grandmother heard them in the yard, half a dozen of them making enough noise for a dozen strong troop of regular marching soldiers. My father and Frank ran for the loft. My mother put my sister and myself sitting on the bottom step of the stairs. She told us to say nothing. My grandmother faced them in the doorway. They pushed her aside and came on in, filling the place with shouting. My mother told them my father wasn't here. My grandmother told them the same thing. Honor, who was two years old, began to cry. I told them my father was upstairs, in the loft. He was still struggling to get the window open when they took him, and Frank.'

'You were six years old,' Faith said. 'You thought your grandmother and I had forgotten he was upstairs. You told me so yourself, afterwards.'

'Afterwards . . .' Liam looked up, into Oscar's attentive face. 'Do you know what they did with him afterwards?'

'I've read of the brutality of the Black 'n' Tans,' Oscar said.

'A man of learning indeed. But before we get to that there's another thing you should understand. You say you met Bernard Corkery? Frank Corkery was his father. Mrs Corkery and Bernard, the youngest of her six boys, were the only two at home when the Tans called there, before they came here. They knew where the two men were and they stood in front of the Black 'n' Tans, the both of them, and they lied, Bernard as good as his mother. He also was six years old, the same age as myself to within a month.'

'He was too frightened to speak,' Honor kept her voice even, 'too petrified even to open his mouth. He's always said as much. Over and over, when we were growing up. It had nothing to do with courage, or lying to save lives.'

For the first time since Liam had begun his story she looked at and spoke directly to Oscar. His face was entirely without expression.

'Bernard doesn't blame Liam for what happened to his father. He stopped all that when they were about fifteen years old,' she said.

'The harm was done by then.' Faith, sitting on a chair by the door, spoke in a flat voice. 'Liam lived his early years with the weight of what had happened heaped on him daily.'

'Your father was shot, Honor?' Oscar said quietly, his eyes on her face.

She got up and walked to the dresser, keeping her back to him when she stood there.

'No. My father wasn't shot. Shooting was what they did to animals, or for the fun of target practice.' She rearranged the cups on the top shelf. Her mother wasn't tall enough to keep them in a row. 'Shooting was too good for my father, and for Frank Corkery.'

What had she been thinking of, letting the conversation get this far? She should never have encouraged it. Too late to draw a halt now. Far, far too late.

'What happened?' Oscar said, quietly.

Liam answered him. 'They tied my father and Frank Corkery to a tree in the middle of a field the other side of the village, then they dynamited them. People were picking pieces of skin and clothing from the hedges and stones around for months afterwards.'

'Didn't even leave us a body to bury,' Mary said.

The dog rolled over and gave a slow, hopeful wag of his tail as Liam stood. When he helped himself to a mugful of spring water from the container by the back door the dog followed him. Liam filled him a bowl and hunkered beside him as he drank, fondling his silky ears.

'Man's best friend,' he said.

'You have my sympathy.' Oscar, standing, spoke to no one in particular. 'I feel . . . unqualified to say more.' He cleared his throat. 'We live in a merciless century.'

'That we do,' Liam agreed, 'merciless and pitiless and hard to see it getting any better.'

'We must believe in God's mercy, even when we can't see his plan.' Mary was shrilly insistent, jerking her head as if suddenly awakening. 'There was good in one of the Tans came to dynamite the Corkery house afterwards.'

'Enough, Mary.' Faith sounded tired. 'The man's heard enough.'

'He should be told the full of it.' The old woman was insistent, looking straight ahead as she went on. 'The Tans came back because Bridget Corkery had lied, not told them her husband was in this house. There were five of them and while they were digging a hole in the kitchen floor for the explosives Bridget decided to take her sewing machine outside, into the yard, to keep it safe. She'd reared a family of six stitching on that machine.'

Honor began clearing the table. It was easier than hearing again another story she'd grown up with.

'Four of the Tans were for blowing up the machine along with everything else,' Mary went on, 'the fifth said no, she must be allowed to have it. He stood by her and he had the day. They blew up the house but left her her sewing machine.' She pointed a finger at Oscar. 'What do you think of that then? Does that make you consider the good in the worst of us?'

'It's late.' Honor cut across any answer he might have given. 'We should leave for the village. I'll get my coat.'

She was passing her grandmother when the old woman's hand clutched at her, capturing her arm before she could move it out of reach.

'You should know what make of a man your German is,' Mary said, 'you should be listening to what he has to say for himself. I told the story of the Corkerys' sewing machine for your benefit.'

'Thank you, Grandmother,' Honor said and tried to pull her arm free. Mary held on, tightly.

'What do you think the story tells us?' She fixed her eyes on Oscar.

'It has hope in it.' Oscar, watching her in turn, spoke carefully.

'Yes?' Mary barked.

Oscar, smiling cautiously, said, 'It indicates that man's humanity to man will prevail.'

'Does it indeed?' Mary Cusack's eyes gleamed and she all but screeched in triumph. 'Well, the end of the story might enlighten you further. That man was the ringleader of those who blew my son and Bridget Corkery's husband to smithereens, and a tree along with them.' She waved a dismissive hand and turned her back balefully on Oscar. 'You understand nothing of war. And less about man's inhumanity.'

'You could be right,' Oscar said.

'Honor could have made things right between the families if she'd married Bernard Corkery,' Mary spoke without turning. 'With the others gone the farm was coming to him. Joining together the two farms would have made a decent parcel of land and we might all have lived a bit better. She chose instead to think of herself and to please her aunt. On her head be whatever happens to us now.'

★ ★ ★

Oscar was quiet on the trip to the village. The road was uneven, with potholes as big as craters, and relentlessly and darkly winding. Honor gave the front passenger seat to her mother and sat in the back with a restless Liam.

'You mustn't mind my mother-in-law,' Faith said as the lights of the village appeared along the curve of the bay. 'It's just her little way. She never got over the death of her son.'

'He was your husband,' Oscar said.

'Yes. And Honor's father. She was two years old when he died.'

'You can drop me at O'Casey's bar,' Liam said, already pulling on the door handle as they came down the hill into the village's main, and only significant, street. 'I'll make my own way home.' He was out of the car before it stopped. 'Or if I don't come tonight, I'll take a lift from you when you're going back to Cloclia tomorrow.'

The village at that hour was quiet, the lights of a few cyclists passing the row of low, stucco-fronted houses, a single donkey-cart drawn up outside a late-opening shop.

Jack Danaher closed his early. His was not, and he was adamant, a huckster shop. It smelled of licorice and camphor and he dealt only in the basics of life – yellow meal, flour, wheat, porridge oats, red lemonade, boiled sweets and a limited line in groceries. He was a quiet man who, since his wife had died, meant it when he said he was pacing himself gently towards the grave.

He made tea, and offered whiskey, but when Honor asked him for a song before she and her mother left he pleaded a bad throat. He glanced apologetically at Oscar.

'Time was when I could sing and talk the night long to compatriots of yours, and others, when they came collecting songs and the like,' he said, 'but I was younger then. And the times were different.'

He was a heavy man, with a jowly face and just two

yellowing teeth. If he missed his daughters' company he never said so, and if he was glad to have Oscar Raeder as a house guest for the night he wasn't revealing that either. He was a man who believed in live and let live and Honor had never, in her lifetime, heard him pass a harsh judgement.

She made up a bed for Oscar in her mother's old room, then sat on it a while and damned the world she'd grown up in. A different one would have allowed her to share the bed with him until morning.

The thought of her arms filled with him gave the room, with its picture of Christ crucified on a cross entwined with snakes, a whole new dimension. It gave it possibilities, a life she'd never before felt there.

She sat on, tracing the pattern on the familiar pink quilt, confronting the fact that she'd stopped circling life, was no longer taking stabs at it and running for safety to her Aunt Grace.

She'd stepped into the ring, at Oscar Raeder's side, and would take her chances with him from now on.

# 18

'I congratulate the Third Army on its success in restoring
to France the historic city of Metz.'

General Eisenhower, November 1944

Liam brought the news of Oscar's arrest when he arrived
back, red-eyed but sober, not long after eight next
morning.

'You're drunk,' Honor said, 'and if this is your idea of a
joke . . .'

'I'm stone, cold sober,' he said.

He was drinking a mug of milk. Their mother was in the
cow shed, milking the two cows Honor had brought in from
the fields earlier. Honor had also, in anticipation of Oscar's
early arrival from the village, taken off her wellingtons and put
on shoes. The place Liam now occupied at the table she'd laid
for Oscar.

She stood in the doorway, her back to her brother, looking
out and across the fields to the winding road, a knot developing in her chest as she prayed fiercely for the Ford to appear.
It didn't.

'Tell me what's happened,' she said.

'I was in O'Casey's back bar. Dan Lalor gave me a blanket
there for the night and was making me a breakfast cup of
tea . . .'

'I'm not interested in your breakfast nor in where you spent the night.' Honor didn't turn around. She made fists of her hands and folded her arms across her chest. 'Just tell me what's happened to him.'

'I'd hardly tasted the tea when Sergeant Healey appeared in the bar, looking for me. He said he couldn't leave the barracks to drive me back himself but wanted me to get back here and tell you as soon as possible.' Liam stopped to pour himself another mug of milk from the enamel jug on the table.

'Tell me what?' Honor moved fast. Before he'd a chance to lift the mug she'd grabbed it, and the jug, and pushed them to the other end of the table. 'Tell me what's happened to him, Liam, or as God is my judge I will not be responsible for what I do to you.'

'I'd to cycle back and I'm not feeling the best . . .' Liam, looking at her face, blinked and cleared his throat. 'Your German friend was arrested at dawn following the discovery of a dead body on the beach a while before that. Sergeant Healey questioned me about the body too. Me! God Almighty . . .' He closed his eyes and shook the hair out of his eyes. 'Bastard wanted to know where I'd spent the night.' He reached out a hand. 'Now can I have the milk?'

'No, you cannot. *What* body? And what does it have to do with Oscar?'

'Another German. Looks as if he was strangled, according to Healey, but there'll have to be a post-mortem to make certain.' Liam leaned on his elbow and rested his forehead in his hand. 'It's looking too as if the body was left on the beach to be taken by the tide.' He paused. 'He'd been dead a while.' He lifted his head and looked at his sister. 'The body was probably brought from Dublin in the boot of the Ford.' He stopped then added, 'According to Healey.'

Honor stared at him. His bloodshot eyes held a simmering fury. Her brother was not half so torpid as he appeared.

'Sergeant Healey's being remarkably efficient,' she said.

198

'It's out of character too for him to be out of his bed and down on the beach during the night.'

'That's what I thought.' Liam dropped all laconic pretence. He slammed the flat of his hand on to the table. 'And that's one of the things I asked him about.' His voice rose. 'He had a tip off, Honor. A concerned citizen delivered a note to the barracks at six o'clock this morning telling him where exactly on the beach he would find the body of a dead German male. This is *not* something you should be involved in. Keep out of it, if you know what's good for you.'

'How's Grandfather? Did you think to call on him?'

'I called. He's not saying much. You know how he is . . .'

A banging on the loft floorboards was followed by Mary Cusack's voice.

'What's going on down there?' she called. 'If the two of you can't speak together without raising your voices then get yourselves outside into the fields and do your arguing there.'

'Who delivered the letter to Healey?' Honor, leaning closer to her brother, whispered harshly. 'Or didn't he think to tell you?'

'It wasn't signed.' Liam's whisper deteriorated into a dry cough. 'His view is that this is a case of thieves falling out, or in this case spies. Christ, I could do with a cigarette . . .'

While he rooted through his pockets, Honor silently lit and handed him one. She waited for him to speak again before lighting another for herself.

'This man's death is no coincidence.' Her brother stabbed the table with a forefinger. 'It's tied to the killing of that woman in Dublin. The underworld of spies and their kind is turning in on itself because of the war ending. Raeder's a part of it. He may not want to be and he's a decent enough sort in himself but he's still a part of it. You'll have to keep away from him from now on. Let them fight it out between themselves.'

199

He stopped and Honor passed the milk along the table. From upstairs there came the familiar sound of their grandmother pulling her chamber pot from under the bed. Liam shook his head.

'We've enough troubles in this house,' he said, 'without you bringing this in on top of our mother.'

'You're right.' Honor stood up. 'I'll leave. You can explain things to her. Tell her too that there's no need for her to worry because Oscar has nothing to do with anyone's death.'

'Where the hell are you going?' Liam's voice rose to a low howl. He stood in her way as she went for the back door and the coats hanging there. 'There's no good you going to the barracks after him.' He grabbed her arm and held on, tightly, as she tried to pull away. 'He'll have been taken to Dublin by now anyway.'

'Let . . . me . . . go . . . Liam.' Honor, facing him, stood very still and said each word slowly and loudly. 'Now!' She wrenched her arm free. 'Don't try to stop me. Look after your own life. That'll give our mother a lot less to worry about.'

'There's nothing you can do for him.' Her brother followed her to the bicycle shed at the side of the house. 'Healey won't let you talk to him. He said he'd be wanting a statement from you later in the day but that for now you should stay around the place here.'

Honor pulled her mother's bike from the shed and frowned, looking at it.

'I'll come with you,' Liam said, 'Might be I can stop you making a complete fool of yourself.'

'No, you won't.' Honor dropped the bike and took the one he'd left leaning against the wall, 'I need this. Tyres are flat on my mother's.'

She knew the road as well as she knew the features on her own face. She knew the potholes to avoid and where the loose stones were most likely to unseat the unwary cyclist.

She knew where to free-wheel downhill and conserve energy for the inclines ahead. She did it all by rote and at speed and arrived in the village without a single conscious thought as to how she'd got there.

The garda barracks in Kilmacreen was a grey, two-storey, pebble-dash building halfway along the main street. It had a dark-blue door which was usually open but which, when Honor pushed it, refused to budge.

She rang the bell and, for good measure, rapped with her knuckles hard enough to dislodge flakes of peeling, dark-blue paint. The air had an edge to it and the sky was a sharp blue. There was every chance Sergeant Healey had taken off to exercise his beloved greyhound.

She stepped back and looked down the street. She had a choice. She could go round the back and see about getting in that way, or she could wait where she was.

'I can't let you talk to your friend.' Sergeant Healey's voice came from behind her. 'But since you're here I'll ask you to come inside and give me your own statement of affairs.' He was smiling fondly at a greyhound on a lead when Honor turned. 'I'd Dotey Black to see to,' he said, 'you might have saved yourself the rush getting here.'

His newly benign mood didn't fool her. Finbarr Healey, twelve years stationed in Kilmacreen, had a wife, no children, and in another four years would be retired with a pension and all the time in the world to devote to the training of Dotey Black. His preferred route was the one of least resistance and the early-morning's activities had seriously upset the tenor of his ways.

'Come round the back,' he said, 'I need to tie up the dog.'

The back of the barracks faced the sea, with a sloping field in between and a stone wall to keep the beach from encroaching. It was only partially effective; the lower part of the field resembled a sand marsh. The beach, a three-mile-long stretch of silvery shingle, sand and occasional rock, was prone to rip-tides and sudden shelving, a notoriously dangerous place to swim from.

'Liam tells me you found a body on the strand.' Honor kept her voice calm. The sergeant would want no part of her hysteria, would be rid of her and the sick worry building inside her if he got so much as a whiff of it. 'A man's body.'

She squinted along what she could see of the wintry beach. The tide was coming in, waves high and crashing white on to the shingle. There was nothing resembling a body to be seen.

'That's right.' Sergeant Healey filled a pot with water for the dog. 'Found him out there in the very early hours, myself and the young guard. Dead as doornails. An ugly sight he was too, and a bit of a shock for Guard Tunney.' He looked up. 'But there's no need for you to know anything more about it.'

He fondled the greyhound's ears and closed the gate on the small compound where he kept him. Honor, only two years before, had seen Dotey Black shoot his head through the bars of the same gate and take the head off a small kitten. She'd found it hard to have warm feelings about the animal ever since.

It was said of the sergeant that he wasn't unkind. She could only hope this was true.

'I don't believe Dr Raeder had anything to do with it,' she said, carefully, as the sergeant pushed open the back door to the barracks. 'I know him. He's a decent man, and good.'

A knot in her chest made it difficult to breathe. The sergeant still said nothing as, taking deep breaths, Honor followed him along the cold stone corridor to the light at the end which marked the public office. The sergeant and Mrs Healey lived overhead and the holding cell, with Oscar inside, was off the dank, back corridor they'd just come through.

'Sit down there and I'll get you a pen and ink and some paper to write on.' Sergeant Healey put a chair beside a square, cluttered table.

'What do you want to know?' Honor sat. When he brought pen and paper she cleared a space for them.

'Just a few facts about why you're here and the time you arrived.' He cleared his throat. 'Why Dr Raeder came with you. That sort of thing.'

'You know why I'm here.' Honor dipped the pen in the ink. 'And you know too that it was early-afternoon when we arrived and called to my grandfather's shop.' When an ink blot fell from the nib on to the paper she did nothing to stop it spreading. 'Am I under suspicion as well as Dr Raeder?'

'It's as well to have the facts, clear and simple and in writing, so as we all know where we are.' He shuffled through some papers at the other end of the table. 'The quicker these things are done, the quicker the whole business will be dealt with and finished.' He straightened up, his head narrowly avoiding contact with the metal shade on the light bulb. 'I have my orders,' he said. 'I'm told it's by way of eliminating you from enquiries.'

Honor put the pen down. 'I'm sorry,' she said, 'I can't just write you a statement like that. Not unless I know what's happened and what I'm supposed to be involved in.' She drew a long breath and looked him in the eye. 'Either that or I'll have to get a solicitor here to represent me.'

'A solicitor! What do you mean, a solicitor? What I'm asking is just simple procedure.' In his agitation Sergeant Healey's head hit the metal lamp shade and he swore. 'Jesus Christ, woman, you know me,' he said. 'We can do this without the fuss of a solicitor. It'll hold things up for God knows how long if you make us go that road.'

'You're right. It will.'

The room was cold, damp turf smouldering in the grate

of a small, cast-iron fireplace. A clock on the wall showed nine-thirty and a greyhound racing calendar hanging beside it had the next three Saturdays circled in red.

Honor went on staring at it until the sergeant said, 'This is what happens when country girls go to live in the city.' He sat down on the other chair in the office, on a chintz-covered cushion put there by Mrs Healey as a 'solace' to his bony behind. 'They get notions above themselves. You know I'm a man hates fuss and commotion. You know that I know you're an unfortunate bystanding casualty in this business. Half a dozen sentences is all I need.'

'No.' Honor didn't shift her gaze from the calendar. 'Not until you tell me everything that's happened and let me talk with Dr Raeder.' She paused. 'Either that or a solicitor. I'd like Mr Fitzgerald from Droom to represent me.' Droom was sixty miles away, Oliver Fitzgerald a busy man with a lively, anarchic way of dealing with the law. 'I'm within my rights,' she said.

'By Jesus, but your aunt's trained you well!' There was more resignation than anger in Sergeant Healey's voice as he lifted a pole and banged on the ceiling, twice. 'I won't deal with that conniving devil Fitzgerald. Cate'll bring us tea and I'll give you the story. You can have three minutes with your man in the cell, not a second more, then you can write out your side of things and be gone. There's an ambulance coming to take the body back to Dublin and a car to take the prisoner.'

'There was a letter delivered?' Honor prompted.

'At six this morning. Mad hammering on the door and then silence. Letter said the writer had come across a dead body on the beach and seen a man walk away and drive back towards the village in a two-tone car. Didn't sign his name, said he had enough trouble in his life.' The sergeant gave a short laugh. 'Probably meant he was after leaving a bed he shouldn't have been in. I could go out of my way and find

204

out who he was but it would all stir up more trouble than it's worth.'

He listened and gave a soft, satisfied grunt when he heard his wife's step on the stair.

'I went out to the beach, taking Guard Tunney with me, and the body was where the letter said it would be, just beyond the shelter of the rocks below Jim Nolan's place. Overweight man, about forty years old, I'd say, though it was hard to tell rightly on account of the discoloration.'

'Discoloration?' Honor's heart skipped an uncomfortable few beats. When it settled into a reasonable rhythm again she repeated the word: 'Discoloration?'

'Death will do that.' Sergeant Healey was impatient. 'You should know, training to be a doctor.'

'Yes. But . . .' Honor began.

'You'd want to go back to your medical books,' Sergeant Healey said, 'because I saw him and he was all discoloured. Rigid as a board as well, but then that's a part of death too. All of it the opposite to life.' He fell silent, sighing as he contemplated death and the changes it wrought. He let out a deep breath and went on in a resigned tone, 'I knew the two-tone car was your friend's so I went down to your grandfather's place and picked him up and brought him here.'

'How was the man killed?' Honor asked.

'I can't answer that.' Sergeant Healey shook his head firmly. 'What in the name of God got you mixed up in this, Honor? Fine young woman like you, your life in front of you. I suppose there's no use my talking to you, warning you about the dangers ahead if you persist in taking this doctor's side, is there?'

'No,' she said.

'You're all the same, you young people. You probably think he's Jesus reborn, this friend of yours. And maybe you're right and he didn't do it, I don't know. It's only the second time in my life I've had to deal with a murder and the other was the result of a drunken brawl. I left Guard Tunney on the beach minding the body. Poor lad's probably numb and hungry as a crow by now.'

He uncrossed his long legs and stood as Cate Healey came into the room with a tray.

'What happens next?' Honor said.

'The pathologist is on his way as well as the ambulance. Dr Raeder's car has been impounded and will be taken away for tests. I've questioned your brother, just to clear up any possibility of his being involved, and Lalor's willing to swear he slept in the back bar under a blanket they gave him when they couldn't get him out of the place. That's my end of things looked after.' He cleared some space for his wife to put down the tea tray. 'If you've any sense you'll keep out of it yourself too.' He glared at her. 'But you've no sense, we already know that.'

'You'll have sugar in your tea?' Cate Healey enquired.

'Just milk.'

Cate Healey poured. Quiet, thin as her husband, she was about a foot shorter and shared his passion for greyhound dogs. The tray held three cups, a teapot, milk in a jug and sugar in a bowl.

The phone, balanced on a small shelf, gave an energetic shrill.

'I'll take his tea in to Dr Raeder,' Honor offered as Sergeant Healey went to answer it.

# 19

Hitler orders general mobilisation of all able-bodied males between 16 and 60.

November 1944

The holding cell had been a scullery/cold room in the barracks' earlier days and bore the signs still. The Victorian house it had been then kept sunlight and heat at bay with a slit-window in the stone wall and low ceiling. The gloom of it all had been moderated by whitewashing the walls, though not well enough to hide the evidence of anterior shelves. A rope mat on the stone flags and a couple of Cate Healey's chintz cushions on the day-bed alleviated the bare look. A naked, forty-watt bulb gave enough light to read by.

Oscar got to his feet with a newspaper in his hand as Honor came in. Sergeant Healey, without locking it, closed the door behind her again.

'He might at least have given you soap and a razor,' she stood looking at Oscar, the knot of anxiety hardening in her chest. He was wearing his glasses, and a dark stubble.

'Probably worried I might slit my throat.' In a cutting motion, he drew a forefinger across his neck.

'Don't,' Honor said, 'please don't.' The dark shadow gave him a haunted look. The newspaper, a days' old copy of the *Irish Independent*, headlined news of the Allied advance on

Germany. 'Oh, God,' Honor said, and his face went out of focus, a blur through tears that came from nowhere. The blur moved and a pair of arms went about her and held her, tight, until she moved her own arms and wrapped them about him so they could hold on together. He felt warm, a surprise in that dank place.

'Sergeant Healey won't let me stay long.' She eased herself back slightly to look up at Oscar. 'We should talk about things.'

'Yes,' he said, and bent his head and kissed her. It was the sort of kiss that made the world outside recede, that moment the only reality. Honor locked her arms about his neck; an anchor to save her from drowning completely.

'We should talk . . .'

It was Oscar who said the words this time, shakily, stroking the hair back from her forehead. Honor stepped away from him, looking around the cell and then directly into his eyes as she said, quickly,

'I don't understand what's going on, nor anything about why these two people have been murdered. But I do know that the guards are going to hang on to you as a suspect until they find the real killer.'

'*If* they find the real killer,' Oscar said. 'The circumstantial evidence against me is strong. It may even be enough to hang me.' He stopped when he saw her face, ashen under the dirty yellow light of the bulb. 'I'm sorry,' he said briskly, 'the macabre keeps surfacing. It's how all of this strikes me. The bodies of the dead embalmed for dissection and the pursuit of knowledge I understand. Medicine must know. But to kill and embalm . . .' He stopped. 'It has to be a madman doing this.'

'Are you telling me the dead man had also been embalmed?' Honor stared.

'I'm willing to bet on it,' Oscar said. 'Something the sergeant said on the phone about its appearance . . .'

'He told me it was discoloured. Not blue, or white. Discoloured was the word he used.' She paused. 'It struck me as an odd word too.'

'He used it because the body will have been an unnatural-looking brown. Unnatural-looking for death, that is. Did the sergeant tell you how the man died?'

'He said he couldn't tell me. Don't know if that means he doesn't know or won't tell.'

'Very likely doesn't know.' Oscar looked thoughtful. 'If he was strangled, as Bridie Keogh was, then embalming would minimise the strangulation marks.'

'Your murdering madman is not so mad he cannot plan,' Honor said, 'nor so mad as to allow himself to be caught.' She caught Oscar by the arms. 'His plan is for you to take the blame. There's no other reason to leave this body on a beach, not a half-mile from where you were sleeping.'

'The case against me holds that I wasn't sleeping. That I was the one put the body on the beach to be swept away by the incoming tide, that I had it timed to perfection but, being ignorant and a city man, didn't realise the body should be placed crosswise and out of the way of rocks on the beach. So it wasn't, in fact, swept out on the tide but waiting for the sergeant when he got there at six this morning.'

'Conveniently,' Honor said.

'If I was in the business of murder and disposing of bodies, I'd have made a better job of it.'

Honor, dropping his arms, all but shouted, 'Don't! There's a murderous madman trying to make sure you take the blame for his vile acts and you stand there being rational.'

'Of course.' Oscar was cool, watching but not touching her. 'What else would you have me do? Only by being rational can I understand how he thinks, what he might do next.'

'Wrong! Madmen *don't* think rationally so that's no way to enter his mind.'

'There are very few genuinely mad people in this world,' Oscar told her softly. 'There are many whose view of life is deformed and there are those who are simply evil. To say such people are mad is an injustice to the few who are unhappily afflicted. It absolves the majority from responsibility for their actions. I don't believe the person who killed both Bridie Keogh and the man on the beach is anything other than evil. And because he is evil he will kill again.'

'Why? Why would he kill at all? And why embalm the bodies? Why set you up?'

Honor was shaking. She couldn't stop herself, not even when she shoved her hands deep into her coat pockets and clenched them until she felt a nail pierce her palm.

'What good does rational thinking do you in the face of all that?'

'There are probabilities . . .' Oscar took her arm and pulled her down to sit on the side of the bed with him. 'He may have killed for love: the eternal triangle. He may have killed the woman he loved because she loved another, and now he's killed that other.'

'I don't think so.' Honor shook her head, then leaned against him. The shaking stopped, more or less. 'I don't believe a jealous murderer would embalm the body of the woman he loved.'

'You may be right,' Oscar spoke against her forehead, 'and I think the embalming is the key. He did it the first time because he thought he'd got the perfect way of getting rid of the body. He did it this time because he wanted both to preserve the body and so as to be able to arrange the circumstances of its discovery to make me seem the murderer.'

'But *why*?'

'Maybe because I'm an easy target, an arrogant German needing to be brought down.' He shrugged, smiling. 'Perhaps I know something I don't know I know. Some espionage secret. God knows my brother has tried often enough to engage me.' He shook his head. 'I don't believe it's anything more than the fact I'm convenient for the murderer's needs – a hate figure of the moment.'

'We still don't know that the man on the beach actually *is* embalmed,' Honor said, 'but that's something I can check on at least.' Sergeant Healey could hardly cordon off the beach, nor stop her from going there. 'I'll do it as soon as I leave here.'

'I would prefer that you didn't have to.' Oscar took his arm from about her shoulder and leaned forward, studying the flagged floor. 'But I admit I'd like to know whether he is or not.' He turned to her. 'You should know what to look for – the body will not be like those in the tanks in the dissecting room.'

'What should it look like?'

'If it's been embalmed it won't look like a normal dead body. As well as being brown it will be hard to the touch. And, as I said before, you won't be able to tell if he's been manually strangled because the embalming will have made the strangulation marks disappear. The post-mortem will tell us, of course, since the hyoid bone is always fractured in manual strangulation.'

'Right.' Honor was businesslike. 'Hard, browny-coloured skin – that's about it?'

'Yes.'

'You're to be taken to Dublin,' she said, 'and so is the body.'

'So I've been told. I spoke with our German Minister, Dr Hempel, on the phone earlier. There's not a lot he can do until the dead man is identified and a post-mortem's been held. I'm to be kept in custody until charged. Or not. I'll be given legal representation. Bail looks doubtful.' He gave her a quick, wry smile. 'All very fair.'

'It would be if you'd done something wrong,' she said. The

knot in her chest had taken on a leaden weight. 'A phone call came through from Dublin as I was leaving the office.'

'Yes?' He picked up her hand and studied it, separating her fingers and closing them again. 'Yes?' he repeated.

'The newspapers know about it.' Honor took back her hand. Sergeant Healey told whichever one of them phoned that you'd be back in Dublin by this evening. He doesn't want this on his doorstep. They'll all be waiting there – the case is being made against you publicly and you're to be punished, guilty or not.' She stood, her arms wrapped tightly across her chest to stop the shaking starting up again. 'People want it to be you. They hear stories about Germany every day, terrible stories about extermination camps and massacres and brutality. It's on the wireless and in the newspapers. They want someone to hang their hatred on, to take away their own shame that they stood aside.'

She stopped at the window and looked through the narrow slit. The sky had become quite grey.

'I know that shame.' She paused. 'I always used to think we were right to stay neutral. Now I'm not so sure any more. We don't know enough yet about all that's happened in this war, but our children and theirs will know. They're the ones will judge us.' She turned. 'But you're being judged now and you'll be hung now because people want a scapegoat. You have to leave, Oscar, you have to get away, out of Ireland.'

He reached for her. 'I can't do that, you know I can't.' He held her to him and kissed the top of her head. 'It'll be all right,' he said, 'they'll get the man who did it. It'll be all right. I've more faith in the Irish system of law and order than you have, it seems. Hempel will sort it out, with the help of a solicitor.'

'You're a fool, Oscar.' Honor spoke softly as a knocking came on the door and Sergeant Healey's voice called out.

'I'll have to ask you to come on out now, Honor, another

two minutes and I'll expect to see you in the office. Do you hear me, girl?'

'I'll be there,' Honor called, and to Oscar *sotto voce* said, 'You're a fool to believe in this country. I know it better than you and there's every chance you will not be all right. Your Dr Hempel may well find he doesn't have as many friends at court as he thought he had.'

'Believe with me, Honor, please.' He traced a finger along her cheek. 'I need you to.'

She laid her head against him again, and spoke to his chest, arms wrapped around his back. 'I'll do all that I can to help. And I'll believe in you,' she said, 'but I can't believe *with* you that you'll be fairly treated.'

She lifted her head and he kissed her, hard, and for a precious minute the words ended and everything else too.

'I'm going to the beach.' Honor pulled away. 'I'll let you know what I find there.'

The sun had gone when she reached the edge of the shore and a soft mist was rolling in from the sea. The tide was quite far in so she walked as quickly as she could along the shingle until she came within view of the dark outlines of the policeman guarding the body of the dead German.

They were on the curve of the beach, just above the line where the tide was dragging the shingle back with it on the ebb. Guard Tunney was pacing, beating his arms about his body to keep circulation going to him. He kept a distance of about two feet between him and the grey blanketed shape on the sand. He faced Honor as she came up close.

'I'll have to ask you to go back,' he said loudly, 'there's a police enquiry into the death of this man and no one's allowed in the vicinity.'

He was wilted and white-faced and no more than twenty years old. Honor smiled at him reassuringly.

'I'm a doctor.' The lie came easily, 'Sergeant Healey asked me to bring you these.' She handed him the bar of Bourneville she'd bought in the village and the last three cigarettes she had on her. 'He said I might take a look at the body too.' She spoke firmly. 'Give him an idea what to put in his report.'

Guard Tunney accepted the chocolate, cigarettes and her word without question. He lit up, with dexterity considering he didn't remove his gloves, and stood silently watching while she crouched over the body, gently lifting the corner of the heavy grey blanket which covered the head and shoulders.

The hair was cut short and the face, at a guess and without its dread rictus smile, would have been heavy-set and good-looking enough. It was hard to tell but he'd probably been about forty years old, as Sergeant Healey had said.

The skin was a muddy, unnatural-looking brown, the body rigid as a board. There were no marks that she could see on the neck.

She slipped off a glove and touched the face. The guard started forward, protesting. But she'd felt what she needed to. The dead man's skin was hard as dried leather.

'Thank you.' Honor retrieved one of her cigarettes from the packet in Guard Tunney's gloved hand, 'I've all the information Sergeant Healey needs.'

# 20

# The Basement

'. . . Above stairs, the ball
Danced to its end, and the host stood alone
On his steps, watching the trees as they sprang
Into the rushing polka of the wind.'
               Bruce Williamson, 'Afternoon In Anglo-Ireland'

E vil is active and there has been another killing. I am now certain of that which I was only almost sure about but prayed was true.

Honor Cusack's German lover, probably unknowingly, has been sucked into the well of depravity over which I've been keeping a vigilant watch. He will, also unknowingly, be the instrument through which I will round the circle, finally expose all and destroy Grace Danaher. And it will be because Honor, her beloved alter ego, delivered him to me.

It's as if God has played right into my hands. Or the devil.

Honor Cusack's trip to the countryside was fortuitous. Her absence left me more on my own than usual and allowed me time for reflection in which some things have become more clear. Her little visits take up quite a bit of my evenings and without them as diversion I've been free to ponder rigorously the reactions of the Friday diners to Dr Oscar Raeder.

Grace Danaher called, of course, to give me the news of the fresh murder. I feigned disinterest.

Small actions, a few words casually said, can say so much more than people intend. They reveal a very great deal when one is already armed with the secrets of that person's life.

I was almost sure, before the second killing, that I'd dined at Grace Danaher's table with the prostitute's murderer. The second killing, committed in a fashion which again makes Dr Raeder the most likely suspect, has convinced me.

My reasoning, based on what I already know, is thus: Dr Raeder poses a threat to the murderer, whose secret he could in the future expose. The murdered couple were very likely a threat too. Their underworld existence made them relatively easy victims but Dr Raeder's disposal would require more subtlety. A state hanging would do the job nicely, and legally. It is not yet time for me to intervene. I will wait a while longer, give the murderer enough rope to hang *himself*, and Grace Danaher along with him.

It was in conversations with Honor, in the days after her return, that I gathered together the extra information I required to reach my conclusions. I spoke to her for the first time after her lectures on Monday. By then I'd listened to most of the available details on the wireless and had read all that the *Irish Times* had to say. I knew then that the second victim was Clemens Hauptmann, lover of the murdered Bridie Keogh and the man for whom they'd been searching.

Honor was short-tempered.

'Algernon's been fighting again.' She frowned crossly at my quarrelsome older kitty. 'His ear's in flitters. Why does he does it?'

'Why don't you ask him?' I said sharply. The cat's fighting life had never interested her before and I was in a mood to ask questions, not answer them.

She knelt down and Algernon, surprisingly, allowed her to fondle his damaged ear.

'Did you do anything with it?' she said.

'These things mend in their own time,' I said, which was not altogether true. As with life, wounds often deepen and become gangrenous. 'Though the situation of your doctor friend may get worse before it mends or gets . . .'

'Worse?' She raised an eyebrow. 'Why would it get worse? He's clearly innocent of murder, or of any wrongdoing. The situation is ridiculous and everyone knows it. Everyone who knows him, that is.'

She looked at me coolly, daring me to say I fell into the camp of those who didn't know and doubted him.

'It must have been a shock for you, all the same.' I sounded sympathetic.

She said nothing, just lifted Walter, her favourite, into her lap. Algernon had taken himself to the window and was looking out, ready to fight again.

'A shock to realise some person, or persons, are so deter-mined to see him blamed,' I went on. I could have said 'hung' but didn't want to antagonise her.

'Yes,' she admitted. 'That was – is – a shock.'

'How did your mother take it?' I asked, politely.

'Calmly enough, she's good in a crisis. She's had plenty practice. My grandfather Danaher was shocked; stupefied really. He didn't want me to come back to Dublin. He's getting old.' She added this last as if it was something she'd noticed for the first time.

'And your brother? How is he? And your grandmother?'

She looked at me suspiciously. My concern was entirely affected but she couldn't be sure so she answered.

'Liam didn't drink for the rest of the weekend and spent the entire time defending Oscar to anyone who'd listen. Just being his anarchic self, nothing to do with believing in him.'

She lifted Walter in her arms and held him tightly against her chest. He squirmed and she sighed and let him go again, on to the floor. Then she told me about her grandmother.

'She's pleased. Says it's the wages of sin. That sort of clap-trap. She could have been worse, though. She went quiet on Sunday, the day of my grandfather Cusack's month's Mass. She's so contrary most of the time you forget she has normal feelings.'

I wondered if Honor felt the same way about me. I was feeling the cold badly that day for some reason, a chill that reached to the marrow of my bones. My weekend of thinking and planning hadn't done me much physical good.

'I'm cold,' I said.

The words were out before I could stop them. She looked concerned and became immediately busy, throwing turf on the fire and making me a hot whiskey. She talked to me as she did so, in quick, jerky sentences. I'd have preferred her sitting opposite where I could have studied her face.

'The guards are keeping Oscar in custody. They're not agreeing to bail. Not yet anyway. They're saying they've enough evidence to hold him for his own safety. Feelings are running high, they say, because of what they're calling the "desecration" of the bodies.'

She gave me the whiskey and stood with her own, looking into the fire. I hadn't told her she could help herself but let it pass. I was tired as well as cold.

'They let me see him for a short while today. He reads. He studies. He tries to occupy himself . . .' She stopped. When she went on there was a slight edge of desperation to her tone. 'The dead man was Clemens Hauptmann, but I suppose you've heard that already. The guards expect me to believe his body was in the boot of Oscar's car for the journey to Cloclia on Friday. They're carrying out forensic tests to prove it. It's ludicrous. It *couldn't* have been.'

'Why not?' I said.

'Because there was nothing in the boot when I put my

suitcase into it before we set off.' She stared at me, hard. 'I'd have noticed a dead male body.'

This attempted bravado was to cover the fact that she was lying; I very much doubted she'd put her own suitcase in the boot. There was no doubt, however, that she would go to great lengths to help her lover. I wondered how far, exactly.

'I'm tired.' She headed abruptly for the door, talking all the while so as to prevent me from questioning her further. She was a bad liar and would never convince the police. 'The 'bus coming back last night was wheezing and cold, like a bronchial old man,' she prattled. 'It got in so late I missed the last tram and had to walk from McBirney's.'

'How unfortunate,' I said, but she was gone, closing the door behind her and clattering up the back steps to the kitchen.

She didn't visit for two days after that and when she did it was late in the evening. She came directly from Lansdowne Road where she'd been visiting old Terence Delaney and his dog.

'The dog in that house has more sense than its master.' She arranged laurel leaves in a vase on the table. She often does this, claiming she's bringing me a breath of life from the garden. I tell her the leaves are dead once plucked but she ignores me. 'He howls and barks until Terence is forced to take him for a walk, which means he has to go outside at least once a day. Terence is so upset he'd sit in that dungeon of his from one end of the week 'til the other otherwise.'

'He's upset about Dr Raeder's arrest?'

'Obviously.'

'I suppose the police have been to the house, searching and pulling things apart and upsetting him even more?'

I said this with a sigh and sympathetic shake of the head. The room was dark apart from the firelight. I wanted it that way. It encourages a certain intimacy and talkativeness. The cats lay close together, asleep in the firelight. The mood was perfect for confidences.

Honor sank to the floor in front of the fire and sat hugging her knees. She appeared no more rested than she had a few evenings before. She seemed to me not to have slept and not to be eating particularly well either.

'The guards have been to Lansdowne Road three times,' she said, 'they even searched Terence's part of the house.' She hesitated then said in a rush, 'They were looking for evidence that the embalmings had taken place on the premises. So one of the guards told Terence anyway.'

She was silent for a while after this and I let her be. Her shocked outrage was clear but I myself thought the police justified in making such a search. They would have been very foolish not to have done so. She spoke in a flat, even tone when she went on.

'The same guard said they'd done a thorough job of examining the embalming rooms and facilities in all three of the city's medical schools. They were satisfied, he said, that none of those facilities had been used illegally. In other words, the bodies weren't embalmed there. He was very clear about that, Terence says . . .'

'But?' I said. Her hunched body had the shape of a large, troubled question mark.

'They discovered more than twenty litres of formalin fluid had gone missing . . .' Again she stopped.

'Need I ask from which school?'

'From UCD,' she sighed, then went on quickly, 'though that doesn't necessarily mean the embalmer is attached to the college. It could be a distraction, a ploy. A lot of medical people would know their way around all three schools.'

This sounded like wishful thinking to me. 'Do the police agree with you?'

'Not yet.' She gave me a wry smile.

A certain ironic detachment is one of the things I've always rather admired in Honor Cusack. It may well prove her salvation.

'The post-mortem results show he died from manual strangulation.' She volunteered this information without my asking. 'Same way as Bridie Keogh. It seems also that he'd been dead a few days when he was found on the beach.'

'So he could conceivably have been transported there later and killed elsewhere?'

'If you're asking if Clemens Hauptmann could have been murdered in Dublin and taken to Waterford then the answer's yes.' She dropped her arms and got to her feet quickly. 'But not in Oscar's car boot. The guards have yet to find out both who murdered him and who brought him to where he was found. There's nothing but circumstantial evidence against Oscar.'

'Of course not.' I was soothing. I didn't want her making one of her hasty exits just yet. 'Does this mean they'll be freeing him on bail?'

'It doesn't mean that at all.'

She stopped and took a deep breath. She was standing very still, hands in the pockets of her coat. It was difficult to see her face but she seemed to be staring at nothing in particular.

'What's happened to him?' I spoke softly. She could so easily be frightened off.

'He's been taken to the Curragh camp. He's to be held there as an internee, like his brother Stefan though without the same parole freedoms. They say it's for his own safety. The German Legation and Dr Hempel have agreed.'

'How odd,' I said. 'All this because of purely circumstantial evidence?'

'Yes.' She moved to the window and stood with her back to me, hands on the curtains as if she would close them, staring into the darkness outside. 'But also because they have discovered that Clemens Hauptmann was in this country unofficially – all German nationals are obliged to report to and keep contact with the German Legation. He didn't. No one knew he was here, officially anyway.'

She looked over her shoulder at me briefly, as if reassuring herself of something, then went on, her back to me again. Though it was very dark outside she didn't close the curtains.

'They think he was on some sort of spying mission. Army Intelligence has become involved and so has the Supplementary Intelligence Service and they're saying that all their intelligence sources, and captured spies, have disclaimed him. None of them knows why he was here since it seems the German spy network in this country collapsed some time ago. Ireland's of no more interest to the Nazi Party and Mr Hitler. They're too caught up with losing the war and salvaging what they can in Europe.'

'That's entirely possible,' I agreed.

'They think too there's something else afoot, and that Oscar's a part of it. They're locking him up while they investigate.' She pulled the curtains closed with a lot more force than was necessary. 'The Curragh's a compromise dreamed up between them and Dr Hempel.'

'You're sure of this?'

I knew she was. *I* at least knew what was afoot. I also knew how desperate the murderer would be to keep his secret and devilish plans from discovery. I was merely curious as to how she'd got herself so well informed.

'I'm sure. Do you want me to feed the cats before I go?'

'Thank you,' I said.

I was silent while she coaxed Algernon and Walter from their place by the fire, kept my peace too and didn't call out to her while she fed them in my small kitchen. I needed to know but didn't want to plead with her to tell me how she'd got so much information.

'I hope you're as sure of your own safety in all of this as you are of your facts,' I ventured when she came back. This was by way of feeling my way towards asking who her informant was. She saw through me immediately.

'My facts, since you're so curious to know, come from Bernard Corkery.' She gave me another of her wry smiles. 'I've never in my life met anyone so prying as you are, Mrs Sayers. You really should get outside more, widen your horizons.'

'You keep my horizons quite wide enough, my dear Honor, with your visits,' I said. 'But satisfy my prying nature, please, and tell me how Bernard Corkery could possibly know as much as he does?'

'Because he's a member of the Supplementary Intelligence Service.' She gathered up her scarf and gloves from the table. 'I'd known he was for a while and gave him no peace until he told me all he could about Oscar's situation and the murders. He swore me to secrecy,' she looked at me, hard, 'but telling you is like telling it to the grave, isn't it?' She stopped talking and gave a rueful smile. 'Crudely put but you know what I mean, Mrs Sayers, don't you?'

'Your secret's safe with me,' I said, automatically. She'd told me as much as I needed to know. 'But you're right, nonetheless. I'm old and near death and need my rest. Good night.'

Bernard Corkery's was a surprise involvement. But then of course he might not be involved at all. Since he wasn't greatly encouraged by Grace Danaher and came infrequently to the house I'd had little opportunity to assess him. I would need to find out more.

After Honor had gone I made my way to bed with the cats. Their warm weight was a comfort as I lay there; her fears and talk of murder had resurrected memories. Too many of them. I lay uncomfortably remembering my own fear in the months after I'd poisoned Lionel.

There had been days then, and nights, when I'd felt the noose around my neck and my tongue choking me, so many were the lies I'd had to tell.

For a while too I had a terrible recurring dream in which I was in an arena, exposed to the sun and a caged pack of wild dogs who awaited a signal from a smiling Grace Danaher to tear me apart. The dream faded when my fear did, which was when I realised no one was ever going to doubt that Lionel, who ate and drank too much and had a dodgy liver, had died from food poisoning while we were holidaying in Vienna.

The murderer of Bridie Keogh and Clemens Hauptmann would be feeling something of the same fear.

Or maybe not. He was a man used to living a secret life and with beliefs that had little to do with care for his fellow man.

# 21

'There is no chance for any country in Europe to save its own culture and religion except through Germany who has been, and still is, fighting to establish a complete and just peace.'

German Radio, November 1944

R ain fell steadily as the bus drove across the Curragh plains. Hard frosts followed by heavy rainfall had worsened the pot-holed, uneven state of the road to the internment camp and the wooden seats and lack of heating in the bus added to the passengers' general discomfort.

None of them complained, least of all Honor. The bus driver, before taking them on board in Newbridge, had made it clear that they were lucky to get transportation at all. They were especially lucky he himself was willing to drive them.

'You won't find everyone as broad-minded and tolerant as myself,' he said, taking ticket money from the fretful queue, 'now that the carry-on of the Germans is getting known.' Most of the prospective passengers were German internees returning to the camp from parole. 'There's nothing but German and IRA fellas out there now and the Germans are still getting a better time of it than our own lot. Only that it's my job of work I wouldn't be for driving out there at all.'

'Maybe you should find yourself another job.' Honor took her ticket from him.

'Would that life were so simple,' he said, without irony.

Stefan met her by the parole hut at the gates as she walked from the bus. He'd brought an oiled cape to protect her from the rain. He wore one himself, its dripping state an indication that he'd been waiting a while.

'Thank you.' Honor draped it over her shoulders. Her feet, in shoes with inch-high heels, would have to take the consequences of the muddy track though the compound. 'Do we have far to go?'

'Oscar's hut is at the far end,' Stefan said curtly. 'Mine's this side. He's confined to his own end.' He took her bag, filled mostly with books and newspapers. 'Divide and conquer.' He shrugged and led the way.

Halfway across the compound, while they stood in the rain, a soldier examined the visitor's pass it had taken Honor two weeks to acquire and searched through her bag. Two weeks without seeing or talking to Oscar, a fortnight listening to bile and bigotry every day.

'Oh, God, I've missed you,' she said to him when he appeared out of the rain from behind the hut.

She threw herself into his arms then and hung on, straining through his coat and her cape, through the falling rain and the endearments he kept repeating, to hear his heart beat. On the other bus, from Dublin to Newbridge, through the crying of a fractious infant and moaning gossip of two women, she'd told herself, over and over, that once she heard his beating heart she would be able to believe again in their future together and in their short past.

'Your heart's intact,' she said when she heard it at last. She looked up at him, the rain falling on her face, smiling madly through tears.

'Yes.' He brushed the rain away then kissed her.

As kisses went it was memorable, hard and long and filled with the furies of frustration and longing. Then the rain came between them, falling harder and down their necks, and Stefan's voice called, 'I've been out here long enough.'

By the time they parted he'd gone inside, leaving the bag with the books and newspapers some feet away on the muddy ground.

'The rain follows us,' Oscar said as he picked it up.

Honor, remembering too the day they'd met, caught his hand as they walked towards his hut. He was thinner than he'd been then and his hair was shorter. In every other way that she could see, he was the same.

He'd prepared for her visit. The bed had been made and the medical books he'd been studying stacked on the floor to make way on the table for a bottle of brandy, three glass tumblers, sliced cold meat and brown bread.

'Stefan knows his way round the system here.' Oscar indicated the food and drink and took her cape. 'Make yourself at home.'

The grey blanket on the bed reminded her of the one covering Clemens Hauptmann's body on Kilmacreen beach, the absence of curtains on the window of the fact that they were under surveillance.

Stefan was stoking the pipe stove and the room was warm.

'I'll leave,' he said, 'if you want me to go?'

'Please stay,' Honor said politely, 'I've brought some newspapers . . .' She spread them on the bed to dry, wishing all the time he would go, that she could rip away the blanket and make quick, delirious love on the bed with Oscar. 'Papers are a bit damp,' she said, 'and maybe you've read them already.' They'd been dry until he had left them on the muddy ground.

'It's true that we continue to hear more news than we used to.' Stefan stood behind her, studying the headlines. 'Now that the war goes so badly for Germany. But we still do not get enough. Our commandant tells us we are better not knowing. I say we are better being prepared. Thank you for the newspapers, whatever your intentions.'

He picked up a copy of that day's the *Irish Times* and sat tight-lipped by the stove reading the news story which put the Allies twenty-six miles from Cologne.

'What do you *think* my intentions are, Stefan?' Honor asked, puzzled. He muttered furiously in German but didn't look up.

'Let him be.' Oscar put her in a chair by the table. 'Morale's seriously low in the camp, we're all a bit nervous about what's going to happen to us.' He poured brandy into the tumblers and held up the bottle. 'It wasn't easy getting hold of this or the glasses.' He pushed one her way and sat close to her, lifting his own. 'To you, Honor Cusack.' He touched her glass. 'My friend,' he kissed her lightly, 'and my love.' He suddenly looked very serious.

Honor blinked away the threat of blinding tears and gulped a scalding amount of brandy. 'My pass says I must be back on the bus in an hour,' she said. 'We should talk.'

'How is your aunt?' Oscar said politely. 'And her friends? The old Mrs Sayers?'

'Aunt Grace is fine.' Honor was impatient. 'She now agrees you've been done an injustice. The others are as you'd expect and Mrs Sayers is as watchful as one of her cats and twice as sharp. But they're not what I want to talk about.' She swirled the brown-gold contents of her glass. 'I've been working on a plan.'

'What made your aunt change her mind about me?' Oscar shook his head and cast a warning look in Stefan's direction.

'Circumstances.' Honor shrugged. 'I told her I would go and live in your house if she couldn't find it in herself to be more understanding, that Terence and the dog would be better company. I meant it. I still mean it and might do it too. She saw reason.' Honor let a breath out slowly.

228

'And Bernard Corkery had a few useful things to say during the week.'

'Bernard?' Oscar said. 'What did he have to say?'

'Well . . .' Honor hesitated. 'It may explain what's going on. If, between us, we can get together some more information we may be able to prove you'd nothing to do with the murders.' She stopped, then went on quickly and in a louder voice, 'Something he said made me think Stefan might be able to help.'

'Who is Bernard Corkery?' Stefan said. He didn't look up from the paper.

Oscar explained briefly. 'Honor knew him before he came to work for the medical faculty. His family farmed next to hers.'

'And why is this man . . .' moving deliberately and slowly, Stefan left the stove and sat at the table '. . . this man whom I have never met, in a position to say whether or not I can help with your predicament?' He began by speaking to Oscar but turned as he finished to Honor. His neck was flushed. 'Perhaps he is more than a medical technician?' The flush spread to his face. 'Perhaps he is part of that worthless band of idiots, the IRA?'

'He was recruited by the Supplementary Intelligence Service to help Army Intelligence.' Honor was curt, 'I've no doubt you're familiar with the SIS. There's nothing very secret about its existence, or even its activities.'

'The Supplementary Intelligence Service is as ineffective and worthless as the IRA from which organisation its members were recruited,' Stefan said dismissively.

'Not so worthless as all that,' Oscar reminded him. 'They were the people who prevented the spy Herman Goertz escaping in 1941. It would help, Stefan, if you would simply listen to what Honor has to say.'

His brother lifted and downed a glass of brandy. 'Please . . .'

He gestured to Honor to continue. The flush had died from his face and for an aching moment she thought he might cry. Then he poured himself another glass of brandy.

'Bernard didn't mean to tell me as much as he did,' Honor said, 'but since I have the information I think it could be useful.'

She told them then what she knew, in more depth than she'd told Lavinia but still keeping back the fine detail of her latest encounter with Bernard and Dandy Lyons. She'd been heading for the bicycle shed when she'd met them. It was dark, almost six o'clock, and they'd finished work for the day.

'I'm in no mad rush to get home to the old trout of a mother,' Dandy raised his hat with a flourish, 'so if the pair of you could be civil to one another for twenty minutes or so I'll stand you both a drink in Hourican's.'

'I think I could manage that.' Honor raised an eyebrow at Bernard who grinned, took her arm, and said to Dandy, 'You're on.'

They got seats in the snug. With an eye on his pint, on the counter settling, Bernard said, 'It's a bad business, this locking up of Oscar Raeder in the Curragh. A bad, bad business.'

He waited while Dandy paid for their drinks and until they were sitting at the table before he spoke again. To ensure they kept the snug to themselves he backed his chair against the door.

'They'd no right to deny him bail,' he said then, 'like any other suspect waiting trial.'

'They're not all that generous with bail at the best of times,' Dandy said, 'and why would they believe he'd keep to a bail bond?' Dandy leaned back and crossed his legs. He'd kept his hat on his head. 'There would be nothing, saving your presence, Honor, to keep him from skedaddling.'

'There's no place for him to go to,' Bernard objected.

'There's Germany,' Dandy said. 'Falling apart, it's true, but there's no better place for a man on the run to hide than in the middle of chaos.'

'He won't run,' Bernard said, 'because he didn't do it.'

'He told you as much?' Dandy enquired.

'I'd put money on it,' Bernard said. 'The man's a pillock but I don't think he's the one killed either of the victims.'

'Why not?' Honor asked the question this time. She asked it casually, one eye on the clock on the wall. As if the time were more important than his answer.

'Because he's not a fool and he's not stupid,' Bernard said. 'It was his insisting we got old Frank Dermody's body into the tank before lunch that led to the discovery of Bridie Keogh in the first place.' He leaned forward, unbuttoning his waistcoat. 'It's hot in here tonight,' he said, and downed most of the pint. 'I'll have another one of those.' He held up the almost empty glass, trying to catch the barman's eye.

Dandy, watching him, smoothed his moustache with a finger. 'How was he to know you'd take a close look at the bodies already in the tank?'

'He wasn't to know but the risk was too big and he's no fool,' Bernard said. 'It would take a foolish murderer too to carry a body to within a mile of where he was staying and lay it out on the beach.'

'But he thought it would be washed out.'

'How many times do I have to say it?' Bernard was still watching the barman. 'The man's no fool. He wouldn't do a thing like that without making simple calculations about time and tide and possible impediments on the beach.'

'I'm glad you agree with me,' Honor said dryly.

Dandy, finger to his lips, silenced her. 'There's more than that to it, isn't there?' he leaned across the small table, stabbing Bernard in the chest with a forefinger. 'It's not simply your fine sense of character analysis helping you deduce things, is it, auld son? You're keeping something from the people who care for you most in the world. If you can't tell myself and Honor what's going on . . .' He left the sentence unfinished.

'There's nothing going on.' Bernard caught the barman's eye at last. 'And if you're all that fond of me you can pay for a second pint.'

'Done!' said Dandy, and Bernard, before he could change his mind, held up his glass and said 'You heard him' to the barman.

'It's my own belief,' Dandy declared, 'that all of this carry on is part of a government plot to distract us from the disaster in the Stadium last night.' He turned to Honor. 'I suppose you're unaware that the heavyweight champion knocked out Ó Colmain, the national cruiser, in the second round?'

'The government has no idea what's going on with Raeder,' Bernard spoke across Dandy to Honor, 'and nor do the guards. The only people up to scratch on what's happening are the army. There's no reason for you to be hopeful your doctor friend will get out of this.' He shrugged. 'There's no reason either to suppose he's their man.'

Honor, drinking a Bulmer's Cider, took her time about answering. When it looked as if Dandy Lyons might start again about the boxing match, she said, hurriedly, 'Thanks for the ray of hope, Bernard,' and looked at him hard. 'Don't suppose you could stretch a point and tell me just what the hell you're taking about?'

Bernard, without answering, hunched moodily into his coat and picked up his glass.

'Tell her,' Dandy urged, grinning, 'tell us both what the SIS has been up to. Jesus, man, if you can't trust her and me, who *can* you trust?'

He stopped grinning abruptly, sounding cool to the point of anger when he went on: 'She's in a lonely enough spot, Bernard. You saw yourself the way they moved away from her in the bicycle shed just now. A courageous lot, the

middle-class brats attending this college. God help tomorrow's Ireland is all I've to say about them. Tell her what it
is you know, man. Stick with your own.'

'It's between the three of us if I do,' Bernard said.

Dandy snorted.

'Anyone needs to know probably does already.'

'It's like this . . .' Bernard cracked his knuckles and lowered
his voice. 'Clemens Hauptmann is unknown to Abwehr, the
German military-intelligence set-up. It's in the same disarray
as the rest of Germany but we've our contacts and they're
telling us they've never heard of the unfortunate sod. They
say there hasn't been a spy sent here in a year or more, that
Ireland's of no more interest to Germany.' He cracked his
knuckles, ignoring Dandy's wince. 'Germany's got enough to
do just trying to survive.'

'Maybe he was a deserter?' Honor suggested. Bernard
shook his head.

'Unlikely. There's evidence he's been coming and going for
the last few years, but no evidence of his ever meeting with our
Dr Raeder.' He shrugged. 'My own feeling on the matter is
that if Raeder were clever enough to cover up his connection
with Clemens for years, why would he behave with such
fucking stupidity when it comes to murdering the man?'

'Language!' Dandy wagged a reproving finger. 'And in
front of a lady too. My old mother would have you across
her knee in double quick time for that . . .' He giggled. 'I
should give you a good spanking myself.'

'What about his brother – Stefan?' Honor said. 'He came
here as a spy. Has he been asked if he knew Clemens
Hauptmann?'

'All of the internees have been asked. None of them had
ever heard of him. Doesn't look great for Raeder. Doesn't
look hopeless either.'

The second pint arrived. Bernard finished the first before going on.

'They mightn't get enough to hang him. The witness who wrote saying he saw Raeder on the beach at Kilmacreen can't be found and the forensic tests on the car didn't come up with blood or anything else either. He could have been transported in some sort of sealed casket, of course. Those Fords have a lot of space. But the old man, Terence Delaney, swears by his mother, father and every Bible ever printed that he spent four days working on the car and Raeder couldn't have nipped down with the body earlier in the week.'

'You're saying they won't get enough proof to hang him?' Dandy pressed.

'I am. But the hounds are baying for blood and they'll have to get someone. The way things are looking, Raeder's likely to find himself facing a very long prison term.'

Bernard had said nothing more, refusing to reveal another word of what he said was 'treasonable information'.

Stefan Raeder listened impatiently to Honor's account of her meeting with Dandy Lyons and Bernard. By the time she finished he was pacing the floor, hands behind his back. Oscar had put some of the bread and cold meat on a plate in front of her.

'The bread's baked here in the camp,' he said.

'They keep us healthy for the work we must do after the war.' Stefan stood over them. 'We have heard that we are to be workhorses for the lazy farmers hereabouts.'

'You'll be paid,' Honor replied curtly, 'but you'll have heard that too.'

'German labour is worth four times that of . . .'

Honor straightened her back. 'Shut UP, Stefan!' She slammed the flat of her hand on to the table, close to screaming. 'Just shut UP!'

234

There was silence while she lifted a piece of bread to her mouth and began to eat. It lasted until she swallowed and went on, her voice lower, 'I didn't come here to listen to your whining hatred and self-pity. If you've nothing to say that's useful then please don't waste my time. You know where the door is.' She turned an angry, controlled glare on Oscar. 'Did you know about Clemens Hauptmann? Did they tell you he was a renegade of some sort?'

'They questioned me about him.' Oscar spoke quietly. 'I had nothing to tell them and they told me very little.' He paused. 'They've left me alone most of the time since I got here.'

Honor couldn't read his expression but no longer cared. The mud and rain had soaked through her shoes and her feet were cold. In twenty minutes or less she would be leaving to go back through the mud, back on to the bus, all the way to Dublin and the endless waiting for something to happen that would get him out of here. She wanted something to happen before she left. If not what she had in mind then at least a step towards it.

'But *you* know about him, don't you, Stefan?' She stood facing Oscar's younger brother. Her feet squelched loudly in her shoes. 'You've been questioned about him.' She made it a statement.

'We were asked,' he said, 'all of us. No one has heard of him. That is what we must say, officially, and what we told them.' He shrugged. 'They don't expect us to tell them anything and why should we? So we deny.'

'You did know him then?' Honor said sharply.

'I met him once or twice, but in Germany. He wanted to be a spy but was rejected by Abwehr. He had great ideas, plans for Germany and Ireland . . .' Stefan thought for a moment. 'I didn't interest myself in him. He was a person of no importance to me. I am sure that whatever brought him here had nothing to do with Abwehr intelligence work. He was not the type.'

'What type was he then?'

'He was an independent. Lazy and fat. Maybe he just came here and fell in love with the woman.'

'Maybe.'

'I don't know anything for sure,' Stefan said, 'and so there is nothing I can tell the police when they ask me. I have been here nearly a year now, everyone else in the camp longer even than that. The war has been planned and fought without us all of that time. Germany may have found a use for such as Clemens Hauptmann in our absence but I very much doubt it.'

He stood with his legs apart and hands still behind his back, taut as a fiddle string and every bit as likely to snap.

'Your friend Bernard is right that they will lock Oscar away for a long time,' Stefan went on. 'The attitude now is "a plague on the house of all spies and those who help them". The deaths of an illegal German and his whore are of no further interest. Why would they waste time and money investigating them when they have a German who may be a spy for a suspect and what they think is evidence?'

'Oscar's not a spy. Why would they think he is?'

'Will I tell her or will you?' Stefan said. His face had flushed again. Honor resisted the temptation to tell him to sit down.

'It has to do with Stefan's intention to recruit me as an agent,' Oscar said. 'Nothing came of it but his notes, and a letter he'd intended delivering to me, were all found when they searched his belongings again, more thoroughly this time, after my arrest.' He glanced at Stefan and away again. 'They say the onus is on me to prove I wasn't recruited.'

Stefan pulled another chair up to the table and they sat, all three of them, subdued and thoughtful, like people becalmed after a storm. The light from a torch, flashing across the compound outside, was a reminder that the day was darkening. And that Honor's visiting time was coming to an end.

'Christmas is coming,' she said.

'Christmas is coming,' Oscar echoed, 'even this year, even here.' He smiled and covered her hand on the table with his. Stefan, trained to observe any nuance, watched her carefully.

'What is your point?' he said.

'Even wars stop for Christmas,' Honor said, 'all sorts of allowances are made in the interests of peace and goodwill.'

'What is your point?' he repeated.

'I think . . .' she hesitated '. . . I think it may be possible for *both* of you to get parole. For Christmas Eve and Christmas Day. It may be possible for you to spend some of the holiday in Dublin. With conditions attached, of course.'

'This is an idea you have?' Stefan said.

Oscar, who had left the table to study a calendar hanging on the wall, said nothing.

'It's part of a plan I've been working on, but I'll need your help.'

'You'll need my help celebrating Christmas?' Stefan, leaning back with his hands in his pockets, balanced the chair precariously on its hind legs. He looked more alive than at any time since Honor had met him.

He knows, she thought. He knows that I'm planning an escape and he's excited. He's like a child and it's a game to him.

As long as he was an obedient child things would be all right.

'I'll need your help to get Oscar away,' she said boldly.

In the silence that followed she looked at Oscar, leaning against the wall with his arms folded and his glasses pushed into his hair, his expression easy to read now. It seemed to her that Stefan was watching him too. She didn't turn to see.

Oscar's voice, like his expression, held alarm. 'I don't want you involving yourself in any more of this, Honor,' he said. 'The Legation and Dr Hempel will do whatever's necessary.'

'The Legation's hanging on by its teeth,' she said bluntly. 'No one there knows from one day to the next what's happening, how much longer they'll be in Dublin, how much longer they'll have a government and country to answer to . . .' She took a deep breath. 'These are not, as they say, normal times – and *they* are right. I can do this for you, Oscar, I can help you get out of Ireland and back to Germany. You can't stop me.'

'Yes, I can,' he snapped. 'You cannot do anything if I don't agree.' He shrugged. 'It would in any case be dishonourable to break my parole. My solicitor says the investigation is open still, that the police need more evidence to convict and they will find the real murderer soon enough. Stefan feels the same way about breaking parole.'

'You don't know that,' Stefan growled. 'What is honourable and what is not has changed for me. Attitudes to our country have changed so that we are considered animals these days. There is no honour in an animal's nature.'

Honor disagreed but chose not to argue his last point.

'You would be a fool not to agree to my help, and what I propose,' she said to Oscar. 'There's every chance you'll get away. I also plan . . .' for the first time that day she was tentative, clearing her throat before she went on quickly '. . . to join you as soon as the war finally ends. At least in Germany we can be together.'

And in Germany she would be free, part of a country being rebuilt, able to begin a new life by his side. They would be just two more people in a world emerging from chaos and destruction, no more remarkable and no more sought after than anyone else.

She could have explained all of this if Stefan hadn't been there, leaning forward on his chair, drumming his fingers impatiently on the table.

'It won't be like you imagine, Honor.' Oscar was frowning at her. 'The hardship to come in post-war Germany cannot be imagined by any of us . . .'

'I know that,' she said, 'why would you think that I don't?'

She knew what hardship was, did he think she didn't? She could take harder than she'd known too, if she had to.

'If there is a way my brother can escape then I will come too.' Stefan had stopped drumming his fingers. He shifted in his chair as he spoke. 'We will work better together. I am trained. He is not. Tell me what you plan.'

'Enough,' Oscar told them, 'this has gone far enough. There will be no more talk of escape.'

'That is not really for you to decide,' Stefan said coolly. 'Not any longer.'

'Stefan's right on several counts,' Honor agreed.

She'd been prepared for their different reactions. Stefan's going along was part of her plan but the idea had to come from him. It didn't take a Dr Freud to see that otherwise he would be obstructive and a liability.

He had to go along because he was a sailor, knew about boats and the sea. He was also the way she would get Oscar to agree. He would go if Stefan went. Would not let her endanger herself for his brother alone. He would go along because only by doing so could he make sure she was safe. At least until they got away.

'You planned this,' Oscar said softly. 'What have you done, Honor?'

'Nothing much, yet.' She looked at her watch. 'I must leave.'

'Go outside and wait, Stefan,' Oscar said. 'You'll escort Honor to the 'bus.'

'Don't lecture me, Oscar, please,' she said when Stefan, without a word, had done as his brother asked. 'You wanted to go home to Germany anyway and this is the only way you're going to be able to. You want to find out about Clemens Hauptmann, why he was here, and clear your name? Well, this is the way. The guards here may take years to do anything. You could be an internee for . . . oh, God . . . who knows how long? It *can* be done. You can get away. The application for your parole is being worked on. So's everything else.' She stood. 'I'll be back next week.'

'You shouldn't have told Stefan . . .' he began.

'Because now we have to go ahead? Because he won't let it go?' She put her arms about him. 'I *had* to tell him.'

They said nothing for a while, hanging on to each other with a tight, feverish need until Stefan's voice called from outside that the bus had arrived at the gate.

'It will be all right,' Honor said as they walked to meet him, 'there's every chance this will work.'

Oscar, as they came up to his brother, took her face gently in his hands and kissed her forehead.

'There's a slim chance,' he said.

# 22

'Christmas has opened with a new and dramatic turn of events on the Western front.'

*Irish Times* editorial, December 1944

G race got a Christmas tree and Yule log from the Turf Bank in Percy Place. The tree was very large and Delia, whose sole interest in life was her pregnancy, said it was as big as the one they'd been putting up in Holles Street Hospital when she was visiting her doctor.

'They have it in the main hallway where it has all the space in the world.' She shook her head, looking at Grace's tree. 'You don't have the same space here. I don't know how we're going to be able to move around it.'

'I can see how you might have difficulty, Delia.' Grace looked from the increased girth of her lodger to the tree, centrally positioned between dining and living rooms and high as the ceiling. 'The rest of us will probably manage.'

'The pine needles will get into everything,' Delia was nothing if not persistent, 'and it's likely to topple over. I'd have chosen a smaller tree myself, for those reasons alone.'

'Smaller?' Grace stood back and studied the tree. 'Smaller would in no way embody the magnanimous and hope-filled Christmas I plan for this year. The Christmas evergreen comes to us from Germany and is a symbol of immortality and the Christmas spirit. The Yule log is another tradition for which we must thank the Germanic tribes. Smaller might suit your aspirations for Christmas, Delia,' she became brisk, hauling decorations from a box at Honor's feet, 'but smaller most certainly does not suit mine.'

'It's true then that you're having the Germans here?' Delia, looking as if she might faint, clutched the back of a brocade-covered chair. 'Have you no fear, Mrs Sayers? And no caution?'

'I've plenty of both but make it a point never to give in to either,' Grace said.

'Will they have a police guard with them? Will they be handcuffed?' Delia sat in the armchair and crossed her legs delicately at the ankle. She pointedly ignored Honor. 'It's a generous and good thing you're doing, Mrs Sayers, but misguided, if I may say so. If the word gets out that Dr Raeder's here . . .'

'I've been busy spreading the word myself,' said Grace, 'so you need have no worries on that score. I've no doubt the spirit of seasonal goodwill will prevail, and of course good manners. This is Ballsbridge, after all.'

'God between us and all harm, Mrs Sayers, we'll be . . .'

'You'll be lucky to survive until Christmas, Delia, if you keep up this lunacy.' Honor blew dust from a trio of wooden snowmen. 'Oscar and his brother will be here for dinner on Christmas Day, that's all. A few hours. If that's more than you feel you can endure it might be a good idea to eat your turkey in your own rooms.'

'It's enough to make a person's flesh crawl.' Delia put a hand delicately to her throat. 'I just can't imagine how you . . .'

'You don't *have* to imagine anything,' Grace was sharp, 'but you *will* have to be less hysterical about my Christmas guests. You could start practising at dinner tonight.'

It was Grace, persuaded by Honor, who had used her influence to get Oscar paroled for Christmas. She'd put a lot of effort, and a great deal of charm, into persuading a senior army officer that she was still the young woman, and he the young man, who'd shared dangerous times together in the early days of the state. She'd even visited the officer at the Curragh camp, thought not Oscar in his hut. That, she maintained, would have been 'a sacrifice too far, and humbling to boot'.

She might have done it for Honor's sake but now, having put herself on the line, she was going to see Oscar Raeder's three days' freedom through to the bitter end.

The brothers would be brought to Lansdowne Road for Christmas Eve, would dine in Clyde Road on Christmas Day and return to the Curragh the next. There would be a guard on both houses at all times.

'Those who aren't with him coming here are against me on this one,' Grace announced on the day, a week earlier, that word of the parole had come through, 'because if a thing's worth doing at all then it's worth doing well.'

'Good to see you holding the old wisdoms.' Honor smiled, relieved but aware that her aunt's motives were anything but pure.

Grace, with her instinct for turning things to her own advantage, was enjoying the uncertain thrills of notoriety. Shocked, sideways glances and hushed admiration in public added as much spice to her midwinter days as did the predictable concern and resentment within her household.

'I hope he's appreciative of the trouble I've gone to,' she said. She'd expected some acknowledgement from Oscar, a grateful letter at least.

'He's too overcome to write,' Honor said. Grace, annoyed, ended the conversation. The truth was that Oscar had scruples about the ruthless use Honor was making of her aunt.

'It's a fundamental betrayal of her trust,' he'd argued.

'Can you think of another way to do this?'

'No.' They were standing by the wall calendar, double

checking days and dates. 'I can't think of *any* way to do it.' He put an arm about her shoulders. 'We could call the whole thing off.'

'Because of my aunt?'

'Because of you. This could ruin your life, Honor. Whether it fails . . .'

'It won't.'

'. . . or succeeds. You're risking everything, including Grace, without even knowing that there will be a future for you. Anything could go wrong.' He turned her to face him. 'Stefan and I might not make it to Berlin. The police may discover you helped us.'

'They won't. Terence is looking after that end of things.'

'The plan may go wrong and we'll all be . . .'

'Do you want to go?' Honor was curt.

'Yes.' He paused. 'I must.'

'And you don't have a better plan?'

'No.'

'Then talking about the pitfalls or consequences is a waste of time.' She wrapped herself tightly in his arms. 'Grace will be all right,' she said. She hoped. Neither of them mentioned Stefan.

Stefan, using a network he was unwilling to discuss, was organising a meeting at sea with a U-boat which would take them to mainland Europe. For Stefan things had gone far too far to turn back now. He would go alone, if he had to. But that wouldn't happen because Oscar, as Honor had known, wouldn't allow his younger brother to go alone.

Christmas Day fell on a Monday. Arriving to dinner the Friday before, Grace Sayers' guests were faced with a large, undecorated tree and, against a wall, the similarly bare Yule log. Grace, wearing a poinsettia behind one ear, explained.

'Honor and I will put the baubles on the tree on Christmas Eve,' she said, 'because that's the German way. The Yule log will not be lit until then either. Our guests must be made to feel welcome, as at home as is possible.'

'They won't be here until the next day,' Florrie Mitchell pointed out, 'so what difference can it possibly make when you decorate?'

'You've really gone out of your way to be disagreeable about my Christmas arrangements this year, Florrie,' Grace complained. 'Doing things at the right time has to do with the *integrity* of our welcome to the brothers.'

'Not disagreeable, dear lady, merely doubtful of the wisdom of your goodness.' Florrie rocked on his heels as he warmed his backside to the fire. 'It wouldn't have done those lads one bit of harm to spend the three days of the festival in the camp. There are enough of their Germanic brethren resident for them to celebrate in their customary way. But . . . thank you, sir.' He took the glass of port handed him by Lennox. 'This is your house, dear heart, and you will do as you will, and must do, in your generous-to-a-fault fashion.'

'Indeed I will, Florrie,' Grace was acid-tongued, 'indeed I will. But my generosity *has* been known to have limits.'

This was a not-so-subtle reminder of an occasion on which Florrie had incurred her wrath by selling a portrait he'd painted of her without her permission and been refused entry to the house for two weeks.

'It is also my house,' Lavinia reminded the table at large, 'and I certainly have no objection to sharing my Christmas dinner with a spy and a murder suspect.' She cast a coolly disparaging glance at the bare tree. 'It should make for quite a diverting time.'

'Thank you, Lavinia, for your support,' Grace said crisply.

Delia and Ernie Gibbons had brought candles.

'A gift from a client and too large for our humble rooms,' Ernie said. 'They'll shine much more brightly in the oak of your fine table, Mrs Sayers.'

'They're church candles.' Grace held them aloft, one in each hand, as if offering sacrifice. 'Are you tailoring for bishops now, Ernie, as well as for the army and politicians?'

'I make for people from all walks of life,' he said, stiffly.

'The cut of the people who come to him is a measure of Ernie's excellence.' Delia gave her shrill laugh. 'That's a good one, isn't it? Cut and measure?' She laughed again, a touch belligerently this time when the others failed to join her.

'You've the country sewn up, Ernie,' said Grace, at which everyone but Delia laughed.

Grace, for this pre-Christmas meal, served braised goose with dumplings. The candles, two-feet-high pillars burning in the centre of the table, lit up the bird's golden-brown skin as Lennox carved. They were to eat by candlelight.

'Goose, though I enjoy it immensely, doesn't altogether agree with me.' Lennox smiled regretfully at Grace. 'But for your sake, my dear, I will risk my digestive system.' He glanced briefly at the faces watching him in the candlelight. 'The goose, my friends, was always eaten at Michaelmas in old Ireland.' He carved deftly, slicing evenly and thinly. 'Eating goose on that day was said to bring good fortune all the year round.' He cut through the leg joints and laid both drumsticks carefully to the side. 'It was known as the "green goose" and very good to eat because it would have fed on the stubble after the harvest.'

'Not so old Ireland,' Honor said. 'We had goose at Michaelmas every year.'

'Good fortune has certainly blessed you,' Ernie said. 'The world awaits at your feet, Honor. It would be a pity not to guard your good fortune. Take care it doesn't become harmed in any way.'

'I'll be careful, Ernie,' Honor said. She helped herself to a couple of slices of goose, then to parsnips and potato from the warm dishes further down the table.

'Sauce?' Florrie held the bowl her way.

'No, thank you,' Honor said. He poured anyway, generously covering her goose.

She wasn't going to be able to eat any of it. Her stomach was in revolt at the sight of the piled-high plate and mud-brown sauce.

Lavinia was watching her. Lavinia to whom she'd given details of Monday's plan. It was safe enough telling Lavinia but if she wasn't careful someone else at the table was bound to sense something was wrong. She speared a piece of goose on her fork.

'Are you doing any interesting research work at the moment, Lennox?' she said. Lennox had been known to talk for twenty minutes without drawing breath once on to a pet subject.

'My work is always interesting.' He looked at her briefly, then shrugged, 'I wouldn't concern myself with it otherwise. My problem is space for my books and collection of folkloric objects.' He sighed, smiling, and looked in Grace's direction. 'My little house seems to shrink by the day. It's severely limiting what I can do.'

'There's a fine house lying idle on Lansdowne Road,' Florrie said. 'You could move yourself and your chattels in there. It's likely to be empty for some time to come, by all accounts.'

'The house is not empty,' Honor pointed out, 'the owner lives there. With his dog.'

'Ah, yes, old Terence Delaney,' Florrie said, shaking his head, 'of course he does. But he's the owner in name only and lives, as he always did, in the basement. He doesn't know what to do with the rest of the place.' His glowing face smiled in the candlelight.

'You're very well informed.' Honor was discouraging, wary of Florrie's opportunistic eye falling on the pictures and *objects d'art* in the Lansdowne Road house.

'Needs must, my sweet child, needs must.' Florrie was eternally cheerful. 'I'm but an impecunious artist and my own sole support and must keep myself alert to every opportunity.'

She was right. He was sizing up Terence's house. She watched him run a fond hand along the sleeve of his velvet, ruby-coloured jacket.

'Appearances are not always what they seem, alas,' he sighed, picked up his cutlery and went back to his food. 'Penury beckons. The picture-buying public is fickle and I must resort to my wits to make money.'

'So you plan, Mr Mitchell, to strip the walls and cabinet shelves of the Leahy home in the way you have done here?'

The hard, cold anger of Lavinia's interjection brought silence to the table.

'You surely know, Mrs Sayers,' Florrie looked at Lavinia over the rim of his glass, 'that anything which has been entrusted to me from this house has been returned in coin, as it were, for the building's upkeep. I sell what our hostess feels she can part with so that she and you and Honor may continue in the life you are accustomed to.'

'Please!' Lavinia shuddered. 'Don't presume to include me in your greedy dealings. They are between you and Grace Danaher. If she believes she can trust you . . .' Lavinia shrugged and went on '. . . I make the point because I am certain you will not find Mr Terence Delaney either as avaricious or as gullible as my son's widow.' She turned a hard glare on Florrie. 'I will be writing to him about your dealings with questionable contacts.'

'You've overstepped the mark, Mrs Sayers.' Florrie looked hurt, and cornered. 'My contacts are above reproach, as are my dealings. I'm particularly distressed that you should impugn my honesty.' He pushed his chair back from the table. 'I really don't feel I can remain any longer.' He stood and turned to Grace. 'I don't see how I can possibly come here ever again, in fact . . .'

'My own character has been assassinated every bit as much by Mrs Sayers as has yours,' Grace snapped. 'Sit down, Florrie.'

She turned so quickly towards Lavinia that the poinsettia fell from her hair. Lennox picked it up.

'Whatever I've sold was mine to sell,' she said, 'and if you've got other grievances or anxieties you want to air then I suggest, Mrs Sayers, that you make a contribution to the season and keep them to yourself until after the New Year.'

Honor moved food around her plate and held her breath. If Grace pushed Lavinia too far there was no knowing what she might say.

Panic, like a bad taste, rose in the back of her throat. She shouldn't have told Lavinia about the escape plan. But she told her everything else and the old woman had always been close as the grave. It would be all right. Please God let her shut up now, let her not say another word.

'*Carpe diem*,' Lavinia murmured and leaned back, closing her eyes. 'You are exposed, Mr Mitchell, and I am weary.'

'Exposed!' Florrie's anger was blurred by an unconvincing show of astonishment. 'Anyone would think I was a common criminal! I cannot stay. I cannot return . . .'

'Still on your feet, Florrie?' Grace smiled. 'Please sit down and finish your food. I've made mincemeat pudding with lemon sauce for dessert.'

'A man must have some dignity, some pride . . .' Florrie, beginning what looked like becoming a speech, stopped when Grace shook her head. She was still smiling and gentle when she said, 'You do what you do, Florrie my old friend, there are none of us perfect.'

'This is preposterous and upsetting. I'm leaving.' The candlelight threw Florrie's hovering face into unreadable shadow. 'I may not return.' He bowed to the table, briefly, and turned for the door.

'A word before you go, Florrie.' Grace's clear voice had become quickly and compellingly icy. 'If you use this small exchange as an excuse not to dine with my Christmas Day guests then you may, indeed, not return to this house.'

'I have never let you down, Grace, never,' he said, and vanished through the door.

The Gibbonses left for their rooms earlier than usual, Delia pleading a headache and a hard day following.

'The shop stays open until six o'clock tomorrow,' she complained, 'but Ernie's taking me to see Noël Coward as Mother Goose in the Royal after. It'll be our Christmas treat together.'

'That's nice.' Grace was distracted, fiddling with her napkin and frowning.

'It will be *very* nice,' Ernie said, loudly. 'An innocent pleasure, in line with the season that's in it.'

'Absolutely,' said Grace.

'Do you think Florrie was more than usually offended?' she said to Lennox when the door closed behind them. 'His leaving like that was unusual.'

'He may have been annoyed that Mrs Sayers . . .' Lennox cleared his throat and nodded at Lavinia, who ignored him '. . . put a stop to his immediate advances on the Lansdowne Road house. I would say he's at this very moment holding up the bar in the Waterloo and that his departure was more about a Christmas pint of the black stuff than anything else.'

'He wants to paint my portrait,' Grace murmured, 'again.'

'The man has taste, I'll grant him that,' Lennox said.

'You've suffered no ill effects from the goose then?' Lavinia eyed the remains of the bird, still in the centre of the table. 'I thought it overdone myself.'

'None so far,' Lennox was resolutely cheerful, 'though of course food can circle the digestive system for twenty-four hours before causing upset.'

'I hope, Lennox, that you of all people aren't going to let me down on Monday?' Grace said.

He took the fallen poinsettia from where he'd left it on the table and pinned it behind her ear again.

'Being prostrate on a hospital bed is the only thing would keep me away,' he said.

'How very reassuring,' said Lavinia.

# 23

# The Basement

'. . . It is doubtful, even,
If there is music left in us at all.'
Bruce Williamson, 'Afternoon in Anglo-Ireland'

The time came, as I have always known it would, and I seized my hour. *Carpe diem*. I have taken action, at last, and the years of waiting will be over in just a few days. I will be avenged, and so will Douglas.

All things, it is said, come to him who waits; another old adage whose wisdom has been proven in recent days.

I knew the time had come when Honor Cusack came and told me about her plan to help the Raeder brothers escape justice. She is using the younger brother, who sounds to be the essence of all that is abominable and loathsome in German youth, the type who answered Mr Hitler's call eagerly and gave him power, to ensure her lover goes along with the plan.

'He will return to the fight,' I said, 'he will be the cause of more killing in this vile war.'

'He will use his contacts with the navy,' she said. 'There's a network still existing and he's a part of it. All he and Oscar have to do is get down the coast to meet a German U-boat on the afternoon of Christmas Day . . .'

'A U-boat!' I was shocked; genuinely so. 'You would encourage those devils to our shores? You would bring the war here, help the Hun in his hour of need?'

'The German counter-offensive is being dismissed, it is over for them, they're in retreat.' She was fierce in her own defence. 'The world knows it. Nothing will make any difference to the outcome now. Stefan will be captured as soon as he goes back into the fighting.'

She was reading reports and listening to the wireless then. She was also hearing what she wanted to hear. But that is the way with the young when they want something in life. She is as ruthless as any of them and just as careless.

'Or he will be killed,' I said.

'Or killed,' she echoed.

'And Dr Raeder? Are you not afraid that he, too, will be captured?' I said. 'That he too will be killed?'

'Oscar does not intend fighting,' she said coldly. 'He is a German citizen and no more a part of this war than many others of his countrymen and women.'

I was silent. As was too often the case, speaking my mind would only endanger her trust in me. So I nodded, as if understanding, and she went on incautiously.

'He will first go to Paris, since it is liberated and he has friends there. He was in contact with his friends just months ago, by letter. He will make his way from Paris to Berlin as soon as is practical. In the meantime he will work in Paris to set up what he can by way of medical help for the people of Berlin when the war ends.'

'Very laudable,' I said.

It was possible Dr Raeder believed this nonsense, that he wanted to help his war-stricken country. It was just as likely that he was deviously escaping the invidious situation in which he found himself in in Ireland. He might well get to Paris. He might just as likely get himself shot *en route*.

I put another alternative to Honor. 'Do you not worry that his brother will betray him?' I said.

'No. In their case, though they bitterly disagree about the

war and National Socialism, blood has always proved thicker than water. They've stood by each other while agreeing to differ.' She paused. 'Stefan is outraged by what has happened to Oscar.'

She believed this, it was very clear. 'You know best,' I said. 'I do, Mrs Sayers,' she said, 'I really do.'

She sat on a footstool and began braiding her hair. It was before ten in the morning and, with the university closed for Christmas, she was restless, unable to stay in the house with her aunt and equally unable to study in the library. She had done her Christmas shopping, which was limited in any event by her lack of money, and told her mother she would not be home for the holiday. There was no one she could talk to about what was planned. I was her last, and only, resort.

'I'm keeping away from Gretta,' she'd admitted candidly when she arrived, 'I'm afraid I might let something slip when talking to her. She's very sharp, you know.'

I did know. I'd experienced the sharp side of Gretta Harte's tongue on more than one occasion.

'I worry about Terence.' She examined the braid, found it displeasing and began to unravel it again.

Her state of nervous apprehension was such that I worried about her endangering the plan. This would not be in my interests.

'Terence Delaney is manifestly well able to look after himself,' I said in my most reassuring voice.

'Of course he is; that's not what I'm worried about.' She divided her hair into two. 'I'm worried about the arrangements he's making with his boatman friend in Poolbeg.' She began, fingers moving in a tense, jerky fashion, to braid one of the sections of hair. 'He was all for helping Oscar get away. Says the state we have in Ireland today is not the one he fought for and that he's got no faith in its law-keepers or law-makers.'

Her fingers stopped moving and she dropped her hands to her lap. She stared blankly in front of her.

'He says Stefan should be left to rot where he is and I suppose you'd agree with that. But Stefan is the only one can get Oscar a passage to the coast of France and so he must go free as well.' She turned to me, still fierce. 'I know you would do the same thing, Mrs Sayers, if you were in my shoes.'

'I would never have got myself into such a ridiculous position in the first place,' I said.

A lie. The situation I'd found myself in had been equally odious, though in a different way, and I'd got myself out of it by equally drastic means.

'What is Mr Delaney arranging? And with whom?' I was curious for more reasons than one.

'He is arranging the boat which will take Oscar and his brother out of Dublin and down the coast.' She went back to braiding her hair. Her nails were bitten and ugly. 'They will be picked up along the river, somewhere by Sir John Rogerson's Quay, on the night of the twenty-fifth, after they've had dinner here and gone back to Lansdowne Road. Terence has a plan too to get them out and past the guards who'll be watching the house. I have to trust in him. What worries me is the way he keeps talking about his days with Michael Collins . . .'

'Collins was dangerously heroic, they say.' I'd been intro-duced to him once, but didn't intend telling her that. He'd bristled with life and an animal energy. An interesting man. And attractive. 'It's possible that Mr Delaney learned a thing or two from him about clandestine behaviour.'

'Terence Delaney is more than eighty years old,' Honor sighed. 'He was old even when he knew Collins, about sixty, so whatever he learned I hope he remembers well. His boatman friend is from the Civil War days too, but younger. He will take them down the coast to meet a U-boat off Wexford. From there they will be taken to Brest, in France, where there is a special U-boat harbour.' She stopped, gathered the second clump of hair and began separating it into three parts.

'Terence says his friend can be trusted.'

'What's this man's name?'

'I don't know,' she said, avoiding my eyes.

There were some things she was keeping from me then, which was a pity. For my own plan, taking shape in my head as we spoke, I would need to know every detail. Needs must, however, and I had more than enough to be going on with.

I inveigled the murderer to my rooms by the simplest of means. On an evening when I knew he was with Grace, and knew Honor to be with Terence Delaney in the Lansdowne Road house, I made my way upstairs. They were surprised to see me come into the drawing room.

Grace Danaher was sitting in an armchair with the wireless on beside her. I listened and watched for a minute before they saw me. She was wearing a saffron-coloured robe, her feet shod in two inch-high satin shoes and her legs in silk stockings. She'd been expecting him then. She'd always dressed for men, even those she'd no intention of taking to her bed. She liked them to be enslaved. Her lipstick was very red.

The wireless was tuned to a German propaganda pro-gramme, which they were discussing. The sense of the broad-cast seemed to be a German hysteria that in a post-war Europe, one in which Germany was defeated, Britain and America would rule the world by economic power and, if necessary, hunger and bombs.

'The military situation is becoming hopeless for Germany,' the murderer was saying, 'and what the speaker fears may well come about.'

He was less flamboyant than usual; uneasy I'd have said. Grace Danaher didn't seem to notice. She fluttered a beringed hand and was about to divulge her views on the subject when I stepped into the room.

'Algernon and Walter became over-excited and knocked over the aspidistra.' I spoke loudly and as if annoyed. 'I cannot get it back on the pedestal. It will die.'

'There's not the slightest danger of it dying,' said Grace Danaher, who had straightened in her seat and looked quite startled when I appeared, 'that old plant is impossible to kill.' She laughed, softly.

'I would nevertheless like it back on its pedestal.'

'I doubt I can lift it if you can't, Lavinia,' she said.

'I saw you arrive,' I turned to her guest, 'I was hoping you might assist me.'

'I'll come down with you.' He was deference itself, bowing slightly as he stood. I left the room and he followed me, one step behind all the way down the back stairs. I didn't like it.

The aspidistra lay where I'd knocked it, clay scattered but not enough to expose the root. I am quite fond of it, as a plant; it was given me several Christmasses ago by Honor.

I brought a pan and small brush and watched while my gallant stood it upright, then lifted it back on to its pedestal. He was very efficient when he put his mind to something, a characteristic I'd noticed before.

'There is something I would like to discuss with you,' I said as he rubbed his hands clean with a linen handkerchief, 'since fate, or the aspidistra, has thrown us together.'

I smiled but he wasn't taken in. He doesn't believe in fate any more than I do myself. Like me he well knows that what happens in life is ordained, and made possible, by the actions of man. Or woman.

'Should I take a seat?' he said and sat down, crossing his legs and letting his hands hang from the arms of the chair. It was the one usually occupied by Honor when she came to see me. He wore a cool half-smile on his face.

'Grace will become impatient if I'm away too long,' he said.

He was right. I would have to say what I had to say briskly as well as very carefully.

'The way I've chosen to live allows me see and hear many things . . .' I began.

'I'm aware of the close attention you pay to what goes on around you,' he cut me short. 'You're an intelligent woman.'

'I'm no longer susceptible to flattery,' I said, 'but you're right, of course. And you, my friend, are an intelligent man and as such will understand why I am choosing to betray a confidence and tell you that Honor Cusack has arranged for the brothers Raeder to escape from Ireland on Christmas Day.' I allowed myself a short laugh. 'So much for parole and the much-vaunted German code of honour.'

I hadn't expected him to display great shock but the stillness, the absence of any emotion with which he greeted my news, was a surprise. When I took a moment to consider this, however, it was in character. He was a man whose façade was so false, who lived such a monumental lie, that the expression of any genuine emotion would have been difficult, if not impossible, for him.

'Please go on,' he said after a minute or two. He had made a steeple of his hands, capable fingers in a prayer-like posture under his chin.

'You are the only one I feel able to trust to do what is right,' I said, 'the only one who believes absolutely, as I do, that the brothers should not be allowed get away. I am an old woman and cannot do what must be done. I can't be dealing with police and army and whomever . . .'

'Tell me what is to happen, Mrs Sayers,' he said. He wasn't rude about interrupting me, just calm and businesslike. I went on in the same tone.

'They will come to dinner that day as planned,' I said. 'Afterwards they will return to the Leahy house in Lansdowne

258

Road from where, after dark, their escape has been planned. Terence Delaney, who may be elderly but is also ruthless and has nothing to lose, is involved in this aspect of the plan. It is my understanding that the brothers will be taken by boat to the mouth of the river and from there out into the Bay and down the coast to Wexford where they will be put aboard a U-boat and taken to the port of Brest, in France, where there is a U-boat harbour.'

I stopped. His eyes, from looking into the middle distance, had now focussed on mine.

'People have been busy,' he almost whispered.

'Very,' I said, 'but, in one instance at least, talkative also.'

'A womanly weakness,' he commented.

'Not all women.'

'Of course not.' He was hastily apologetic. 'There are women will take secrets to the grave with them.' He smiled. 'As I'm sure you will, Mrs Sayers.'

I let this go. 'I will deny everything if you tell Honor I betrayed her,' I said. 'It will be my word against yours – but by then justice will be done and we will all of us have other things to contend with.'

'Why would I tell her?'

'In the event of anything going wrong,' I said, 'you might want to . . . explain things.' By betraying me, I might have added but didn't. I didn't need to. We understood one another well enough.

For my part, knowing his secret, I knew he could be trusted to go to the police. He had to; he couldn't allow the brothers Raeder to return to Germany where there would always be the danger of one or other of them exposing his links with Clemens Hauptmann. Great socialiser that he was he would know exactly who to inform, what person among the Irish authorities could most efficiently act to prevent the escape.

But for my purposes, and his own, he would have to do it

259

secretly, after the manner in which he'd let the police know where Clemens Hauptmann's body lay on a beach. A similar anonymous note couldn't be ignored, given that the earlier one had given correct information.

'I do realise,' I spoke regretfully, 'that you will not be able openly to inform the police. I am sorry to put you in such an invidious position with Grace, who would never forgive you were she to discover you were the person who betrayed her niece's lover. It would, of course,' I appeared to be musing though what I'd to say to him had occupied my thoughts the night long, 'suit Grace very well to have the young men escape. It will give her back her niece, return Honor to her studies and give Grace peace from the worries of recent months. That will be your unsung gift to her. On the other hand, as long as the doctor is incarcerated here, Honor will be distracted, obsessed with fighting his cause.'

'As I said earlier, Mrs Sayers,' he smiled without showing his teeth, 'you are an intelligent woman who pays close attention to all that goes on around her.'

'And then there is always Grace Danaher's sense of drama!' I allowed myself a small laugh, followed by an indulgent shrug of the shoulders. 'Once they've gone she will enjoy the vicarious thrill of involvement by proxy, the daily waiting for news, the woman betrayed who offered hospitality and trust. It will be quite like her younger days again, when she endangered life and limb for Irish freedom.'

I must not have kept the derision from my voice with sufficient caution for he looked at me sharply, a sudden cold light in his eyes.

'I sounds to me, Mrs Sayers, as if you would *prefer* me to act in secret fashion,' he said.

I caught the emphasis and drew back into myself and my more usual, slightly dismissive persona. He was not a fool, as I well knew, and I was in danger of betraying my hand.

'I have been overly preoccupied with this dilemma since Honor confided in me,' I said. 'It has amused me to look at the problem in the round, so to speak. I naturally considered the effect on your situation when I decided to trust you with her secret.'

'Very thoughtful of you, Mrs Sayers.'

He sat in silence after that, contemplating the middle distance once more. I understood his dilemma. Now that I'd told him he would have to act, even without altogether trusting me. He had no choice. It was in his own interests, whatever way he looked at it.

'You're right, of course,' he said at last, 'I will have to tell the guards indirectly.'

He smiled again, still without uncovering his teeth. It was not a smile Grace Danaher would ever have seen. 'The Raeder brothers will not be allowed to escape the island and Irish justice. You've no need to worry any more.'

'I'm glad to hear it.'

'This will, of course, remain a secret between us.' His tone was pleasant enough. 'It wouldn't do, as you've said, for Grace to find out I was the one told the police.'

'I will take it to the grave with me,' I said reassuringly, 'if only because I've no intention of alienating Honor and exposing myself to Grace's vengeance for what's left of my life.'

'I'm glad to hear it,' he echoed me, smiling.

Once the brothers were back in custody I would betray him, tell the police *he* was their informant and that I was *his*. Once revealed he would be subject to intense scrutiny by the army and SIS. Honor's admirer, the young Mr Corkery, would be more than keen to push the inquiry. My murderous gallant's German activities and associations would be bound to come to light then, his links to Clemens Hauptmann exposed. He would be destroyed.

And so, by association, and with the help of the malicious gossip which holds what passes for society in this city together, would Grace Danaher.

'Thank you for righting my aspidistra,' I said.

He stood and looked around my accommodation. When his eye fell on the portrait of Lionel he walked closer and studied it for several minutes.

'He was a handsome man, your husband,' he said. 'You must miss him.'

'Not any longer,' I said.

'I suppose not. He's dead how many years now? Eleven, is it?' He kept his back to me, looking and looking at the portrait, blocking my own view of it.

'More,' I said. He well knew how long Lionel was dead.

He sighed, his shoulders rising and falling as he took the breath in, then let it out. 'You've had your share of tragedy,' he said, 'as well as secrets to keep.' I said nothing and he turned. 'We all have secrets.' His face was a perfect blank. He wasn't even looking at me.

'It's part of the human condition,' I said. Was he threatening me?

'Indeed it is. But you and I will be well able to continue keeping one another's secret, Mrs Sayers, won't we?'

'Of course,' I said.

262

# 24

'The menace of Germany's under-sea fleet is real and continuing.'

Churchill/Roosevelt statement, December 1944

Gretta Harte was in two minds about the wisdom of Oscar Raeder and his brother spending Christmas Day in Clyde Road.

'It would be less trouble for everyone if they stayed where they are in the camp in Kildare,' she said, up to her elbows in fruit in the hot, small, overcrowded Turner's Cottages kitchen.

Her nephews, idle and unbiddable, eyed her progress with the sherry trifle, one of them wheezing every time the wind down the chimney sent smoke gusting into the room.

'But then Christmas is a time of goodwill and charity and all of that,' she whacked the creeping fingers of another nephew as they edged towards the cut fruit, 'so I suppose we should put up with whatever bother it'll bring.'

'You're not being asked to put up with anything,' Honor pointed out, 'you don't even have to see Oscar. Unless you want to.'

'I wouldn't mind meeting him again,' Gretta said, carefully. 'He was a decent type of man.' The kettle, suspended over the fire, began to whistle. 'I'm still finding it hard to believe he got himself caught up in this murderous carry-on.'

'He *is* a decent man,' Honor said, 'and nothing's been proven. The case is still open.'

'Jesus God, but you're touchy today!' Gretta glared at the nephews and lifted the kettle in one fluid movement. 'A cup of tea with something to bolster it might help. Out, out!' She swooped on the small boys, ushering them protesting into the frosty street. 'Lazy little buggers.' She made the tea. 'Sitting with their tongues hanging out as if they hadn't had a bite this morning. The oldest one's decided there's no Santy and he's infecting the others.'

'How's your mother?' Honor asked.

She shouldn't have come. Gretta would sense there was something wrong. Any minute now and she'd be asking questions, probing until she got answers. That was the real reason she'd put the boys outside.

'My mother's not the best.' Gretta scalded the tea-pot. 'First Christmas Eve of her life she hasn't been up at cock-crow.'

It was half-past eight. Tilly Harte was eighty-three and, usually, a vigorous housekeeper.

'Maybe she needed the rest,' Honor said.

Greta poured the tea, added whiskey, and put the cup forcefully into Honor's hand. 'Sit,' she commanded.

Honor sipped but remained standing. 'I'm in a hurry,' she said. Gretta was watching her, and waiting. 'I've shopping to do.'

'Shops are closed,' her friend said. 'It's Sunday.' True. There had been a small outcry to have them opened but it would have meant changing the law so the *status quo* had prevailed, even though it was Christmas Eve.

'I forgot,' Honor said.

'What's on your mind?' Gretta probed.

'Everything, I suppose.' Honor smiled uneasily. 'All that's happened.'

'I'd expect to be told if anything new was stirring,' Gretta warned her. 'Drink your tea.' She drank her own, quickly, and went back to cutting fruit for the trifle. 'When do the brothers get here?' she said.

'About midday.' Honor put the bag she'd brought on to the table. 'A car from the German Legation's bringing them to Lansdowne Road. I brought some presents for the boys,' she indicated the bag, 'for you too. I must go now.'

'I'll be here when you want to talk to me.' Gretta's tone had softened. 'I need to wrap the present I got for you so I'll give it to you tonight. You'll be going to Midnight Mass, I suppose?'

'Yes.' Honor hadn't thought beyond midday. She'd spent the night, and the early hours, in useless activity. Being here now was more of the same. Anything to avoid thinking, to keep worst possible scenarios at bay.

'Where will you be?' Gretta asked. 'In Lansdowne Road?'

'Yes.'

'I'll call for you there. It'll give me a chance to wish Oscar a Happy Christmas.' Gretta nodded to herself, seeming very happy with this arrangement. 'I'll call about ten o'clock. That'll give me half an hour before we head for St Mary's in Haddington Road, you and me. Unless Oscar and his brother want to come along too. Are they Catholics?'

'No. Protestants of some sort.'

'No point asking them to come along so,' Gretta said, sounding relieved.

'I suppose not.'

Terence Delaney was pleased to see Honor. She could tell by the way he touched his hat when he opened the door, by Setanta's quick bark. They were very attuned to one another these days, the man and his dog.

Terence had fires lit everywhere. Like her, he'd been up early, unable to sleep. 'It's the devil's own work trying to get a bit of rest with all this going on,' he grumbled, 'and the guards around the place make me uneasy.' Angry too from the look of his tightened jaw as he stood in the window. 'There's plenty real work for them to be doing in a country as corrupt and sliding as this one.'

Standing beside him Honor could see a garda stiffly pacing under the trees opposite. 'Is that all there is?' she said. 'Is he alone?'

'All of them there's on view.' Terence's voice was harsh. 'You can be sure there's a few more scattered around. In the upstairs window of one of the nearby houses most likely, in the back laneway, at the end of the road. They're about all right. They've a dangerous murderer to watch.'

Honor moved back into a room which looked no different from when she'd seen it first, a lifetime before, with Oscar's books on the table and stacked on chairs, pictures on the walls still dusty, clock an hour fast on the mantle in front of the great, gilded mirror. She turned the pages of a book lying open on the table.

'Maybe they'll be tired of watching by tomorrow,' she said. 'Maybe there won't be so many of them willing to work, it being Christmas Day.'

'Won't make any difference,' Terence said, 'the lads'll be gone by then.'

Honor's stomach gave a small, sickening lurch. She stared at the page under her hand. Oscar had been reading up on the anterior wall of the abdomen.

'By tomorrow night, you mean?' she said.

'They'll be out of here by tomorrow morning,' Terence said as she turned to face him, 'there's been a change of plan. They're moving out tonight.'

With his back to the window it was impossible to see his face. When, obligingly, he moved into the room and sat by the fire there was little discernible difference. He was flesh made stone, his expression as revealing as a granite cliff-face.

'Why?' Honor said. 'Why have things been changed?'

Change wasn't good, it made things uncertain and unstable. Change brought confusion, increased the risk of everything going wrong.

'Things have been changed for the best,' Terence reassured her. He was looking at the dog, lying with his head on his paws, apparently asleep. 'Your help will be needed with the earlier part of proceedings.'

Honor's stomach didn't relax so quickly this time. 'When was the change decided?' she said. '*Who* decided?'

'You don't need to know. All you need do is be available.'

'There's been no change, has there?' The realisation came like a blow, taking her breath away. She stood. 'It was always going to be tonight only you didn't trust me enough to tell me. That's it, isn't it, Terence?'

'There's no good half the world knowing what's going on,' he said, 'a shown hand is a bad one. Best to keep your cards close to your chest when you're engaged in work of this nature.'

'Is that so?' Honor said. 'Well, I need to think about this.'

In the high, draughty hallway she walked up and down, slowly at first but then furiously and fast. Terence Delaney hadn't trusted her, pure and simple, probably because she was a woman. He'd reverted to his guerrilla ways, deserted reality for the mythology and memory of his glorious, fighting past. He could ruin everything. Could already have ruined everything. He was a menace, a geriatric lunatic. God alone knew what he'd arranged for tonight. God alone knew who else he'd involved.

'Who else knows?' Back in the room she stood in front of him, mouth dry with fear and anger. 'What have you *done*, Terence?'

'You'd best go down to the kitchen and plunge your hands into the bucket of cold water there,' he was kindly-sounding, for Terence, 'best thing in the world for cooling the head. Go on now,' he made a shooing movement with his hand, 'I want your head easy when I'm talking to you.'

She went, both to mollify him and because he was right. She needed to calm down. The water was icy and she stayed on her hunkers beside the bucket for several minutes, watching her hands whiten as the blood vessels closed down, then redden as they opened up again with the increased blood flow. She felt calmer, probably because of the time spent considering her blood's behaviour. She dried her hands and went back to the sitting room.

'You didn't trust me,' she said again accusingly.

'You're right,' Terence said, 'I didn't trust you. Why would I?'

The question wasn't rhetorical. He was sitting with his back ramrod straight and eyes fixed on her face. He looked more alive than she'd ever seen him.

'Is it because I'm a woman?'

'That's a part of it,' he said, 'but it's more to do with you having no experience of this business.' He looked away from her, lost in his own private world again. 'You've no practice at it. You might talk, without meaning it, to the wrong person. What you don't know you can't talk about.' He paused. 'The fewer people know the better.'

Honor walked to the window and stood there with her hands against the cold glass, cooling them again.

How could he know? Sweet Jesus, how could he? Lavinia couldn't have made the journey here to tell him and there hadn't been time, since Honor had confided in her, for a letter to be delivered. Terence couldn't have visited Lavinia either, without everyone in Clyde Road knowing about it.

'I'm not saying you'd have told anyone, mind,' Terence's

voice said behind her, 'or that you've done so. Just that it's better you didn't know to avoid any chance of you being indiscreet.' The kindly, patient note disappeared and he was his irascible self when he added, 'Sit back down, woman, closer to me where I can see and be sure you understand what I have to tell you.'

Honor sat at the table. She could see he'd have preferred her closer but this was as near as she was going. He knew her too well already.

'My sources tell me the guards aren't expecting the lads to make a run for it.' Terence spoke clearly and concisely. 'They're banking on the German code of honour to prevail, so we've their sloth and stupidity on our side. The night's set fair with few clouds forecast which is unfortunate for our purposes but there's not a lot we can do about it. My man will pick them up halfway down the south wall, near the mouth of the river, at twenty-four hours thirty. The tide will be ideal at that time.'

'How are they going to get there?' Honor said.

'The latter part of their journey needn't concern you,' he said, 'just the first bit, and getting them out of the house here. You'll go with the pair of them to Midnight Mass in St Patrick's church in Ringsend. You'll have to explain to the guard outside what you intend. They may let you walk, escorted, or they may take you there in a car. It's of no consequence. You'll leave it a bit late setting out, so that the church will be packed when you arrive and make it harder for the guards to keep a tight surveillance on the young men. Are you with me so far?'

'Yes. But Oscar and his brother are Protestant,' Honor said. 'Why would they go to midnight Mass?'

'Because this is a Catholic country, Miss Cusack.' Terence was testy. 'They're naturally anxious to show their gratitude and take part in a traditional Irish Christmas. Tell it to the

269

guard in whatever fashion you wish but try to keep your wits about you.'

'I'll try,' Honor said.

'Stay well inside the door, but not too far into the body of the church. You'll see a pillar to your right with a listing of the times for the novena to St Jude pinned to it. Stand as close to it as you can. Don't take a seat, even if offered one. The Mass will end shortly after midnight but before it does, at the time of the second gospel, the drunk and the half-sozzled will make for the doors.'

He stopped, checking that she was listening attentively, before he went on.

'One such drunk will push you against the pillar. He'll be as rough as he needs to be to cause a commotion. By the time you gather yourself together and get outside the church Oscar and his brother will be on their way to their pick-up destination.'

'The south wall?' Honor said.

'Wits, Miss Cusack, use your wits! Might as well put them standing in the middle of Croke Park as expect them to find cover on the south wall. No. The man who'll lead them from the church knows the river and basin well and will take them to a spot offering plenty of shelter. They'll be met there. My boatman knows his business.'

He put the pipe in his mouth and began a root for matches, finding them in his breast pocket.

'What then?'

'There's no more you need know.' Terence held a match to the pipe bowl and began to suck.

'There's something *you* should know,' she said. 'Gretta Harte and I have arranged to meet tonight at eleven to go to Midnight Mass in St Mary's in Haddington Road. She'll think it very odd when I insist on taking Oscar and his brother to Ringsend. She's not a fool.'

'You're right about that,' Terence spoke with the pipe between his teeth, 'she's not. A practical kind of woman. Only kind worth having around. Runs that post office like a military installation.'

He stopped, frowning in thought. Honor didn't help, or add anything more. His admiration of Gretta was a revelation but not, when she considered it, much of a surprise. Gretta was, in some ways, a younger, female version of Terence: both of them liked to be in charge.

Terence Delaney was the man here and he'd taken charge of things. She could only pray he was as much in control as he seemed to think he was, that his planning was as tight as he said it was, that the people he was dealing with could be relied upon.

'There's no harm done,' Terence concluded eventually. 'In fact Miss Harte's presence could be all to the good.' He brought his closed fist down on his knee for emphasis. 'It will look better, the two of you going with the lads. Christmas Eve bringing the world together in prayer.' He chortled, a gravelly sound deep in his throat. 'It goes without saying that I don't want you to say a word about anything to Miss Harte. She doesn't need to know.' He fixed her with a stern eye. 'We work, always, on a need-to-know basis. It's the only way.'

'Okay,' Honor agreed. 'I've no argument with that.'

Nor had she. She couldn't, in any event and not even to save her life, have told Gretta what was going on. Also, she had a deep certainty that her friend would disagree on principle with either of the Raeders fleeing the country and its justice.

Gretta Harte was different from Terence Delaney in one respect: she didn't share his anarchic streak.

'There are a couple more things.' Honor spoke quickly when Terence showed signs of getting out of his armchair. 'Gretta is going to know afterwards that there was something

271

afoot all along. There'll be the commotion in the church, then the police search when they're found missing, then the questions . . .' She hesitated. 'She'll know then it was all planned.'

'She will indeed, since we're agreed she's no fool. But she'll have no information to give anyone who questions her because she'll have been told nothing. Am I right?'

'I won't tell her anything,' Honor said tartly, 'but I can only hope the people you've involved can be trusted . . .'

'Each one of them knows only as much as he needs to know,' Terence repeated, 'and in any event, money talks. Not a man among them gets a penny until the job's oxo.'

'You're *paying* them all?' Honor stared at him.

'Did you think they're doing it for love, like you?' Terence was impatient. 'Or even some sort of belief? By God, but you've got a lot of growing up to do, Miss Cusack. It's only a fool or a romantic helps another without payment these days.'

'Which are you then?' she said.

'I'm not romantic,' Terence growled, 'that much is certain.' He began easing himself out of the chair. The dog got up too, just as slowly. 'I was making a pot of soup when you arrived,' he said, 'I'll carry on with it; they'll be glad of something hot when they get here.' He straightened up, shaking a forefinger at her. 'The body must be kept nourished. Nothing is possible if the body is not fit and well.'

# 25

'The German Army . . . has been sorely depleted by its
losses in Poland, Czechoslovakia, Hungary and Italy . . .'

*Irish Times*, December 1944

There were dark depressions under Oscar's eyes, perfect
half-moons which made it look as if he'd been in a fight.
Or hadn't slept for a week.

'I've had too much time to think about this thing. The
chances of its not working out are high, the risks to others
unfair . . .'

'Are you for abandoning our plans then?' Terence stopped
in the middle of the garden path. 'Because if that's the case,
you'd better speak up and be quick.'

'No point.' Oscar tightened his hold on Honor's hand.
'Stefan's going ahead, alone or with me it doesn't matter to
him. I've wasted endless time trying to talk him out of it. My own
thinking is that there's a better chance of his getting away if I go
with him, or that hopefully I can save his skin if we're caught.'

'You could be right,' Terence walked on, slowly, 'but it's
your own skin you should be concerning yourself with. I've
been talking to an acquaintance about your prospects. Seems
it won't be easy for the government to get you back here for
trial without a firmer case than they have at present. To
get you back they'd obliged to carry out a more thorough
investigation. While if you stay . . .' he gave a derisive snort

'. . . you'll be an easy scapegoat, someone to punish for the sins of the losing side. Bully boys, all of them. If the Germans had won they wouldn't be so quick to condemn. Then again,' he beat a low branch out of their way with his stick, 'the world would be in a bad way if they'd won.'

'War's not over yet,' Honor reminded him, tiredly.

'It is in all but name,' Terence said.

It was seven o'clock, inky dark with a scattering of stars, the ground underfoot crunchy and frost-bitten. Seasonal and peaceful enough to have enticed Honor and Oscar into the icy garden for a hopefully private, if not intimate, breath of air. That hope had died with the stomp of Terence's hobnails following them out. He stopped at the end of the garden and turned to look back at the house where a stiff, square-shouldered Stefan stood watching them from an upstairs window. He'd turned the light on, making sure they saw him.

Stefan hadn't left Oscar's side since the car had delivered them from the Curragh, five hours late. He'd followed his brother from room to room and stood within earshot of any attempted conversation with Honor. Getting him to stay in the house while they took a walk in the garden had taken some blunt speaking which Terence, who must have heard it, chose to believe didn't apply to him too.

He'd already closed Honor out of the kitchen while giving the brothers instructions for the night's escape plan and wasn't going to risk Oscar telling her more than she needed to know.

'That lad's a bit of a worry,' the old man said. 'Hasn't let you out of his sight since arriving.'

'True.' Oscar looked up at his brother, who stood motionless. 'He slept in my hut the last two nights, or paced the nights away to be more accurate, and that's my bedroom he's in now. He's losing his nerve. Either that or he's already lost it. But he won't face the fact and he won't back away from what we've planned.'

'He'll be a liability,' Terence warned. 'There may come a time when you'll have to go on without him. To leave him behind.'

'I'm going so as to with him if things become difficult,' Oscar said, and began walking back to the house.

Honor, her hand still tightly held in his, felt her heart do a peculiar, fear-induced somersault. By the time it had steadied itself again they were in the kitchen.

'This is all happening very fast and we're not going to have any time together,' she murmured.

'Not tonight anyway,' he agreed.

They stood very still, not touching and not speaking, the chasm between them filled with hope and wordless terrors. The frosty moonlight through the window lifted the planes of Honor's face and lent a sparkle to her tears when they fell, slowly.

'Don't, please.' Oscar held her face in his hands and brushed away the tears with his thumbs. 'Don't cry for me, Honor, please. Nor for us.'

'I can do anything but that,' she said, 'anything but that.'

'I *will* be back . . .'

'No, I'll come to you. Immediately it's over. The very day it ends.'

Terence's boots crossed the threshold as they kissed. It became a long, silent touch, not desperate exactly but full of things useless to say. All the time they held each other carefully, cherishing the warm familiarity of bodies that had loved. All the time Terence hovered.

Honor had decided against calling to the cottage to tell Gretta about the changes to their arrangement. Gretta Harte, with time to think, would have too many questions to ask. Might even find some answers to them herself.

She arrived at five minutes to ten. Honor told her they would all be going together to Ringsend Church as she was shaking Stefan's hand.

'All of us?' She smiled, eyebrows disappearing under the rim of the navy blue beret Honor had given her for Christmas. 'You too, Mr Delaney? The Lord loves the Prodigal, they say.'

She didn't add that the Catholic church was notoriously unwelcoming of its Protestant brethren, nor ask for an explanation of why the Raeder brothers weren't visiting St Matthew's in Ringsend, which was of their denomination. She stood waiting while Oscar gave her the explanation she wanted.

'The only Prodigals going along tonight will be my brother and myself,' he said. 'We have always honoured our Irish grandmother's faith at Christmas.'

Gretta looked at him for a minute before answering. 'That was nice of you,' she said, 'and it's a good thing to keep up family traditions.'

'We'll have a Christmas drink together first.' Honor stood over the silver tray on which she'd placed six glasses, the extra one for the guard standing inside the door who would be driving them to the church. 'Then we'll be off.'

She poured the whiskey carefully, less into Stefan's glass than anyone else's, more into Gretta's to soften her bite. The guard, whose name was Nolan, was easily persuaded. They drank to the year ahead, to peace and the end of war.

'Why are we going to Ringsend church?' Gretta said in the small silence which followed. 'I thought we'd agreed on St Mary's? It's closer.'

'Our grandmother often spoke of Ringsend, and of the church there,' Oscar lied with apparent ease. 'We would like to go there, if that's all right with you?'

'We'll be driven,' Honor said, and stopped. Best not to

276

overdo it. Too much chatter and Gretta would smell a rat.

If she hadn't already.

The church was crowded when they got there with people still arriving, a good quarter of them drunk, good-naturedly pushing and shoving a way inside, most hoping for a seat in a pew or, the very least, a wall to lean against. Or a pillar. Hundreds of candles made for a flickering, shadowy light and added to the warm swell of body heat. An organ hummed.

Guard Nolan went into the church with them, making light of his presence, saying he 'needed to get Mass anyway'. A second and third guard took up positions outside, on either side of the gates. One, who had been waiting when they got there, touched his hat and wished them a Happy Christmas when they passed.

Honor squeezed Oscar's hand to get his attention as they moved in a closely pressed group through the open doors and into the back of the church.

'Stefan's too tall,' she mouthed softly when he turned to look at her, 'he's head and shoulders above everyone else.'

'He'll have noticed that,' Oscar smiled. 'He'll know what to do . . .' He stopped when Gretta, on the other side of Honor, looked at them with a quick, sympathetic smile.

'You've a better chance of finding a seat together up along the side of the church,' she whispered. 'Follow me.'

'We'd best stay together, here at the back,' Honor said quickly. 'Guard Nolan would prefer it that way.'

'I'm easy.' Guard Nolan, without appearing to listen, heard her. 'I'll stand here, at the end row, and ye can forage a way to a pew.'

If they did that they would have to pass him to get out and he would, literally, be standing over them for the duration of the ceremony. Guard Nolan was neither so easygoing nor so credulous as he seemed.

'For me, this is far enough.' Stefan leaned apparently idly against a pillar. 'Any further and I would feel myself altogether too smothered in the Papish embrace.' He smiled. 'I prefer to remain a little distant.'

It was the first time Honor had seen him smile. An odd, truncated movement of the mouth, it disappeared as quickly as it appeared. She felt a rush of sympathy, and touched his hand.

'We're all staying here,' she said.

Taped to the pillar was a listing of the evenings and times of an upcoming novena to St Jude.

'You can feel quite safe wherever you choose to plant yourself.' Gretta, with a sharp look at Stefan, spoke in a hissing whisper. 'There's no one here going to break their neck signing you up for church membership.' She adjusted the beret with a quick, angry movement. 'This is a flawed country but at least it's a free one.' She blessed herself quickly, moved her lips in a silently muttered prayer before adding aloud: 'We'll stay here then, if it'll keep you happy.'

Stefan, arms folded and looking with vague curiosity round the church, ignored her.

'My brother didn't mean . . .' Oscar, attempting to mollify her, was stopped dead when Gretta put a finger to her lips.

'The priest's on the altar,' she said, 'it's customary to respect him with silence and attention.'

The congregation rose to its feet before falling to its knees as the priest ascended the altar and choir and congregation broke into a fast and lusty rendering of *Adeste Fidelis*. Honor, the habit of a lifetime impossible to resist, joined in.

They were on the second verse when Oscar, leaning close to her ear and with head bent, began to sing quietly in German. They sang together, softly. Once, when she cast a quick sideways glance his way, Oscar seemed to her very young, lonely and foreign.

A few heads turned. Guard Nolan, his hat clutched against his chest, cleared his throat and touched Oscar on the shoulder.

'It might be best not to attract too much attention,' he said.

'I agree,' Stefan said, frowning.

The sermon, when it came, was on Christ's forgiveness, the celebrant's voice echoing through the shadows and rising, just about, above the coughs and whispers and creaks of the old wood pews.

'. . . Christ forgave his enemies, those who trespassed against him,' he reminded the congregation, 'and I would ask you to reflect on this tonight and tomorrow and in the days and months to come. There will be much to forgive in the year ahead. On this Christmas Eve above all others, my dear people, with the end of the war in Europe in sight, I give you the words of the Bible to dwell upon, the wisdom which tells us that the leopard shall lie down with the kid; and the calf and the young lion and the fatling together; and a little child shall lead them.'

Honor and Gretta were the only women in the male stronghold to the back of the church. It was as Terence had said it would be, as Honor had known it would be: the favoured location for those dropping in after the pub to do their 'Christian duty' and aiming for a quick exit.

At the Consecration, when the priest turned to raise the monstrance and the congregation bowed its head in shuffling, murmuring prayer, Honor searched for her likely assailant among the lowered faces around her. It could have been any of them.

'I'm sorry,' Oscar said softly, 'for involving you. For having to leave you.'

She held his hand tightly and nodded. She couldn't speak. She hadn't even noticed the man standing next to Gretta.

He was barrel-chested and short, a cap in his hand and pate bald and shiny enough to reflect the candlelight. His nose had the flattened ridge of many breaks, his blood-shot eyes full of an anger waiting to be incited. She couldn't understand, afterwards, how she'd missed him. Not that it would have made any difference.

She couldn't have, and didn't, see his nose and eyes anyway until he raised his head and went to work on the job Terence Delaney had paid him to do. Or at any rate got down to his understanding of what he'd been told to do.

Without either turning or looking at Gretta he brought his shoulder up and rammed it into her arm. She gave a small cry and tottered sideways, clutching at Honor for support. She was still clutching Honor when his next move, still with his shoulder but followed by a meaty hand on her back, propelled her forward. Her shocked scream was cut short by the sickening collision of forehead against stone pillar.

Honor screamed, 'What the fuck did you do that for?'

Supporting a collapsing, bleeding Gretta, Honor heard the man's snarl above the general commotion and clamour of concern, saw in a blur its owner clamp a hand on the small man's shoulder, saw the small man turn and grunt and lunge, head first, at the owner of the hand.

The rest was pandemonium.

Honor, half carrying Gretta, shrieking at the crowd to keep back and make way, pushed for the door. Other hands helped her, lifting Gretta's feet and clearing a way out and into the blessed sharp cold of the night air.

The Mass had come to a halt, the priest calling for calm 'in the name of the good God and Mary His mother'. The choir, at his signal, began a bouncing rendition of *Away In a Manger*.

Honor, for the rest of her life, would hear the hymn and shudder, remembering and seeing again Gretta's head in her lap, her terrifying stillness as blood from the wound on her forehead ran in grotesque patterns into her hair and down one side of her chalk-white face.

'The doctor's coming,' a woman said and knelt beside them, rosary beads in her hands. 'Is she . . . ?'

'She's not dead,' Honor said thankfully.

The wound was reasonably superficial: the beret had acted as a buffer and lessened her impact with the pillar. An excess of blood was to be expected in a wound of this nature, with the edges gaping the way they were. An X-ray would be needed but with luck, concussion should be the biggest problem.

'Pray for her,' Honor said to the woman.

'There's an ambulance on its way.' Guard Nolan hunkered down and put a blanket over Gretta. He was ashen.

Oscar was gone. Honor had felt him leave her side immediately the bald man moved and been aware of a wrenching pain in her chest, a desolation so physical it must surely have torn at her heart muscle and tissue and everything else in her chest cavity too.

When she could breathe again, half normally, she looked around. Stefan was gone also, his tall form nowhere to be seen.

A frosty moon shone, far too bright, on the streets and roads leading to the river and sea.

# 26

'. . . our Führer, Adolf Hitler, has fallen this afternoon at
his command post . . . fighting to the last breath . . .'

German Radio, 1 May 1945

G ood weather towards the end of spring brought cyclists
out in great numbers and highlighted the lack of space
in the bicycle shed. With not enough room for the extra bikes
retrieving one at the end of the day became a marathon, a
fraught battle with unwieldy steel.

Honor, attempting to free her own from behind a pyramid
of at least six others, lost patience and kicked at the one
nearest.

'Damn you and damn all bikes and damn this shed to
hell . . .' She gave it a second kick and stood back, leaning
against the wall, counting to ten, then to twenty. By the time
she'd added another ten and got to thirty she'd made up her
mind to give the owners five minutes to retrieve their bikes
before beginning a serious assault.

'Patience is, and always was, a virtue,' the voice in her
ear said. 'But if you were to compose yourself and be nice
to me, I might be tempted to get the bike out of there
for you.'

'Don't patronise me, Bernard.' She didn't open her eyes.
'I'm not in the mood.'

'Your mood's fairly obvious,' Bernard Corkery said, 'but

that's nothing new.' He paused. 'I'll buy you a drink, if it'll help.'

'Thanks. It wouldn't.' Honor opened her eyes. 'But thanks again.'

He'd grown a beard during the months since Christmas. Luxuriant, a darker red than his hair, it suited him.

'A coffee then?'

'Thanks, but no. I'll just get my bike.'

They disentangled the piled bikes together, in silence. When hers came free Honor hung her satchel on the handlebars and began to wheel it away.

'How long are you going to go on like this?' Bernard fell into step beside her. 'It's not doing anyone any good, least of all yourself.'

'I know that,' Honor said.

'You haven't heard anything then?'

'No. I haven't heard.'

She'd lived through the five months since December suffering a recurrent nightmare. In it Oscar and his brother walked forever through a black and desolate winter along the wrecked German roads to Berlin. They walked alone, and silently. Their own people turned frozen, starved faces away when they came near; Allied forces pursued them with guns which shot bullets that never killed them. Oscar stopped, often, to look back. Stefan never once did.

'Maybe now I will,' Honor added, 'now that the war's over.' She shrugged. 'Maybe I'll go to Germany myself, now the war's over.'

'The Red Cross is looking for doctors and nurses from all over the country to make up a team to go to Germany,' Bernard said.

'So I heard. But I heard too that they've had more than two hundred applications. Far more than they need.'

At the Lesson Street intersection they stopped on the

283

footpath, waiting for a tram to pass. It was six o'clock, the air still warm and the sky cloudless. Honor's lectures had ended at four and she'd been in the library since then. Bernard's working day had ended at five. She was aware he'd waited for her.

He'd been a loyal and friendly source of news and support until early-April. Since then, with no word of either Oscar or Stefan, with Cologne and other captured cities in blazing ruin and the German leader ordering their useless, last-ditch defence, he'd been seeking out her company on a more personal basis. She couldn't encourage him.

'I'm thinking of going to Germany anyway, on my own, later, when I finish my exams. I'll wait until then to hear from him. It's my line in the sand. Maybe he's a POW, or in hospital, injured, using another name. Going as part of a Red Cross team might hinder my search,' Honor said.

They stood watching the tram pass. Transformed by the summer weather, the passengers wore summer frocks and shirts and smiling faces. Those on the top, open deck were laughing loud enough to be heard above the rattle and clatter along the tracks.

'Being with the Red Cross would restrict me,' Honor said, 'limit what searching I could do.'

'The Red Cross itself might find him for you,' Bernard pointed out.

'I don't see how they could, he'll have changed his name so it would have to be somebody who knew him in Dublin and could recognise him. That's if he's still alive.' She stopped. Her knuckles were white on the bars of the bike. 'You've got a sudden and great faith in the Red Cross, Bernard Corkery.' She raised sceptical eyebrows at her companion. 'My aunt is helping out in one of their gathering and distribution depots and says there's nothing but bitching and faction-fighting going on all day.'

'She's at the centre of the excitement herself,' he said. 'I've seen her a couple of times in Lincoln Place. She's not a lot of good at being a team player, our Grace, likes to take the lead.'

'I can imagine . . .' Honor smiled.

The tram had gone and they crossed the road.

'Thanks again.' Honor turned the bike for home when they got to the other side, 'I'd better be going.'

'I've something to tell you,' Bernard said.

'You have?' Warily.

'I can walk with you and talk or we can have that coffee?'

'We'll walk.'

Gretta was expecting her to call and Honor kept every promise, big or small, she made to her friend these days. Gretta had a scar on her forehead, not big but noticeable, that she would carry to the end of her days. She claimed the scarring of her betrayed trust in Honor went far deeper.

'I'll wheel the bike for you,' Bernard said as they walked on, up Leeson Street, avoiding the homeward-going crowds by sticking to the outside of the footpath.

'I'll wheel it myself,' Honor said, adding a 'thanks anyway' to lessen the impatience in her voice.

They walked in silence for a while with Bernard, head down and hands in the pockets of his cord trousers, savagely kicking at loose stones in his way. They were crossing Leeson Street bridge, and his boot had just sent a stone spinning in front of the bike, when Honor said, 'What is it then?' and looked sideways at him. He'd stopped and was looking down along the canal. He didn't hear her. 'What did you want to tell me, Bernard?' She shook his arm, gently. 'Bernard?'

'You're right to say that I'm interested in the Red Cross.' He went on looking down the canal. 'A matter of *self*-interest, you might say.'

He stopped talking. A couple of stately swans sailed from under the bridge and on down the canal, one behind the other.

'The Red Cross,' Honor said. 'That's it then? You're going with them to Germany?'

An odd sinking feeling in her chest surprised her. When she tried to put a name on it, so as to pin it down, the only word that came to mind was bereft. She would be bereft without him. Bereft of what she wasn't prepared to think about.

'Close,' he said, 'but not quite. Can we walk by the canal? It'll only take you a small bit out of your way.'

'It's on my way, as it happens.' Honor turned her front wheel toward the towpath. 'I'm calling on Gretta on the way home.' She was also delaying the hour of her arrival in Clyde Road.

Delia Gibbons' baby boy was two weeks old and colicky. He cried for large parts of the night, and a great deal of the day too. Delia's solution was to walk with him in her arms throughout the house, cooing and coaxing and extolling his wonders. This worked, intermittently, but was hard on the nervous systems of those around. Grace had taken to locking the drawing-room door and turning up the radio.

He was a beautiful, dark-eyed baby who had been given the name Clyde by his proud parents. 'After the road where he's to grow up,' Ernie said, 'as we promised.'

Honor rarely called on Lavinia Sayers these days, except to make sure she was well and had all she needed. Lavinia's betrayal of the escape plan to the police, who'd excused their Christmas Eve laxity by explaining they'd been expecting and prepared for the Raeder brothers to escape on Christmas Day, had created a rift between them.

Unlike Gretta, who was prepared to forgive if not forget how she'd been betrayed, Honor was not about to be mollified or won round by the old woman. She no longer trusted her.

She was also, since the betrayal, half-afraid of Lavinia and the underground world of dark confidences she'd created around herself.

Honor gave the bike to Bernard when they reached the towpath. He seemed to need something to cling to; maybe clutching the handlebars would make it easier for him to say whatever it was he had to tell her.

The trees along the canal banks, only recently exploded into pale green leaf, allowed dappled sunlight on to the water. Ahead of them, as they walked, the swans continued their imperial way along the centre of the canal.

'Well?' Honor was gentler.

'I'm leaving the university. I'm fed up with everything here so I'm clearing off, out of it altogether. I'm going to France, to start with anyway.'

He stopped and Honor, with sharp impatience, said, 'Go *on*, Bernard.' The bereft feeling grew stronger.

'You were too preoccupied towards the end of last year to remember much about an earlier Red Cross recruitment campaign.' Bernard had become businesslike, pushing the bike faster than before. 'It was for medical staff, nurses and doctors, to work in a hospital to be set up in a small Normandy town by the name of Saint-Lô. The place was almost bombed out of existence by the Allies trying to get the occupying Germans out of it. I applied but they wouldn't take me.' He shrugged. 'Not qualified enough.'

He skirted another couple of pedestrians with the bike and increased the length of his stride. Honor, running to catch up with him, asked him to slow down. When he didn't she trotted alongside. There were times when a person just couldn't hear.

'Well, I thought to hell with that,' he went on, 'and went another way about it. Brunt of it is, I'm to drive a couple of lorry loads of supplies over to Saint-Lô, delivering preliminary equipment for the setting up of the hospital. The bulk of the rest will go in August. I'll just make the two trips but at least it'll give me a chance to see the lie of the land, so to speak.

Then I'll pack my bags and be gone for good. There's nothing left for me in this Godforsaken hole, I'll be glad to see the last of it. I'm going to be part of the new world being built across Europe and in America.'

'I'm sorry I couldn't be more fond of you,' Honor said impulsively. Fondness was all he'd ever asked for, never love.

'You couldn't help it.' He stopped walking and turned to her. Buried in the beard there was a definite smile. 'Any more than you could help yourself falling for Oscar Raeder. I'd find him for you, if I knew where to look. I'd like to see you happy, Honor. For old times' sake.' He paused. 'For your own sake.' He touched her hair, lightly. 'Maybe we're alike, the pair of us. In one way at least, without knowing it. Maybe we both want what we half-know we can never have.'

'I thought I could have Oscar.'

'But you helped him get away.'

'Yes. Because I thought it would ensure we could be together, eventually.'

'Did you really think that?'

'Yes, I really did.'

'Well then, maybe it'll happen,' he said. 'If it's what you want.'

'It is.'

## 27

'The dead are piled up so thickly in some parts of Berlin that they may have to be buried in mass graves.'

*Reuters*, May 1945

The weather continued fine. The city was transformed, consumed by a latinate air that consigned the long winter, and longer still period of sitting out the war, to the distant past. The new growth all around was encouraging too, blossom everywhere and, along Clyde Road, leafy trees sighing in warm breezes.

It was altogether so pleasant that Grace got the deckchairs out and served a cold meat and salad buffet in the garden three weeks later. It was the first Friday in June.

'We need cheering up,' she announced, which was true, 'and the garden's putting on such a glorious show we've a duty to enjoy it.'

The garden was in danger of taking over the house. The rhododendrons which had once bordered the end wall had taken magnificently to neglect and now reached halfway up the garden. The hydrangeas had been similarly encouraged and mingled their blue and white with the rhododendrons' purple.

Grace spread the deckchairs in a circle on the grassy patch remaining between the kitchen door and encroaching jungle. For Lavinia she put out a straight-backed armchair; her increasing frailty made lounging impossible for the older woman. The food was laid out on a makeshift velveteen-covered table in the centre, the wine and other drinks in a box beside Grace's own deckchair. To keep it from toppling over and spilling into the grass, she said.

Everyone, including Lavinia herself, knew the real reason was to stop the old woman helping herself to more than was good for her. She'd twice recently fallen off her chair at the table and had to be carried downstairs. She was no lightweight and Ernie had complained bitterly of his back after the more recent episode.

Florrie had brought along a brand new gramophone player to replace the old EMG with its horn. He'd sold a painting, he said. The fact that no one even pretended to believe him, Grace openly and dryly wondering if she should check the silver, was part of a sea-change in the gathering. A lightness had gone, and a sense of fun. Familiarity had bred contempt and the game was coming to an end.

The gramophone was streamlined, with a silver arm, and they were listening to a Count John McCormack record supplied by Ernie Gibbons. He was singing '*Oft in the Stilly Night*'.

'You'd miss Lord Haw Haw,' Grace said. She was wearing a white linen hat trimmed with artificial grapes.

'You would indeed.' Ernie was solemn. 'The man had a point of view not often enough expressed. He wasn't taken in by the propaganda about why the Yanks were put into Northern Ireland. No, siree, not William Joyce.'

'Some of us don't miss him at all,' Lavinia said. 'Perhaps because we were never taken in by him or his vile propaganda.'

She had aged over the winter; withered the way a hydrangea does, Honor thought, with the grand outline still there but the skin thin and crumpled as charred paper. She wore black all the time now too, always with jewellery. It further emphasised how faded she'd become.

'One listened without necessarily being in agreement,'

Grace said, 'simply to inform oneself. He could be very amusing, unintentionally of course, and his performances will be remembered . . .'

'Indeed they will,' Lavinia, cutting her short, shouted loudly, 'for his lunatic treachery!' Her outbursts of temper had become more frequent. Often more unpleasant too.

'Please, let us have peace among ourselves.' Florrie yawned. 'I'm too exhausted for all this principled agonising. Joyce will be tried for treason and hung and that'll be the end of him. A very fine ham, this.' He displayed a pinky-blue slice of meat on the prongs of his fork. 'You're to be congratulated, Grace, for your insistence on only the best.'

'Which is why I continue to have you as a guest, my dear Florrie.' She smiled tiredly. 'Only the best in all things, including dinner guests.'

Hers was a brave face for an occasion which had lost its sparkle since December, when the police enquiry into the disappearance of Oscar Raeder and his brother had aborted Christmas Day's dinner.

The brothers' complete disappearance had convinced the police they'd escaped by boat but they'd persisted with their inquiries for months, agitated both by the escape itself and the misleading tip-off giving false information about the timing of the escape plan. Honor hadn't been accused, directly. No one had. But the sulphurous odour of unease and betrayal settled slowly over them and refused to go away.

Grace and Honor filled the plates and handed them around. Lennox poured the wine he'd brought with him; it was harder to get than before but he could still be relied upon. It was just eight o'clock.

'Is this dinner you've served?' Lavinia, looking at her plate, was acid-tongued. She waved a black lace Spanish fan vigorously in front of her face.

'Oh, shut up, Mrs Sayers.' Honor was weary and abrupt. Lavinia folded back into her armchair and was quiet.

'I've asked Bernard Corkery to join us,' Honor said. 'I told him eight o'clock but he'll be late. He's late for everything . . .'

'You've invited Bernard?' Grace interrupted. 'Why would you do that? It must be . . .' she paused, thinking '. . . a good two months since he called and you weren't what I'd call encouraging then. He's not unwelcome, of course, but it's not exactly typical of you to ask him.'

'He's got some news might interest you.' Honor looked around the table. 'Might interest you all.'

'It will be a change to have him actually speak to me.' Her aunt sniffed. 'We met once or twice when I was working with the Red Cross people. He'd hardly a word to say to me then.' She flapped at a hovering fly with her napkin. 'Of course, he got on with the people there better than I. They weren't my type of person at all. Bureaucratic and self-righteous, the lot of them, quite unable to take advice.' She looked at Honor. 'I must admit I was surprised to see Bernard there.'

She stopped, waiting to be told his business with the Red Cross.

'He'll be here shortly,' was all Honor said.

John McCormack finished singing and bird song filled the silence from somewhere in the middle of the rhododendrons. Algernon skulked on his belly under the leaves. Delia got to her feet.

'Clyde is far too quiet,' she said, 'I'll go inside see how he is.'

'You could bring him outside now,' Ernie said, 'the worst of the day's heat is gone from the sun. He'd be safe enough outside at this hour.'

'Best to leave a sleeping child lie,' Lennox said.

'I'm not sure he's actually sleeping . . .' Delia began.

'Then he should be,' Lennox said. 'It's my view he doesn't

get half enough sleep for his age.' He was wearing a straw boater and off-white suit, and raised his head to gaze at Delia from under its brim. 'A child's brain grows while it sleeps. Medical evidence is clear. You do not, surely, want to be responsible for retarding his mental development?'

'I don't want to be responsible for harm coming to him through neglect,' Delia snapped, 'and if you don't want the bother of him here you should be the one to go inside.'

'I was trying to be helpful,' Lennox protested.

'I understand how Mrs Gibbons feels,' Lavinia said, dreamily. 'I used to fret terrible when Douglas was out of my sight, and silent. Being a mother is never easy. She and I can vouch for that, can't we, Mrs Gibbons?'

Delia stared at her. 'Yes, I suppose we can agree on that much.' She turned to Grace who had crossed her legs and put down her meal, unfinished, on the grass. 'I'll wheel him out here in his bassinette, Mrs Sayers, if that's all right?' she said. 'I'd feel much better if he was beside me.'

'Motherhood certainly must not in any way be maligned.' Grace's face, under the linen hat, had flushed during Lavinia's intervention. 'Please bring your son out to join us.'

The bird sang on, joined by several others, as Delia went through the French windows and into the house. Algernon had disappeared but Walter jumped on to his owner's lap. He stared straight ahead while Lavinia stroked him, her rings loose and tapping against one another on her newly thinned fingers. It wasn't yet nine o'clock. There was a lot of the evening to be got through yet.

'Should I keep a meal for Bernard?' Grace was casual. 'What time did he say he would join us?'

'As soon as he could,' Honor said, 'he's a bit tied up.'

'I always thought him a pleasant young man,' Lavinia said, 'and without guile. A man without guile is worth ten of the other kind.' She turned to Honor, her hand on the cat's back becoming quite still. 'That's a piece of wisdom you should take to heart, my dear.'

'Thank you, Mrs Sayers, I'll do that,' Honor said. 'I'll go even better and ensure my women friends too are without guile. Now, if you'll excuse me, there's someone knocking on the front door.'

She walked without hurrying through the kitchen and along the hallway to the front door. Looking around as she went she almost felt nostalgia for the old place. Soon she would be gone from here. Soon. Soon.

She would be sorry to leave Grace to Lavinia's whims and poisonous ways. Since the old woman's betrayal of Oscar and Stefan she'd had a sickening sense that nothing was as she'd thought it was. She'd believed in Lavinia, thought theirs was a special friendship. But she was certain the old woman had told the police, got a note to them somehow, about the Christmas Day plan. She denied it, of course, but Honor wasn't a complete fool and Lavinia had been the only person, apart from herself, who'd believed the escape was going to happen on Christmas Day.

Thank God for Terence, his guerrilla training, his caution. If the original plan had been the real one and had gone ahead, Oscar and his brother would be in prison now. So would Terence and, very likely, Honor herself.

As it was, and no thanks to Lavinia, they'd escaped. To God alone knows where or what.

Bernard was wearing a brown sports jacket with leather buttons. Otherwise he was the same as always, except for a suspicious and faint whiff of what might have been *eau de cologne*.

'Thanks for coming,' Honor said.

'The things I have to do to get a smile from you.' He touched her cheek.

'You'll get something to eat too, if you play your cards right.' Honor led the way down the hall.

In the kitchen, before they stepped through the door and into the garden, she stopped.

'You haven't changed your mind?' she said. 'You're not going to do an about turn and take Grace's side? She'll be dead set against this thing.'

'Why would I do that? I don't want to do this but I said I would and, by Jesus, I'll keep my word. You know that, so why the hell are you . . .'

'Just afraid.' Honor put a hand on his arm. 'And trying to figure out who to trust, and worrying about guile . . .' she could see a puzzled anger growing in him and went on, hastily '. . . sorry, Bernard, I'm truly sorry. I should have known better.'

Baby Clyde Gibbons had decided to cry again. His mother was pacing with him in her arms, his father making pacifying, clucking sounds from his deckchair.

Bernard perched on the edge of the chair he was given and ate his food quickly and in silence.

'Eaten like a man who appreciates good food,' Florrie said when Bernard put down the plate.

'Like a hungry man, Florrie,' Bernard corrected. He got up and went to the table to help himself to brown bread and tomato. 'Like a very hungry man.'

'There's no shortage of anything here, thank God,' Grace joined him at the table, 'so help yourself. Would you like more potato salad? Or meat? I can get them from the kitchen.'

'I'm fine, thanks. That lot calmed the hunger nicely,' Bernard said, smiling. He gestured with his glass to Lennox, pouring a refill for himself. 'But I'll have another glass of wine, since you're offering.'

'Of course.' He checked the bottle's level. 'We need replenishments. Be back in a minute.'

'Thanks,' Bernard said, and then, half-apologetically, 'I seem to have developed a taste for the old grape over my time in France.'

'You were in France?' Grace said, adjusting her hat so that the grapes hung more jauntily to the side. 'That was . . . courageous of you, Bernard.'

Lennox had stopped, bottle in hand, to listen. Florrie, in need of a refill, rolled impatient eyes at the clear blue sky and sighed.

'Why was it courageous?' Bernard was blunt. 'France isn't the moon. Just the nearest bit of the wreckage that's the mainland of Europe. Could it be, Grace, that you don't expect the likes of me to travel beyond their own back yard?'

'You're so sensitive, darling Bernard.' Grace patted his arm and went smiling back to her deckchair. 'You always were.' She shook her head, sighing. 'I merely meant that, with all the truly terrible things which have happened to France over the last years, it must take a genuinely brave soul to go willingly into the bleak and desolate aftermath of war.'

Her delivery was slow, perfectly pitched, and sombre. When she stopped she kept her gaze gravely on Bernard. Honor almost expected a round of applause from Florrie and Lennox, Ernie too.

'There are quite a few of the brave souls you're talking about knocking around France at the moment,' Bernard said. 'Rescue and rehabilitation operations are getting under way. They've been in the planning stages for months, since it became clear which way the war was going to end.'

'You're very well informed,' Florrie said. 'Are we to understand that you've become part of these operations?'

'You could say that.' Bernard became suddenly cagey. 'I've been there and know what's involved,' he looked at Honor, 'and I'm going back.'

Grace saw the look.

Very slowly she unwound herself from her deckchair and stepped outside the seated circle. She stood with her back to the garden, the untamed growth a back-drop to the gold of her frock, the white linen of her hat. Lennox watched Grace. So did Florrie.

Ernie had one eye on her too when he said, 'Very fine and noble, I'm sure, but it's your own country you should be putting first, Mr Gibbons. We've sixty-two thousand men and eight thousand women unemployed. Our industrial production is down by thirty percent. Emigration is rising. There's plenty to be done here at home by the fit and able like yourself.'

'I don't doubt it, Mr Gibbons.' Bernard spoke evenly and formally, sitting forward with his hands on his knees. 'But my visit to France has given me an admiration for the endurance and courage of the French people. We've escaped the destruction, starvation and massacre suffered by the rest of Europe. It's time we looked beyond ourselves.'

'True,' Grace murmured.

'There's a man working as a storekeeper for the Red Cross in Lincoln Place,' Bernard went on. 'His name's Beckett and he's lived in France for years and intends going back there. He says he prefers France at war to Ireland at peace. I'd no idea what he was talking about until I went there.' He paused. 'There's no one looking over your shoulder, for one thing.'

'There's nothing wrong with this country!' Ernie Gibbons sounded shrill. 'We stuck to our guns when our backs were to the wall. We kept ourselves pure from a war between major powers wanting world domination.' His son's cries growing louder with fright, he raised his voice to a shout. 'The evil stories we're hearing of the carryings-on of the Nazi regime and extermination camps all had to do with a struggle that had nothing whatsoever to do with Ireland.'

'You're upsetting Clyde.' Delia had taken their son from his crib and was circling her deckchair with the baby over her shoulder. 'There's no point in this kind of argument any more, Ernie, people will think what they want anyway.'

She had grown plump, and her face flushed as the heels of her high-heeled shoes sank into the grass.

'Maybe Bernard has a girl in France.' She gave a sharp laugh. 'Nothing like wanting a woman to give a man principles.'

'When do you go back, Bernard?' Grace said quietly.

'The wrong side won!' Ernie cried. 'They're all shouting out about the camps, places like Auschwitz and Belsen. But what about Dresden and Cologne? Weren't the horrors done to those cities by Allied bombs equal to anything Germany did as part of its battle?'

'Be quiet, Ernie,' Grace said, 'Bernard has something to tell us.' She was standing absolutely still.

'Newsreel films of Belsen are nothing but propaganda.' Ernie was out of his seat now, fist in the air. 'All faked up by the British. I have it on good authority that the people we see in those films are nothing but starving Indians . . .'

'Be QUIET, Ernie,' Grace shouted. 'Or if you cannot do so then leave my garden. Immediately. You're nothing but a fool and a nuisance.'

Ernie Gibbons stood and rearranged the knife-edge crease in his trousers before he said with cold precision to Delia, 'Come! There is no place for us here.'

'Go on your own.' Delia didn't look at him. 'You brought it on yourself.'

Ernie turned on his heel and disappeared into the house through the French windows. His son whimpered on his mother's shoulder.

'The floor is yours, Bernard.' Grace spread her arms wide. 'Please speak to us.'

Bernard studied his empty glass and glanced at Lennox. When the latter made no move to get more wine he shifted in his deckchair and began.

'I took a lorry load of supplies to Normandy, in northern France, for the Red Cross. There's a hospital being built there . . .'

'I heard about it months ago,' Grace interrupted, 'but no one said anything to me about supply lorries going there.'

'Things have moved on since you left Lincoln Place.' Bernard didn't look at her. 'The people on the ground in Normandy needed something to cook on, as well as refridgerators, bedding, that sort of thing. Someone had to take it there.' He looked straight at Honor. 'The town of Saint-Lô, where the hospital will be, has been flattened into the earth. Bombing has left nothing but rubble and created a diseased, rotting landscape across which are scattered wooden huts in which the people who are left and those who have returned live, and in which, even now, some go on dying as a result of the war. Others live in the cellars of their bombed houses, under the rubble, with rats for company. We live in a paradise by comparison.'

'We've had our share of suffering in Ireland too,' Grace put in.

'I agree,' Bernard said, 'and I agree there's work to be done here. But by others, not me.' He looked at his silent listeners. 'In Saint-Lô, and the other parts of France I passed through, there is a pulling together by the people, a driven determination to rebuild. I will be staying there to help in any way I can. You could say that in deciding to look beyond my country, I've learned to look beyond myself.'

'Very profound,' Lennox put in, 'very profound indeed, Mr Corkery.' He clapped his hands, twice and slowly, a half-smile on his face. 'But is this what you came to tell us? You wished to unburden yourself of your sudden philosophical turn of mind?'

'I last drove into Saint-Lô in the early-evening.' Bernard looked at Lennox as he went on. 'The light was fading and lines of men walking along the road stopped to let me pass. I slowed down to ask for directions to where the hospital was being built. The men were German POWs and had just come from there. They were helping to build it. I turned the lorry and went back towards the hospital.'

He turned his gaze on Grace.

'A couple of hours later I was taking the air, and a smoke, after unloading the lorry when one of the men I'd passed on the road approached me. I didn't recognise him at first, in the dark and with his hair cut short. But when he spoke I cottoned on to him fast enough.' Bernard cleared his throat. 'Dr Oscar Raeder is alive and well and helping to build the Irish Hospital in Saint-Lô.'

In the still silence Clyde gave a snuffle or two against his mother's neck and was quiet. Delia, sitting down carefully in her deckchair, kept her eyes on Honor's face and murmured 'sorry' when she moved and the canvas gave a protesting creak. A car backfiring somewhere in the neighbourhood was like a cannon shot.

'He's being held as a POW,' Bernard explained.

'Well, well, I'm not one bit surprised.' Lennox shook his fine head and turned to Honor. 'Your Dr Raeder had an air of great resilience about him. I told you, my dear, that your adventure wasn't over, did I not?'

'You were very reassuring,' Honor agreed.

'Reassuring my arse!' Florrie gave a snort. 'Deluding more like. You're not surprised, Lennox, because outside of being killed, Raeder's turning up a POW in Normandy was the most likely outcome of his gallop for home. Chances were high that he and his brother would be picked up once put ashore along that northern coastline.'

He got out of the deckchair with surprising agility for a man who'd earlier complained of exhaustion.

'I'll get you a brandy.' He put an arm about Grace, standing ashen and immobile with her hands to her face. 'A brandy's what you need.'

'Thank you, Florrie.' Grace's voice was steady, her face bravely smiling when she took away her hands. 'A brandy would be nice.' She kissed her fingertips and put them to his mouth. 'Only be quick, there's a darling.'

Honor wrapped her arms about her knees and leaned forward. 'I'm glad to see you're all as delighted as I am that Oscar's safe.'

'Don't play games, Honor, please,' her aunt said. She turned to Bernard. 'Tell us about his brother. What happened to Stefan?'

'Stefan is dead,' Honor answered for him. 'He tried to escape capture and was shot.'

'May the Lord have mercy on his soul,' Delia said.

'Amen,' Lennox added.

They were quiet while Florrie crossed the grass with a tray carrying the brandy bottle and glasses. No one said anything either while he poured a glass each for Grace, Lennox and himself. No one else wanted one.

'A hard thing for Oscar to bear,' Grace said.

'Hard, yes,' Bernard's voice was flat, 'but in a way useful too. He goes by his brother's name. He's a POW because he was captured in the company of a German army unit his brother had joined. When his brother was killed and it became clear that those captured were to be sent as POWs to Saint-Lô it made sense as a way of hiding himself until some sort of order is restored. He intends working then to prove himself innocent of the murders.'

'He must have been shocked to see you,' Delia was wide-eyed.

'Not really.' Bernard shrugged. 'He'd reckoned on someone who knew him arriving eventually, though he thought it would be later rather than sooner. There are a thousand German POWs working in Saint-Lô, any number of French, Italian and Algerians too. I'm the only person so far who's recognised him. Now all of you know who and where he is,' he looked slowly at the faces of his listeners, one after the other, 'and one or more of you may feel duty bound to inform the guards.'

Honor found their general, murmured dissent less than encouraging. She knew, on the other hand, that even if Grace or one of the others went to the police the complications were such that Oscar was likely to be left where he was for a while to come. What Grace and the others didn't know was that he'd already made contact with friends in Paris where legal manoeuvres had begun to get him back to Berlin. She had no intention of telling them that. Terence was right about it being better to operate on a need-to-know basis.

It was Florrie, surprisingly, who made the common-sense point.

'Don't see why any of us should involve ourselves further, child dear,' he smiled at Honor, bloodshot eyes steady, 'since it's only a matter of time before someone else exposes him. He's not going anywhere and will become a bone of contention once revealed. The Germans will want him for killing one of theirs. We'll want him for killing one of ours. Allegedly . . .' he held up his hands in surrender when Honor would have protested '. . . allegedly killing. Just putting the case, that's all. He'll be in Normandy for a while to come, is my guess, and his chances of getting home to Germany and his case sorted out are better there than here.'

'Bit of sound thinking behind that, Florrie.' Lennox gave

302

him a look of mock surprise. 'The old mind's not completely sozzled then.'

'No more than your own,' Florrie said, suddenly sour.

'Well, I think the good thing is that there's been nobody else killed since he left,' Delia said, 'we can all sleep safer in our beds.'

'You're a woman of astounding subtlety, Delia,' Lennox murmured.

She smiled at him. 'Thank you, Lennox.'

'Why didn't Oscar write?' Grace asked.

'I intend asking him that myself when I get to Saint-Lô,' Honor said.

# 28

Whatever you do, do cautiously, and
look to the end.

(Anon. Chronicle *Geta Romanorum*. cap. 103)

Daybreak over the French countryside was one of the
most beautiful Honor had ever seen, sailing as a slow,
dark gold into the indigo night sky and turning it palest blue.

The boat had berthed in the night at Cherbourg and she'd
driven with Bernard through the dark: her first ever sighting
of a French landscape was by the early light of dawn. The
sun, a bright gold and warm by seven o'clock, shone on an
endless sea of still fields and trees and occasional rivers. Wild
flowers, in their irrepressible way, shot beads of colour into
the browny green of it all.

Nothing moved.

It was a landscape struggling with ruin, fighting for renewal
against the overriding marks left by war. Broken, still malignant, the hulks of tanks littered fields gaping with bomb-
craters. Rusting guns and helmets lay in piles by the roadsides;
swathes of earth stretched razed and barren. Most desolate
of all was the sight of pulverised villages and farmhouses,
occasional walls and chimneys and even spires still standing.

'We've never known this,' Honor said.

'No,' Bernard agreed, 'only starvation and cruelty and
repression.'

'That's all,' Honor said. It was growing warm in the cab of the truck but the cratered, uneven road made sleep impossible. After a minute she added, 'Do you think we've learned anything? Do you think anyone has?'

'I'd like to think so but I'm not sure. No one wants another war, for now. Everyone's for peace and a life thereafter – but we'll see.'

'Yes,' Honor said quickly, not wanting him to go on, sorry she'd started a conversation she lacked the heart to pursue. After a while she added, 'I'm sure that's the way it is.' Too late. He didn't answer. He was easily put off intimate conversations these days.

She was tired. The sea had been rough for their crossing and she hadn't slept. She stared through the windscreen, forcing herself to concentrate on what she could see, not to anticipate the meeting with Oscar.

There was an old man ahead of them on the road. He was bare-headed and empty-handed, aimless-looking. Another ruin on the landscape.

'I'll see if he wants a lift.' Bernard pulled up alongside and called down to the man whose voice, calling back, was hoarse. When he spat on the lorry Bernard drove on.

'What did he say?' Honor said.

'No idea. But he preferred to walk.'

She would have asked Bernard to stop, let her get out and walk too, if she'd thought for a minute he would do it. She knew he wouldn't.

He'd been driving like a fiend, and cursing the inadequacies of the lorry, since they'd disembarked at Cherbourg at three o'clock. He was bringing her to Oscar because it was the right thing to do, not because he wanted to. He'd told her about meeting Oscar for the same reason. He wanted to get her to Saint-Lô and Oscar, have the deed over and done with, as quickly as possible.

Only now she was afraid. What had seemed imperative in Dublin, the thing she must do without question, was becoming more doubtful by the kilometre. What if Oscar hadn't written because he didn't want to? What if he just wanted to be free of Ireland and all that had happened there?

She needed time to think out an approach. During the long three days she'd waited for Bernard to be ready all she'd done was react. She'd burnt her boats and had no idea what she would do if Oscar didn't want her, if he'd changed. She'd waited until the last minute before writing to tell him she would be arriving with Bernard. She hadn't wanted to give him time to write back telling her not to come.

'How much further?' she said as they drove through the rubble of another village.

'We'll be there in an hour or so,' Bernard said. 'Saint-Lô is bigger than this place, flatter too. More in the nature of a cemetery for the living dead.' His sideways glance caught her swallowing, the too-bright shine in her eyes. 'I'm sorry,' he said, 'this must be hard on you too.'

He pulled in to the side of the road, opposite a track leading through trees to a house with the beginnings of a new roof.

'Wait here,' he said and was gone, through the hedging and along the dirt-track to the front door. She could see him gesturing when it was opened, then going round the back with the owner. When he returned he had plums, pears and grapes in his pockets. They breakfasted sitting on the running board of the lorry.

'Resourceful people, the French,' Bernard said. 'I like them.'

'You seem to have picked up a good bit of the language.'

'I looked through a couple of books,' he said diffidently, 'I've been teaching myself.'

A couple of books. Teaching himself. She didn't know him at all, this determined man with his beard neatly trimmed and French canvas shoes on his feet.

'Dandy'll miss you,' she said.

'He will. I'll miss him too, mad bastard that he is. I'm thinking I'll move on to Paris. There's plenty of work there. He can visit me, bring the old mother along if he likes.' He paused. 'There's one or two people will miss you too.'

'Funny thing is,' Honor said thoughtfully, 'there are only one or two people I'll miss myself.'

She'd said goodbye to Gretta the night before leaving. To everyone else too but Grace, nevertheless, turned up at Alexandra Wharf to say a 'final farewell'. Lennox drove her, along with Delia. Florrie came too but Ernie was working on a 'crucial order' and couldn't take the time, Delia said. She'd left Clyde with Lavinia in the basement.

'She wasn't too pleased but she does nothing all day and I thought I'd be brave and give it a try,' Delia said. 'I weighed it up and decided seeing you off was too important to miss.' She smiled, waiting to be told she was a good girl.

'That was good of you,' Honor obliged.

'It's not too late to change your mind,' Grace said, brightly. 'You could jump in the car and come home with us and all will be forgotten in a week.' She was dressed in black, with a mantilla on her head.

'I'll write,' Honor told her.

'I've promised your aunt I'll arrange a trip to see you later in the year,' Lennox said. 'That's if you're still in France.'

'I'll write,' Honor said again. 'We may be in Berlin by then. But you could visit us there.'

'He's a wanted man,' her aunt persisted. 'You don't know where you'll be.'

'He's not guilty,' Honor said. 'The police file is still open, you know it is.' She hugged Grace and was surprised to find her shivering. 'Truth will out, Grace. You used say that to me when I was younger, and I believed you. You'll have to believe *me* now.'

Grace Sayers threw her arms around her niece and clung to her for several long minutes before letting her go.

'May God go with you, my lovely child, my Honor.'

Florrie moved forward and took Honor's hand. 'I'll look after your aunt,' he promised, 'she'll be all right.'

'Thank you, Florrie.' Honor looked at him gratefully. Grace would indeed be all right: Florrie and Lennox would battle beside her for years to come. She would miss her aunt, but not a lot.

Her mother had been more resigned. Faith Cusack had given Honor her string of pearls and her blessing to sell them if needs be.

'If you're not sure of him when you're there, then leave him,' she said. 'You'll be all right, Bernard will look out for you.'

Liam had refused to say goodbye. So had her grandmother. Looking back from the road, before turning her bike for the village, Honor had seen Mary Cusack's white head peering from behind her mother's dark brown one.

She would miss her mother.

She regretted saying goodbye to Lavinia. She'd waited until the last minute, aware of the old woman watching from the basement window as she came and went from the house, refusing to be drawn back into her web either by pity or by guilt.

'I think your going to France is a bad idea,' Lavinia said when Honor at last went to see her, 'it can only end in disaster.'

'Why should it?' she said. 'Now that he's out of Irish jurisdiction it will take a while to get him back, especially with the case against him not proven. We'll work together to prove his innocence. Oscar has always believed the key lies in Clemens Hauptmann's background, in whatever reason he had for coming to Ireland. He has lawyer friends in France and Germany who will help. Now he'll have me too.'

She stopped, realising she'd fallen into the old trap of talking too much to Lavinia. Not that she'd told her anything which was secret; Oscar, innocent and, looking into the background of the man he was supposed to have murdered, whose lover he was also supposed to have murdered, just made common sense.

It was more that Lavinia unnerved her, looking at her with that fixed stare, body rigid and hands blue-white against Walter's fur.

'You don't look well,' Honor said.

She looked terrible. Grace couldn't get her to see a doctor; she'd had Dr Lamb call once and Lavinia had hurled a plate at him. The drinking was about pain, in her mind as well as in her body. But there was nothing Honor could do for her now.

'You'd better go,' the old woman said, 'but remember, I tried to stop you. Remember you wouldn't listen. On your own head be whatever happens.'

Honor wouldn't miss Lavinia, not one bit.

By nine o'clock they were on the outskirts of Saint-Lô. The weighed-down lorry had taken six hours to cover one hundred and fifty miles.

Bernard had been right about the town having suffered greater destruction than most others. On first sight it seemed nothing but a vast, straggling field of rubble, piled as high as twenty feet in places, with pillars and the odd wall rising higher here and there. When they came closer Honor saw there were pathways, even roads, between the piles, that the pillars had once been chimney breasts, the walls all that remained of larger buildings.

People were out and about, most of them men pulling down what still stood and creating more and higher piles, carrying bricks in wheelbarrows.

Bernard lit a cigarette for each of them. 'Saint-Lô – or what's left of it.'

Honor opened the cab door and climbed down. A warm breeze blew dust about her feet and, when she stood leaning against the front of the lorry, she found herself inches deep in a soft, ashy-coloured clay. It was everywhere and covered everything, from the ground under her feet to the rubble people were making their way through. The air carried a vague, indefinable stench, as if a recent, unmentionable smell was slowly dying.

She pulled on the cigarette. 'It's very quiet,' she said, remembering Bernard's remark in the garden in Clyde Road about Saint-Lô being a cemetery with living ghosts.

'Gets livelier as the day goes on,' he said. 'The baker's back in business, using American flour. The train station's open, rail lines running from Paris, Cherbourg, Caen . . . other places too. Farmers have started to bring produce back into town. There's even a provisional Mayor and town council.'

'Town?' Honor echoed. 'Where do people live in this town?'

'In cellars. In makeshift shelters against anything that's left of the walls of their homes. In wooden huts. Some of them live with farming families outside the town who escaped the worst of it. Wherever they can.'

'Where am I to stay?'

'In converted outhouses in one of the farmhouses. I'll take you there after you've seen Oscar.' He grinned and gave a small shrug. 'I know you're secretly concerned about me, so you should know I've a place where I bunk down in the hospital stores.' He raised his hands as if fending her off. 'Just in case you need me, you'll know where I am.'

'I'll remember,' Honor gave a wry smile, 'though God knows you've done enough already.' She touched his arm and smiled. Then she asked, 'Where do the German POWs live?'

310

Bernard opened the cab door. 'I'll take you there now.'

It wasn't possible to drive through the town and it took half an hour's manoeuvring around the outskirts before they got to the long, low huts housing the more than a thousand German POWs. These had been constructed on a slope, the ground between them cleared of debris and levelled off. It was nothing at all like the Curragh camp.

The armed guards dotted around the perimeters outnumbered the prisoners who were visible.

'Most of the men have been taken off to whatever work they're doing by now,' Bernard explained.

Honor got down from the cab. When she went on standing there, too long, Bernard followed and took her arm.

'He's coming.'

He turned her so that she was facing a passageway between two rows of huts and the man running in their direction. Then he let go her arm and stepped back. When she began walking to meet Oscar, Bernard climbed back into the lorry and started the engine.

'You didn't write. You didn't contact me.' Honor stopped when Oscar did. They stood about two foot apart.

He was breathless from running and different-looking. He was thinner, but she'd expected that. His hair was short; she'd expected that too. She hadn't expected him to look so much older, nor so worn. Her heart cried out when she met his eyes. They were where the real change was. It was like looking into a dark ravine with no way out.

'I'm sorry,' he said.

'It's all right.' She tried to smile. 'I forgive you.' He would need her.

They walked to where a grassy patch overlooked the town.

'I can offer panoramic views but nothing to sit on,' Oscar said. The grey dungarees and shirt he was wearing hung from his bony frame like a shroud but looked newly washed.

'I like sitting on grass,' Honor said, and sat with her legs tucked under her, running a hand over the yellowy green. 'Feels warm already. It's too dry and a bit scratchy but it'll do.' She reached out her hand to him. 'You didn't know I was a grass expert, did you?' He took her hand and sat beside her.

'I don't know what music you like either,' he said.

There was still so little they knew about one another. About their likes and dislikes, fears and dreams. About what had happened in the months since December.

Honor looked away from him. 'I'm sorry about Stefan,' she said. Below them she could see the lorry making its winding way down the slope.

'Stefan knew what he was doing, he didn't want to live with defeat.'

'Are you saying it was suicide? That he wanted to be killed?'

'He knew how he wanted to live his life,' Oscar said, 'and that included knowing how to end it.'

'All very fine and fancy,' Honor wanted to cry, 'all very fine and fancy.' It was a phrase her grandmother used, she'd never thought much about it until now. Oscar still had told her nothing about himself, or how he felt about losing his brother, or about the loss to the world of millions and millions of Stefans.

'He was so very young,' she said, 'only a boy.'

Bernard, in the lorry, was heading towards a large and relatively clear area of ground.

'A boy is what he was,' Oscar agreed. 'The war was a playground to him.'

Honor took his head in her hands and kissed him on the mouth. His arms circled her. He felt warm and alive. She pulled back a little, looking at him. His eyes had life in them now. She smiled, ridiculously happy.

'I thought I'd never see you again,' she said.

He didn't answer, just drew her to him and kissed her again. For a long time. When at last he let her go, he said, 'Do you have any idea how much I love you?'

'None,' she couldn't stop smiling, 'but I'm willing to listen, and learn.'

He held her against him with one hand. The other played with her hair, then pushed it back from her face and traced its outlines. 'Then you will be instructed,' he said, 'there is a lot I must teach you.'

The sound of an explosion made them part. It wasn't close, but was loud enough and visible in the erupting earth in a field outside the town. Oscar stiffened.

'They're clearing mines,' he said, 'there are a lot of them to clear.'

When she checked Honor saw the lorry had come safely to a halt. She could see Bernard walking across a clearing, stopping to talk to another man.

'You've seen the war,' she said.

'It changes you.' Oscar followed her gaze.

'In what way?'

'In every way. Fundamentally.' He struggled to find words. 'I used to think I understood death, but all I knew was the mechanics of it. I used to think too that there was a great divide between life and death. Now I know there's hardly any distance at all between them. A hair's breadth. War is the death of life itself.' He paused. 'I don't know how I didn't know all this before. How it was that I didn't think of it before.'

'You didn't have to,' Honor said, 'and you didn't want to.'

'You're right that I didn't want to,' he said.

They sat for a while longer on the grassy look out before a French soldier came to tell Oscar politely he would have to join his work team. To Honor he said that if she cared to see

Oscar again that evening then she was, *naturellement*, at liberty to return.

'The French have a fine sense of priorities.' Oscar, with a smiling shrug, helped her to her feet.

They walked to the edge of the camp, close enough to touch but made suddenly self-conscious by the young Frenchman's presence.

'Come about seven.' Oscar spoke close to her ear, his arms tight around her again. 'There's a lot you need to know. I want to tell you about my friends in Paris, the legal manoeuvres they've got going.'

'I can help now I'm here,' she said. 'I'll be your courier.'

'You are my life,' he said.

The soldier looked away while they kissed. Even so he was an inhibiting factor and Honor, whispering against Oscar's mouth, said, 'When will we be together?'

'Soon.' He let her go, smiling. 'The French, as I said, have a fine sense of priorities. What will you do now?'

'Sleep. Go to my lodgings. I can see Bernard from here.' She shaded her eyes with her hand and squinted to where the lorry had stopped. 'I'll walk on down to meet him. He's taking me to where I'm to stay.'

The site on which the Irish Hospital was being built had been covered in allotments before the war. The serious work of erecting the wooden hospital huts had yet to begin and all Honor could see when she got there was a rubble-free area of ground with the beginnings of foundations in place.

Bernard was waiting.

'I still have to unload,' he said. 'The stores are a half-mile out the road, and where you'll be staying in St Pierre's a half-mile further on. I'll unload, then take you on to St Pierre.'

The hospital had been given use of the lofts over the stables of a stud farm for storage. Bernard's accommodation was a bed in the corner of a loft, its ventilation a gaping hole in the roof. It also, he assured her, gave the best night sky views in northern France. There was chair, mirror, razor and wash basin.

'Quite a home from home,' Honor said.

Bernard, with the help of two German POWs supervised by another rifle-carrying French soldier, unloaded an electrical generator, fumigator and the basic necessities for the medical and administration people due to arrive in a month.

Honor studied the blue of the sky through the bullet holes riddling the roof and wooden walls, ignoring a familiar-sounding scrabble until the culprits, a couple of large rats, sprinted across the floor a couple of feet away.

When the cat's away . . . she thought and decided she would get Bernard a cat, for both company and protection.

St Pierre, when they got there, was a hamlet of several bombed houses and a few relatively unscathed farmsteads, the outhouses of which had been converted into dormitory accommodation.

Honor was to share a room with four other women and three small, happily insouciant children. Two of the women were as old as her grandmother, the other two the sad but fierce-eyed mothers of the children. Everyone was polite and curious but spoke no more English than Honor did French. Sitting unsteadily on her narrow, white-covered bed, she felt too faint from tiredness to find a way to tell them all she wanted to do was lie down and sleep. One of the older women solved things when, with a sigh and a shrug, she motioned Honor off the bed, turned down the covers and indicated, with brusque kindness, that she should lie down.

She was dreamlessly asleep when Bernard woke her.

'Come outside,' he said, 'I need to talk to you.'

He was standing in the shade of a tree, leaning against the trunk and smoking, when she joined him. The sun was still high, and hot, as she crossed the yard. Checking her watch, she saw it was five o'clock; she'd been asleep for four hours.

'What's happened?' She took the cigarette from his hand, pulled on it long and hard and handed it back to him. He was much too angry-looking for the news to be anything but bad.

'We weren't alone on the boat.' He stopped, slapping with deadly accuracy at a fly on his bare arm.

'I noticed that,' Honor said.

'We weren't the only ones coming to see Oscar Raeder.'

'Who else is here?' She was calm. Detached. Not really believing things were going wrong again, not so soon. They couldn't be.

'That self-righteous bastard Lennox Mangan is here!' Bernard kicked a stone the length of the yard. 'He boarded the boat after us, with your aunt's blessing, got himself a cabin and arrived here by train three hours ago. He's already paid visits to the Mayor and to the commandant of the German POW camp. What they didn't know before about Oscar Raeder they sure as hell know now.'

'Why?' Honor felt the icy chill of premonition taking over, making her shiver. She pulled her cardigan tightly across her chest. 'Why would he do a thing like that?'

'He says it's to save you from yourself. Says that your aunt wanted him to come, that he couldn't bear to see her heart broken, and that Oscar's a murderer who should be exposed. Says he's a danger to the French and they should know it.'

'Lennox speaks French then?'

'And German. A very learned fellow, our Lennox. Highly principled too.'

This time he picked up a stone and threw it full force at the bucket hanging over the well. The clang echoed down the shaft and brought the elderly French-women into the yard.

'I went against what's natural in me to bring you here,'

Bernard said, 'fought with myself to hand you over to Raeder. And what happens? That worn out, lecherous bastard ruins everything, in his own interest!' He took a steadying breath, looked at her quickly and away again. 'I did what I did in my own interest too,' he said, 'I want to see you happy.'

'I know that,' Honor said. After a minute she asked, 'Where is Lennox now?'

'The Mayor found him a room in one of the small houses left standing on the other side of town.'

'When were you talking to him?'

'About forty-five minutes ago. He turned up, in a taxi, at the hospital site. Raeder was working there, laying foundations with the other POWs. I was giving a hand. Mangan was quite Bolshie, telling Raeder he should make a run for it while he could, make life easier for everyone, including you, by really disappearing this time. Struck me he might be regretting his gallant action, worried your aunt might think he'd gone too far. Either that or . . .' He stopped, scratching his beard and frowning.

'Or?' Honor prompted.

Bernard lit a cigarette before answering. When he didn't offer her one Honor shook out her own and lit up. She didn't care for the pungent French brand he'd taken to anyway. The smoke got rid of the circling mosquitoes and other flies. The elderly French women muttered together and watched.

'The "or" is a crazy idea,' Bernard said. 'Let's forget it.'

Bernard had had plenty of crazy ideas in his time so Honor was prepared to do just that.

'Where's Oscar now?'

'The soldiers let me take him back to the camp. I left him with the commandant, trying to sort things out.'

'Will you take me there too?'

'Why not?' Bernard shrugged. 'You'll walk there anyway, if I don't.'

# 29

Bernard came with her, into the POW camp and the office of the commandant, a small man, grey-haired and neat. He spoke good English and was quite clear on the issue of Lennox Mangan versus Oscar Raeder.

'Stefan Raeder, or Oscar Raeder as I'm now told he is, has not been proven a murderer. He has not been proven innocent either, of course. I understand from him that he wishes to return to Berlin. I am concerned only with the men legitimately under my command. Since he is not a soldier he can no longer be held as a POW and is free, as far as we in this camp are concerned, to leave and take his chances in the world of civilian justice.' His expression discounted any belief that this would be fair.

'Has he left?' Honor said.

'He is packing his belongings. He is in hut number four. I have taken away his brother's papers and given him an emergency set in his own name. He is to report to the Mayor and police of Saint-Lô. They are expecting him.' The commandant's expression this time indicated it was of no real interest to him where Oscar went once he left the camp.

The trousers and jacket he'd worn leaving Ireland emphasised how thin Oscar had become. Since everything else he owned was winter wear, a couple of jumpers and a long coat, he left the camp still wearing the POW shirt under the jacket. Bernard drove him with Honor to the loft over the stables where he'd made his own quarters.

'Candles are about all I can keep here because of the rats,' he said, 'but I'll get what food I can in the town and be back. We'll talk about what's to be done then. In the meantime,' he produced a bottle of Calvados from beneath the blanket on his bed, 'help yourselves to some of this.' He grinned. 'It's used here as an anaesthetic when the real thing's in short supply, which is often.' He paused at the opening at the top of the stone steps leading to the yard below. 'I don't know how the hell you're going to sort this one out, Raeder,' he said, 'but I'm taking Honor home if she'll come with me.'

Honor stood in the opening and watched as he turned the lorry and left a trail of dust on his way to the narrow road.

'He's a good man,' she said.

'A very good man,' Oscar agreed. 'You should think about what he just said.'

'Don't be ridiculous,' she answered.

They sat on the bed and drank the Calvados from the bottle. An absence of any glasses indicated this was how Bernard enjoyed it too.

'God, it's strong,' Honor said.

'Wait until you try Schnapps.'

'Are you inviting me to come to Germany with you?'

'I don't seem to be able to get away from you.' He held her against him. 'We'll go to Paris first and from there, with the help of friends, to Berlin. Once there I'll know how to set about finding out who Clemens Hauptmann was and what he was doing in Ireland. Then I'll know what the murders were about and the murderer will be revealed. It's the only way.' He sounded very certain.

'I hope you're right,' Honor sipped from the bottle. 'Lennox is a a self-righteous shit. I do *not* want to see him: I won't be able to restrain myself from physical attack if I do . . .' She sipped again. 'How could he have done this to you? I always thought him a self-regarding old rake but . . .' She held up the bottle. 'I like this. The situation's becoming more agreeable with every drink.' She shook her head. 'I haven't eaten since early-morning so I'd better not have too much more. How long do you think Bernard will be?'

She turned to him. Her eyes, as she began unbuttoning the buttons of his shirt, had a glazed intensity.

'Not long enough,' Oscar took her face in his hands, 'not half long enough.'

He kissed her, gently, and pulled her down to lie beside him on the bed. They lay for a while in the silence, both of them very still. A dog barked in the distance and a second dog echoed him. There was another explosion. Everything seemed very far away.

'Is Terence well?' Oscar said.

He's trying to keep me awake, Honor thought, but I would dearly love to sleep, here and now and for a long, long time.

'Terence is Terence and he's fine. You should have let him know you were safe.'

'It was all or nothing. I wanted you to get on with your life, without me. Terence would have told you I was in contact.'

'No, he wouldn't.' Honor shook her head adamantly. 'Terence is an outsider. It's the only way he knows how to live. He'll keep secrets and do things his way until the day he dies.' She paused. 'In some ways he's like bloody Lennox, stubborn and secretive . . .' She stopped, considering something which had just occurred to her.

'What's Lennox secretive about?' Oscar prompted.

'I don't know,' Honor continued thoughtfully, 'it's only just occurred to me that there's always, at the edge of my mind, been an awareness that Lennox isn't what he seems, that there's another man behind all the polish. Same thing with Florrie Mitchell. Funny how you know these things but never really think about them. It's the Calvados. It's made me woolly-headed. Dissecting Lennox's personality is hardly top of our present agenda.' She stopped again then said sleepily, 'I'm rambling on, I know I am.' She shook her head and rubbed her eyes. 'All I seem able to think about are secrets . . . people with secrets. Lennox and his secrets, Terence and his secrets, you, me, Bernard, Lavinia . . . all of us. What do any of us really know about each other, when all's said and done . . .'

The question was rhetorical and Oscar didn't answer. Instead he said, 'Goethe says that none of us knows ourselves, and that God forbid we might.'

'That's all fine and fancy,' Honor straightened, wooziness becoming agitation, 'but secrets can warp the mind. Evil secrets can harm others.'

'Lennox's coming here may not be the problem you think it is.' Oscar was thoughtful. 'I'm out of the camp, I've got my emergency papers and we're on our way. All his coming here has done is make things happen more quickly.'

'How will we get to Paris?' Honor asked.

'By train. We'll need Bernard to drive us further down the track to catch one. The Mayor and police may decide to come looking for me, though I doubt it. Digging this town out of the ruins is all anyone's concerned with at the moment.'

'I hope you're right,' Honor said again before, warm, hungry and tipsy, she slept.

Shadows were lengthening across the yard below when

Bernard arrived back in the lorry. Oscar, crouched watchfully in the doorway at the top of the steps, muttered to himself before calling to Honor. When she didn't waken immediately he went to rouse her.

'Bernard's back,' he smoothed the hair back from her face, 'and he's not alone.'

She sat up. 'Not alone?'

The cab door on the lorry banged and voices carried from the yard. The loft had darkened while she slept and the fumigator, in its shadowy corner, taken on the shape of a giant, hovering beetle. There was a chill in the air and, quite close by, distinct scrabbling sounds. Honor looked at Oscar, back watching at the opening.

'Who's with him?' she said.

'Lennox Mangan. They're both coming up here.'

Bernard's corner of the loft was crowded with the four of them standing there. Lennox, smiling and cool-looking in cream-coloured trousers and jacket, upturned an empty crate and sat with his back to the door. He crossed his legs and rested his hands elegantly on one knee. The light behind him made it hard to see his face.

'Honor, my dear, I'm very glad to find you safe and well,' he said. 'I've come hoping to persuade Dr Raeder to do the right thing and return with you and me to Dublin.' He turned to Oscar. 'It would be better for yourself, Dr Raeder, and for any future you might hope to have with Honor, if you returned and faced Irish justice. It would be the honourable and manly thing to do.'

'Oscar has made his own decision about where he will get justice,' Honor tried hard to control her temper, 'and he doesn't believe that will happen in Dublin. We're going to Berlin, together, to find out about . . .'

'I've been trying to tell Mr Mangan he should get the next boat home,' Bernard interrupted.

'Indeed you have, Mr Corkery,' Lennox said, 'indeed you have. But before I do anything I think the four of us should have a chat. We might as well be comfortable so please sit down, all of you.'

He gestured invitingly towards the bed and a second upturned box. No one moved.

'Oh, dear,' Lennox sighed, 'I hope this isn't going to be unpleasant. I didn't expect you to be overjoyed to see me, Honor, but I didn't expect antipathy either. I'd hoped common sense and the greater good might prevail.'

'*Your* idea of common sense and the greater good, Lennox, not mine,' she said.

'Of course.' He smiled. 'What else is there? Once one finds the answer to life's chaos one would be a great fool to abandon it for the feeble notions put forward by others.'

'Adolf Hitler thought he'd found the answer but was proved wrong,' Oscar said carefully.

'Not proven wrong, Dr Raeder.' Lennox shook his head, smiling. 'Temporarily defeated. His ideas and principles live on.'

'National Socialism is dead.' Oscar was watching him closely. 'Europe and Germany will rebuild and move on.'

'You're quite wrong, my dear Dr Raeder.' Lennox shook his head gently. 'The ideals and truth live on, as does the work of giving them life.'

'What ideals are you talking about, Lennox?' Honor demanded. 'What truth?'

Bernard, watching quietly, lit a cigarette.

'You say you are going to Berlin, my dear?' Lennox said. 'Your aunt will be disappointed when you don't return with me.'

For minutes, while he looked at each of them in turn, the only sound in the loft was the scrabbling of rats. Then Lennox shook his head in resignation.

'There is so much to be regretted about what has happened,' he said. 'But you are determined to make things difficult, all three of you, I can see that. Even so,' he brushed fussily at his lapel, 'I will not be deterred. Like Mr Hitler I will "go the way Providence dictates with the assurance of a sleepwalker". Providence has brought me here and I am prepared to do what has to be done.'

'Have you completely lost your reason, Lennox?' Honor kept her voice calm. 'You can't force Oscar to go back.' When Lennox didn't respond she said slowly, less certain of him every minute, 'I didn't know you were such a great admirer of Adolf Hitler. I don't remember your speaking about him . . .'

Lennox waved a dismissive hand. 'His ideas became obscured in the confusion of war and he ceased to be suitable dinner-table conversation. In any event, I didn't want to ally myself with that idiot, Gibbons. Nor did I wish to show my hand. My work is too important for that. No one could be trusted, not even my beloved Grace.'

Honor's world shifted on its axis. Show his hand? Work too important? Lennox had become a raving lunatic. She wrapped her arms about herself and tried to hang on as everything she'd been sure of began to retreat.

'You had no business coming here.' She was almost shouting as she took a step towards him. 'This is my life, Lennox, and where I go and what I do is none of your affair. You had no right to follow me.'

'*Au contraire*, my dear Honor, I had every right,' he said. 'You are misguided and must be saved from yourself, for your aunt's sake if nothing else. Dr Raeder is a double murderer and must be brought to justice.'

'But those aren't the real reasons you're here Mangan, are they?' Bernard, leaning against a beam, lit a cigarette. 'Would I be right in thinking you came here on the track of something else altogether?' He dragged on the cigarette, the tip of it glowing red in the shadows.

Lennox sniffed deeply and stood up. 'Cigar tobacco is so much more satisfactory than the variety used in cigarettes. You should try it, Mr Corkery. Perhaps right now? I'm going to have one myself.' He turned towards the opening. 'I'll need some light.' He walked to the doorway and stood with his back to them

'He found me in the town.' Bernard's voice was a low growl. 'I couldn't get rid of him. He'd been pushing his case to the Mayor and the camp commandant.'

Honor, her mouth dry, watched Lennox while she listened. Even with his back to them she could see him going through a routine she'd observed a thousand times: extracting a cigar from his inside right-hand pocket, snipping one end and holding it in his mouth while he took a lighter from his inside left-hand pocket.

'They're busy men,' Bernard went on. 'Mangan's got no authorisation for what he's doing and they weren't inclined to listen to him. All that counts, as far as they're concerned, is that Oscar's admitted to being himself, not his brother. I'm the only other Irish person here at the moment and I've denied knowledge of everything.'

Lennox had the cigar lit and was now pulling on it, hard.

'Strange things happen in wartime,' Bernard was saying, 'the commandant knows that, so does the Mayor. No one here's interested in a couple of murders in a neutral country which took no part in the fight. A couple of murders against millions dead . . .' He took a breath then muttered, 'Everything, as they say, is relative. I'm beginning to learn the truth of it.'

Lennox put the lighter away and his hand back into his right-hand pocket.

'He's got a gun!' Honor cried, suddenly and too late

understanding her fear, knowing it had come from the realisation that everything about Lennox was wrong, all utterly changed.

'He's got a gun!' she cried again, desperate and frightened this time and filled with a sickening comprehension.

Lennox had murdered Bridie Keogh and Clemens Hauptmann.

'This has all become a right *dîner de chien*,' Lennox threw the cigar down the stairs and held the gun with both hands, 'and things could so easily have been otherwise. I was, however, afraid of this happening and came prepared.' He moved forward until he was only five or six foot away. 'On the bed, all three of you. You, Honor, will sit in the middle. Quickly, my patience is nearing exhaustion. Too much of my time has been wasted already.'

Oscar, wordlessly but without taking his eyes off Lennox, caught Honor's arm and pulled her down to sit on the bed beside him. Bernard didn't move.

'Don't aggravate me, Corkery.' Lennox didn't shift his gaze from Honor and Oscar. 'And don't underestimate me. I've too much to lose and you're too insignificant to give me pause for thought.'

'You're mad, Mangan, a fucking lunatic . . .'

The gunshot was ear-shattering in the confined space, exploding the quiet like a bombshell. Honor screamed. She went on screaming when Oscar caught her against him, turning her head from the sight of a slumped, groaning and bloodied Bernard.

The gun was pointing again at Honor and Oscar on the bed.

'Come on, out of there, Corkery.' Lennox was brisk. 'Get yourself over to the bed. No need to climb on to it. Stay on the floor, but line yourself up with the other two.' Bernard, holding his bloodied and shattered leg, looked up at Lennox.

'You fucking bastard of a madman . . .'

The second shot tore at an angle through the floorboards beside Bernard's good leg.

'I warned you not to underestimate me,' Lennox said. 'The first shot got your calf. Nothing fatal intended. You'll walk again. The second hit what I wanted it to hit too. If I've to use a third, I'll kill you.'

'You're going to kill us anyway.' Bernard, stone-eyed and ashen, began pulling himself towards the bed. A trail of blood followed him. 'What else can you do?'

'Oh, we may be able to strike a deal of some sort,' Lennox said. 'Depends what level of understanding we reach.' He waited until Bernard had propped himself against the bed. His trouser leg was a blood-sodden mass and the stain was spreading.

'That needs a pad pressed against it . . .' Oscar said. 'I can use his shirt.'

'Save your energy, Dr Raeder,' Lennox said, 'you may need it for yourself. You're the one responsible for all of this. If you'd kept your hands on your microscope and off your students none of this would have happened. You can take your hands off her now too.' His tone became irritably fastidious. 'Sit up straight, Honor, your clinging to him like that is a most unattractive trait. That's better. Now, where were we?'

'Exactly *what* is Oscar responsible for?' Honor sat upright and alert. Bernard's head lolled against her leg, blood soaking in a semi-circle on to the floorboards from where he was clutching his leg. Honor touched his head.

'Don't touch him!' Lennox didn't raise his voice, much. It was enough. Honor removed her hand and he went on, 'To be fair, my dear Honor, you were just as much to blame as Dr Raeder. If you'd kept your mind on your studies I wouldn't have had to involve him at all. It could all have been so very different.'

327

'Clemens Hauptmann . . .' Oscar began.

'Of course. Clemens Hauptmann.' Lennox kicked forward the upturned box and sat on it. His movements were precise, his manner detached. He didn't once take his eyes from the bed. 'I knew you'd come round to Clemens Hauptmann sooner or later. Later wouldn't have mattered if Germany had won the war. As it is,' he gave a barely perceptible shrug, 'later had to be prevented so I had to find a way of getting rid of you too. Having you put away for the murder of Hauptmann and his silly whore, or better still hung by the neck, was a very convenient way of solving things for all concerned.'

'You didn't want me to go home to Berlin because I might find out who he was and why he was in Ireland, and that would have exposed his connection to you,' Oscar said. 'That's why you're here now, too. You couldn't get me brought back to Ireland, so I'm not to be allowed to go on.'

'That's it, more or less.' Lennox sounded apologetic. 'I'd every faith in your putting it together before . . .' He stopped, his expression still apologetic.

'Before you killed me?'

'I'm afraid that's on the cards, yes,' Lennox said, 'though we may of course be able to talk things to a different conclusion. I've always had hopes of you. I've followed your career, you know. You're an intelligent man. Altogether more intelligent than your brother, though misguided in a way that he was not. I'm sorry he's dead.'

'No, you're not,' Honor said, 'you've no real feelings about anything. You don't care that he's dead, any more than you care about poor Bridie Keogh or Clemens Hauptmann.'

'You're right.' Lennox shrugged, 'I don't. There are plenty more like him to take his place.'

'How did I never see what you are, Lennox Mangan, how did I never *know*? How did Aunt Grace never know?'

'Grace knows me very well.' Lennox made a sound which

might have been a chuckle. 'She knows what she needs to know very well indeed. Your beautiful aunt is both intuitive and intelligent, an example of what is best in our race. Intuition has given her healing hands and a way with men but she has used her intelligence to ensure she gets what she wants from life. An admirable woman. And what do you think I am, Honor, now you've seen the real me?'

'You're a monster. A lunatic monster who strangles people then fills their bodies with embalming fluid. You *have* to be lunatic to do that.'

'Wrong,' Lennox leaned forward, the gun very steady in his hands. 'I am a man who believes in an ideal which you, and others like you, would have come to know and believe in too, given time.'

'What ideal . . .'

Bernard fainted. He fell forward with a small sound and then slumped sideways against Honor's legs. She fell to her knees beside him.

'Leave him where he is and get back on the bed,' Lennox fired another shot into the floorboards, missing her hand by inches. 'That leaves me with three bullets in this gun. Which means, of course, I've no more to waste. Each one expended from now on will have to account for itself fully.'

Honor sat back on the bed. 'He'll bleed to death.'

'He brought it on himself. Please try to behave with more intelligence than he did. It's getting dark. Soon be a resolution to all this. Light a candle, my dear.' He nodded at a candle in a holder and matchbox on the floor by the bed. 'It would be nice to see each other while we chat.'

'Why did you kill Bridie Keogh?' Honor said. She lit the candle and sat back on the bed. 'Why did you embalm her? Why did you kill her boyfriend?'

'Profound questions. To understand my answers, dear Honor, you will have to bear with me while I go back in time, to when you were a babe, in fact, and to my meetings with the most remarkable of men. But we still have time, and I would like both of you to understand the tragedy to come.'

'What tragedy?'

'One question at a time.' Lennox all but wagged the gun at her. 'And please allow me to begin at the beginning, not the end.'

For a moment, fleeting and frightening, he seemed lost. The frightening part was the realisation that he might, and could, do anything, in a moment just as fleeting.

# 30

'I set my face
To the road before me,
To the work that I see,
To the death I shall meet.'

Padraic Pearse 'Ideal'

The candle flickered. A rat ran across the floor. A star came up and a draught of cold night air gusted through the door below and across the room.

Lennox Mangan talked, quite animatedly, while continuing to hold the gun in both hands.

'I've always had a talent for turning life's predicaments to my advantage,' he said. 'An early and fine example of this was when I found myself unsuited to the study of medicine and turned instead to gathering folklore material for a doctoral thesis.'

'Is it necessary to give us your life story?' Honor interrupted.

'It's interesting,' Lennox looked displeased, 'and, yes, necessary. In part, at least. You in any event have the time to listen.' He stopped to order his thoughts and went on. 'My studies brought me into contact with German scholars in the same field. I was in Berlin in the late 1920s researching fairy tales, superstitions and the like when I was given a copy of *Mein Kampf*. I was enthralled. Some ten years later I attended a speech in Vienna given by Professor Eduard Pernkopt in which he called on physicians to promote racial hygiene.' He raised one eyebrow at Oscar. 'You are no doubt familiar both with the professor and the ideal, Dr Raeder?'

'I've heard of the theory, yes.'

'I thought so.' Lennox turned his head, slightly. 'For your enlightenment, my dear Honor, Professor Pernkopt believes in the elimination of those who are racially inferior.'

When Honor remained silent, he shrugged.

'After listening to him I was inspired to develop a theory of my own merging medicine and folklore, my two fields of knowledge. My research showed that the Aryan races, who do not rely on dull empiricism like the British, needed to develop their intuitive powers in line with their rational ones. I came to believe too that the Celtic race, and in particular the Irish, would benefit greatly from developing their rational qualities and controlling their intuitive ones.'

He shifted his gaze from Honor's to Oscar's face. There was a boyish triumph in his voice when he went on.

'I have been at the very heart of research and work being carried out by an elite organisation under Professor von Kleist of the SS, aimed at ensuring the development and controlled use of intuitive areas in both races.'

He stopped. Honor, who had been watching Bernard with a quiet desperation, said, 'He's bleeding to death.'

'Have you been listening to me at all?' Lennox sounded peevish.

'Please continue,' Oscar said quickly.

'I may not have made it clear that our organisation includes philosopher members of the SS as well as physiologists, all of whom believe that the part of the brain devoted to intuition could be more developed in the Germanic peoples. By "Germanic peoples" I mean, of course, the races who are defined by Herr Hitler as Aryans and thus superior.'

He glanced briefly at Bernard, waxen-looking and breathing shallowly on the floor. 'We believed,' he sighed, 'that the Celtic race would come into its own again once Britain collapsed. Though we were aware, of course, that the people of Ireland would have to be properly controlled and governed if they were to achieve true greatness and take their place in the world.'

'But Britain has not collapsed,' Honor pointed out. Lennox looked at her with distaste.

'A victorious Germany,' he enunciated each word slowly, 'was set to ally herself with the new Ireland. Through careful breeding over a few generations, a genuine Celtic master race would emerge, one in which the German strength of rationality would control the Celtic intuitive one. Our work will continue.' He stopped tapping with his foot. 'Do you understand, Honor, anything of what I have been telling you? Anything of what I . . . we . . . are about?'

'I know what you're telling us, Lennox,' she said.

'Good. And you, Dr Raeder, do I have your attention?'

Oscar nodded. 'Has your work gone on throughout the war?' He spoke carefully.

'Of course. I thought I'd made that clear?' Lennox betrayed his irritation. 'Discreetly, of course, I continued to keep in touch with my counterparts in Germany, passing on my ideas and in turn enjoying the fruits of their research.'

He paused and looked from one to the other of them, frowning. He ignored Bernard.

'You are too close to one another,' he said, 'move apart, please. Further. That's it. You will be as close as you want to be, soon. But for now I want your undivided attention, no distractions. Yours especially, Dr Raeder, since you seem to have no idea what was mapped out for you.'

'Apparently not.'

'Don't, please, resort to the clever riposte,' Lennox sighed. 'We had great things in store for you. All of this,' he gave a small shudder, 'is so very unfortunate. We had been aware of your presence in the medical department for a number of years. You were chosen as an ally for when the war was over.'

'I needn't have bothered making plans of my own then . . .'

'I warned you, Dr Raeder, against sarcasm. You would have learned, in time, that the greater good always comes before personal preference. A large part of our post-war work would have utilised the facilities of your dissecting room.' He smiled pleasantly. 'I had nominated you as the person to oversee that work. You would have made brains available for dissection and helped with studies for any kind of concordance in size and structure between Aryan and Celtic brains.'

'It's not an area of work which interests me,' Oscar said.

'It would have, in time, when you came to see its value. You have a good mind. You would have been unable to resist the excitement of discovery, the possibilities of perfecting the race.' Lennox shrugged and his foot began to tap again. 'That was then, however. Things changed with the progress of the war. It became more and more apparent that our work might have to be postponed, for a while, when the battle ended.'

'Bernard is coming round!' Honor cried.

Bernard's eyes were open and he was looking at her. She moved as if to go to him.

'Stay where you are or I'll shoot him dead,' Lennox said calmly.

'He's going to die anyway, from loss of blood,' Honor was harsh, 'we have to do something.'

'You're right,' Lennox said.

He fired the shot which killed Bernard Corkery without appearing to take aim. The bullet went through the middle of the sternum, around the area of the fourth rib. It would have gone straight into his heart.

He died instantly, the hand he'd been trying to raise falling

334

back to his side as he groaned, softly, and lay still. Honor screamed.

'Don't!' Lennox shouted when she would have gone to Bernard. 'Stay where you are.' He lowered his voice. It was no less threatening.

Honor, face buried in her hands, felt her heart lose its rhythm then start up again, slowly and with a hard, sick-feeling thump. 'Oh, Jesus! Oh, God, no . . .' She rocked back and forth.

'He was a distraction,' Lennox said, 'he was always a distraction, forever interfering where he wasn't wanted. His precious SIS made things very difficult for me these last months. He should have kept his nose out of things which didn't concern him.'

'Such as what Clemens Hauptmann was doing in Ireland?' Oscar said.

'Precisely. Hauptmann, as Corkery discovered, had been operating outside the regular spy network, so to speak. He was the means by which myself and Professor von Kleist communicated our research and ideas throughout the war years. He was well paid. Very well paid indeed. But he was lazy and greedy, and as things began to go badly with the war, money just wasn't enough to satisfy him. Bridie Keogh was another distraction.'

'So you killed her?' Oscar said.

'He broke the rules. He was told never to have anyone in the room I rented for him in Dublin and not to become overly fond of any woman. He did both of these things, with flagrant disregard for established procedures.'

He made an exasperated 'tsking' sound and raised his voice.

'Stop that snivelling, Honor! It won't bring your friend back and I at any rate want you to listen.'

Only when Honor, stony-faced and still, had taken her hands from her face did he continue.

'I made an unscheduled call one morning and Miss Bridie Keogh was there, alone. It was clear she'd been staying there. She recognised me. Had seen me in the Shelbourne Hotel, with Grace as it happens. I merely made a virtue of opportunity and removed her from the equation by strangling her. I waited for Hauptmann outside the building and sent him on his way back to Germany post haste, with a promise that I would look after his whore. He'd broken the rules and was told not to come back.'

'Then you embalmed Bridie Keogh?' Oscar said.

'Seemed a shame not to. There are very few young, healthy female bodies available for dissection, as you know. She was both. She was also dead in a room to which I alone had access. Getting the fluid was an easy matter. Knowing my way round and having a set of keys greatly facilitated her disposal in the tank. *Carpe diem* and all that.'

*Carpe diem.* His rallying cry at her aunt's table. Honor shut her eyes and saw him, saw them all in the candlelit, gossiping community of Friday nights. She had listened, all those years, and truly heard nothing. What had her aunt heard? What had Lavinia and the others heard?

'Did you not think she would be found before she was dissected?' Honor found her voice again. It sounded distant to her.

'No, I didn't,' Lennox seemed surprised by the question, even affronted that she had asked it. 'That was Corkery again, of course, new and enthusiastic as he was.'

'You didn't expect Clemens Hauptmann to come back for Bridie Keogh either?' Honor hazarded a guess.

'Irrational behaviour on his part,' Lennox agreed. 'He left, using the well-established channels we'd set up. But he didn't stay away. He was, it seems, fond of Miss Keogh and returned with the idea of taking her to Germany. He of course discovered her death and found the embalming necessities in the room. I had no choice but to strangle him too. Not difficult since he was overweight and had been drinking. I had the facilities to embalm him to hand this time, but couldn't use the dissecting tank to dispose of him, naturally enough.'

'So, since you'd already got the police focussed on me as a suspect, you went a step further and put the body on the beach at Kilmacreen when you knew I would be nearby?' Oscar said.

'Just seizing another opportunity.' Lennox smiled. 'It was a very simple matter to interest the guards in you as a suspect. A word here, a word there. You know how it is.'

'I know how it is,' Oscar echoed.

'Your secrecy about your brother was a God-send, it made them hugely suspicious. You also, of course, had access to the dissecting room.' He shook his head, regretfully. 'You see, Dr Raeder, your developing friendship with Honor made you of less and less use to me. Made you a threat, in fact, with your talk of returning to Berlin together after the war. The chances of post-war exposure by you were too high. It would be fatal to our plans if I were to be exposed before our little organisation had retrenched.' He shook his head. 'I couldn't let that happen. Putting the blame for the murder of Clemens Hauptmann on to you was perfect. It meant you would be either hung or imprisoned. It would also put an end to your friendship with Honor.'

His expression, when he looked at her, was that of the wryly humorous dining companion she was used to.

'I've no doubt, my dear, that you consider the fortuitous circumstances which came my way a case of the devil looking after his own?'

'He didn't do such a good job of it, did he?' Honor said. 'Oscar and Stefan escaped in spite of your worst efforts. Why . . .' She stopped to take a steadying breath. Lavinia's

337

betrayal was all the worse now she knew exactly to whom the old woman had divulged the escape plan.

'What is it you want to know, my dear?' Lennox spoke softly.

'Why did Lavinia Sayers tell you what I told her in confidence about the escape?'

'Why, indeed?' Lennox smiled. 'A very good question.' He glanced quickly about the loft and stood. 'She told me because she knew I would help.'

'How did she know that?'

'Why . . . how . . . too many questions.' Lennox looked annoyed. 'She knew I would help because she knew about my work. Her late husband Lionel had an interest too in the early days. He was a dilettante, and in any event he died. Lavinia Sayers and her secrets are an irrelevance. They belong in another place and very definitely in another time. It's late. I must be going.'

He moved away, out of the candlelight and into the shadows.

'I want you to believe, Honor my dear, that I am truly sorry for what has to be done. The cause is greater than my affection for you, or even than my love for Grace. I have, as the poet said, "set my face to the road before me".'

'You're going to kill us?'

Honor heard herself say the words without consciously thinking them. She felt her heart beat too, loud and fast, and her mouth go dry again, her palms become cold and clammy. All in seconds. I'm terrified, she thought. A man I have known for years, a man I thought was a joke, is about to shoot me dead. And Oscar too. And I'm like a bloody rabbit, frozen and dazzled by fear and unable to think of a single thing to do.

Lennox sighed in the shadows.

'It's dark enough now for what has to be done,' he said softly. 'There will be a fire in the loft. Fire-fighting facilities

338

are limited in the town and in the dark it will be difficult to improvise. This building, so far from the centre, will not in any event be a priority.' He gave a short, dry laugh. 'It would seem, Honor, Dr Raeder, that the devil has thrown his hat into my ring for a final flourish.'

'So it would.' Honor, eyes scanning the shadows for his outline, felt the stifling fear in her die, slowly. 'But you've made too many mistakes. You'll be caught anyway.'

Anger, every bit as cold but ruthlessly calculating, took the place of fear. Her thoughts were clear now, and very fast. All she needed was to know what he planned. It wasn't in her to give up her life without a fight. She wouldn't let it be taken from her so easily, and by a madman.

'Why not drive off in the lorry, Lennox?' she said. 'Just leave us here? We'll take our chances, you take yours. You've done enough killing.'

'These are strange times we live in,' he said, 'and die in. There are too many dead everywhere – what matter a few more bodies, as your friend Mr Corkery pointed out. War draws a thin line between morality and depravity.'

'There's no need to kill Honor,' Oscar insisted.

'Your gallantry is understandable and quite pointless.' Lennox's voice was dismissive. 'I'm moving on and cannot have her putting the hounds on my tail. Because of you two I have had to leave Grace behind me. Because of your turgid little romance I will be an exile for the rest of my life. But I will also be free to pursue my work. Stand up, both of you, away from the bed.'

The command was rapped out. Oscar took Honor's hand and they stood together.

'Step over the body,' Lennox ordered.

They stepped over Bernard's body. But not his blood which had spread in a clotted, oozing mass. It was sticky and squelched underfoot.

'Pick up the candle, Honor,' Lennox ordered.

She knew what the plan was then.

He was going to shoot her first, as soon she had the candle in her hand. When the bullet hit her she would drop the candle and a fire would be started. Oscar, distracted by the flames and her being shot, would have no chance to do anything to save himself before he was shot too.

But Lennox only had two bullets left; maybe he could be made to waste one. She had nothing to lose, not even her life. She would lose that anyway if she didn't do something.

'Pick it up!' Lennox was almost shouting.

There was a click in the dark and his lighter came on. He held it above his head, gun held now in one hand only. He wasn't going to rely on just one fire then, he was going to start a second.

But she now knew precisely where he was. Thank you, Lennox, she thought, for the opportunity I am about to seize. *Carpe diem*, Lennox, *carpe diem*.

When she slipped her hand out of Oscar's he turned to her, then quickly towards Lennox. She felt him move from her side even as, in one fluid, desperate movement, she picked up and hurled the candle at Lennox.

Everything which happened then happened, it seemed afterwards, together and in the same few seconds.

The gun went off. Honor screamed. Flames leapt from the eaves behind Lennox. Oscar hit the floor. The gun went off a second time. Oscar's arms went around Lennox's legs. Lennox roared and lashed with the gun at Oscar's head. The flames grew higher. And hotter. Honor felt a knifelike pain. Then nothing.

She was in the yard, at the bottom of the stone steps from the loft, when she regained consciousness of a sort. Oscar was hauling her to her feet and draping her arm about his shoulder when her eyes flickered open.

'Try to walk,' he said, 'I'll help you.'

She walked, painfully dragging her steps, half lifted along by Oscar. The stables and loft blazed, clear red flames fed by tinder-dry wood and straw, molten heat on their heels and backs as they made for the outside wall.

It went on burning after they got there, crackled behind them when they stopped to catch their breath on the other side, threw mile-high sparks while they crossed the road into a field and lay, watching it burn and burn with Bernard's body inside.

'The lorry . . .' Honor gasped 'it wasn't in the yard. He got away, didn't he? Lennox got away?'

'He took the lorry,' Oscar said, 'but I doubt he'll get far.'

He set about tending to her wound then, making soothing medical sounds all the time. The practical and tangible gave her something to hold on to, kept hysteria at bay.

'Bullet passed through the muscle and soft tissue.' Oscar tore the bottom off his prison camp shirt. 'It's nothing to worry about really.' He tied the cloth about her arm, putting pressure on it to stop the bleeding. 'It missed the brachial artery . . . lucky for you it was on the outside of the arm . . . no nerves or tissue of importance there.'

'I suppose you could say we're getting round to that extra class after all.'

Honor smiled at him before she lapsed into unconsciousness again, vaguely aware as she did so of the distant wails of a police car and ambulance and, much further away, another mine exploding.

# 31

# The Basement

'Fold up the deckchairs, dear. There will be some
Not needed next year, no matter how warm the sun.'
Bruce Williamson, 'Afternoon in Anglo-Ireland'

M y time came, and now it is gone.
The waiting was long but I always thought it worth while. Revenge, as they say, is a dish best tasted cold. The preparation and seasoning of my chosen dish gave me the greatest pleasure. But I am glad, in many ways, that the waiting is over. It has tired me out.

I knew, on the night long ago that my late husband told me about his and Lennox Mangan's obscene ambitions for an Irish/German master race, that I would use their mad scheme to revenge myself upon both Lionel and Grace Danaher. The idea that selective breeding between the savagely primitive Irish and the foul, overbearing Germans could produce anything other than a ghoulish nightmare was, of course, insane.

I used a trip to Vienna, where Lionel went to meet luminaries of their organisation, to see to my husband.

He was a drinking and gluttonous man, though never fat, and left me alone in our hotel for days and nights while he dined with those he'd come to meet.

The truth, which I recognised and which Lionel, as always, chose to ignore, was that his associates had increasingly begun to see him as indiscreet and a dangerous liability. Also, the money he'd given them was all spent.

They didn't want him around any more than I did.

Lennox Mangan, with his medical knowledge, helped me organise a solution which suited everyone's needs. Lionel was dining with his associates when he died, at the dinner table, from the inevitable effects of cyanide administered by me as directed by Lennox Mangan.

Lennox applied all he knew of evil, which was considerable, to help me. What he proposed was, he said, a gamble but one worth the taking. He called on the death of the mad monk Rasputin for inspiration.

Rasputin, he reminded me, was given cyanide but did not die immediately. This, he explained, was not the miracle many thought it to be but due to the little-known fact that the Russian, a heavy drinker, suffered from alcoholic gastritis, a condition which delays the conversion of potassium cyanide into lethal prussic acid.

Lionel, who constantly complained of indigestion and stomach discomfort, had all the symptoms, Lennox assured me, of alcoholic gastritis. His stomach was, most likely, in the same state as Rasputin's had been.

I put the amount advised by Lennox into Lionel's glass and we had a last drink together before he left for the dinner. I couldn't have borne to be at his side when he died, or to have the police come to our hotel room and question me. Things were much better left in the hands of Lennox's organisation.

They were indeed most helpful afterwards. A doctor among them pronounced their colleague dead from a heart attack; a legal member helped his desolate widow get him coffined and home. Lennox Mangan offered to embalm the body for the journey. It was a kindness too far and I refused.

But death was too good, and too easy, a punishment for Grace Danaher. Knowing she realised nothing of Mangan's

343

mad plotting was, in the beginning, a pleasure in itself. By the time I'd ceased to enjoy my observations of the ignorant pleasure she took in cavorting with a cunning lunatic, I'd arrived at a way of destroying her.

The war had started by then and Lennox Mangan's alliance with Mr Hitler's cohorts had become a very dangerous pastime indeed. I never doubted a situation would arise which would allow me to expose him, and in the process destroy Grace Danaher. But I would have to be careful; a cornered and betrayed Lennox Mangan would reveal me and my secret.

I was right. Evil begot evil when Clemens Hauptmann and his prostitute lover were murdered. I recalled Lennox Mangan's predilection for embalming the dead and knew, after the first death, that things were going wrong for him.

Dr Oscar Raeder, when he appeared as Honor Cusack's beau, was a threat which Mangan, in his madness, dealt with by attempting to have the doctor hung, or at the very least imprisoned, for the murders.

The mess of pottage was bubbling nicely and my plan to expose Mangan, and by extension Grace, coming quickly to the boil.

What I did not foresee were the consequences.

The Raeder brothers' successful escape was my first indication that things might be beyond my control. Lennox Mangan was not pleased, and let me know it. I lived in fear of him in the months which followed.

I lost Honor Cusack's trust and was surprised at the cost to me, both of her company and her usefulness. She knew I wasn't well and still she stopped coming to visit. She told me, in a newly cold and precise voice, that this was because I'd betrayed the Raeder brothers to the police. I told her she should learn from the experience, that I had at least taught her not to trust *anyone*.

The will to revenge myself on Grace Danaher didn't

weaken, but my body did. When my daughter-in-law brought a doctor to see me I hurled a plate at him. That was the end of him, and of any other doctor. Brandy and other alcoholic drinks, in ever-increasing amounts, became my solace in the continuing wait.

I saw justice and the end come in sight again with the news of Dr Oscar Raeder's safe whereabouts.

I had never stopped watching Lennox Mangan at the dinner table and, when the war ended, could see by his increasing calm that his position had become desperate. I knew Mangan could not allow Dr Raeder to return to Berlin where, in time, he would discover Mangan's secret and connections with the SS and others who by then would be *persona non grata*.

I didn't need to do anything further. He did it all himself, becoming the instrument of his own destruction when, in the lorry in which he was trying to escape his murderous attempt on the lives of Oscar Raeder and Honor Cusack, he drove over an unexploded land mine.

But I was wrong about Grace Danaher. He served her well to the last. When her suitor was revealed as the murderer who embalmed his victims, as well as an active advocate of Adolf Hitler's master race policy, my son's widow left the country. Before going she gave newspaper interviews in which she said the shame and disgrace were too much to bear. She would devote the rest of her life to humanitarian work in a decimated Europe.

She was labelled a heroine. A tragic, well-meaning woman whose generosity had been exploited and good nature taken advantage of.

She now lives in Berlin, where her niece and her new husband have set up home. Honor Raeder, who has softened and now writes to me, says her aunt has settled well and entertains a new group of friends to dinner each Friday.

Honor herself seems happy; perhaps I was wrong and her feelings for her German are lasting and true. I no longer go upstairs in this house.

Delia Gibbons is mistress there now, her acrid little husband its master. Grace Danaher, after persuading Florrie Mitchell to sell every picture and *objet d'art* which was hers to sell, gave the Gibbonses charge of the house, rent-free. The condition was that Delia took care of me.

Delia Gibbons is insolent and steals from my rooms. Ernie plays the gentleman and is a fool. Their child howls incessantly. When I die Grace Danaher will no doubt return and sell the house.

All that I lived for, all those years, is gone. But I live on, still waiting. This time for death.